PRAISE FOR
SALT OF THE AIR

". . . Cautionary, sensual stories of love, reversal and revenge upend fairy tale conventions in Nazarian's lush collection. . . . Sumptuous detail, twisty plots and surprising endings lift these extravagant tales."

—*Publishers Weekly*

"These are beautiful, haunting confections, reminiscent of Tanith Lee's erotically charged tales in **Red as Blood** and elsewhere. . . . And while Nazarian thus strikes fresh notes off old vessels, she provides the template of sword-and-sorcery with new glitter, new power. . . . Fine shades of emotion, mythic grandeur, crystalline prose, sharp revisionist intelligence: these are Vera Nazarian's hallmarks, signs of a strong emerging talent. **Salt of the Air** is her best, most representative book so far."

—**Nick Gevers**, *Locus*

"She writes with an elegance and grace that is at times ethereal, picking out other worlds in soft watercolors with an impressionist's brush. At other times, her writing is penetrating and sharp, piercing to the heart of a concept or a theme. Or you. . . . I recommend savoring **Salt of the Air**. Leave it on your bed stand. Each night, perhaps with a nice cup of tea, delve into one of her stories. Enjoy them slowly, even skipping a night or two here and there to make the collection last longer. Let the reflections and worlds contained in each story creep into your brain. Then dream remarkable dreams."

—**Deborah J. Brannon**, *Green Man Review*

SALT OF THE AIR

Vera Nazarian

Cover Art:
"Phoenix" Copyright © 2009 by Ahyicodae

Interior jewel emblem detail:
"Reading a Book," Rudolf Ernst (1854-1932)

Cover Design Copyright © 2009 by Vera Nazarian

ISBN-13: 978-1-60762-036-5
ISBN-10: 1-60762-036-7

Revised and Expanded Reprint Edition
Trade Paperback

April 15, 2009

A Publication of
Norilana Books
P. O. Box 2188
Winnetka, CA 91396
www.norilana.com

Printed in the United States of America

Salt of the Air

Norilana Books

Fantasy

www.norilana.com

Other Books by Vera Nazarian

SALT OF THE AIR

Vera Nazarian

Introduction
by
Gene Wolfe

"The World is shaped by Two Things—Stories told
and the Memories they leave behind."

—from Dreams of the Compass Rose

Contents:

INTRODUCTION

GENE WOLFE

Fantasy is the least understood genre. Horror is nearly as bad; give it second place. Science fiction fans quarrel endlessly over exactly what constitutes science fiction, but everyone knows. Call it a weak third. Mainstream, romance, mystery, and western are all well understood.

But what is fantasy? Must it have elves? Unicorns? Are ghost stories fantasy? Some people feel utterly and unshakably certain that any story with a witch in it is fantasy—yet I have had witches give me their business cards.

What has all this to do with the book you're holding? Nothing, perhaps. You must decide.

Vera Nazarian wrote this book. I once wrote one whose cast included a witch and a private investigator, and was told very firmly that I could not do that. Witches and private investigators did not belong in the same story. I protested that there was an unemployed salesman in my book, too. That was all right, my inquisitors said. Salesmen were real, some were unemployed, so I could have one in a book that included a witch.

The yellow pages of any big-city telephone book will supply column after column of private investigators, and one of my daughters is a former private investigator.

Fantasy, you see, is really about things that are not believed; and the reality or unreality of those things has nothing to do with it. Ghost stories are fantasy *as long as you do not believe in ghosts*. If you see a ghost—but do not believe it— ghost stories remain fantasy. For you. As long as you reject the thing you saw.

If I could compel you to read the stories in this book in whatever order I chose, I would compel you to read the first story first. Its title is "*Rossia Moya*," and it is a very good story indeed. I would compel you to read it first not for any benefit Vera or I would derive from your act, but for your own good. Let me tell you a story.

"Once upon a time there was a boy who was very smart in school but was often ill. One year it happened that he was ill on the very first day of school. When he was well again and came to school, he found there was a new subject that he could not grasp. He read and reread his textbook, questioned the teacher, and questioned other students. He could not understand the textbook. Nor could he understand the teacher's answers, nor understand the answers he got from other students.

"Eventually he realized that something had been said on the first day of school which he had not heard, and indeed that he had never heard in all his questioning or read in all his reading."

Try to remember my story, please, although it will not be numbered in this introduction. You may call it Story Zero.

The second story in this book—the one that follows "*Rossia Moya*"—is "Beauty and His Beast." Although it is not the story of Sleeping Beauty, it recalls it because it is a story of the same kind, a story told by mothers (more often by their mothers) to teach young men something they should know. You are advised to read it; if you are young and single, male, and given to reflection, you are advised to think about it a great deal.

The third story is "The Young Woman in a House of Old." When I had read half of it, I wished that I had thought of its idea myself. When I had finished it, I was glad I had not. Vera handled it better than I could have, and every good story deserves the best possible handling. Do they still sing *Old Soldiers Never Die* in the U.S. Army? I doubt it, but hope I am wrong. This story made me recall that song.

The story that follows it is a retelling of "The Princess and Pea." It is a rape story, and a good one. Good rape stories are very rare.

The next story is "Bonds of Light," but I am not going to tell you about it. It will be much more fun for you to read the stories and compose your own capsule description of each. What I am going to do instead is tell you why this excellent book is so good. There are two reasons.

The first has to do with the nature of fantasy. The background of nearly all our fantasy is Western European. We draw on familiar fairy tales, Greek and Roman myth, Norse myth, Celtic myth, and so on. We do not believe in Morgan le Fay, in Woden, or in Minerva. Vera Nazarian was born in Russia, and her mythic background is Eastern European, not Western. *She does not believe in different things.* (It is a troublesome concept, but try.) That is the first of the two things I mentioned.

The second is Vera herself. Could another writer from the same background have written this book? Absolutely not.

Could another writer from that same background have written one as good? It is possible—Russia has produced some superb writers—but highly unlikely.

We are come at last to the closing paragraphs of this too lengthy introduction. Here I was going to explain the significance of the story of the boy who was ill, of Story Zero. I had planned to illustrate the parallels between a book of stories and a course of study. And so on. And so forth.

Upon further reflection, I will not. If you do not understand why I told that story already, no explanation I could provide would help.

I trust you do.

Gene Wolfe

ROSSIA MOYA

"Russia is dead!" cried the old beggar woman, looking at me. *"Ti shto, baba? Zachem priyehala?"*

Why had I come indeed.

I stepped off the last rung of the detachable rolling staircase that was docked with the transcontinental airplane, using my right foot to make the first step onto land, for good luck.

Underneath me, underneath the concrete, ancient Moscow earth.

Fifty years stood between my last step and this one. Fifty years ago, as a girl of eight, I had taken a similar step, right foot first, upon the superstitious urging of my mother, onto an old Aeroflot plane. At the height of the Cold War, I was leaving the country of my birth forever, with all its stagnation and rancid Soviet decay.

And now, here I was again, at the time of Closing.

The land beneath me was still the same, the one from which I had sprung.

But the desolation was different.

Yes, I had prepared myself psychologically, knowing what lay ahead, knowing what to expect. I had taken the inoculations. I had brought the extra protein-rich rations, and the chemo-chlorine for the drinking water. The water I had been told to avoid, and to consume only bottled imported liquids.

I had also calmed myself with the hypnotic self-induced trance of indifference that I had practiced during the long flight, the visualization of things through a fine inner film of apathy.

I stood now, and felt a moment of vertigo, as the land spun beneath me while the milky sky stood still—or was it the sky spinning? For a moment I couldn't tell, because the long stretch of concrete between the plane and the airport building was charcoal gray, spotted with puddles of the recent rain, and the sky was lighter slate, so that the two blended.

Early fall. . . .

The old woman just before me, holding out her palm in automatic supplication, had come out of nowhere, and was ignored by all passengers descending from the plane.

Maybe I had been the only one who momentarily glanced her way. Or maybe she could tell that I was the only one of all those people who was actually Russian?

Whatever it had been, she homed in on me and uttered her tirade, then stood aside, her palm still outstretched.

"Pomogi chem nibutz . . ." she added quietly.

Help me.

"I am sorry," I said, averting my eyes. I switched automatically into Russian, feeling oddly self-conscious about the manner in which it slid off the tongue. "I am sorry, I don't have much. . . ."

Bullshit.

I had everything. It was just the sudden panic coming over me, the old habit dying hard. Refusing beggars is a habit they teach you inadvertently, a habit of fear. Whether you have something to give or not, just mumble anything and step away. Or else pull out some coins or a bill, and hand it to them with the superiority of those who can afford it.

But not here. Here was different. There had been no beggars in the memory of the 8-year old girl that was myself. Or rather, she could still remember two separate shocking instances, the sight of human beings covered with an unmistakable sheen of gray, of dirt, sitting on the street, wallowing in it, while all around, busy feet of pedestrians, and her father's cautionary voice explaining in her ear, "These are *neeshii*. These people have no home. . . ."

There had been no beggars in Russia, officially, under the Soviet regime. Everyone was guaranteed a home no matter how crowded or poor.

After the collapse of the Soviet Union in the latter part of the twentieth century, chaos came to reign, for the repression-pustule had burst, and with sudden freedom, all screaming hell had come loose. Beggars became the norm, as the doctors and engineers and scientists, all members of the intelligentsia, joined the factory workers on the Mafia-ridden streets and openly asked for handouts from the pitying foreigners, though rarely from their fellow countrymen.

Hell had come to Russia and as months and years went by and workers were living on IOUs with no salary in sight, the ruble rode waves of devaluing fluctuation, and food became scarce, even in the form of relief aid from the West.

And after that, the negative birth rate took its toll. Together with the despair, the unrelieved hunger, and the children being born with severe birth defects from malnourished parents, the population started to decrease at an alarming rate. In the year 2000, when other countries merely worried about technological compliance, Russia was on the brink of a down-spiraling irreversible trend.

And the following several decades did not change the rate of extinction.

And then. . . .

And then became and now. The times have swept through me, and with the memories emerged shame and wonder at myself, at what I still carried inside after all these years.

"I am sorry," I said again, this time locking my gaze with the watery eyes of this nameless stranger. "I am very sorry."

And then, I stood aside, allowing the stream of passengers to walk past me to the airport building, while I put down my carry-ons, rummaged through my purse, took out several bills of International Market Currency and handed them to the woman. She was not that much older than me, maybe in her early seventies. And she was dressed decently, not like a beggar at all.

She took the IMC, without a thank you. It would not be of any use to her after what was going to happen in three weeks—we both knew—but for now it still had significant value. She then turned, and I expected nothing more, for it had been her right.

And yet, the woman had stopped and stared back at me, and her lips moved, as though with a muttering.

I was not sure if it was a curse or a blessing.

Or maybe it was just a wetting of the lips.

I was stopped at the customs check-in window, like all the other incoming passengers, by two officers. They were young boys, in my opinion, with pink sickly spots on their sallow faces, and the same watery eyes. They checked our papers, and put stamps on passports, and then asked the same question.

"What is the purpose of your visit at the time of Closing?"

Everyone's answer was: "Business."

They were all here to close their bank accounts, finish deals, remove belongings, do any other number of last minute chores, before the final Closing of the country to the rest of the world.

My reason was personal. But, "Business," I lied to the soldier-boy. Only no, he was not a soldier—times blurring again—he was just a youth in a civilian government uniform, wearing the drab colors of an impotent nation. A glorified clerk.

He did not look at me twice, but stamped my papers, turned to his fellow and said, *"Yeshe odna po delam."*

One more on business.

And yet, maybe my reason was not so personal. Maybe I had unfinished business to complete, just like all the others.

The second customs worker glanced at my passport, and then, noticing my name, said to me, *"Vi russkaya?"*

"Da, molodoi chelovek," I said. He reminded me of my cousin, fifty years ago, fresh out of the Soviet Airforce Cadets, with a chin nicked from clumsy shaving, and the acne of a boy.

"Zachem vi zdes?"

Again, that question. Why am I here? Why?

"Business," I said again, this time coldly, this time in English. "These are all my papers. I will be leaving again in exactly two weeks, just like it says here, a week before the Closing."

He did not look at me again. He simply showed me to the door leading inside, to the rest of the airport.

To the rest of Russia.

Around me, tall buildings of at least five stories, and of several hundred years—greenish tan, beige and pale brown, aged cream and dusk, rusty brick or deep-baked mauve, with ornate fronts, doorways topped with sculptured reliefs, with fleur-de-lis, and windows framed with carved panes—in the venerable heart of Moscow. I took an old creaking trolley bus directly to a dilapidated hotel with an old rusty-red front and faded gold trim. There, I left my bags in a dimly lit room with a musty smell of several centuries, a combination of czarist and Communist and post-Soviet scent that was imbedded permanently in the patterned paper of the walls.

And then, still walking in a trance, I came outside. I stood breathing the air after the rain, early evening, with the sun that had eventually come out, hitting the glass of the windows in the houses around me with sharp violent blots of golden orange glow.

The glow fractured, and triggered memories of a painfully sweet newness, of a time when I had a fresh cavity within me and bubbling faraway futures ahead, when my mind was young, a clean white vista of hope, and I could see only tomorrow . . .

You notice, I hardly mention people.

Yes, they were there, but like drab peculiar shades, ghosts already. They walked the streets, pedestrians and occasional cars turning corners, running on the last of the hoarded old-style gasoline. I tried to ignore them, avoided looking at their emaciated faces and their pale Slav eyes, because I knew that if I did look, if I did stop and pause, something within me would be displaced, like a changing of a gear.

And so I ignored the people. . . .

Let them walk past me, take my bags, obscure my sun for a moment, displace the air molecules around me. Let them move in their coats and with their *ushanki* over reddened ears and flax hair. Let the old women in patterned flower-shawls and huge furrows of wrinkles cutting up their faces hurry past me, carrying rope-sacks of potatoes, just like they did fifty years ago. Let the young street punks with heavy makeup and untreated acne wander aimlessly in their skin-tight or baggy jeans and leather miniskirts showing thin high-heeled legs, and imported Western jackets with corporate logos advertising products most here had never seen. Let the occasional bareheaded member of the criminal underground saunter lazily and stand outside the doorways, waiting for a classic obsolete Mercedes to roll up grunting on dwindling gasoline, choking on exhaust fumes. . . .

They were all dead. None of them real. None of them from the same world as myself. I say this figuratively, and yet, the psychological door was shutting already, even before the formal act of Closing—the formal political recognition that there was nothing more the world could do for Russia, that the global community, otherwise linked into one vibrant entity, was powerless to avert the extinction of a people.

In the middle of the seventeenth century, when Pyotr Pervii, known in the West as Peter the First, the Great, carved a so-called window into Europe and opened uncouth Russia to the rest of the "civilized" Western world, it was thought he was committing an irreversible act.

And now, in the first quarter of the twenty-first century, the window was closing up again. And it was taking all the centuries of clamor with it. . . .

I began to walk aimlessly along the street. One block, three, thirteen. I moved forward because there was a need, and no one paid attention to yet another middle-aged woman in drab foreign clothing—they all wore it, the clothing of the West, the last vestiges of Western humanitarian aid. I may have stood out only in the slow confident carriage of my straight back, but they did not observe too closely.

At the corner of *Kropotkinskaya* I hailed a cab, raising my hand to wave in the old Muscovite manner, not with the American thumb. Eventually a private vehicle stopped—cabbing was a second income for many—and I was given a cool stare, and a "*Kuda?*"

"*Novoslobodskaya*," I said, giving him a rolled up wad of IMC bills, "near *Butirskii Val*."

I got in the car, and was not surprised to find it a European model. But it was the old gasoline-engine kind, since

Western compu-electrics had not been financially feasible in this place of encroaching decay.

I had also forgotten how noisy the gasoline engines were. We drove, rattling north past *Sodovoe Koltso*, and finally onto the street I had specified, and I stared, and searched my memory, and recognized absolutely nothing. Finally, the cabdriver dropped me off, and then took off into the long shadows of encroaching evening.

I was crazy to be here alone, with night coming on.

And yet. . . .

This was the moment it all slammed into me, the enormity of it. I stood on the washed-out pavement, across the road from the corner with a six story house that led off into a small side street, lined with tall deciduous trees, golden-orange with the ruddy fall.

I am supposed to know and remember that side street, that *pereulok*.

I was born here.

All I had to do was cross the street, and walk past approximately three buildings, and on the left would be the five-story building where I had lived my childhood. Across from it would be the tall deep red-brick housing complex with glass windows that I would stare at as a small child and see brilliant reflected sunlight. The sidewalk itself may still have traces of the hopscotch game the children would draw on it with colored chalk, and then jump on one foot to navigate a hockey-puck or *shaiba*, or even a shoe-polish can, through each of the ten cells. And if I walked along the sidewalk before my building, there would be the tall maple trees on the edge of the pavement, and the earth underneath them would be littered with a thick detritus of fallen leaves, sienna red, orange, pale yellow, variegated shades of autumn.

I used to rummage through the leaves, and kick them up with my little shoes, and watch them rise up like flimsy paper and then settle down again. Underneath, the earth would be moist and cold. And if this were spring or early fall, there would be bumps and small cracks in the rich black soil, where I knew mushrooms were rising—mushrooms that I would proudly dig out, and bring back home so that my mother would add them to a buttered pan and fry them, sizzling and fragrant.

I stood frozen, and watched the street corner across the intersection. Then, instead of crossing the street, I started to walk in the opposite direction toward the grounds of the abandoned women's monastery which had been converted to a public park.

"*Mama! Mama! Smotri, eto ne vorobei!*"
I sat on an old park bench, feeling the cold hard slab of stone through my pants and coat, and watched the little girl point out to her mother a small unidentified bird flitting through the orange leaves of the nearest tree.

Overhead, the sky was milk-gray, darkening. Before me was the round rim of a dried-out pond. The shallow concrete reservoir of the pool had just a puddle of rain water on the bottom, and was instead filled to the brim with the leaves of fall. At the center of it was an old rusty fountain spigot, but I had never remembered the fountain working, not even as a child.

However, the bench underneath me was familiar. I just didn't remember it being so small.

Everything—the park, the trees—they were so small. . . .

The little girl with a reddish-blond braid ran ahead, splashing through the fallen leaves, and her mother stood watching her tiredly. The girl was no older than six. The woman was young, probably in her early thirties, and wore a simple beige coat with a wool shawl covering her hair. She never looked at me, and instead focused vacantly ahead of her. She was clutching a small bag in her hands.

They were pale, emaciated, her hands. Just like the sickly color of her skin. Her sunken face.

The little girl was thin too, pale and bleached out like a doll. And yet she was alive, smooth, full of energy, as she thundered through the clearing between the trees and the walkway.

At one point she neared me, and smiled, and I smiled back at her, and said, "*Kak tebya zavut?*"

"Lena . . ." she replied, a little shyly.

"What a beautiful name you have, *Lenochka*," I said, while times blurred around me, and I remembered another child with that name, also with a golden-orange braid, a little girl I used to play with.

I was about to say something else, but the little girl was already gone, having run off toward her mother.

Overhead, the small grayish bird flitted through the trees.

I never did go to see the house of my childhood. Instead I had returned to the hotel and gone to bed that night. But first I had made a phone call to America, using my credit card, on an old-style phone without a video display. After three bad connections and hangups, I finally heard John's familiar voice through the crackle on the other end, telling me to come home, that he was worried for me, worried there might be travel complications related to the Closing, and that I had gone at such a bad time.

"Not a bad time, but the last and only time," I said, with a smile. "Besides, you always worry. Please tell Andrew and the other kids that all is well. I feel great, no arthritis flareups. Everything's okay and I'll be back soon. I just had to do this, you know. Early retirement gift to myself. The way things are going, it's now or never."

"I still wish you'd let me come with you," he said.

"No, it's better this way. I need to be alone to do this."

"So, did you see it? Your house?"

"Not yet. . . ."

"Why are you doing this to yourself?"

No need for a video display. I could imagine his tense expression so well, knew it like the back of my hand.

"Don't worry about anything. Enough. Love you, and see you soon," I said, and hung up before I could start feeling.

The next week I spent wandering Moscow. And I mean, wandering, on foot, dragging myself aimlessly along *Tverskaya* which used to be called Gorky Street for a while during the Soviet days, past the half-empty storefronts. Here, I could see slightly out-of-style Italian, French, and American fashions through the window glass, that no one could afford to buy, and other luxury items gathering dust.

I passed by bookstores with gaudy displays of translated Western thrillers, the so-called "blood and porn" *boyevik* videos and books with topless bimbos and guns on the covers, and noticed, huddling in the back, old unwanted classics. Occasionally, there were cafes with big commercial neon signs of western soft drinks, and inside, one or two customers drinking tea or coffee before stand-up counters.

My eyes paused on one young bleached-blonde woman with heavy makeup marring her attractive face, dressed in a fake leather jacket. She was having tea from a tall glass at the counter, and I watched her skinny throat move as she swallowed. With a flash my vision blurred, and her throat became smooth and adorned by a glittering choker, while her features superimposed upon another face, without a blemish or a trace of artifice, a young bare-shouldered woman in a dress of *Ekaterina*'s court, with her powdered hair gathered in a twisted beehive crown above her forehead, with sculpted locks and flowing folds of silvery satin over a wide flaring crinoline skirt. . . .

Something was happening to me, and I had no words for it.

Instead, I blinked it away, gathered myself, and followed *Tverskaya* haphazardly on to the Red Square.

Here, I stopped and stared at the grand expanse of empty open cobblestones beneath a pale blue-white sky, and my childhood pierced me so strongly that for a moment I felt dizzy.

Times blurred, and the rose and brick-hued stones fell into a mosaic at my feet. I stared at the patterns they made before my eyes, and for a moment saw shadows of old giant banners of Lenin's face hanging from the *Kreml* walls in the distance, and the huge seal of the Soviet Russian Republic with the braided wheat pattern over the sickle and hammer, *serp y molot*.

High noon and strong wind. The square was nearly empty, except for some bedraggled gypsy-beggars, a couple of peddlers of the last of Western imported goods, with small carts, and occasional hurried passerby. I saw a tall young man walking fast, in an old worn-out army uniform. Once again the odd stupor came upon me, and I blinked away the vision of him as a soldier in the White Army over a century ago, an elite guard of the Tsar—an image which was immediately superimposed by another one of the Red Army green uniform, and a decorated World War II soldier, and then a disenfranchised unemployed soldier of the Commonwealth.

I continued staring, drunk with the high cool wind in the square, and watched his quickly receding back, and he was still morphing before my eyes, falling in and out of time.

Before me in the distance, *Sobor Vasilia Blazhennovo*, the ornate cathedral with its rainbow-colored zigzagging onion domes, like a great gingerbread and jewel toy. All around, *Kreml* walls of rose-hued brick, crenellated on the top. Off to the side was the old *Mavsolei* building.

I never did see the embalmed corpse of Lenin lying in state, never had been inside the Mausoleum, even as a girl.

"Some other day," my parents would tell me. "Today the line is too long."

But the line had always been too long, and so I had to satisfy myself with watching the changing of the guard, as every fifteen minutes they marched before the Mausoleum like clockwork soldiers.

There was no honor guard now, nothing to protect in the small rose brick building. The Mausoleum had been converted into a bland museum of Sovietica circa the year 2007.

And today, only pigeons circled the expanse overhead, and there were hardly any visitors to the old sites.

I ate one of the ration packets I had brought with me, while watching a *Vremya* newscast on the flickering hotel-room TV. They were speaking of the Closing, of the measures the country was taking to stay afloat in its imminent complete isolation. Not a word about American or European reactions. Preparation was discussed in isolationist terms, as though the Closing had happened already—in terms of heightened economic production, of a self-contained ecosystem of supply and demand. Images of factories and farms and corporations were interspersed with faces of emaciated peasants in the small remote towns, as they were shown plowing their tiny plots of land with borrowed archaic tractors.

Chewing the unpleasant protein-rich canned food, I considered momentarily what might happen were I to go downstairs and buy some simple bread and cheese in the grocery store from across the street. Would I get sick immediately?

I stared at the can of imported soda sitting on the table before me, and longed to try some hot tea. Indeed, I craved hot tea. The one Russian thing that had truly stayed with me, even after all these years, was my love of plain black tea. I'd been given it in a baby bottle! And even as a refugee, I never switched to coffee.

But to drink it, I would first have to chemo-chlorinate the water. Blech.

So I tried not to think about it, and finished my meal.

Tomorrow would be another day. I had already spent plenty of time walking, and now would try something new.

Tomorrow.

I took a ride in a small *kater*, one of the cruise boats that moved relentlessly along the brown-green waters of *Moskva Reka*, or Moscow River. There were only a few passengers on the boat with me, mostly families with small children, wearing American sports jackets, and huddling from the chill autumn breeze. I watched the swampy waters churning, and the high banks on both sides, the occasional swooping ducks and swans.

"Nu shto ze budit posle Zakritiya?" one woman in the boat was saying to her husband, what would happen after the Closing?

Zakritie. That word was translated as Closing, or a shutting down.

The man proceeded to say he had no idea, that maybe phones would not work and they couldn't call outside the country, that computer networks will be severed, and planes would not fly except across Russia. There would be no more imported food or clothing, or technology and machinery. No more humanitarian aid.

At that last bit, the woman sucked in her breath sharply, maybe because that was the only thing that really sunk in, the only thing that mattered to her, was understandable, personal. All else—computers, worldwide networks, high tech—all else was abstract and remote. It did not affect her or her children directly.

Or so she thought.

I wanted to say something to these people, but had no idea what it was. What had I to offer? Sympathy?

Instead, I kept quiet.

After the cruise was over, I got off the riverboat and wandered some more, this time taking a taxi to one of the Metro stations. For the rest of the day I would ride the Moscow Metro, and get off at every *stantsia* and look at the fine inlay mosaic decorating it, and the gorgeous rows of lanterns that were different at each themed stop.

"I don't like this at all," John was saying to me on the phone, "Listen, come home early, please. There's bad stuff going on, you should hear what's on the news here, the kinds of sanctions discussed. Congress is withdrawing all diplomats even from the surrounding countries, the little ones immediately bordering Russia. Obviously extreme measures, but still—"

"Not yet," I said, "I haven't seen my house."

"Why the hell not? You've been all over town for more than a week now! What's wrong with you, really? I don't understand what you could be thinking at a dangerous time like this."

"I am a little scared," I said. "If I see it, and if what I see is different from what I remember having seen, it would upset me. I don't know. I will do it soon. Today maybe."

"Do it! Promise me!"

I nodded silently, forgetting we were not on videophone, then said softly, "Yes, okay."

And so I took a taxi back to *Novoslobodskaya* and *Butirskii Val*.

This time I steeled myself, became absolutely calm and apathetic, and I crossed the street, and entered the *pereulok* or side-street of my birth.

It was one of the last clear days of fall. Overhead, the sky streamed outward with a warm autumn glow, and the tree crowns were high and still sparsely full of gold and orange leaves.

I walked and counted houses.

It would be on my left.

A tall five-story housing complex, painted bland off-white, with five or six *podyezdi* or front entrances. Our apartment had been on the first floor, in the third *podyezd*. In front of each would be a long entrance, and a bench or two on the side, where the old women, our *babushki*, would congregate every evening when it was warm enough, until the sky became indigo and twilight enveloped all. We kids also used the benches to plan our games, to gather and count off and decide that one of us was "it," and then we'd go running like the wind, and hold our breath while we hid in the hedges and bushes lining the house, or around the corner in the back—which was a whole different play world—or inside the different *podyezdi* under staircases. . . .

There it was.

My house.

As I approached it at the corner, I glanced for a moment to the left, to the place where there were a couple of tall trees and then beyond it the backyard area. The tallest tree that still stood immediately before me, after all these years, used to hold one of our makeshift swings. Once, someone had climbed up and drawn a tall rope, and from it we hung a wooden cross bar, and then eventually an old car tire, so we could swing on it. The old *babushki* would come yelling at us to stop, telling us we would ruin the beautiful tree, and that we were little barbarians who broke branches and pulled leaves. And so we'd take down the rope, and then when the old women were gone, we'd bring it back again, and swing like monkeys, until the next warning.

Memories came falling like blocks upon me, slamming. . . .

I walked on the sidewalk before my house, and saw that its paint was peeling, and had not been refinished. It was merely young or middle-aged, in house years. But it was as old as I was, nearly sixty, built in the same year as I was born, just months before.

I counted three entrances, each one raised up about three stairs. Then, I stopped.

I stood facing the first window on the left, half a flight above ground level. There were pastel curtains on the other side of the window pane. And underneath, the flowerbox had something colorful growing—not like our own had been, empty, with just a couple of chive onion bulbs. . . .

I stared relentlessly at that wooden flowerbox, and the peeling paint.

After a while, water came streaming out of me.

It pooled in the corners of my eyes, while pressure built inside, and I was holding it, still and poised for something. My features did not move, but the waters were running, running. . . .

At some point, the doorway of the *podyezd* opened, and a little girl of about seven came outside, carrying a jump rope. She had short chestnut brown hair and a round face. She hopped down the last two stairs, then started to move away, and suddenly saw me.

She paused, staring at my face.

"*Tyotia, shto takoe?*" she said.

What's the matter, aunt?

I looked at her, feeling my face in that instant loosening, suddenly collapsing into a quivering mass. And then I drew a paper tissue out of my purse, and I put it over my face. I hid beneath it for a second, wiping away the water and the contorted expression that had broken through for one second only.

"Oh, nothing, my dear," I said. "I am only a little sad, because I am visiting here from very far away, and I used to live here long ago, when I was a little girl like you."

"Really? You lived here?" said the girl with a genuine look of wonder. "Where?"

"In that first apartment, right here. See this window?"

"Oh!" she said. "That's my home! You lived in my home? How weird! Do you wanna come inside?"

My heart, my head, my breath, all was spinning. . . .

"If it's not too much trouble," I said.

"Of course not! *Pozhaluista*, come in! My mother and grandpa are home, and you can have some tea. . . ."

Sitting in the room with familiar greenish-tan wallpaper with a tiny pattern of fleur-de-lis, looking at strangers—a tired woman, an old man, and a little girl's welcoming faces—I put the glass to my lips, and swallowed.

I didn't even think twice.

The water was hot, nearly scalding, untreated with chemo-chlorine. It tasted like a shock of reality, an immediate quenching of a forgotten need. Water had been shed, and now it was being replenished. The pungent aroma of plain, freshly brewed tea leaves struck me with an essence that was deeper than any other thing, any memory.

I was tasting it again, the water of my Russia.

Rossia moya.

I was home.

"What the hell are you talking about?" screamed John's voice on the phone. "You are crazy! Absolutely insane! I knew I shouldn't have let you go there all alone, vulnerable like that! I blame myself—"

"Listen," I said. "My dear, dear sweet one. It's really something that was going to happen one way or another. Besides, these are silly precautions. Silly, idiotic, uncalled for. It's been two days, I am still perfectly healthy, and there was nothing wrong with that water."

"You were damn lucky there was nothing wrong! But that's not the point! The point is, you're supposed to be leaving tomorrow, coming back, getting on the plane, and now they're not going to let you! They'll scan you and find local contaminants in your system! Do you know what that means?"

"Yes, I know. They will keep me here for a couple of extra days, that's all. There's plenty of time."

"There isn't any time! In less than a week is the goddamn Closing!"

He paused, and I could hear his stifled breath coming in gasps on the other end. I felt vaguely guilty for causing him to be worked up like that, knowing how easily he could get excited, how much it hurt him. . . .

"That's it," he resumed, catching his breath at last. "I'm coming to get you! I'll be on the next available flight to Moscow—"

"No!" This time it was I, breathing shortly, madly, swallowing air. "If you do that, then I am not coming back at all! Ever! Let me be, John!"

I heard a shuffle on the other end, other voices arguing. Then there was Andrew on the line, my son.

"Mom!" he said. "Please, come back! I don't know what happened, okay. I don't know if you and Dad have a problem, I had no idea—but please, you've gotta come back home, okay?"

"Andy," I said, "there is no problem. None at all, you hear? This has nothing to do with me and Dad, nothing. All is and has always been perfectly fine—"

"Mom, please . . ." Andrew was suddenly crying, his man's voice cracking. Hearing it made me go cold and hot in flashes. "*Mama! Mamochka!* Please!"

He had switched to the Russian I had taught him, the couple of words of his childhood. . . .

"I'll be home," I said, hearing him through the fabric of a dream. "I promise you I will be."

And so I was.

Today was the day of Closing.

John's fears had been justified, and after a customs health scan had come out positive for certain substances, I was officially delayed. Not for a couple of days, but indefinitely.

Which now meant forever.

I had not called them again. It was no use hearing their agony. But oddly, I felt no guilt. Something had happened to me. Indeed, something. Ever since I had drunk the water.

Today, exactly at six at night, the international phone lines will be shutting down. And with them, the planes will stop. The computer servers will terminate interlinking nodes.

In the morning I had gone to a still functional ATM at an international bank and converted several thousands of IMC in my personal savings account to the Russian local equivalent, the almost worthless ruble. What I was going to do with it, with myself, somehow did not matter.

I spent the afternoon wandering the streets, listening to people talk, and gave away my remaining IMC bills to random beggars, who I knew would rush to convert them before the end of the day.

The day was not cool, once again, a remainder of the early fall. The wind blew fresh in my face, and there was an odd singing in my blood. Surely, a madness.

I paused before Pushkin's monument in the square of the same name, gazing at the statue of the famous beloved poet, the one who epitomized the fathomless soul of Russia, just like Shakespeare in the West.

Legend has it, Pushkin's great grandfather had been a man of royal Abyssinian descent, and was honored at the court of Pyotr Pervii. Even now as I looked, the vibrant pliancy of the African heritage was pronounced in his otherwise Slavic features, in the tight curly locks of his hair, in his sultry eyes.

The statue spoke in my mind, and I was dizzy. Spots of color began to dance before my eyes, superimposed against the clear blue sky.

I thought I heard verses of poetry, immortal words of childhood.

> *U lukomoria dub zelyonii.*
> *Zlataya tsep na dube tom.*
> *I dnem, i nochiu, kot uchennii,*
> *Vsio hodit po tsepi krugom. . . .*

At the shore of the sea stands a green oak, sang the words, and on the oak, a great golden chain. Night and day, a clever learned cat walks round and round upon that golden chain. A cat who sings songs and tells ancient tales. . . .

Legendary words, the heart of the Russian fairy tale.

Every child knew this poem, and the elements it evoked. It was a kaleidoscope of all the figures of ancient Russian folklore, unforgotten through the centuries, older by far than any of the reforms of Peter the Great, older than the Communist blot upon the history, older than the millennium.

I continued to look, and Pushkin's statue opened its eyes in mischief, and winked at me.

I blinked, but again, it was but solid cold stone.

The time was late afternoon, past four.

Two hours before the Closing.

There was no guilt at all inside me. I was a monster. I checked myself, looked for it earnestly, wanting to feel it, wanting to be wracked by it, torn to pieces, savaged, for abandoning those I loved.

I walked past groups of people huddled around small boombox radios, listening to the last international transmissions from the outside. Soon, a sonic interference barrier would be put in effect, and only crackling silence would come.

"*Umryom mi vse!* We're all going to die!" someone cried.

I walked, not looking back, and heard some shots ringing out, from illegal handguns, even now contraband.

But mostly, people were serene.

I moved, seeing peaceful emaciated faces, tired receptive eyes. They were ready for anything, the people of Russia. They had always been. Ready for anything, resigned to it all.

I took a taxi back to the street of my birth. And then at the corner I once again walked in the other direction, to the old monastery grounds, and that little park where I used to play.

I wandered past an old metal swing, which surely was the same one I played on, and then found the stone bench before the old dried-out pond.

Here I was not too surprised to find the same little girl and her mother, walking along the path.

The woman greeted me this time, with a light smile, and the girl waved and started to run, kicking up leaves.

After a minute or two, the woman came back toward me, stopped, and sighed.

"*Nu, vot, Zakritie uzhe sluchilos,*" she said softly, tiredly.
The Closing has happened.

"I know," I replied. "I am sorry."

"It's all right." She shrugged. "Really. We can manage on our own—Russia always has. I think nothing has changed. We're still the same, aren't we all? The sun shines. The children run and play. See, my little girl. . . ."

And she smiled.

And indeed, as I looked, the thin pale little girl, Lena, ran with hands upraised, like a bird, and giggled, and made noises.

There was a high wind, a gust.

Somewhere in the distance, I thought I heard the sounds of the bells in the *Kreml* Watch Tower.

Only, it couldn't be. It was much too far from here. The sound would never carry.

"Can you hear it?" the woman said. "Odd, isn't it? But now, I am sure, it is really six o'clock."

"*Oi! Mama! Smotri!*" suddenly cried the little girl. She had stopped running and was frozen, pointing with her finger up at a nearby tree.

We turned, her mother and I, since we heard a fluttering, a beating of heavy wings.

"*Smotri! Zhar-Ptitsa!*"

A bolt of lightning-flame, orange and persimmon and gold, like a small dislocated sun, had erupted from the very fabric of the air, and burned in the branches of the old maple, so that for a moment I thought someone had set it on fire.

At the heart of the fireball, was a white incandescent outline of a bird. The bird swept its wings, beat once, twice, then suddenly burst forth and rose from the branches like a meteor, an impossible sight.

It rose just over our heads, and then circled the park, while sparks of colored fireworks came down from it, sparks of legend, of a non-scalding fire raining over our heads.

Zhar-Ptitsa.

The firebird.

"Oh my god!" gasped the woman, crossing herself. "*Ghospodi pomilui*, look at that! What is that?"

But before she could say another word, the air shimmered on the other end of the park, and a golden chain appeared, glowing with impossibility. An unnaturally great black cat, the size of a panther, sprung forward, like an animated creature, and balanced along the golden links, swinging lightly. . . .

And immediately all the other trees started to creak, to ring like gentle bells. And out of nowhere, faerie female voices arose with a clamor, as *rusalki* of lithe pale skin and long wood-brown tresses were suddenly visible among the branches. And there was a whisper of *leshii* of the forest, a movement of gnarled muscular limbs. . . .

Then, behind us I heard the sounds of a horn blowing, and a tall white horse came galloping upon the leaves. Mounted upon it was a *bogotyr*, a warrior knight out of legend—great, blond bearded, with sky-eyes of an earnest dream. Immediately behind him came the ghostly rumble of other approaching horses, a great army.

"*Mi sdes, matz svyataya Rossia!*" He brandished his spear and cried in a bass that burst through my head and made my ears ring. "We are here, holy mother earth, mother Russia! Never again will you be alone, for we are with you, unto the end, and now at last you're free!"

"Then go forth, and God be with you," said the giant black cat suddenly, shockingly, in a quiet rational voice of power. It blinked once, widened the slit of its golden eyes into a warm sphere of intensity.

And as I stared, caught up in the unreality of this, the little girl reached up with her hands high above her, straining, while the firebird arose higher and higher, circling over the park, lighting up the early-evening sky of indigo like a phoenix rising out of the ashes. . . .

My Russia was alive again.
Somehow.
Rossia Moya.

BEAUTY AND HIS BEAST

She would watch them, sideways out of her cold clear eyes, the lovers walking with hands and gazes entwined, among rose-briars and thick verdant foliage of the gardens. These were her gardens, and they, the ardent young trespassers, were now and then made *aware* of her, when she allowed it to be. It was but a reminder, lest they forget, that this marvelous idyll, this wonder of a natural Eden, was but a small place within her abode, a place she chose to share. And the lovers, many of whom often came here at a whim, knew in the back of their minds that upon any random turn of the meandering path, beyond any thicket revealing a secret niche, they might come upon her, grimly horrendous and shadowy, the dark queen they all came to know as the Beast.

The gardens—lustrous eyelashes around a glittering eye—sprung forth in abundance to encompass the Palace of the queen. This queen, an oddity, was of such an acutely noble ancient lineage that due to an unpredictable genetic quirk she had been born a monster. She was, at the age of twenty-three, and at the time of her coronation, exactly six-and-a-half feet tall, hunchbacked, her muscular and fleshy hominid body covered head to toe by a thick growth of dark bristly hair—including the face—and her head was misshapen and oversized like a boulder. The head grew sable hair which fell in a fearful mane from the scalp to her waist. Amid the thicket her facial features were hardly distinguishable—indeed, no one ever ventured close enough to try. But her eyes, those were bright, coldly intelligent, *human.*

When she spoke, her voice also was frighteningly human, rich and deep and plush as ermine. It carried also tones of remarkable education—faultless really, except for the occasional moments when a hollow wheezing would overcome her—for the queen suffered from a chronic and inborn lung ailment.

The queen inherited her full rank at the moment of her father's death, then proceeded to institute major changes. The now-deceased king had been a grim shadowy man—although physically normal by all means, as human beings go. In his day, the kingdom lay under the miserly clutches of gloom and decay, under a strict control. With his passing, the gloom and decadence suddenly took a different form, emerging as creative energy. A new pulse-beat was given to the land by the beast-queen. But the control remained. For, she was strong, strong as a Minotaur, by the sheer force of her will contained in the horrendous body.

Brought up and educated as a normal girl-child of her position, the Beast with the given name Vinnaea (which no one cared to use behind her back), held a fine court in her opulent Palace. She was a connoisseur of the Arts and Sciences, patron to those who excelled in such. And she was above all, a subtle lover of beauty.

And this, of all things—some speculated—was the reason for the open gardens and the opulence and the exquisite people surrounding her. They said, the queen wanted the harmony of line and sound and thought to envelop her completely. They said, she wanted to drown in it and lose her *self*, and cease being the Beast—for she knew very well what people thought of her.

When appearing to the court, the Beast wore voluminous robes to cover as much of her grotesque form as possible. And always, the grand chandeliers were raised, and the hall dimmed before she would make her presence.

The bright lights, it seemed, hurt her abnormally sensitive eyes.

In the rich thick darkness of the gardens, the queen would find peace more often than elsewhere. She spent her days here—when the sun burned overhead, she would hide in a grove of maples, or near the weeping willows by the brook, or would lose herself in the artificially sculpted thicket of the Maze. When it rained, she crouched, reading in one of her favorite grottoes, books of philosophy, or else, jotted down acutely beautiful thoughts in her leather-bound diary, with her clumsy black-maned hand.

At other times, when the sun spilled itself in an amber sunset, or clouds came to shadow the horizon, the Beast would watch those who strolled in her gardens.

They were beautiful, those young men and women, as perfectly formed to her as any amber sunset, and even more *alive*. The Beast loved to observe them strolling in couples, whispering to each other words of intimacy (which she would guiltily overhear, while a new feeling—one she could not verbalize to herself, but one that appeared persistently—would insinuate into her inhumanly *innocent* heart. It, this feeling, lingered there and occasionally made her soul-sick). But their presence here, no matter that it stirred alien longings in her, made her oddly content.

Until one day, a youth plucked a single bright crimson flower from her most treasured place, and thus there was to be no peace for the Beast.

"Oh, how pretty! How large that one is, I want that one!" cried Aysnera, pointing to the lush exotic flower whose name she did not know, growing larger than the rest on the branches of the tree.

"I'm not sure, lady," Moere said thoughtfully. "I don't know if it would be right to pick the flowers here."

"Why not?" the lady cried, in her petulant lovely voice. "There are so many here, who would notice? Or care? Or are you afraid of *her?*"

Moere colored lightly. So easy it was to observe the changes on his fair light skin, fine and delicate as porcelain— each blush, each faint blooming of veins under the cheeks, left his face flaming as the dawn, and then, as quickly, pale again. Aysnera was not the only one charmed by his exquisite sensibilities, his curling honey-locks, and his gentle introspective eyes. In their circle of friends, he was affectionately teased with the nickname "Beauty," by both the ladies and the young noblemen.

"Well then," lady Aysnera said. "I will pluck it myself!" And she proceeded diligently to make the attempt, stretching up her bejeweled hands for some time, and finally gave up, saying: "This stupid bush! It's too tall for me! But oh, how nicely that bright red thing would sit in my hair. If only you were kind to me, Moere! You're tall enough."

The young man gave in, and plucked the blossom. He could not explain it to himself what made him uneasy about doing this—almost, a feeling of being observed.

And the next thing he knew, Aysnera was busy clutching her skirts to sink into a deep reverential curtsy, sudden alarm written on her face, and uttering "Your Majesty," while his own pulse first swooned, then also gained speed (in fear, and from some other feeling he had no words for). Just before he too lowered himself into the proper courtly bow, his glance froze upon the great dark hunched form suddenly looming before them out of nowhere, and he had a glimpse of cold-burning *human* eyes. The blossom on its stem was still clutched in his trembling hand.

"Rise," said a deep voice of power. Controlled anger was in it also. "Rise, and do not ever do this again. Who taught you manners, lady?" The latter was addressed to Aysnera, who trembled.

"Oh, I am so sorry, Madam! Oh, so sorry—"

As though there existed such an unwritten law, they both stood now, yet neither dared raise their eyes to look at *her*.

"What is your name, girl?" said the Beast.

"A-aysnera, Your Majesty. Lady Aysnera Hild. I am so sorry—"

"When you allow guests into your house, Aysnera Hild, do you also expect them to appropriate the silverware from your dinner table, or the tapestries off the walls? These are my gardens, and you are my guests. This particular flower—although for weeks now beloved by me—has no great value really. It is but the careless attitude which you display, lady, that disturbs me. Your *carelessness* in taking it."

"I am the one to blame . . ." the young man blurted suddenly. "I took the flower from the branch." And his gaze rose to meet the Beast. "Moere Deiwall, Your Majesty, at Your service."

"Yes," said the Beast after an instant in which he thought his mind would explode from meeting the gaze out of the hooded darkness. "Only—it was not your intent. I know, for I have been observing the two of you contemplate my favorite flower."

And just as suddenly, the queen addressed Aysnera again: "You are dismissed, lady. And I have forgotten the incident." And then, to Moere: "But not you. I want you to come with me."

Such a cold wave of fear engulfed him then, that the young man, in a chill daze, never heard the crinkling of starched skirts as Aysnera curtsied in a hurry, and nearly went running down the path. She also, never looked back.

Moere stood alone with the Beast.

The fear accompanied him as he followed the dark hooded form (not knowing what lay underneath the rich heavy brocade of the Beast's cloak, having seen but the *eyes*), as they walked the twisting garden paths, to an unknown destination. He walked as though under a geas, pulled by an intuitive sense of obligation, and some strange new excitement.

"I want to show you things you have never seen before." The Beast spoke as they walked. "You, unlike these others, I must show."

And it never occurred to him to ask her "why."

They passed through groves of maple and oak and birch, and the Beast spoke to him of the perfect sound that leaves make, falling, and the murky breathing of the earth. They glanced into each one of the running streams, and she explained how it is possible to count every single pebble on the stream bed, at a glance. She showed him the patterns of lacework that the sun made through the fine leaves and branches of the weeping willows by the water's edge, and then he realized that, indeed, he'd seen the lacework before, woven into the artful court tapestries.

Next they wandered in the grottoes where he observed the rock formations give off light, eerie and hypnotic, and the occasional streamlined and elegant shapes of the bats evoked in him no longer the customary revulsion and fear, but an odd gentle pity. Indeed, he noticed, that fear which had followed him was no longer with him, and instead, a lively curiosity had taken hold. Above all else, he wanted to hear the voice of the Beast.

It was at that moment that she stopped, saying: "The sun has almost set, you must now leave, Moere. Keep the flower you have plucked, as my gift. Return here again tomorrow, at the place of our meeting, and I will show you more."

Wordlessly he nodded, knowing that he must.

M oere Deiwall returned the next afternoon as he was told. And then he did so the next day, and the next. Each time, the Beast would take him along with her, and would speak to him, and would *show* him, until it seemed he no longer could keep track of time, and instead began to see the gardens all around him as if they were a transparent lacework dream, while the wind seemed to him solid, and the sun was a golden incandescent vapor in the ice of the sky. Each night he would return, before sunset, and friends would greet him, noting his vacant non-presence, and his pallor, and his sightless eyes. "What is it, Beauty, what is it with you?" they strove to know, for his eyes indeed seemed to look elsewhere when he looked at them.

And when they found out that he had been spending time with the beast-queen, odd pitying glances, lacking any comprehension, followed him, and they whispered to each other of madness.

Months had thus passed. The seasons changed, fall replacing summer in the eternal ring dance, replete with its golden decay and ripeness. And in the winter, when the gardens were bare of leaves, and sparkling ice crystallized on the branches, still Moere would go to meet *her*. Breath freezing on his lips, freezing would he stand, as he listened to her words and to her voice.

And slowly, he found himself speaking also, telling her who was forever hooded in velvet darkness, many things he had never told even himself. It was then that she listened gravely, intently, and he was able to catch yet another rare glimpse of her acute, clear, *human* eyes. And afterward, every time, he would beg to remain with her an instant longer, beyond the moment of sunset, not understanding why it had to be thus. But the Beast insisted, with an urgency he could make no denial to, that he leave.

In the meantime, those he called friends would confront him, question him until he wanted to run and hide and make himself small somewhere. "What is it that you speak with *her* about, Moere? What is it that you *do* with her?" Aysnera and others of her kind asked.

"Nothing," he would say. "Nothing *real* . . ."

And when he saw how unclear his words were, even to himself, and how they provoked even greater suspicion, he would add: "We discuss—philosophy, yes. Her—Her Majesty is very interested in these matters, and in me she has found a good verbal companion."

"Ooh!" Aysnera would cry. "How *can* you? How can you be with the *Beast?*"

And for the first time in months, Moere would flush bright crimson with anger. "Do not call her that. Her name is Vinnaea. And she is our—queen."

"Hah!" Aysnera mocked. "She is, too, the Beast! And what a Beast! You must have gone blind all this while, to have gotten used to the ape-ugliness!"

"I—do not ever—*see* her." And as he said those words, he knew suddenly how odd it was indeed, that he had never even thought to wonder what lay underneath the dark hood, besides the eyes. It came to him then, as though a mental lens had insidiously changed focus, that in truth it was most bizarre, this whole thing. . . . All these days together, and never did he wonder *why*, why all they did was aimlessly wander the grounds, why did she not let him see her, why could he not stay after dark, and finally, hadn't she, the queen, other things to do?

He had been living in a spell, it occurred to Moere. His vision had been—due to that spell—forever doubled. Even now, as he looked at the elegant brightly-lit chamber around him, at Aysnera in her lovely jewel-dress, he could see, like a superimposed image hanging in his *other* mind's eye, the semi-transparency of all these things, the dimness (despite the bright chandelier illumination). And almost, he could see *through* Aysnera herself, to the other wall behind her, for she, too, was only half-corporeal and half-shade, and there was, in fact, less and less substance in her, the more he looked. Another instant of this vision, and she would fade. . . .

He tried to blink this away, drowning in a wave of fear— for he was being engulfed by something far greater than he could ever conceive. And for a while it would recede, and things came into focus the *normal* way—that is, the one and only way he had once perceived them. Maybe it was true then, he was losing his mind.

"Do not go to see *her* anymore . . ." Aysnera whispered then, urgently. "Come instead, with us, we shall celebrate tomorrow, riding in the Dragon-sleds! Come with us, this once!"

"But—" he protested, a dark faint soul-sickness entering him.

"There'll be minstrels and song, and tambourines and fools with bell-caps, and we'll ride faster than the wind! And you'll smile and laugh once again, Moere! Come away, and remember how you once had been! So easy to do this!"

"But I promised *her* I will come. As always. . . . She would not know what happened—she will—what if she is hurt by this?"

"Are you *afraid* of her then, Moere?"

Again, that taunt. He thought then, with intensity.

"Not to see her, only once. Maybe that would not be so bad. She would know I had other things to do. She should guess, by gods! I, too, have my life!"

Only, at that instant, it was as if his inner *vision*, the one that teetered on the edge, doubling constantly, giving him four-dimensional sight, went dim all of a sudden, retreated, and narrowed. And then Moere could only see the normal bleak solid opulence of the room, and Aysnera's attentive eyes.

Somewhere else, placed in the exact same glass vase as it had been many months ago, the crimson lush blossom, the Beast's gift—one that oddly went unnoticed by any and all, except for Moere, and one that never lost its bloom—suddenly shuddered faintly, as though kissed by the wind.

And the next instant it stood dry and death-brown, charred out of its timelessness into instant decay.

The Beast stood alone on the dreary path of her garden. All about her the winter wind blew, tugging crudely at the nude black branches, and sending snowflakes up in drifts of crystal white.

She stood and she listened, and from somewhere far away, carried by the icy gusts, there came to her the sound of laughter, young lovers celebrating the great Ride of Winter. Hoofbeats drummed against the frozen earth, and the wild wailing of reed pipes and beating tambourines rose high on the wind. Wild exuberant joy was upon them, and with her *vision*, the Beast could see *him*, surrounded by laughing young maidens and other youths, their cheeks burning scarlet as dawn from the frost. Young he also was, fresher and fairer even than any of them, and his golden laughter rode the winter wind.

The Beast watched the softly inflamed look in his sparkling, gentle eyes—so intimate, so dear to her, ever since the first time when she had seen him, terrified yet steadfastly clutching the flower in his chill, pale hand. It was then that she had seen the *kindness* in those eyes, odd and sympathetic, unlike anything she had ever experienced. And the look of them had perforated the innocence that walled her in, cut through the invulnerable diamond of her soul-heart, all the way to her deepest soft core of rainbow and mother-of-pearl. And it made her bleed with a feeling that she never fathomed before, and to which she could give no name.

She watched him who was Beauty, as they had gotten out of the Dragon-sleds, wreathed with streamers of scarlet and persimmon gold. He was laughing, and then reached with one gentle warm hand to hug a lady's fine waist—while the lady, Aysnera, trembling with frost and joy, threw her arms about his marble neck, and lightly brushed his soft honey-curls.

There was a wetness in the *human* eyes of the Beast; for a moment her *vision* blurred, and the cold wind froze the drops that came down her cheek of bristling sable fur.

She had never once told him that she loved him. She had never again told him that he must come back, or she would die.

There was no need for it, for she had taught him to *see*.

And again the Beast saw through the blurring mists of immense distance, and heard the singing on the wind. And Beauty's head, she saw, was leaned closely to the maiden's breast. She could see every softly rounded contour of his profile, soft as porcelain, and the rose dawn—his sweet blushing skin.

And the Beast saw the gentle kind look in his eyes, the same intimate vulnerable look that he had once given her and one that now he just as simply and genuinely gave to another.

It was then that something deep within the Beast, deep within the furred, muscular, hunchbacked body, broke at last. No sound she gave, but the strength, the immense *strength* of the Beast had left her. She was now only a crippled thing, wrapped in dark pitiful garments, weightless and slowly sinking in a hunched embryonic heap onto the clear stark-white snow.

Flushed with happiness of the Winter Ride, Moere returned only to see his secret enchanted thing—the one that burned like a beacon in his vision—the flower, standing black and wilted in its vase of glass. And now he remembered how, all through the Ride, in the back of his mind, he had felt it, *dying*, flickering out, and sometimes, oddly, he would see two clear intense eyes of the Beast, clear and sharp as day, in his mind's eye. But never has he seen them thus—they were crying. It had bothered him then, but he let himself be carried by the joy-tide of the moment, made himself not care.

And now, in a wave of darkness, he *allowed* himself to *see* once more, and as his vision once again unfurled, warped and doubled, expanding as it once had been, he knew what he had done.

The gardens stood silent and white, and silver-violet dusk hung in the air. No sound, not even the wind. All was motionless, hazy.

His pulse raced with soul-sickness, and breath came short in the icy air, as he ran. Twists and sharp bends of the garden path, branches striking his face. Another turn, and with a swooning in his head, he saw *her*, or what he knew to be her.

The pitiful heap of darkness sprawled on the path before him, next to the tall familiar flower-bush. A powdery fine sprinkling of snow already had dusted lightly the black fabric. Somewhere, protruding, he saw a small dark-furred shape resembling a hand—rheumatic and knotted, with longish animal nails. Odd, how he had never noticed her hands before, ghastly and black-haired and sad.

Moere fell on his knees in the snow, next to the Beast. One instant he thought she was only a corpse, but then a faint difficult sound came to him, a light wheezing breath of one dying.

In the next instant, the sun spent its last ray, fell behind the rim of the world, and evening darkness, like a curtain, was about them.

Moere knew a sudden instinctual but unreal fear. He lowered his ear to her chest, to listen for a heartbeat, faint but present.

The Beast's face was, strangely, still hooded. Moere's peculiar unemotional response began to frighten even himself. Again, it was as though a spell engulfed him, only this time he saw and heard everything, but could not *feel*.

He gently removed the hood, and this time, the evening twilight rushed in, black, as though to take its place, and again he could almost see nothing, unless he made his searching gaze burn through the smoke-darkness.

Silent, he at last observed before him the Beast's face, like a caricature mask of horror worn at a carnival. And still, he did not feel.

Her eyes, closed before, came abruptly open. And his heart, which was a second ago calm as ice, now swooned in shock.

For, her *eyes* were *different*. Red and burning volcanic pits met him, and after a long moment of recognition, she whispered: "Moere . . . You have come. But oh, not now, no. It is—after dark. And as you see, it is when I lose the last of my humanity. After dark."

She breathed, struggling with effort, and watched with her burning gaze his frozen receptive eyes for any sign of reaction.

"I am—sorry," he whispered. "I had to be away—"

"Yes. How true, away from me. It is only natural, dear Moere. I—I would be surprised if you—always came here." And the Beast-face attempted to smile.

"I—"

"Say no more." She breathed with a harsh, rasping rhythm. And then she bared her long teeth in a horrible mockery of a grin. "Well, Beauty. Now that you see me the way I am, my horrible, my ridiculous face and form, what do you think? And don't be afraid to tell me the truth. I'd know if you tried to lie, you realize. I know you—too well. I am the Beast, my dearest Beauty, and as they say, I can tear you *apart*." She spoke fiercely now, with mockery, with a peculiar pride, and waited.

"Don't ever call yourself that!" he exclaimed, bolting into a true waking state.

"And why not, my fair one? I am the Beast indeed. The queen of all Beasts. . . ."

Something began choking him, deep in the throat, and blood rang in his head. He looked at her in silence, unsullied by words, simply as he always had—looked.

"Well," said the Beast. "What do you *see?*"

And then Moere cried. Silent streaming tears came down his cheeks, freezing and hurting his tender skin, sharper than blades of steel. "I don't—know!" he repeated over and over, "I don't see! I don't—"

He never could express himself eloquently, as she could.

And then, as his head was about to explode with the overflow, the pain, of emotion long suppressed, he cried: "Don't *you* yourself understand? Don't you know what I see, you who showed me that other *vision?*"

And then he gulped, choking on his tears, and continued: "When I look at you, Vinnaea, if you must really know, I only see one *thing*, that which I've *always* seen—not this black form that you wear! No! Not this sad shape of darkness that you somehow—long time ago, before you were even born—planned to put on yourself! It is but an incorporeal shadow, like those all other things I see around me! No, you are not *this*—a light! You, my queen, are the most bright glorious form of *light*, more definite to me than the sun, or any of these poor souls that surround me.

When I look at them long enough, they fade into nothing before me. And if I pretend to myself not to *see*, then I also, begin to fade, like them. But not you! You are the only one the sight of whom blinds me, you are the most concrete form in the world!

"And yes, my shining one, I was once, and still am afraid of you, and to some extent, always will be. For, you are so much brighter than my own being. . . . I can feel how you can burn me away, and yet, I must be, forever be with you—"

And he pulled himself close, underneath her velvet cloak of darkness, and his arms came tightly, inevitably, to embrace the black fur, while his face with its crystallizing tears, buried in the crook of her swarthy neck, and his form shook with weeping.

"Then, my life has not been in vain," said the Beast, soft as falling snow, holding him tight to her. "For, my gentle Beauty, you who are my soul-half, I had indeed been born the Beast only for this—to help you awaken your *vision* of the way things *are*. And that, you have done. . . ."

And at that he wept even harder, and suddenly his constantly wavering sight came into a single great focus, so that he could see *her* fully—bright as day in the middle of night, and more beautiful than he ever suspected. While, he also now saw all things to the farthest reaches of the land, and "inside-out," as though they were faceted crystals, and he was looking out from within each one of their glassy rainbow cores.

The cold had gone from the night, as they embraced, two forms of pure energy fused into one.

And somewhere far away, in a cold incorporeal chamber, Moere thought he saw from his unnatural distance, a tiny but brightly glowing form of a lush crimson flower, superimposed in his true *vision* over a dark decayed husk in a vase.

And he thought he could see, next to the great flower on the stem, there had opened a new young fiery bud.

THE YOUNG WOMAN IN A HOUSE OF OLD

The young girl lived in a big stone house with ivy-covered walls and with old men and women who were all her kin.

When she was a very tiny little girl, she remembered adult faces looking down at her as she lay in her crib, warm wrinkle-framed eyes of tired aunts and grandmothers and cousins and second-cousins and great-aunts and uncles-twice-removed and great-great-grandfathers, and even creatures so old and wrinkled and small that she mistook them for dolls until they moved and she saw that they were ancient kindly goblins and gnomes with white cobwebs for hair and eyebrows.

Her parents were no longer in this world, she was told, and instead, here were her closest kinfolk, all taking care of her.

The little girl had no one to play with in the big house. She did try to play with the grandmothers and the cousins and the aunts, but they all had rheumatism or gout or bad knees or asthma or shortness of breath, and tired soon after. They never ran to catch the ball she threw, and did not even walk to retrieve it more than a couple of times. Nor did they laugh too loudly, only smiled at her with weary fondness. Some tried to trick her out of playing games that required physical exertion by telling her intricate stories, but fell asleep before they ever finished them. Many of them offered to read to her, but there is only so much reading to a little girl can tolerate.

And so she went outside in the tree-lined streets, and sometimes she met other children who lived in the neighboring houses, and together they played lively games of chasing balls and hiding from one another in the overgrown alleys and narrow passageways between houses.

The little girl ran around and played in the sun, and when the shadows grew long towards evening, she returned like all the other children to her own house where the old aunts and uncles sat at the dinner table. There she took her place, and ate the hot dinner, and took part in the grown-up talk.

The older people always talked to her as though she were of an age to understand the table conversation even when her head barely reached the top of the table. And somehow it indeed came to be that she understood them perfectly and even formed opinions.

"What do you think of the current weather?" they asked her. And she smiled back shyly and slurped her soup. "I think the heat is too much for the roses. That's why they curl up and wither before fully opening. And the wind is unusually dry for such early spring."

No one ever told her that slurping was impolite. Indeed, many of the aunts and cousins and grandfathers slurped too, loudly and tastily, as they ate their soup. Some of the really old ones often picked up their bowls and drank the soup as though it were tea, spilling much of it on their withered chins. The white-mustached goblins poured much of it in the thicket of their beards and down their napkins. As dinner progressed, lights were turned on in chandeliers. Evening shadows turned deep blue to displace the golden pinks of the fading sunset.

Then came tea. It was poured from fine porcelain pots, and creamy desserts were served by other old cousins. Everyone laughed with shaky old voices, and the conversation grew as animated as it could be, considering the elderly participants, and eventually there was more fragrant tea. The teapots emptied, and soon someone would call for another pot, and, you guessed it, there was even more tea, pots and pots of it, of different varieties and crops, from India, the Caucasus, Sri-Lanka, with the rich dark leaves and the flavorings like oil of bergamot, or citrus or even some dried raspberries tossed in.

The little girl got tired of it after a while, full to bursting with the pastries and the hot soothing tea, and yet no one ever told her it was time for bed. So she sneaked away, pushing her chair in quietly, and ran to the library where the lights were dim. Here, she dug around in the musty stacks, and selected books with big decorative covers and cursive type that looked like it was a part of the border design. Those were usually the kind to have pictures, and she stared and pretended she was in the pictures, pretended to be the beautiful woman or man or creature drawn with such bright colors and wearing such sweeping robes, caught at a moment when the wind lifted their hems and tangled gauze sleeves and veils and billowed them like sails.

Time then became endless and blurry, its passage convoluted, so that some pictures took forever to examine, while some pages flew past her at the speed of thought.

And then it was very late indeed, and she noticed that all the lights in the house were out except for the faint brown-gold nightlights in the hallways, as the old grandmothers and uncles and cousins had gone to their beds, and all the doors were locked.

The little girl went to wash her face and brush her teeth and braid her hair into a looser soft braid for the night, and with a glass of water she came to her great bed that filled most of her room. She put the glass on her table, pinched the wick in the lamp with a pair of pincers to extinguish the flame, and then rushed to jump under the safe covers that now spread over her like magical layers of a warm protective ocean.

Unlike her cousins and aunts and grandfathers she did not immediately fall asleep but lay there in the warm semi-dream state and allowed images of godlike women and men and creatures to blossom in her vision. Sometimes her eyes remained open for a long time, and at other times she closed her eyes and observed things against the velvet backdrop of her eyelids. The images stood up before her in faraway brilliant color—lands of incredible sunsets and green forests, with running water in mountain pools, with crashing ocean waves of silver against a brilliant white sky, with beautiful ancient ruins and temples of goddesses and fair gods, with flying beings like angels and yet, with other beings, that were like darkness, which struggled with the angels, and which. . . .

She finally slept, and the next morning she carried the dreams with her. She did the same thing every day and looked forward to the following evening.

The girl grew and reached school age. One clear early autumn morning, two of her aunts accompanied her on her first day to school, and then left her there. The girl was told to be good and to listen to the teachers, and to pay close attention. She was also told that here in the school she would be referred to as Miss Marianne Mornay because that was her given name. The girl sounded out her given name and it seemed nice but a bit odd, since no one had ever called her by that name before. Indeed, the idea of having a name was a bit odd too, because in her old stone house with ivy-covered walls her aunts and grandmothers and cousins never mentioned their own names. It was rather unnecessary since everyone always seemed to know who everyone else was referring to.

"Miss Mornay," said her teacher, a serious middle-aged woman with glasses and auburn hair taken up in a tight bun, so that the girl started at being directly addressed. "Miss Mornay, here in school you will learn how to read and write and count. You will also learn history and the arts and the sciences. You will play with your fellow students only during recess and lunch, and you will obey your elders promptly."

And with that, school started.

The girl whose given name was Marianne Mornay attended her classes, and sat at a desk next to other students her age, and when the day was over she came back home where her grandmothers and cousins and uncles had the dinner ready, and everyone was waiting for her so that they could begin eating.

"I am going to learn how to read and write and count!" said Marianne, when asked how her day was.

"That is wonderful, Dear," said an elderly cousin, and several of the old aunts and grandfathers and goblins and gnomes with white eyebrows echoed the sentiment.

Then the soup was served, and the dinner-table conversation started.

The next morning the girl was back at school, and the teacher showed them the first three of the letters of the alphabet, and drew them on the blackboard with dusty yellowish chalk. The letter "A" was made up of three lines, two propping each other up, and the third lying flat and trying hard to keep them apart from the middle. Marianne held her pencil in her fingers and tried to draw the three lines just so.

Next to her another little girl who was addressed by the teacher as Miss Lily North, with pale blonde hair, much lighter than her own, was having a bit of trouble. Her three lines did not seem to connect properly, and the middle line was always lopsided.

"Here," said Marianne to Lily. "This is how you do it." And she drew the three lines just so, exactly how the teacher had drawn them on the blackboard.

On the other side of her sat a boy with dark hair and clever cool eyes. "Show off," he said to Marianne.

But Lily only smiled to her and said politely, "Thank you."

"Dummy," said the dark haired boy to Lily.

But Marianne and Lily ignored him, and instead they listened to the teacher who showed them how to draw the next letter.

When school was over and Marianne had come home, she told everyone in the old house how she had learned the letters "A," "B," and "C." The old ones applauded, and a grandmother with spectacles patted Marianne on the cheek as she poured her the soup.

Later, as tea was served, Marianne slipped away after only one fragrant cup in order to run to the library. Here she selected her favorite book with great colorful pictures, and for the first time she did not look at the pictures first but at the squiggly lines underneath that she now knew to be writing.

She looked at them, and sometimes she found the letter "A." Often the letter "A" came at the beginning of lines and sometimes it was very big and colorful, with green vines creeping around its edges and crimson roses peeking around its top.

"A," said Marianne. "A, A, A," she read over and over, quickly turning the pages while excitement built inside her so that she suddenly wanted to know what all the other squiggles were. Then she looked closely and found the letters "B" and "C" hiding among the squiggles. They popped up unexpectedly, like treasures. And once she knew they were there, she saw them on every page in many places.

Marianne could hardly contain herself and went to bed early so that she did not have to wait 'till tomorrow to learn the next letters.

The next day Marianne's class learned "D," "E," and "F," and as the week progressed, there were more and more letters, and the teacher showed them how to put some of the letters together to make magic in the form of words.

Marianne was one of the quickest in the class, and she drew the prettiest letters just so, exactly as the teacher. Next to her, Lily had trouble with some letters, and Marianne was happy to help her draw "G" and "C," so that they did not look alike. During recesses Marianne and Lily sat beside each other often on the steps of the school, and they drew the letters together. Sometimes Lily would get tired and she'd draw a stick person instead and giggle.

The dark-haired boy who sat in class on the other side of Marianne and whom the teacher called Mister Robin Noggins, often ran by with his friends and stuck out his tongue at Lily and Marianne. Sometimes he threw a rock that clattered at their feet, and at other times he pulled Marianne's braid of chestnut-brown hair.

Once during lunch, as Robin Noggins came by and dropped a bug on Lily's head, Marianne stuck out her foot just as he was running past them, and Robin Noggins fell down flat on his face in front of them and started to cry. He'd skinned his knee and torn his sock, and got himself a big red bruise covered with playground dirt.

The teacher came quickly and shook her head at the three of them. Lily had gotten up and was screaming and batting at her blonde hair to get the bug off, Robin was wailing on the ground where he now sat, and Marianne remained in her spot with a glowering look.

"I don't know who did what, and which of you started it," said the teacher. "But all three of you are going to stay an hour after school and do your homework right here with me. Now, go inside and clean your knee with soap and water, Mister Noggins. And Miss North, leave your hair alone, there is nothing there. As for you, Miss Mornay—"

But the teacher did not have anything to say, only looked at Marianne reproachfully. "Really now, I'd have thought better of you, Miss Mornay," she finally said, at which Marianne blushed.

After school, Marianne, Lily, and Robin remained seated at their desks, and worked on their letters, occasionally staring meanly at one another. In the front of the class the teacher sat in her chair reading, her spectacles having slid down to the tip of her nose.

When the hour was over, they were excused, and Marianne rushed home. This was the first time that she had not been home in time for dinner, and she knew that her old aunts and grandmothers and cousins must be terribly worried.

And she was right. The house was oddly quiet and everyone was seated silently at the dinner table before empty dishes—not empty as in eaten, but empty and squeaky clean as though dinner had never been served. The soup had grown cold in the kettle, and some of the oldest grandmothers and aunts were nodding in their chairs. The goblins slept with their faces down on the tablecloths, and one or two were snoring softly.

As soon as Marianne had entered the room, everyone woke up however, and one old granny said, "Ah, there you are, Dear! Where have you been? Do you realize the soup has gotten cold! And it is not even gazpacho or that newfangled vichyssoise soup but string bean, pea and carrot, which means that it needs to be eaten when piping hot. Well, never mind now!"

Immediately an old cousin got up and began to ladle out the cold soup to all, and as though nothing happened, the usual conversation started up.

"I am sorry," muttered Marianne, but only one grandfather heard her, and he nodded at her and winked, and then dipped his spoon into the soup bowl and began to slurp hungrily.

Later that night Marianne sat in her usual place in the library. She held a book in her lap, and she could read most of the words in it. But tonight she was unable to concentrate, and instead continued to think about her old grand-aunts and cousins and great-great uncles and all the rest of them. What if she were to be late again for an hour, and what if something happened and she was really *really* late? Or, what if she did not come home at all? Would they all go hungry on her behalf?

The next morning during breakfast, Marianne said to a second-cousin and uncle, "Cousin, Uncle, please promise me that if I am late coming home again that you will go ahead and have dinner without me?"

"Why would you be late again, Dear?" said the uncle with a toothless smile as he buttered his muffin and then added a large spoonful of apricot-pineapple preserves on top.

"Well," said Marianne, "I don't know. What if the teacher makes me stay after school again?"

"That wouldn't be a good thing at all," replied her second-cousin in a tremulous voice, as she poured milk into her bowl on top of some sugary cornflakes and loudly scraped the sides of the bowl to stir it.

"But what if it happens?" persisted Marianne. "Would the two of you please make sure to let the others know that it's OK and that you should just eat without me?"

"Oh," said the uncle, biting his muffin, "I suppose we could do that, couldn't we?" And he nudged the second-cousin. "Could we?"

She started in alarm and dropped her spoon into the cornflakes. "What? What did you just say?"

"I said, we need to make sure to let the others know that she—that she—" The uncle looked back at Marianne and said, "What was that again, Dear? What are we supposed to say?"

"Oh, never mind," said Marianne, frustration breaking into her voice. "I won't be late again, I promise."

"Late?" said the second cousin. "Who is late?"

The uncle just shrugged and scratched his wrinkled cheek. He continued to chew his muffin and smacked his lips loudly.

In no time at all the school year drew to a close. Marianne could now read all the words in her primer with a fluent speed that left most of her classmates behind, except for Lily and Robin. Lily could read very well indeed because Marianne always made sure she could, and Robin was not going to let two girls get ahead of him. In addition to reading and writing, they also learned numbers and counting and formulas with mysterious x and y values they had to solve for. They used rulers to make all kinds of interesting angles, and protractors to draw circles, and even started on degrees. There was also history, where Marianne suddenly recognized references to some of the godlike people in the books at home, and knew now that many of them had been real people who lived a long time ago, and that the books simply portrayed them as divine because this is what often happens in history books to people who are popular or strong or brave. In addition to history, they had art, where everyone got to draw objects and still lifes, and where the teacher let them look at even more amazing books filled with pictures of ancient white marble statues and intricate paintings of the great masters.

Marianne could draw very well, just like she could form the letters, and she was better than everyone else when it came to drawing faces. One painter called Rembrandt interested her in particular because he portrayed old people with deep lines in their faces and dark brown shadows and darkness and dim lighting. No one else drew such real-looking old grandmothers and grandfathers, and for a moment Marianne thought some of them looked awfully familiar. Indeed, the more she thought about it the more she came to the conclusion that some of the old relatives living in her house were just like these people in the paintings. They had the same depth of wrinkles and the same shrunken skin and deep hollows.

Marianne took her sketch pad and her art pencils home with her and during dinners when everyone was gathered, she made some quick drawings of an aunt or a cousin or grandmother. Since it was now summer and school was out, she had plenty of time during the day to stop in various rooms of the house and draw a napping white-haired goblin here and an old granny there, while in yet another room she found two or three withered uncles and a gnome playing dominoes, and a cousin or two reading in the library.

By the end of the summer, her sketchbook was full, and the only thing left to do was to return to the library every night or lazy heat-filled afternoon, and to read and look at pictures that she already knew so well, and to dream of ancient times and faraway places all over the world.

When school resumed and Marianne brought her sketchbook to class, the teacher took a long careful look at the images and then stared back at Marianne. "Hmmmm," said the teacher. And then added, "Very well done, Miss Mornay. You appear to have a great facility for character portraiture. I will put you with the advanced class this year."

Marianne blushed with pleasure, and later showed the sketchbook to Lily and even to Robin who had stared over her shoulder for so long that she had thought she might as well let him peek.

"Why did you draw all these old people?" asked Lily. "It is really all very good, of course, but why did you draw them?"

"These are my aunts and uncles and cousins and grandparents," said Marianne. She was a bit taken aback by the question.

"How come they are all so old?" said Robin in a sharp snotty voice.

Marianne shut her sketchbook with a snap. And then she said, "Sorry."

"It's OK," said Lily and smiled her usual kind smile. They all forgot this in a matter of minutes, but Marianne could not. The pleasure at the teacher's comment was somehow diminished now, and Marianne suddenly no longer wanted to draw anything at all. In the next art class she drew a boring still life with roses in a vase.

And she continued to think about what Lily and snotty Robin had asked when she got home. Why did she have so many old relatives? Where did they all come from? What kind of a house was this anyway?

As everyone ate dinner, she wore a frown on her face, and even some nearsighted cousins noticed.

"What's wrong, Dear?" a couple of them said with warm concern.

"Nothing," replied Marianne.

"Well then, have another piece of potato pie, Dear," said a grandmother with a pretty lacy collar around her skinny neck.

And then Marianne cleared her throat loudly and gathered her courage. And she asked everyone at the table: "Excuse me, but why do I have more than two grandmothers and grandfathers? And *who* are all of you?"

The question resulted in silence. Old wrinkled faces stilled in amazement, in surprise, all flavors of it. One or two grannies adjusted their hearing aids, and at least three great uncles set down their spoons or forks and put on their spectacles as though that was going to help them hear better.

"Ahem, Dear?" said one goblin at the end of the table, his voice so shaky and weak that he had to put his withered hands around his mouth to be heard. "What was it that you said?"

Marianne bit her lip. "Who are all of you?" she said again. "Why do you all live here with me? Why do I live here?"

"What kind of a silly question is that, Dear?" said one great aunt. "Why, we are here because this is our house! Goodness, where else would we be?"

"Don't call me 'Dear!'" exclaimed Marianne. "My given name is Marianne! Why don't you ever use it? And why don't any of you have given names of your own?"

"Well, of course your given name is Marianne," said a grandfather, scratching the top of his balding head. "We all know that, don't we?"

"Of course we do," replied several cousins, nodding.

"So why should we have to use a given name when we all know what it is?"

"Exactly," echoed two aunts.

"Would be a waste of words, wouldn't it?" muttered a second-cousin twice removed.

"Say, what's the main course there?" said another tiny aunt, and immediately the dinner-table conversation resumed where it had left off. Meanwhile the old uncle on the right of Marianne patted her hand, saying, "There, there, Dear. Main course will cheer you up in a minute!"

"I don't need cheering up," whispered Marianne. "I need to better understand! For example, Uncle, what is *your* name?"

But the old man had already turned his attention back to his plate and with shaking hands was cutting a piece of lamb chop into little easy bite-size pieces.

The school days stretched forward without end and Marianne lost track of the many things she was learning. Several times Lily invited her home for dinner, and to study together, but Marianne always declined politely, saying that she had to be home that night. More than once there had been splendid birthday parties and her classmates asked their friends to come, and sometimes she was invited. But always Marianne would think of a good excuse why she could not go. No one at home had ever told her she could not attend; she just *knew* she could not.

On such nights she would come home and brood after dinner, sitting alone in her room or the library, while the evening shadows progressed. She imagined the children playing together and opening birthday presents, mountains of them, and running and laughing. Not that she wanted these presents in particular; she just wanted to be there when it was done, to hear the gasps of wonder, and the ripping of bright gift paper, and to imagine what was inside.

Once Marianne asked during dinner when her own birthday was and why did they never celebrate it.

"A birthday?" said one great-grandmother, pouring a cup of tea. "Why, what a lovely idea!"

"Why, yes indeed," replied many of the cousins and uncles and great-grandfathers.

"We will have a birthday party!" said an aunt.

"What a splendid thought!"

Marianne frowned amid their clamor, and then she said, "No, that is not what I meant! I want to know *when* my birthday is! I didn't say I wanted to have a party! I want to know how old I am, and on what day I was born, and how it was, and about my parents—"

"How about tomorrow?" said a second uncle. "We can have the cake ready, don't you think? And there will be time enough to have presents!"

"Why, of course there will be presents, what kind of a birthday party doesn't have presents, silly?" said a cousin.

They went on and on. But Marianne was not listening. A cold strange feeling she had never had before was filling her, and she felt a vertigo, a stifling sense of futility.

And so she left them all arguing about the flavor of cake icing and the color of the ribbons, and she went to her room. There she sat down and thought.

In the morning Marianne went to school, and during recess she told Lily that she was getting a birthday party of her own, and that Lily was invited. Marianne thought with a strange wicked glee that she was just going to have Lily show up at her house unannounced and see what came of it.

"A birthday party?" said Robin, who happened to be walking by just then. "Hey, everyone, Marianne's having a birthday party! And you're all invited!" he said very loudly and stuck his tongue out at Marianne before running off.

"Oh, hush!" said Marianne, but it was too late.

And so as a result, later that night a group of schoolchildren knocked at the door of the old stone house with ivy-covered walls.

The door was opened by one of the grannies who then opened her eyes, too—wide in surprise—and said "Goodness!" before letting everyone in.

The children walked through antique corridors and into a dining room filled with old aunts, grandmothers, great-uncles, second cousins, and others. Marianne stood near the table, and there was a large two-tier birthday cake decorated in lovely off-white roses made from butter icing and covered with candles.

"Happy birthday!" everyone cried, tremulous old voices mingling with bright young children's voices—flat notes mixed with sharp—and gifts were deposited one by one on the side-table nearby.

"Oh, what lovely children!" exclaimed one great-aunt, and she pinched Robin Noggins on the cheek. Robin grimaced but stood his ground, and Marianne noticed that he had brought a present too, although it was a small one, and he stuck it discreetly behind the other boxes.

"Let's have tea and cake!" exclaimed a great-grandpa. "And then we can play!"

At his words, two cousins in aprons carted in a tea-service with several china pots and lots of other pastries and finger sandwiches. Marianne stared with amazement at the extraordinary delicacies that were piled on the tea cart. But she did not have time to gawk, because she was handed a silver cake cutter while a portly second-uncle waddled up and lit the candles on the cake, and then Marianne was told to make a wish and blow the candles out.

Marianne stood and thought, and for a moment her mind was perfectly blank. And then it came to her that what she really wanted above all else was to *know*. And with that in mind she took a big breath and blew out all the candles, while Lily and her classmates and the others clapped, even Robin.

"Now, cut it! Cut the cake!"

And so she did, cutting huge creamy pieces, and seeing that the insides were filled with vanilla custard and strawberries and sponge cake and flaky cake and marzipan and berry preserves and all kinds of amazing things. Two cousins helped her cut the rest of the cake, and although the pieces were all enormous, there was enough for everyone in the room.

Soon everyone had settled around the room, in easy chairs and at the table, and tea was poured and more cake was consumed in large quantities. Lily had settled near two of the grannies one of whom was now braiding her pretty blonde hair, while the other was pouring her more tea. Robin was talking to three of the great uncles twice and thrice removed, who were telling tales of sailing ships and wicked one-eyed pirates and stolen gold, and they had pulled out their domino set and were setting up a game. The other children were also preoccupied with an old cousin or aunt here, or an uncle or grandfather there, who told them stories and patted their heads, and gave them spontaneous squeezes and hugs. Marianne sat down next to a tiny wizened granny goblin, who smiled at her and chewed a piece of soft cake with her gums. "Happy birthday, Dear!" she whispered. And then, as though just remembering, "Why, aren't you going to open your presents?"

In that moment there was a chorus of voices in agreement, and Marianne had no choice but to start tearing the pretty paper boxes and pulling the ribbons. She found inside dolls and books and even a music box from Lily. Robin's small present contained a pencil set of fancy watercolor pencils.

"Thank you, thank you, thank you!" Marianne repeated to all as she opened the gifts. She had expected a fiasco, but instead this had turned into an odd but amazing birthday party.

The hour had grown late, and eventually it was time for everyone to go. The children lingered, many hugging the old great aunts and second and third cousins, and receiving pecks on the cheeks from great-grandmothers and grandpas. Lily in particular hugged one of Marianne's grandmothers, saying, "You are just like my own granny Beth!"

Robin conceded to a hug from a great-grandfather, and blushed when his hair was ruffled.

Eventually they were all out the door, and Marianne and the old relatives stood on the ivy-covered porch waving goodbye.

Marianne took a big breath and a profound inner smile filled her, all the way down to her toes. "Thank you, Granny," she whispered to the nearest old one at her side. "Thank you. . . ."

"Why, Dear," the granny replied, "thank *you*! Those were all such lovely children, your friends. I am so glad to have seen them, they seem so familiar. I think they all remind me of you."

Time swept along so fast then that summer and winter came one after another, with no time for spring or fall.

Marianne was growing taller, and she was learning all kinds of things in school. She learned about ancient invasions and world wars and religions with many chaotic gods and one just god, about deserts and cold ice-covered lands and the reasons why rain fell and what made wind and about the wonderful new energy called electricity and how the earth was a ball that hung in a vacuum and revolved around the sun which was nothing but an average star in a universe filled with billions of billions of stars just like it. She learned that human beings had probably originated from other animals called primates and how those in turn came from tiny amphibians that came out of the ocean. She learned that science was the study of patterns in the universe, and she learned the methods that science used. And although there were so many things, so many amazing details in her different classes, and no one really mentioned this, it began to seem that so many things in the world were connected along various lines of meaning and pattern and organization.

At night, after her homework was done she hungrily read the books in the library, and had gone through several of the shelves there, reading the books from cover to cover. There were books on history and travelogues and philosophies of ancient wise men translated from long-forgotten and long-dead languages. And there were books of stories and novels that told one long complicated story of selected human lives.

Strange intangible things were in those stories and novels—things that science seemed to pass by, maybe because these things were unquantifiable. Science had no true methods for organizing emotions and predicting behavior, although it tried. There was no way to catalogue loyalty or friendship, nor to predict love. No way to measure or avoid fear and despair, and no cure for loss, no salve for anger, no consolation for anxiety. And yet all these things that slipped through the cracks of school studies, they were all here, analyzed and portrayed in the stories and novels, underneath the trappings of history or adventure.

Marianne filled her mind and her dreams with the intangibles, and there was always room for them right beside the numbers and the dates and the historic figures and the scientific details of the natural world.

Marianne thought about her own intangibles, and her own feelings and curiosities and her own fear. Because deep down there it always was, a fear of that which made no sense, of her own tiny microcosm in which she had lived since earliest childhood.

Why, for example did her best friend Lily live with a mother and a father, and why did Robin, now a gangly teenager, have a younger sister? And why was it that Marianne lived with so many old relatives who were, to tell the truth, mostly senile, and who seemed to subsist on nothing more than the food they grew in the garden behind the house, and if so, where did they get all those things they had for dinner every night, such as chicken and beef? Was there an old age pension coming to some of them? Yet why did the mail never come to their house? Whence did the money come to buy new clothes for her growing figure and to buy school supplies? And who in the world were these shriveled, grotesque, vaguely human creatures that could barely speak for their age, and how was it that after all these years none of them had ever required a doctor?

And finally a question occurred to Marianne that was the most disturbing of all. She asked it at dinner one evening, sitting in a chair that was much too small for her, since she was now a budding young woman, and all these old grandfathers and great-aunts and cousins and shriveled gnomes appeared so much smaller than her.

"My dears," said Marianne, clearing her throat after her first swallow of asparagus cream soup. "If I may ask, do any of you require a doctor for things such as aches and pains? And this is a very difficult thing for me to say, and possibly impolite, but how old are all of you? And—and—I wish you all the grandest health and many many long happy years, but when was the last time anyone in this house . . . *died?*"

She expected there to be an immediate silence, and there was. Only a couple of the most shriveled, most hard-of-hearing gnomes and great-aunts at the end of the table continued to clatter silverware against dishes.

Everyone else had stopped eating and talking and was staring at her or at each other. And then a cousin twice removed coughed into a napkin, and said, "My Dear, what an interesting question indeed. Aches and pains? Why, there are always aches and pains, and it's normal for old people to have them, is it not? Though, if you drink plenty of fresh hot tea and eat your vegetables, and take long walks every morning and evening, and if you laugh a whole lot and breathe deeply, then I dare say the aches and pains can be quite bearable. Really, my rheumatism goes away after breakfast, as soon as I take that walk!"

"You know, you are so right!" said an aunt. "I hardly get achy at all if I drink plenty of liquids every day."

"I don't know about you ladies, but a nice full pipe does the trick for me," said a great-grandfather with a hoary long beard and whiskers splattered with asparagus soup. "I smoke a full pipe, and pouff! No more bad knee for the rest of the night!"

Marianne stared at them all with the usual sense of inevitable frustration, as the various aunts and cousins and goblins with bushy cobweb-eyebrows started to tell their own stories. And then, just as she thought that it was hopeless to get any sense out of them, one great-great aunt said, "Goodness, didn't anyone get sick enough around here to have to stay in bed? How odd!"

"Yes," said Marianne, and forced herself to be brutal. "How odd indeed. Did anyone here ever get so sick that they stayed in bed for a long time? And did they then continue to only get sicker and sicker, and never recovered, and eventually died?"

Silence returned. Their faces were all puzzled, but some of them bore evidence of thinking very hard and in earnest.

"Died?" whispered a granny in a frightened tremulous voice, echoing Marianne. "Someone died here? Did anyone ever die?"

"You know, I don't know!" said one very hard-of-hearing uncle in a very loud voice. "By golly, I don't think anyone's died! Why, what an idea!"

"Well, yes," said another uncle, raising his brows with the effort of remembering. "And to think that I've been here forever, and I am older than a rock! I've never seen anyone die!"

"Me neither!" cried a gnome cousin.

"Nor me!"

"How odd and amazing!"

"Indeed, considering how long we've been here!"

Marianne took the opportunity to ask. "And how long exactly would that be?"

"Goodness," said a great-cousin, "I have no idea, but it must be very long indeed, since I don't remember being anywhere else but here."

"Neither do I," said a grandfather. "I've always been here in this house!"

Marianne stared and thought, and felt sorry for the looks of fear and confusion in all their sweet old faces, and the cold abandoned dinner on their plates. She felt vaguely guilty for having brought this up, but she could not stop now.

"Do you not remember being young?" asked Marianne.

They looked at her silently.

"Is it possible," said Marianne, "that all of you are dead already? Maybe—could it be—are you strange corporeal ghosts?"

"Oh!" exclaimed a great-aunt. "How terrible! How awfully frightening, and I certainly hope that's not true! I don't think I am dead, and I certainly don't want to be!"

"But how can I be a ghost?" said a third-cousin and lifted his fork to brandish it in his bony shaking hand.

Marianne rubbed her temple, and bit her lip. She just didn't know what to think, and it was obviously making everyone upset. "I am so sorry, my dears . . ." she managed to whisper at last. "I love all of you very much, and I don't think any of you are dead or ghosts, really, and I wish for you all to be happy and healthy always. It's just so very odd, this—this house of ours."

"Ah, Dear, well, we love you very much too, you know," said one dazed granny finally breaking into a smile of relief. "Don't we?" she added, and was echoed by a chorus of old voices.

And then another granny got up and came to Marianne's side and kissed her soundly on the cheek with a loud smack.

Marianne felt a sudden unquantifiable intangible. It came in the form of tears welling in the corners of her eyes.

The years went by swiftly after that, like blinks of an eye. Marianne finished school, and she and her friends were all grown up. Lily became a lovely young woman with soft unblemished skin and a slender figure. She was to go to a university and her family was proud that she was going to become a teacher herself. Robin was a tall serious young man with dark hair and a strong face, and he no longer made fun of Marianne or Lily and instead spent afternoons in the summer in long talks about interesting intellectual subjects. He too was to attend a college all the way across the country, and planned to become a scientist.

Marianne herself was now a dark-haired tall young woman with an intense expression in her inquisitive eyes and a pair of spectacles that she now had to wear because her weaker vision required it. On the evening before he was to leave for college, Robin came to Marianne's house to say goodbye to his friends, and to let them know that he would not see them for the next four years unless he came home on the holidays.

Lily cried into a napkin and Marianne tried not to, and bit her lip, and then Robin was gone. He did promise to write, and he did, over the next several months, then years. Meanwhile, Lily went to the university and studied to become a teacher. Marianne thought about them both, and about how neat it would be if she could also go to college. But to do that would have meant leaving home, and leaving behind all her old relatives in this house with ivy-covered walls.

"Go to college, Marianne!" Lily wrote her in many letters, repeatedly. "You were always smarter than me, and it would be a shame if you didn't—there's a world of things you could do! As for your old relatives, do what we did with my grandma Beth. Have a nurse come in to look after them, or else there are always the old folks homes and nice convalescent homes and elderly retirement communities. Really, you have many options. Grandma Beth is now living in Cherry Hill Gardens, a very nice facility, and we visit her often . . . or at least as often as possible."

Marianne thought about it as she came home every night from her day job at the local library where she shelved books and watched the stacks to make sure everything was in place.

And once she asked during dinner, "My dears, how would all of you feel if I went to college?"

A familiar silence came to the dining table, the same kind of silence that had come only two or three times before in Marianne's life, when she had asked them her most difficult questions.

"To college?" said a toothless cousin. "And where would that be, Dear?"

"I am afraid," said Marianne, "it would probably be very far away and I would have to move to another city."

"But," said an uncle, "would that mean you would leave us?"

"Well, yes," said Marianne. "But not for long! The program is only four years, and I would come home on all the holidays!"

"Four years!" said a great-grandma with amazement. "Oh, what a very long time!"

"Where would you sleep, Dear? Your room would be so empty without you there. . . ."

"And how would you eat all your vegetables without us making sure you do?" put in an aunt thrice removed.

"And how can we be sure you're all right?"

"Your dinner plate would look awfully lonely on the table with you not here," said a goblin grandpa. "Terribly lonely. I don't know if I'd be able to eat my own dinner, seeing it."

Marianne pulled at a lock of her hair in frustration, and then said, "I will miss you all terribly, dears, but what I am more worried about is how will you do without me being here. Will you make sure to start eating dinner? And what if something happens to any one of you?"

More silence.

"Well, I guess we'll just have to manage somehow," said a cousin eventually. "Won't we, I suppose?" and she looked around the room at the other old folks.

Everyone started to nod, and the conversation resumed as it normally did.

The next morning Marianne gathered her courage, and took a day off work to ride the train downtown and make arrangements for a day nurse to drop by the house that afternoon and make sure the old people were comfortable. And then she rode the train for several hours and arrived at a beautiful university campus in a nearby city, and made enquiries about admissions. When she was finally done, and took the train back home, it was very late and dark. Much later and darker than it had ever been.

As she walked up the path to the ivy-covered front porch, Marianne noticed that all the windows of the house were dark, and the front porch light was out. On the front door was attached a large envelope with a note from the nursing clinic. Marianne took the note as she entered the house and turned the hallway light on. The note was from the nurse and it said: "Dear Ms. Mornay, I certainly hope this is the correct house, and if this is not Ms. Mornay, then pardon me and disregard this message. As instructed, I arrived at 4:30 PM promptly and knocked for a long time but no one came to the door. However, knowing that some old people can be infirm and hard of hearing, I tried the door and forced it open, and then I went inside. This is a very large house, but no one was here, and I checked every single one of the rooms on all the three floors, and the large dining room, as I was told it is a favorite gathering place. I am at a loss as to what to do, and will be leaving another message tomorrow at the clinic where I may be reached. Yours truly, Beverly Halden, R.N."

There was a cold feeling inside Marianne as she walked through the dark house, turning the various lights on, and finally came to the dining room.

The room was dim, smelling of melted candle wax—dim except for two small candles in the table centerpiece that had burned down to the bottom, and by their flickering vestiges of light Marianne saw all of her old relatives. They were seated around the dinner table, most with heads down, some leaning back in their chairs, and many snoring. The kettle of the usual soup stood ice-cold, and the plates were clean and unused.

"Good evening . . ." said Marianne.

And at the sound of her voice they all started to wake up.

"Dear, there you are!" cried a granny and hobbled over towards Marianne. "We were just waiting for you so we could start eating."

And then Marianne screamed. A fit of madness had come to her, an impossible storm that had to have an outlet, and so she screamed and tears ran down her face in a torrent and she could not stop, not even with the terrified old faces all around her, and the soothing hands with withered skin as they came to console her.

"No, no, no!" shrieked Marianne, beating them away, hearing her voice as she had never heard it in her life. "Where were you? And why are you all here now? Why, why, why? What—"

She beat her chest with her fists, and pulled at her hair in an attempt to wipe her nose and she cried, "Why didn't you have dinner without me? Why, why, why? Didn't you remember what I told you, that I would be gone all day, and that you must eat and drink and live without me? And where were you when the nurse came?"

And then Marianne sat down on the floor and she wailed anew, "Oh, God! What have I done to be burdened with this? Why me? What do you want of me, you crazy old seniles? Why can't I go about my own life? Do you expect me to come to dinner and be here with you for the rest of my existence? Do you expect me to rot here forever?"

"What has happened to you, Dear?" said one great-aunt, also beginning to cry. "Why are you so upset? And why are you so late to dinner? The corn chowder is all cold, you know." And she sniffled dejectedly.

"No!" screamed Marianne again. "You crazy old ..." She held her head and she shut her eyes tight, and she was choking on her own tears.

And in a moment between breaths, she heard sounds of sobbing coming from all around the room as old great-aunts and -uncles and second-cousins and grandmothers and great-great-grandfathers and cousins twice removed and shriveled goblins with dried-apple faces sat down or stood around her, crying, weeping, shuddering, like old elm trees and maples sighing in the winter wind.

The sound of their absolute desolation reached Marianne, and she held her breath. It was a sound of cold deepest December, the sound of midnight and the sound of the twelfth hour.

And Marianne took deep breaths and with an immense force of will she stopped crying. Then she took one long last juddering breath and she whispered in a voice made thick with tears, "I am sorry. I did not mean it. . . . I am so sorry . . . my dears."

And at the sound of her lifeless resigned voice they came to her, coarse lukewarm palms stroking her hair and withered chests hugging her, the smell of old dried violets and soap and ancient tobacco on some, the whiff of vanilla and flour on others, the faint echo of lamb's wool and oak, and the soft cobwebs of pale goblin hair touching her at the edges of time fading away into the mists of memory.

"I'll never leave you, I promise," whispered Marianne to them all, cradling old heads with paper-thin skin and sparse hair, and stroking bent backs and fragile shoulders.

"Never," she added, getting up, and starting to light the candelabras around the room.

Four years later, Lily had graduated from university, and Robin was on his last year of an extended program in physics. Robin wrote to Marianne unfailingly, and he came to visit on many holidays, and Lily also.

One summer afternoon, Robin knocked on the door of the old stone house with ivy-covered walls and when Marianne came to the porch, he smiled at her shyly, and asked if he could speak to her about an important matter.

As they passed through the hallways of the house, the sleeping gnomes and withered grannies woke up in their rocking chairs and waved to Robin gently, then resumed their naps. Marianne stole shy glances at Robin, since she had not seen him for several months at a time, and each time she did he looked more handsome and confident. Robin's hair was so very dark and his profile noble and gentle. He was dressed a bit formally today, with a suit and tie, and Marianne who only had a summer dress on was wondering what he was up to.

In her room, Robin closed the door, then all of a sudden it seemed he had nothing to say, except that his breath had quickened, and his face was paling and then blushing.

"Marianne," he said then softly. "My Marianne."

And Marianne laughed suddenly, because for the first time it occurred to her that her given name sounded very much like the name of Maid Marian, the beloved of Robin Hood from the old legends. And here in front of her stood Robin Hood himself, dashing and beautiful and kind.

But Robin Noggins, her silly childhood friend, her Robin, was not smiling. "Marianne," he said, and his voice was alien in its intensity, "I love you, Marianne, my dearest friend. Will you be my wife?"

Marianne heard the wind of summer blowing the pale satin curtains at her window. And she felt the kiss of the sun upon the nape of her neck.

Here was her Robin, ready to take her away.

And Marianne came forward, and she put her hands up, and she took her Robin and held him and her fingers slipped around his neck while her head lay resting against his chest.

"I love you," she whispered. "I love you, my Robin."

And she stayed that way, pressed against him, for a long glorious span of moments, while a distant grandfather clock in the hallway rang the hour.

Robin reached deep into his coat pockets and he brought out a ring with a pale transparent stone that carried in it sparks of the sun. "This ring is yours now," he whispered. "Once it was my grandmother's. We can live together and dream and do the things we've always wanted. If you like, we will have children, or we can travel the world, or do whatever you like, but we will be together now, my Marianne. Say yes, and we can be off tomorrow, on a trip of a lifetime! I know how you've always wanted to see the world!"

"For some reason," said Marianne softly, "I've always thought it'd be Lily. I thought you loved Lily that way, not me . . ."

Robin laughed. "Ah, but I always loved both of you, Lily as a sister, and you as the one for my heart."

"Like the letter 'A,'" whispered Marianne.

And when Robin glanced at her upturned face in surprise, she explained. "Remember when we learned to write the letter 'A'? There are three lines, two always coming together, and one always piercing the two to keep them apart. At one point or another in our lives, Robin, we've served as any one of the three lines. At first you were our foil, between Lily and me, when we were children. And now . . . I am afraid that Lily was never good at drawing that middle line and now you are asking her to be the foil, to stand between us and serve as our balance."

Robin's face became very still and he continued to look at her. "I am not sure what you mean, Marianne . . ." he said.

"I mean," she replied, "that maybe it's best that I be the foil, and I be the balance. I love you so much, my Robin Hood, and I love Lily, and I know you love her also. Go and marry her, Robin. Because in my life, I've discovered that I can only be that middle line. I will always stand firm and loving between you, not to separate you but to prop you up. Otherwise your two lines will just fall into each other, and there will be no letter 'A' at all."

"What are you talking about?" exclaimed Robin. His fist clutched the ring and his other hand bit into Marianne's shoulder painfully.

"I can't marry you, Robin," she said, while water pooled in the corners of her eyes. "I can't go off with you into the great wide world, and I can't have children, nor grow old with you— or with anyone. Go on and live your life, and marry Lily, and the two of you come and visit me sometimes, between the passage of the years."

"Marianne!" he cried.

"You will have lovely children," she whispered. "Light and dark coming together. Now, go, my dear, my dearest dear, and give a great big hug and kiss to Lily, on my behalf."

And saying that Marianne let go of him, and put her hands down at her sides and just stood there, watching his familiar agonized eyes that she'd known for so very long.

"Why?" he whispered then, one last time, bewildered and grown dark and pale and heavy in spirit.

But Marianne just stood there in silence.

Robin turned away and he walked out of the room, closing the door silently behind him.

Later Marianne found out that Lily and Robin did indeed get married, and they were traveling the world together before settling down to a life and daily routine in a distant university city. She did not see them again for many years.

Marianne continued to work at the library where she was eventually promoted to head librarian, and she spent long days in a world of books.

Every day she came home promptly for dinner, which was always waiting for her, and the old cousins and grandmothers and great-uncles and -aunts and the goblins and tiny shrunken gnomes laughed and smiled at her, seeming to be more boisterous every day.

Marianne sat down at her place, and adjusted the spectacles on her nose, and then smilingly began slurping her soup. She only slurped the soup when eating dinner at home, since she had learned it was impolite to do that outside in company, but she also knew it would be impolite not to do it with the old relatives around her.

And sometimes, after a very long day, as she finished her second or third cup of after-dinner tea, there would be an old goblin at her elbow, and she could almost hear a muttered "Thank you, Dear."

"Thank you for what?" said Marianne involuntarily, but the tiny shriveled creature winked at her and nudged her arm gently and then said softly in the general noise of the table conversation. "Thank you for being you, my dear. Thank you for being here. Thank you for being. There's no one else, you know, only you. No one else for us. Like the letter 'A,' your favorite one. You are the horizontal line, the foil and the strength and the succor."

"What do you mean?" Marianne would say in alarm, in wonder, but the old gnome would have turned his back on her, and be poking around on his plate, and mind wandering.

And so it went on. Time flew by, and the dinners and the years melted into one. The world was changing all around, and the young woman Marianne was now stately and middle-aged. The library was a place of ageless wonderful daydreams for her, and she worked, then came home to her own library with its old books filled with cursive writing and magical pictures of godlike women, men and creatures out of legend. Sometimes she would find pictures of Robin Hood and Maid Marian, and with a pang she would remember old intangibles unquantifiable by science. And she would pause and wonder, and then turn the page of history and legend gently.

The old stone house with ivy-covered walls seemed to be in a pocket outside of time. It was always the same inside, with the smells of fresh cooking and sounds of old voices raised in tremulous laughter, soft shufflings of old slippered feet against wooden floorboards—the same feet and the same voices, for no one ever left here, and no one ever died. Indeed, it seemed that every day there were more and more of them, old relatives whom she had never seen or remembered seeing before, old women and men with gentle comfortable faces and half-senile kind smiles, and very little memory of anything else.

Maybe they came here from other places, Marianne wondered, because she thought at one point she saw Lily's grandmother Beth whom she recognized from a photograph she had seen once a long time ago.

But really, it no longer mattered. They were all hers now, and since no one else wanted them, or maybe because they had no other place to go, not even unto death, she would be there for them. Someone had to do it; and now she knew it, recognized it for what it was. She always did make a good bottom rung and middle line to keep things in balance—not because she had to but because she could.

Indeed, after the accumulation of years the young woman was now fading and feeling tired and old herself, with shortness of breath and pains in her joints. Often she sat with a book on her lap and watched them giddy with energy, as her old ones frolicked in the rooms of the house, galloping in abandon, with wrinkled faces set in permanent smiles.

"I love you, my children," she said when no one could hear her, the young woman who was so very old, and fading by the second.

And yet, fading meant gentle regrets but slipping away was a different choice altogether, and there was to be none of it here.

For she was so young, so very young at heart always, just as she will ever be for them, in the house of old.

ABSOLUTE RECEPTIVENESS, THE PRINCESS, AND THE PEA

I watched from my secret place as they opened the grand Palace doors to the flood outside. There was nothing to see beyond the opaque grey sheet of the downpour. Out there, the whole world ended. All was dissipated half-light, falling steel, and silver. Fine quick rivulets of rainwater slid down like eels upon the ebony grillwork of the doors.

And then, she came in.

She was like gossamer. And she had come out of nowhere. One instant there was a maelstrom of whirling silver dusk wrought of sky water. And the next, she stood in the doorway, drenched like a gentle twig of white baby's breath.

Her skin was succulent white. It was the first thing I noticed, for I had a weakness for porcelain skin in the ladies of the court. They did not know it yet, though some had begun to suspect as of late—just as they suspected that I perused their plunging decolletage and the swelling half-moons of their chests with more than a boy's curiosity. For, I would be turning sixteen winters this very month, and my Birthday would be declared a National Holiday, while a Grand Ball would take place in the Royal Hall of mahogany. There, my father would present me with a Medal and sash of violet satin, and I would be treated to exotic delicacies and champagne and dancing with my choice of the most beautiful young debutantes. And, as rumor would have it, among them would be a fair number of foreign Princesses in disguise. . . .

I stilled in fascination, watching her take a few tentative steps, dripping water upon the lacquered parquet floor. Her long hair was plastered to her delicate skull, thus appearing hueless, while filaments of it stuck to her swan's throat like wettened cobwebs. Her dilated eyes were utterly beautiful and vacant.

Their receptive vulnerability elicited in me what only could be called a pang of arousal. It was a sadistic immediate urge for which I hardly had words.

The two Doormen shrank away from her in distaste. Here they were, in their impeccably fitted uniforms of heavy brocade, their necks sunken like monstrous stamen amid frothy petals of collar lace. And they were reasonably unwilling to get themselves wet.

But it was the First Butler himself who noticed that she was about to fall. He came forward just in time to have her fade into a bundle at his feet, a marionette suddenly devoid of strings to uphold her.

She fainted like a felled blossom of a hothouse carnation, swooning down gently in a limp puddle of woman and water. . . .

It all shimmered half-real in my unfocused mind, dislocated images of faerie movement, of her falling. . . .

Her limbs were barely covered as she lay, in a fine soft cloth of dove grey—or maybe lilac—which clung to her form with the intimacy of skin. I was not sure of its color, for the lighting here was poor, and the mother-of-pearl glow from the outside was deceptive, a tumult of storm silver.

There were images of her skin, or possibilities of such.

The doors were shut immediately thereafter, while the Butler leaned nonchalantly over her motionless body and called for assistance in a measured tone, even now retaining his polish.

"Poor child!" said a sudden familiar voice, and I saw the lean aging form of my father, the King himself.

Making his way through the corridor, and on to the Library, he had paused at the sight of her lying on the parquet. A careless commonality, his velvet evening jacket was slightly askew at the collar, while his belt sash had come undone and trailed on the floor behind him like a flaccid appendage of mulberry silk.

Yes, such was my father.

"Poor soggy child..." repeated the King, muttering under his nose hairs, and then gestured with one commanding finger, "Take her to a clean bed, and have my Physician look at her. Hurry, now!"

And with that, he again turned, shuffling, and was gone, while the whole household went into an uproar. It was a pointless flurry of activity, as chambermaids were called, and valets went running up and down the curving stream of carved oak stairs like roaches colliding with each other, while the floors shook under their aimless movement.

The Physician was nowhere to be found of course—though unlike everyone else I remembered very well that he had gone to town to fetch some fragrant smelling salts for the King's plethora of incomprehensible ailments. But the Queen was immediately notified. Or rather, my stately stepmother knew that something was afoot from the noise in the hallways, and she instantly sent out her First Lady to snoop out the gist of the matter.

The Lady-in-Snooping did not lose a moment in informing Her Majesty that a mysterious, young, female creature, cold and dripping and now in an inviolate faint, had been allowed into the Palace.

"What idiot footman opened the door in such a storm and downpour?" said the Queen archly.

But she came downstairs nevertheless, quite in a hurry, it might be observed. She was trailing her onion-skin layers of skirts, while her gelatinous chest, uplifted by a tight corset was set to bouncing and quivering with each step, on the verge of spilling beyond the tight confines of ivory lace.

It was at that point that I came out of my secret hiding place within the walls, and moving aside the tapestry curtain stepped silently into the corridor. Then I approached them—a matter of apparent coincidence—and made my presence known.

"Ah, Prince Glorian!" exclaimed my handsome stepmother with a little stiff smile, and made a slight inclination of her Royal head to myself, as Heir Apparent. As Her Majesty moved, I watched with perfect discretion the jelly of her Royal Teats set in motion.

"Ah, my Dearest Mother," I retorted with an equally tiny charming smile, "What has happened here?"

"Your Highness," said the First Butler, "Apparently, this poor girl has been taken ill at our very doorstep, and His Majesty happened by, just now. His Majesty has commanded that she be cared for immediately."

"Then proceed," I said without a seeming care, giving the fallen stranger an indifferent glance. And with a charismatic nod to my stepmother, I walked past them all. In doing thus, I was demonstrating a purposeful destination, but in reality was on my way to God knows where in this labyrinthine Royal structure.

Later that very same evening, when Supper was served in the Carnelian Hall Dining Room, I came downstairs in my usual dark velvet, without having powdered my hair, nor having taken up its long creamy blond mass in a queue.

I was nonchalant and yet impeccable, and I entered the drawing room only to see my Royal father, stepmother, a number of court ladies and lords, and the fragile stranger—dressed quite differently than she had been when I had first seen her—all seated on the chairs and grand sofas. Seeing her, my heart did a strange thing in my chest that resembled a pang of alarm, and drew me up short of breath for one instant. I hid it well however, under a veneer of cold Princely polish.

"Come in, my dear boy," said the King, sitting up in his pillowed chair, and giving me his gentle phlegmatic smile. "Look what a delicate young creature the fates have brought to our doorstep! It turns out that not only is she of noble stock, but a Royal as well! I present to you, Princess Vialethe!"

At the very beginning of his words, the stranger rose before me, daintily holding her silk crinoline skirts, and curtsied.

Her movements were impeccable.

I almost stared, because she really was different, striking, in her borrowed finery. Her hair had been hidden by a lustrous powdered wig hung with pearls—a wig I had recognized as one of my stepmother's own. Her dress sat low on pristine white shoulders, and the corset strangled an already tiny waist and a nearly flat virgin chest. Her neck indeed was long, swanlike, utterly beautiful, upon which reposed an oval face of unearthly refinement, crowned by a rosebud mouth and great eyes, like smoke. . . .

Those receptive eyes.

"Your Highness . . ." she whispered to me in all her faint lovely femininity, with a voice of submission.

Hearing it, that soft tone, brought sudden disjointed images of her sprawled against pillows on my bed, sheets tangled about her, barely concealing her white porcelain limbs. . . .

And then I heard my stepmother's voice, and the visions were gone with a single swipe of reality.

"A Princess indeed," the Queen was saying. "We cannot know, of course, whether what she claims is true. But surely, breeding and other details of her comportment are strongly in her favor. No one we know has been to Graefaetania, the land she supposedly hails from. . . ."

The stranger, who was surely a Princess if there were any justice in heaven, turned to my stepmother, and with another polite curtsy, said delicately, echoing my own hidden sentiment, "I assure you, Madam, I am a Princess, if any such exist."

I watched her neck and lips move as she spoke thus, watched the fine down of pale hair, fine like smoke that had escaped from the nape of her baroque wig. . . .

And somehow, in that very moment, I just wanted to walk up to her and put my mouth there. Naturally I detained myself, and yet knew that my forehead was burning with imagination.

Saving me in that moment, Supper was served. The King rose, and with him all of Court, and he presented his arm to my stepmother, in order to lead her into the Dining Room.

I followed immediately after. Without any hesitation I offered my arm to the fair stranger before me, feeling again a pang in my chest—which then echoed down into my lower extremities—when Princess Vialethe rested her long, slender, almost incorporeal arm encased in a glove, against mine.

With that delicate butterfly touch, I was branded. All my senses had become atrophied; the whole world receded, except for that spot on my arm, from which radiated an aura as wide as the whole universe. Supper was one flippant memory, and I don't think I touched anything on my plate, nor did I drink more than a few swallows of the pale ocher wine in my goblet.

She sat next to me, and I observed with my insanely heightened peripheral vision the slimness of an elbow, and how her tiny wrist moved to hold the silver utensils, how she barely made any effort to cut her meat, and occasionally lifted her fork and placed it against her lips, and then her swan neck would move slightly, and her throat. . . .

And only later, after the plates were removed, and the candles burned low, did it occur to me that neither one of us had said a word all throughout the evening.

After everyone arose to move back to the drawing room for tea and pastries and rose confiture, I again had the sensual pleasure of holding her by the arm for at least ten steps from the table to the salon. Here, the pale stranger excused herself, curtsying delicately before the King and Queen, and pleaded forgiveness for the need to retire early, due to utter weariness.

"Why, of course, my dear!" said my stepmother with a smile as fine as a rose petal, and as flimsy. "Before you go, let me personally make sure that your sleeping quarters are comfortable for the night."

What? I thought, since when does my Royal stepmother make herself into a Lady of the Chamber?

And indeed, I noted something in the short look she threw my father, a kind of slight, cloying illness covered by charm, before she motioned for the lovely Princess to walk behind her on their way upstairs.

Stepmother was obviously up to something.

As a result, I did not tarry long in the drawing room, seeing that my father was occupied by dull customary talk of foreign politics with two of his oldest crony advisers, and that the remaining older ladies and lords had fallen into a post-meal stupor.

Rising almost unnoticed, I slipped out of the hall, and stood for a moment considering my next course of action in the dimly illuminated corridor. So that the doormen would not think it odd, I started walking with my usual semblance of purpose, until I turned the corner and was out of sight.

And then, I stopped. I stood and considered the antique slightly frayed tapestries hanging on the wall. Reaching behind one in a familiar spot, I found what I was looking for. I pressed inward, pushed, and felt the wall give way before me. Quickly, before anyone would walk by, I moved behind the tapestry, and entered my secret place. . . .

Twists and turns in the darkness. Moving by touch alone. Counting steps while the ground rose before me. . . . Eventually

I had reached what I knew was the upper level, a place where the Royal bedchambers were situated in sprawling old luxury.

I could second-guess my stepmother very well by now, after three years of observing the Royal Second Marriage. I knew exactly where she would place the beautiful stranger for the night—a small bedroom with the walls painted the same pale succulent shade of green as fresh pea soup, and a fringe of gold relief on the corners of the ceiling. The bed there was a wide four-poster with a shallow but soft mattress that could be layered with more or fewer thicknesses of fluffy down, with great feather beds and comforters, and fine silk sheets, according to the guest's preference.

And here indeed was my stepmother, waiting in the room impatiently, having called servants to her, while the Princess Vialethe stood a bit to the side, soft and pale and vacant in her receptive loveliness.

In a matter of moments, chambermaids arrived, carrying a mountain of bedding, for the guest's perusal and selection.

"Excellent!" exclaimed the Queen, "Place it all here, on the bed."

"All of it, Your Majesty?" said a maid in surprise.

"Yes, all of it, girl. And then bring more!"

And then the Queen turned to Vialethe and remarked with a light smile, "Would you step outside for a moment, my dear? We need to get this room ready and comfortable for you."

"I thank you kindly, Your Majesty," said Vialethe, curtsied delicately, and then walked with utter obedience outside into the corridor so as not to be in the way of the hurried servants.

I watched them move around the room, piling mattresses upon mattresses, until the level of the bed reached half way to the ceiling, and definitely near the height of the velvet bed overhead canopy.

A most bizarre sight. What was the reason for such dramatic layering of down and pillow opulence?

And then things became even more strange.

The Queen turned to the nearest empty-handed maid, and announced, "I want you to go to the kitchen, and fetch me a single uncooked, dry, and perfectly round pea."

"Your Majesty?"

"You've heard me. Fetch me a pea from the kitchen!"

The chambermaid stood for an instant too long with her mouth open. She then collected herself, curtsied hurriedly and went nearly running on her bizarre errand.

While she was gone, the Queen stood fanning herself with a light feather fan, and irritably tugging at the edge of her long evening gloves that started to roll down just a bit at the edges, the more she fussed.

The last of the bedding in the form of fine satin sheets, was placed atop a mountain of down mattresses and comforters and quilts. In order to reach it, the servants had to fetch a stepladder, and rested it against the edges of the mattress.

Meanwhile, the maid had returned with the pea. She carried it upon a small silver tray, with the solemnity and bewildered ceremony worthy of a page bearing a wedding ring. With the same confused but well-trained composure, she paused before the Queen and announced, "Your Majesty—the pea. . . ."

At this point I nearly burst. Sick neurotic laughter seethed within me, rebounded from a leashed well of energy. But instead I stifled myself into silence, and remained poised to watch the rest of this impossible scene.

My stepmother took the pea without another word.

For a moment she squeezed it between her thumb and forefinger, and then raised it up to the light as though it were a Caribbean pearl.

"You may all stand witness," she announced suddenly, in such a voice that the servants fell into instant attentive silence.

"Behold," continued my stepmother with a barest sheen of sarcasm, "As I perform a test of True Royalty."

And with those words, the Queen walked up to the mountain of mattresses, and motioned to the servants. "Lift these half way, so that only the very bottom layer remains."

The maids obeyed, and it took five of them to slowly tip the mattress contraption without overturning it, and another two were called to support it from the opposite side.

"Look, all of you," continued the Queen, "I place this tiny pea upon the middle of this bed."

And saying this, she did. She laid the dry pale green globule upon the white fabric. It sat there, winking like a single jasper eye.

"Now, you may replace a single thin mattress to cover it," said the Queen.

The maids were only too happy to oblige, and the first thin mattress on the bottom made contact with the bed, followed of course by the whole heavy layer of endless thin mattresses which were piled back upon the bed, one single thin mattress at a time.

"Excellent," said my stepmother, fanning herself lightly. And then she turned, and walked to the doors and glanced outside into the corridor.

"Come back in, Princess Vialethe, your bed is ready."

My fascinating stranger entered the bedchamber, and then I noted her blank gaze stilling in gentle surprise at the sight of her towering bed.

"Now then, my dear," said the Queen, ignoring her slight hesitation. "You are deathly tired, you've been through a harrowing experience, an icy drenching, and I leave you now to a wonderful night of rest. Your nightgown is right here, dear child, and if you require anything in the night, you need only but ring for a servant. And now, come, let me kiss you and wish you sweet dreams!"

And with those saccharine words, my stepmother leaned forward—her tightly corseted and lightly powdered chest once again nearly spilling out against the lace—and placed a brief kiss on Vialethe's pale forehead.

Then, with one motion of her hand she left the room, followed by all the servants except one who was to help the Princess undress for the night.

I paused only for a moment at the peep hole into the chamber, and then rushed back into the darkness of the secret passages. Running, I was downstairs before my stepmother, and then emerged nonchalantly from the corridor. Then, I returned into the drawing room, taking my customary place, as if nothing happened.

The Queen entered soon after, and everyone rose politely, including myself and the King who then immediately plopped back in his chair and continued his talk of import and seafaring taxes with old Lord Bretaine.

"Our dear guest is bundled for the night," my stepmother said, taking a chocolate truffle from a silver tray, and receiving a fine china cup of tea from a servant.

"Marvelous, she's a sweet child," replied my father absentmindedly with a smile, turning back to her. And then, seeing myself, he pronounced, as though coming awake all of a sudden, "My boy, how well did you like her, this Princess Vialethe?"

"Well enough," I replied as blankly as possible.

The Queen stared at me.

"It occurred to me," continued my father, "that she would make you a lovely bride. Would you like that, my boy? I mean, she is lovely, isn't she? Lovely and young, just like your mother had been—God rest her poor soul. . . ."

"Why—we hardly know anything about her, my love," the Queen said with an odd little smile and a hard stare which I somehow could read very well, even though my father never could—he'd been besotted with my stepmother from the start and saw only such things as he thought should be there.

"What do we need to know, but that she's a Princess?" said the King.

"Indeed," my stepmother said. "We shall know it for a fact in the morning."

"How is that?" said my father.

The Queen lifted her cup of tea to her lips, and took a dainty sip. "Knowing you might ask just that, knowing your utter gentleness of heart, and hence your propensity for trust and for lovely young things, I've contrived a test for the little visitor of ours."

"My dear?" the King said, raising one graying brow. "Go on."

"In the morning," continued the Queen, "when the dear child comes down to breakfast, you must observe her. If she is comfortable and looks well rested, then she is not a true Princess, and has been insolently lying to us. In which case, she must be severely punished for making us a laughingstock. But if she looks worn, with circles under her eyes, exhausted and sickly, then she is indeed a true blue blood. And remember, merely asking her how she's been is not enough—for she will very likely be polite or devious in either circumstances and retort that all has been well. What we must do is observe her condition."

"But, what guarantee is there of her being worn-out or not?" the King said. "I am somewhat confused, my dear, as to how a night's rest might reflect on her being a liar or a true Princess."

"I placed a single hard pea under her mattress," my stepmother said with a fine smile. "The mattress is very thin, and if she is at all delicate—as all True Princesses are known to be delicate—then she would be quite bruised in the morning."

Such a marvelous liar my stepmother could be. And yet, a stickler for literal detail, I must hand her that much—each of the mattresses on that bed were thin, considering on an individual basis.

"Ah, I see," my father said. "A brilliant idea, my dear. Though, I do pity the poor thing her upcoming torment of a night."

And with that, my father turned back to Lord Bretaine and continued a stale forgotten conversation.

I meanwhile stared down into a cup of cooling tea, and thought furiously upon the events that had just taken place.

My lovely Princess, my almost-bride, has been given a stack of thin mattresses reaching nearly to the ceiling. Not only would she be as perfectly comfortable as anything upon that wonderful down-and-feather mountain, but she would probably wake up with roses on her cheeks.

And then, not only would she never be my bride, but my dearest stepmother would make sure she is severely punished.

I had to do something. . . .

When everyone had retired for the night, including myself, I disrobed without the help of a valet, and was all alone in my grand bedchamber. I lay staring at the abysmal shadows on the ornate ceiling that loomed over my head like a canopy of perfect ebony dark.

I was naked to the waist, and had pulled down the satin coverlet, for in the cool air, my flesh burned.

I was burning with her memory. . . .

What was she doing now, my effervescent pale stranger? How had she managed to climb atop that cumbersome mountain of mattresses? Was she asleep now, thrown into a dead slumber of exhaustion, or maybe, a neurotic faint from which she would wake up oddly refreshed in the morning?

The fever rose within me.

Eventually I sat up, hearing from somewhere far the hallway pendulum clocks strike two past midnight.

And then, I threw back the coverlet, and stood up, dizzy for a moment in the darkness, and having to grab the bedpost. Underneath, I still wore a pair of breeches—for somehow, even then, I had known I would be doing this.

What was it that I was doing?

Or, what was I about to do?

No, it was not that. There was no point in touching myself in the darkness, like I usually did—first light as a feather until that part of me below danced with an onrush of subcutaneous currents of blood, then eventually stroking it hard and violently in a frenzy, while it grew improbably, and became a stiff burning coal in my hand, and eventually erupted. And in that one moment of elusive sweet agony I would lose my mind. . . .

No, tonight, none of that.

I was a man, had long been thus now, no matter that my body was virgin to a woman's intimacy.

And now, I will go to her.

There was a door in the walls leading directly into her bedchamber from my secret place. I moved like a shade, barefoot, wearing only my thin breeches, my long pale hair loose from its queue. Night drafts slid against my fevered skin, and yet I was invincible to it, for I carried the sun itself within my flesh, ready to flare outward. . . .

I moved the tapestry, and suddenly was inside the guest chamber.

Before me, towered the mattress mountain. In the shadows, it resembled the marble base of a monument, upon which reposed some unknown, a deity. . . . Next to it stood the step ladder.

In this boudoir, only silence.

I stilled, and forced myself to hear preternaturally the beating of her heart, her soft exhalations.

Or maybe, it was but the ringing in my own temples.

I approached the step ladder, and taking hold of its cool wooden sides and rungs, I climbed it. I was a Prince going to his Bride.

Eternities came and went within the span of moments, and at last I was near the apex, having scaled the down mountain, with my head nearly hitting the ceiling canopy in the darkness.

So dark, that I almost did not see her sleeping form.

But there was no need to see, for I *knew* she was there, I knew with an extended other sense that she lay before me.

Here, must be her head, resting against the pillows, shadow hair strewn like dandelion. Below, her fine swan neck, flowing into a perfect shallow breast, a soft torso, parabolic curves of waist, then hips. . . . Farther down would be long fair limbs, thighs, then legs, then slim feet right there at the edge, yes. . . . And then, returning back up, in the very middle of it would be a place of warm silk, a place of moistness, of dark engendering.

Here, would be her receptiveness.

I scaled the ladder, and like an incubus, descended upon the shadow dark.

Landing roughly, sinking immediately in the mountain of down under my own weight, I felt a slight body falling deep into the mountain beneath me. She was slightly cold of skin, this Vialethe, and yet lay without the nightgown that had been given her.

And as I expected, there came a gentle scream that I immediately stifled with my strong burning palm across a soft rosebud mouth, while at the same time I straddled her, held her pinned down by my powerful thighs, and felt that part of me below grow and break free of the breeches that had a convenient slit opening in the front—ah, now only did I realize the extent of that convenience!

She struggled only for a moment, poor butterfly, while I held her mouth cupped with my fierce strong hand, and the other moved in idiotic clumsiness through her hair, against her neck, then found the small breasts and curve of waist.

"My Princess, you must promise not to scream, my Princess—" I was whispering hoarsely, over and over. "If I let you go, promise you will not cry out. . . ."

But then it occurred to me that, after that initial cry, she neither struggled, nor made a sound. She lay beneath me like a cool-skinned marionette, and the only reason I knew she was alive was because of the shallow rising of her slight chest.

Joy surged through me—my Princess was not going to cry out or resist! My Princess will be silent and I will caress her and she will not object, but will instead allow me to do all that I wanted, to explore her strange alien body—a woman's body, and to touch her, and stroke all parts of her, and to find that dark place that was moist, and was receptiveness itself somewhere in the middle of her. . . .

"My Princess Vialethe, my beautiful Bride!" I whispered, releasing her mouth, and then helplessly lowered my own face to smell the cold porcelain skin at her throat—skin that was beginning to warm up in fact, though it was still invisible in the dark.

Down in that place below, my secret man's place, I knew I had grown impossibly big, and that I was burning, and very near that occult moment of explosion. I reached forward with both hands, and felt her, looking for her corresponding secret place, searching for the warm moist receptiveness in the violent dark.

"There, there, yes, here you are," I was saying like a stricken half-wit, and then, when I found soft female silk, I knew what had to be done, by instinct.

I lifted myself, still clumsy but fierce and young; I thrust, and was imbedded. Just then, I thought I heard her make another sound. Only this one other time did she make a sound, and then again grew silent and motionless.

Soft Receptiveness was engulfing me, was all around me. For a moment I was still, and then was overcome with the Instinct of the Ages.

I began to move, and it sounded to me like someone else, not myself but a stranger was groaning deep in the throat, and it was all like a pendulum—it still is, in my mind, that first true man's memory, the most vivid, violent yet maternal experience of that agony pleasure—

But I digress.

I moved, and then within moments only, I had Exploded. My mind left me for an instant and then surged back with heightened clarity. Only years later would I know about endurance, continuance, rhythm, reciprocation, the true coital dance.

But now all I knew was that a secret part of me had fit a secret part of her like a glove, and that I was encased tight and perfectly within a female womb.

It was my first time, and I cried. Cried, without knowing it. Only later, as I withdrew from her, and felt the hot dripping wetness of my own juices down there, did I also know that tears had been running down my cheeks.

The Princess lay before me lifeless, and yet she breathed. My pale beautiful stranger, my marionette.

It occurred to me finally that I had just used her.

And then it occurred to me that not only had I done that, but I also forced her. And that the reason I had told myself I had come here in the first place was to make sure, in my own sadistic brilliance, that my Princess was sufficiently bruised and worn out in the morning.

I was to learn later that this act carried another dark word, rape.

But how can one be accused of raping a marionette?

My Princess Marionette lay silently, limp and unprotesting.

And in that instant, I suddenly hated her.

Not because I knew what it was in fact that I had done. But because I felt that somehow something was not right.

Absolute Receptiveness was not right.

And so, I put my hands against her throat, and I held her tight, and I squeezed certain parts of her limpness, and began to pinch and knead with sadistic glee, while a song of wild burning arose in my mind, and my man's organ was once again growing, and I knew at last what I was capable of in the violent dark.

Well then, at least there will be bruises in the morning.

Morning came and there were no bruises, only milk-white twilight. I opened my eyes and found myself lying in my own bedchamber. How I had gotten there, I did not remember. Indeed, the memories of the tumultuous darkness and what took place in it were very disjointed, uncertain.

My God!

I sat up, reeling from the force of the sudden understanding of what I had done. I had forced her in the night, forced and hurt and raped my beautiful, soft, unprotesting Princess, the creature out of the storm.

Or, had I?

Suddenly, because of the gentleness of the pale pre-dawn light outside the window, I was no longer sure. There was no room for violence in this primeval calm, in the soft reeling moments of coming awake into a new day.

And then I thought, I will find out for a fact, when I come down to breakfast.

But breakfast was so far away. And so, I lay for hours, dozing lightly, sinking in and out of neurotic sleep, jerking myself awake with a painful memory, then sinking again into a slumber. In the meantime, light traveled past my curtained window, daylight bloomed, intensified, and finally bright late morning sunshine painted the curtains blood orange.

When I finally arose and came downstairs, everyone had already gathered there, and my father was biting into his last slice of puff pastry.

I never lifted my eyes, but sat down at my place like a frozen mannequin. What did I expect?

I didn't know if *she* was there. I looked neither right nor left, but just ahead, at the whiteness of the tablecloth, and the polished gullet of the silver tea decanter. In it, I could see my own reflection, upside down, or merely distorted, as though I had a huge horrendous head, a bulbous nose, and tiny beady eyes.

And then I heard my father speak, "How was your night, my dear? Did you sleep well?"

My heart stopped its beating. Or maybe I only willed that it had.

I continued to examine the dwarf's reflection before me, while I heard *her* surprising bright voice.

"Thank You, Your Majesty, I had a lovely night," spoke Princess Vialethe, while the dwarf stared back at me from the teapot with a grinning scowl.

And then she added, "Though, I did find this odd thing underneath my mattress, Your Majesty. Imagine my surprise, but it was a dried pea! It was horrid and hard as a rock, and I immediately located it and removed it from under the bedding. I wonder how it got there? Well, the rest of the night was wonderful."

I could stand it no longer, and looked up.

My lovely Princess was looking directly at me.

She was attired impeccably in a morning dress, and her porcelain skin was succulent white, and utterly unblemished, while there was more than a hint of roses on her cheeks.

She was beautiful beyond belief.

And in her beauty she terrified me. For, I continued to look, no longer wary of any consequences, continued to look, and was unable to understand. My eyes darted around the grand breakfast table, and I noted my father's right brow had risen in a bit of perplexity. For, in the pragmatic simplicity of this solution, he was unable to decide whether he had been tricked, or whether this indeed was a Princess.

I noted also that my stepmother was nowhere to be found.

As though recognizing my trek of thought—God forbid!—the King turned to me, and cleared his throat, then said in the same awkward tone as he did when my stepmother had made unreasonable demands upon his patience.

"My boy, your Mother is somewhat ill this morning, and unfortunately she is unable to join us."

"What is it?" I mumbled. I had become artless and stupid.

"Nothing too unpleasant, I would hope. She merely asked to remain in bed longer, seeming to be rather pale and indisposed."

"I am sorry with all my heart that Her Majesty is not well," Vialethe said. "And I hope her malady is neither severe nor lingering. Her Majesty has been more than kind to me, and I simply cannot bear to know that she is indisposed."

"What a sweet dear girl," said the King, smiling helplessly, forgetting all of the suspicions instilled in him by my stepmother the night before.

And then my Princess said something else that made both myself and my father stare at her.

"Before I leave," she said, "I would like to pay my utmost respects to the Queen."

"Leave?" my father said.

"Leave?" I echoed.

"Why, regretfully yes," Vialethe said, and for the first time there was a kind of forcefulness, a sharp fey edge to her tone.

"But—Where will you go, dear child?" said the King. "I thought you would now stay with us, and maybe even—Ahem, well, my boy here is about to turn sixteen, and you know how it is—"

In that moment all further ramblings were interrupted by the entrance of my stepmother.

Seeing her, I stood up. Truly, I couldn't help myself, couldn't help bolting into a vertical position, while everyone else around me reacted similarly, of their own volition, and hardly because of Royal Protocol.

My stepmother was clad in a diaphanous lovely dressing gown, but she was walking with a limp, dragging one foot behind her.

There were deep horrible blue shadows of bruises on her half-swollen face, despite the thick plaster-layer of powder and makeup. For once, her bulging chest was somewhat obscured by a tall hedge of lace and smothered with white powder—yet even there, there were visible shadows of unspeakable violence done to her skin.

Violence done by someone. . . .

"Good God!" the King exclaimed in honest confusion, examining his wife in the light of morning. "What happened to you? I had no idea how badly you've been stricken, my dearest! We must get my Physician—"

But the Queen motioned him away with one weak hand, and her eyes instead eagerly sought out the Princess.

Those of a madwoman, my stepmother's eyes. She shuffled near, eagerness and hunger in her gaze, and squinted in order to see it in all clarity. Seeing only perfection in the young woman before her, she couldn't help but smile widely, and I was certain of the kind of thoughts passing through her mind at that point—cold triumph at the results of what she had orchestrated.

"How did you sleep, my dear?" she said, gleeful breath nearly choking in her throat.

The Princess curtsied deeply. "Perfectly well, Your Majesty," she said. "That is, as soon as I removed the pea from underneath the mattress."

And then she added, "But Your Majesty, on the other hand—"

Her words trailed off. She was holding out her tiny white faerie hand, palm upward, upon which gleamed a tiny round globule of pea green.

My stepmother froze like a basilisk.

We all looked at them. There was no need to end the sentence.

My father the King snorted, then blinked sheepishly, several layers of ignorance beyond us all, then cleared his throat. I stared back and forth from porcelain beauty to gelatinous bruised flesh, while another brand of mad thoughts spun inside my own mind.

Even now, all I could think of was Absolute Receptiveness.

Absolute Receptiveness had not been right.

Absolute Receptiveness had not been real.

But then, like a bit of faerie blowing in from the storm, it never is.

BONDS OF LIGHT

This is a tale of myth and madness, of prophecies fulfilled and unfulfilled, and of hands white and fine like silver. The hands belong to the seventh son of the West Emperor, the one given the name Erester which in that tongue means "light," while some say it also means "destruction," and a curse of uncontainable power upon the imperial line. With those white hands he was known to harness light, to hold it and to wield it, as one would mold a thing of the earth. And because of these hands, these hands cursed with light, some said, Erester the seventh son—who was really half-mad—would speak prophecy.

The West Emperor lay dying, having himself long ago prophesied his death moment—for such knowledge was in the blood of this imperial line. And he called his seven sons to him, to declare his successor.

Long he held each of his sons' two hands in his wrinkled own—once also pale and silver—and at last his hands came to clasp those of Erester. The other six sons looked on, some with haughty wounded hearts, others with knowing humility, and one, the oldest, with righteous anger. Many had been hoping to the last. Yet it was no surprise to any as to the final outcome.

"Things come full circle . . ." whispered the old Emperor, his breath and voice issuing as though out of the deep faults of the earth, the final crypt. With trembling fingers he removed a seal-ring from his hand and placed it in the hands of his seventh son. "Take this, and let this help you know truth that will emerge from madness. There must be no conflict between the seven of you. . . . You, Erester, you will be the one. My child of light. You, with the doe-eyes of the innocent. And yet, it is not all complete. Promise me . . . one thing. There is a woman, who even now comes to you, from the solar plexus of the East. She comes to you in state, for I had called upon her thus. . . . She comes to wed you. You must now consent to have her. Speak!"

The seventh son lifted the gaze of his onyx eyes, filled with *otherness*, wildness, and yet gentle wisdom. "Why, Father? Why must I take this—queen of queens—this woman? I cannot consent until you tell me why."

"And I cannot tell you why. Only that . . . things must come full circle. Trust my wisdom and agree to this thing. Quickly now, for I have very little strength left. . . ."

A slowly blooming star of defiance came to the unearthly eyes of Erester, but he was wise indeed. Averting his gaze he spoke: "This wedding, Father. It must not be . . . And yet, only because I respect Thy Wisdom, Lord, I . . . consent."

Those words were the last the old West Emperor heard on this earthly plane.

A rirante rode a stallion hued like silver. Its trappings were precious leather and gold, and pear-drops of opal and topaz hung from the beast's neck. The woman herself wore no adornment, only black and gray warrior's garments. A single ring of metal was on her right hand, and that only to bear the seal of state. Her hair was bound tight in a circlet of pale silk, and braided into three strands that swung to her waist: one strand for the South, one for the North, and one for the East. The Western strand she could not add yet.

Behind Arirante came her warrior escort-train. Ten thousand were in that train, and they filled the road far to the eastern horizon.

At the gate of the great West City, they were welcomed with strewn rose-petals and scattered amber. The young West Emperor himself stood waiting, and as Arirante leaned down from the great height of her stallion to grasp his pale exquisite hand, her living gaze met the remote twilight of his. But then, as she came to stand before him, tall and straight like himself, Erester lifted his hands—finer than the purest ivory she had seen—and simply placed a garland of white flowers around her neck. Light appeared to spring forth from that garland, to dance for an instant with sublime madness, and a shiver went through her at its touch. From that moment on, Arirante, who had never loved before, loved, without knowing why, this twilight-eyed man who could not be and yet had to be her husband.

Three days hence, in a monolithic temple of gold and granite, three Archpriests married the queen Arirante and the young West Emperor. And on the night of the third day, after their secluded fasting and cleansing rites, Erester and Arirante were led to a single room in the deep vaults of the Palace, and left alone.

Twilight shone dimly in the chamber, throwing long eerie shadows on the bare walls and the great ancestral bed that was in the center. Arirante stood before him in a white shift, half-faint with hunger, and with resigned haunting eyes that for the moment lacked the usual energy. Her hair, unbound, was like a sunset. And her hands, Erester noted, were pale and elegant, and very much like his own.

And although something acute and warm stirred in him then, at the sight of her, and he yearned for this woman, Erester stood coldly, and watched her with unyielding eyes. "My lovely queen," he said. "How well my Father chose for me. And yet, I must decline this pleasure. I'm afraid, Lady, that we cannot be joined now as they expect us to be. You see, 'things must first come full circle.'"

Arirante's surprise lasted only for a second. How well she had anticipated that this one, the seventh son, would be *different*. She looked into his unreadable eyes, her gaze also focused now, and said: "I see. . . . Then this wedding was not of your design. Well then." She straightened her back. "To tell you the truth, Lord, these woman's clothes do not really suit me at all. Nor my hair, hanging wanton and loose like an army harlot's. Indeed, it is highly regretful that the irrevocable ceremony has been completed and you have not explained yourself to me earlier. Which, by the way, is the only thing about this matter that I don't understand."

"Then it appears we both regret the misunderstanding." He smiled, like a razor. "But—let me explain. My Father, before he made me his successor, asked me to agree to this marriage, as a condition. I have done so, although he would not explain his reasons. I am now the West Emperor."

He paused, his eyes searching hers for the impact of his words and also for some other thing. And then his expression focused, intensified. "However," he said. "To marry you was the *only thing* I promised to a dying man. It was his choice made *for* me. And I always keep my word, Lady. Only—in all things I choose for *myself*."

"And you would not have chosen me. I see now." Arirante was pale as the shift she wore. "Then, my Lord, I can only despise you," she said. "For, unless you're as innocent as a caged songbird, you have misled me as well as yourself, in this game. You have sold yourself for the throne, not even knowing what the future of the throne was to be. And now, let *me* in turn explain your old Emperor's reasoning to you: Only some time from now, your old ailing father was secretly faced with an imminent war—not with my own Eastern Empire, but with the barbaric nomads from the far south, those peoples without a name that the Empires must fight, from the dawn of our history. Knowing his own weakness and the weakness of his army, and knowing the power that lay in the East, the West Emperor made a deal with me, Erester. He gave me his son, yourself, his fair successor, as he had long known he would through his gift of prophecy. And together with you, Lord, he *gave* me the West Empire.

"Only—my fair Erester—I have never asked for you, you who welcomed me with white blossoms. I agreed to this marriage, my husband, because this was the most peaceful and simple way to unite our two Empires. There was no need for any marriage. Indeed, the old West Emperor's heir and his six brothers would have been welcome as honored generals in my army. Or—" and Arirante's eyes flamed with power—"they just as easily would have graced the cells of my dungeons, for disloyalty to their new Empress!"

As she spoke thus, Erester's manner grew frozen and even more remote. "Stand away from me, woman..." he whispered then, wildly, with unnatural affect. And again she saw the telltale signs of peculiarity in him, the oddness that the old Emperor himself warned her about.

"You sicken me! I welcomed you then on an impulse of madness... In that madness I thought I recognized in you something, a light... But oh, how we have both been deceived! Locked in an accursed marriage that stands before us both as a fact, to encircle and strangle us! And I am to be your obedient slave! Oh, Gods!" And the young man sat down on the bed, putting his pale ivory hands on his head. He went still, his shape vulnerable, desolate.

"So, I sicken you?" whispered Arirante, angry that he drew so much response from her, and thus more harshly than she meant. "Well then, words I have not to express what I feel at the sight of *you!* Especially since I came to you with an open soul.... In the East there is honor and sanctity that is expected of the union of a man and woman. I see now, there is none of that left here. . . ."

With a sigh, the woman gathered her long radiant hair, and with fingers that also seemed to send forth light, she began to braid it into one long rich strand. "No matter, then," she said coldly, in a voice of power. "Know, then, that Arirante needs no more reluctant slaves. You are free to go and be as you wish. Our marriage vows, meaning nothing, I now declare broken— just as my deal with your father. Also, Lord West Emperor, I throw back in your face your West Empire. It might be madness and pride on my part, but I have no need of it, Lord, since I already have *three* Empires. I leave this City tomorrow, and wish you all the luck . . ." She laughed then, proud, herself confused, wild-eyed. "And you will need it, seventh son and wielder of light, when tomorrow or the next day all the hordes of nameless rabble come knocking on your Empire's door!"

Erester looked up, his twilight gaze also focused with all the blackness of the night, and not a trace of gentleness. "When they do come, I shall not need *you* to help me keep them out," he said rationally. And then, with a stab of sarcasm: "And by the way, my Lady, thank you for graciously giving me back my Empire."

And then he paused, stricken, like a child, as he looked at her pale fine hands, pale and white, as they moved pleating the hair. In that moment a sense of certain things came to him, and he knew true prophecy.

He continued, in a different tone, looking at her with puzzled eyes. "However, I see, it is easier said than done . . . My thoughts wander. I have always had too much honor for my own good. Also, I admit that—my mind is not always my own. And now I'm afraid we cannot nullify our marriage, no matter how much we both wish it, simply because I have given *my word* to my Father. I *see* now that the game he has been playing is not yet complete, and I know also that, like my own half-glimpses of truth, he was always guided by a greater knowledge. 'Things must come full circle,' he said. Gods only know what he meant, but I do know one thing—all of the prophecies are converging upon us now. This has indeed been prophesied as a time of madness. A time when East and West, North and South, shall be one, like the strand of your silken hair, Lady. . . . When seven make eight, which in turn makes one. . . ."

Arirante, who only an instant ago was ready to storm out of the chamber, watched him weary and blank-faced. "And what manner of madness do you speak now? I thought I married a weak-minded coward, but now I see I married a blathering idiot! What prophecies? What mean you by all this?" She spoke meanly thus, because there was an inkling of truth to what he said. A truth she had long feared.

And then she sat down with her back towards him, on the other side of the great bed, and, surprising even herself, started to laugh bitterly, shaking off that fear in one blow. "We are, both of us, blathering idiots," she concluded. "Throwing an Empire back and forth between us, in a childish game of pride."

She looked back over her shoulder, once more poised and serious, almost gentle. "This night has been full of surprises, my Lord. Fasting has made me light-headed. And it put me off-balance. It seems fated then, that we keep this bargain made with a dead old man. Let us start anew. If you wish—I ask forgiveness for my rash stupid words. Words not worthy of myself. You need ask no forgiveness, having been made a victim of my and his scheming."

She got up then, and neared him. As he stared upward, curious, into her pale strong eyes, Arirante leaned and placed a cool sealing kiss on his forehead. "No bargains will be broken, thus. And yet, '*husband*,' I too have honor. We will be bound only in name. This kiss is my word to you that you are *free of me as a man*." And turning away, she quickly left the chamber.

Erester sat, stricken for the second time that night, because where her lips had been, his forehead burned as though branded, and he knew no words for the feeling that filled him at that touch.

The enemy, when it did come, attacked from all sides. East, West, North, and South, the barbarians seethed—their number like grains of sand on the seashore—and they lay siege to the West Empire. The Emperor and Empress rode at the head of an army of many thousand. Pennants of fire and silver flew high in the wind.

Arirante, grim in her stark steel armor, atop a war-stallion, carried a razor-tipped lance. A broadsword of black metal hung at her side, but was not half as sharp as the look of her pale relentless eyes. Sorrow she hid in them, deep where none would see—for none could face her imposing gaze long enough to know her.

Erester, the seventh son, wore armor of light. Whiteness seemed to gleam from his polished steel, and congealed about him in a manner almost material. Cold-eyed and feral, with none of his former gentle manner, he never once turned to look at Arirante. His habit now was to pretend she was not there. And occasionally his fingers wandered to tighten reassuringly over the ring given to him, the one with the seal of state.

His broadsword, like a dark beast, was in his pale elegant hands—white and fine like silver.

One of the six sons, the eldest, neared the West Emperor. "Our armies stand ready to fight for you, Brother." He spoke tonelessly, and Erester thought how this one too had never learned how to speak to this brother of his, to the seventh son. Blank and remote he seemed to Erester, like the other five of his brothers.

"It is not for me that you will fight," replied Erester, looking him in the eyes, with a glimmer of the old softness. "It is for *her*. To her you now answer." And he moved one pale white hand, newly gloved, in the Empress' direction, and whispered oddly: "She has usurped me. . . . I no longer have a sense of self."

From the corner of her eyes, sharper than a hawk, Arirante saw the gesture, and she heard the words. "It is not for you *or* for me that these soldiers fight," she said in a loud voice that was heard among the ranks. "It is for this land that we will all shed blood." And she thought. *For a land to which I somehow bind myself. . . As I bind myself to this mad one.*

Erester's lips curved in a bitter smile. "Truly you speak now, Lady. For indeed, blood will be shed today. I have seen one of us, children of this imperial line, lie bloodied and lifeless, as the others look on and weep. . . ."

"Much good your prophecy does us now, fool!" exclaimed Arirante, inflamed. "Indeed, tell all of us how we all lie dead and cold, and that right before the battle! Hah! I have had enough of this, all of this, I spit upon any and all prophecies!"

And with that, she spurred her stallion ahead, while trumpets rang to announce the battle.

Erester looked in her wake with grave intensity, and uttered quiet words to his eldest brother, before they also followed: "She might scorn the prophecy, but she does not know that the dead man I speak of will be *myself*. . . ."

A rirante fought like one possessed. White light and silver rang in her mind—as always during battle. She did not know the limbs she severed, never heard the cries of agony as her broadsword struck, again and again. She fought for this land—only remotely her own—and for the man with the gentle eyes who had put a garland of flowers about her neck. And it was the gods who now acted in her stead. The barbarians fell back, clearing the way before her and the imperial army.

On the other side of the battlefield, Erester burned like a beacon of wild light, and the slaughter wrought by him was also superhuman. Long had he ceased to wield the battlesword, but instead grasped the source of Whiteness itself, the sun, in his hands, and he struck them down with raw energy. Dark beastly faces of the enemy, barbaric shadow forms—no longer even remotely human—came flickering by his eyes, and the battle was now only a whirling dream.

I do not need you, woman! he cried within his own mind. Echoes of chaos answered him. And it seemed to Erester that not only must he die today, but he must take her with him, this woman who was bound to him unspeakably, unto death, he now knew, by an empty promise. Yet, how could that be? He hated her like he hated the madness imposed on him, and he hungered for her, like he hungered for the other side of his self that had also been imposed upon him—prophecy and truth.

And through the raging battle—that was long since concluded in their favor, and yet which went on continuously now in his mind—Erester came through the field of slaughter, searching for her who held him in more ways than one.

Arirante, helmet unlaced, stood in numb silence to wipe the sweat from her face. She was unarmed when he came from the back upon her, to strike. And yet, the white light still sang warning in her head, and the last traces of battle gave her a sixth sense. Just enough to know *him* coming.

She whirled, grabbing the sword at her feet, and parried a deadly blow.

"Die!" he cried. "Die with me now, and let things come full circle, at last!"

"You don't know what you speak, Erester!" she cried in turn, striking back at him.

"I know only that I *make my own choices*, woman! Oh, how he tortures me, the old one in his grave . . . Oh, how he stifles me now, with a promise that presses upon me like a curse! He gave me the ring and told me to look at it to find truth. There! I look now! And where is truth to be found?"

"Is it your pride that wounds you now, or your madness? Can you not bear that a single Choice has once been made for you?"

"I am the seventh son, woman! The seventh is always said to be blessed by the gods—or damned and bound, as in my case! And you are my curse!"

"I'm no such thing, you dramatic fool! Listen to me! I am—"

Their broadswords shattered as one. Only hilts remained in their hands. The man and the woman crouched, facing one another, both mad-eyed. But the woman knew her own madness, while the man did not.

Instead, he began to ply the thin air about him, with his hands, pale and fine like silver, until a blade of light appeared, solidified. And he raised it, to strike.

But the woman raised her own hands up, in a timeless gesture of defense, and where her hands had been—pale and fine like silver—grew a shield of light. When the two sources of light met, there was only *sun*. It blazed behind their closed eyelids. And then, in their minds, thunder.

And afterward, there was nothing. Erester stood with pale lifeless hands, staring in silence at Arirante who also stood before him, drained of light.

"You are now no longer the seventh son . . ." she whispered then. "And you are therefore free, of both the blessings and curses." She stretched out a trembling hand with her seal ring on it, and took his own ringed hand, so that he could see that the two rings were identical, like their hands were.

"There had never been a seventh son, Erester. Instead, the seventh labor of your mother resulted in twins. We are not really alike, you and I. Indeed, if our Father had not decided it was *time*, and told me, and showed me my own truth, I would never have believed this yet another tale of madness, in which I had to lie and lie. . . .

"They had to separate us, Erester. Two children like us, together, bore too much light and destruction for one land to contain. And yet, things had to be resolved ultimately, to come full circle."

"A sister . . ." Erester looked at her with thrice-stricken eyes. "And I wed you!"

"And yet you have not. . . . You had known, always, deep inside. It held you back. Only—your madness developed instead, as a result of our separation. The power that ran through us was hungering for the other, was never complete. . . ."

Erester was looking somewhere into the distance. "I feel it no longer . . ." he whispered. "The sense of prophecy. It is gone now, like the wildness in my soul . . ."

He exclaimed, "Why then did I not die? I saw it clearly, my bloodied corpse."

"Because, my beloved-hated brother, half-prophecies never tell more than half-truths. What I saw before the battle was yourself, *reborn*. And that was my side of it. Our Father 'wedded' us symbolically, I now see—for that was the only thing I did not understand even then. I too had been made insane by the power. It clouded my reason and hid half-truths from me, while I hungered for Empires. . . . I had lied so much to you, attempting to disguise my self—forgive me!—and yet *you knew me*, even back then, the only one who knew me ever."

Erester, with onyx eyes of the doe, looked into her eyes. "I am no longer sure if I even know myself, or am capable of Choices. Only one thing shows me what I am now, one place— the reflection of myself in your eyes."

Then the six brothers of the West Emperor approached them, through the empty battlefield, and the eldest one reached out, welcoming, with his own fair and silver-white hands. His expression as he spoke, was more clear at last to Erester than it had ever seemed before: "Welcome back, Sister, Brother. We have waited so long for madness to recede, and for things to come, at last, full circle."

THE STARRY KING

It was on one of those nights when stars reveal their true nature as naked living souls that the woman came walking through the sleeping town. She walked with an apparent lightness, an infinite poise in her statuesque figure. And yet, though none would know it, each step she made was like a burden of lifting up a world.

At first glance she was young—slender like any girl of twenty winters, if only taller. In the first tavern she entered, they noticed, under the cheap illumination, that her clothes were masculine and modestly threadbare. Her face and hands, it was observed, were pale as a smoky dream, colorless, lifeless, drained of everything that was of the soul. It was only the heavy look of her blue eyes that spoke not only of a great life-will, but of burdens unspeakable, and of power even beyond.

And thus they all noticed her.

As everything happens in such intimate towns as this, rumors spread fast. Some said she was a great noblewoman, masquerading for her own private reasons. Others, after discerning the deadly-beautiful blade among the folds of her cloak, spoke of warrior women from the East. She dressed, indeed, as some former aristocrat who's seen better days. Yet, others claimed, there was gem-light of rings about her fingers! She could have bought the whole town with them, if she tried.

The woman had old eyes. It was, if anything, the heavy expression which made them appear thus. No one she had to deal with quite fathomed these eyes, since none met her gaze longer than necessary.

And then, one day, someone had seen her take the hood off her hair, and this was when rumors went mad. Her hair, like long filaments of exquisite satin, was white as death.

She said that her name was Nellval, and she was looking for the starry king. At this point, many laughed in her face, while rumors also quieted, seeing before them only a madwoman.

As children, all had been told the tale of the "starry king," and as adults, could only scoff at any who might even suggest a belief in such things. Who, being sane, would credit as history the story of an ancient king's son loving his bride to the extent of interring her dead body with himself in a stone tower? Who could believe that he stayed alive with the lovely corpse for more than a month, without food, or water? Legends said that for over three months his sobs and moans resounded through the tower, as he tried to breathe life into her, until remnants of his own left him slowly and with placid cruelty.

And then, when the moon waxed and waned thrice over, they said, and his soul departed the grief-wrecked body, there were odd occurrences all throughout the land.

The sun rose one morning, redder than a rose. The great river that flows to the sea, changed its course—yes, verily!—and branching, gave birth to a twin. Far West, snow, like silver, fell prematurely over the tall mountains. And one night, when people looked up, they saw a new constellation formed in the heavens, stars sprinkled over the black abyss of sky in the shape of a man.

The Starry King, they called it. The man-shape wrought of pin-point lights had its one arm outstretched in silent longing, a circlet-crown of greater stars traced his brow, while his eyes, yes, the eyes of the starry king, seemed to weep—sadly the two eye-stars flickered, in semblance of fluid motion. They looked down at the world, and old folk said that the Starry King's great love had, through its suffering, taken in and contained the burden of primeval sorrow that was originally fated for mankind to bear. He, the starry king, had not died, they said. And if one could but find him, somewhere in this world, then one's sorrows and burdens would depart, a cleansing. . . .

"A pretty story, is it not?" a tavernkeeper said after lengthy recounting, to Nellval, feeling sorry for the mad one. "Almost makes you wish you had lived in those days, when people made up such things. And believed them too."

Old-young eyes met his. And the tavernkeeper also never quite fathomed that gaze. "Would you like to hear more?" he asked, pitying her, and thinking of gold.

She shook her head negatively. "I would like, but I have no time, my friend. I must go on." She spoke in a soft voice, kindly, and then left his tavern. Several blank or mildly charitable eyes turned in her wake.

Nellval went to see an old sorcery-woman of this town. "How can I find the starry king?"

The expedience-inclined hag did not even blink— although she too had heard of this mad one's search. "How much are you willing to sacrifice of yourself, to obtain this meeting?" she said harshly, her black eyes like sharp agates, and gold dangling about her gypsy-hands.

But when the younger woman raised her heavy gaze, and threw the hood off her white hair, the black agates narrowed in sudden understanding of the uniqueness of these circumstances.

"The Starry King . . . does not take all burdens indiscriminately," she whispered in a different intimate voice. "He also has a limit, a price. . . . Do you really think you can—"

"Enough. What is *your* price, old one?"

"What is your burden?"

Nellval shrugged and then got up. She turned to leave.

"Wait!" said the woman, eyes lusting after the precious rings on her fingers. "No questions, my pretty, no more. That blue stone—give me—"

With utmost indifference Nellval removed the ring, dropped it in the wrinkled clutching palm.

"A-ah," the sorcery-woman cackled, fingers closing over the thing. "What you search can be found but in a graveyard under a full moon, when the white star-flower blooms."

"Indeed . . ." For the first time, something almost like sarcasm came through Nellval's tone. "But—I believe you."

When that month's cycle came to the moon's apex of fullness, Nellval set out in the early evening to a nearby old graveyard on the outskirts of the town. She was accompanied at first by careful crowds of tentatively cruel laughing urchins of this town, for she was an object of peculiar half-mockery. Soon, with the coming twilight, the children dropped away, and she continued unaccompanied, along a winding path, among hills, birdsong, and rhythmic cicadas. The graveyard lay in a clearing, old tombstones half-sunken among wildflowers and brush, and overhead the sky streamed endlessly outward, lightly hued with silver on the horizon, and black as ink at the zenith.

Nellval stood among the gravestones. Then she began to pace, limber as a shadow, yet tall with her mysterious power. She continued to pace thus, her soft boots marking the anemic grass, as the moon floated at last over the horizon's rim, round and bright and perfect, like the sun's shadow.

It was then that the sunken earth all about her started to move and quiver, like waves on a high sea, and the grave-stones began shifting. Pale lotus-hands thrust through the dark earth, reached out, followed by waxen faces with vacant or feverishly burning red eyes. The dead were emerging, with moans like siren-song. And they reached out to her, inevitable in their approach.

Only, Nellval brushed the pallid hands away with the firm leather of her boot, her face blank, almost disdainful, and with some secret pity. If *they* continued, insistent, then she bared her sword blade, and had but to touch the dead flesh with its radiant sharpness, for *them* to give way. But most often, it was only the look of her heavy eyes that made the burning red ones cringe, look away, and conceal themselves back in the abysmal earth. And thus Nellval quietly paced among the graves and silver grasses, and the softly wailing dead.

When the moon-disk soared straight overhead in a dome of night covered with a trillion stars, a shadow of silver came to stand like a haze over the earth.

Nellval looked about her, and her gaze swept the ground. She saw small pale blossoms opening their hearts to the moonlight, at the precise moment of the moon's zenith. The cicadas grew silent, and the last night bird held its breath. Even the dead sank away once more into oblivion.

The star-flowers growing among the graves, tiny, delicate as gossamer, seemed to reflect in them identical shapes, the lights of each individual star.

Nellval felt something equally delicate snap within herself, deep, as she watched the stars and their shadows, star-flowers, begin an interplay with moonlight, so that after some moments, her honed, tense vision began to *perceive*. She saw lines, or rays of silver moon-form, reaching from each one flower to each single star, a bond of one-on-one, spanning the limitless airy expanse of night.

And suddenly, she began to make out a solidifying outline of a constellation in the sky, a man-shape with a crown. The stars congealed about *him*, adding features and light to the form, and the eye-stars were now supernovas.

There was a feel of many souls, of power in the air, and a tingling in her blood. Throwing back the cloak, so that her white hair billowed like nebulae, she turned her pale face to the skies, and looked in *his* eyes.

"O, starry king!" Nellval cried, a hollow empty voice, then whispered, ". . . starry king. . . ."

She blinked but once (was it the moistening in her eyes), and a man stood before her, on the human grass.

He was half-corporeal, half-night. His outlines were of moonlight and starlight, and like an exquisite ghost, tall and majestic, he wore garments of ancient glory, wrought now only of mist.

He took a step, shadows shifting all about, in liquid silver. Nellval watched the dully-gleaming crown on the light silk of his hair, the haunting face.

Surprisingly, he had a deep voice, solid and ringing with power, as a mortal man—a lord among them.

"I am he. What would you have of me . . .?"

The words were kind, yet they echoed inhumanly with the emptiness and eternal expanse of night. (His face, oh, the beauty of his face!)

Nellval looked at him, and her lips quivered. "Starry king," she said, oddly passive, "look in my eyes. . . . What do you see there?"

Eyes of shadows and stars met mortal eyes of pain. For an instant, only.

"Bitterness," he said. "Blood and death—on your soul. Anger, burning within you, a cauldron of boiling poison-hate. That, deep under the surface of your placid outer shadow. You are but a shadow, woman, nothing any longer touches you. An outer husk you bear, of soft-spoken apathy."

"Hah! My greatest burden, you have guessed it— apathy!" Nellval cried, in a suddenly sarcastic, agonized voice turned hoarse by a lack of breath, so that her own heart jerked at the hysterical sound of it. She faced him who remained unperturbed.

"What else do you see, starry king? How deeply *have* you looked? My eyes—" and she took a step forward, almost touching the ghostly man (but he was oh-so solid, so real)—"Do you see my parents, my brothers, among the ravaged dead? And what of my child, whose *beheading*—a foul mockery of the word—I have witnessed myself, powerless to stop the madmen? Or—" and her eyes now filled with a congealing light of so many stars—"the eyes of the man whom I had loved, cold and indifferent, as he turned to love another? And the convulsing hands of the hanged man who had fought at my side as my brother? Or, the beggars on the filthy town streets, who always raise their hollow martyr eyes at me, when I hopelessly drop a coin into an emaciated palm?

"And what of the *pain*, the *horrible agony* of those I myself have killed, betrayed, destroyed, or harmed in any other way??? It is *their* eyes I remember, their cringing. . . . The eyes of the king I—betrayed. And—just as *he* had cringed, whom I loved and pursued—in my damned possessive obsession, his fear, his eyes—"

"Enough," said the one called the starry king, and there were no words to describe the nature of the understanding that had passed them. And he added, "Your hair is white as a dream. . . ." And suddenly then his voice was but a whisper.

Nellval looked at the face that was neither old nor young, neither of the fancy, nor truly corporeal. She too, whispered, urgently: "You understand then, what my burden is."

In answer, waxen lips smiled with gentle sorrow.

"Will you . . . cleanse me, Lord of Stars?" said Nellval.

A pause of silence then, as all the night waited for the *answer*.

His lips moved.

"First—take the seal of silence off your heart. Weep . . . O woman."

She shuddered, letting in a sudden flash of memory of *something* so far gone, so far. . . . "I can't. It—it would *hurt* too much." she concluded, knowing the stupid helplessness of her words. "I don't—cry anymore. I—don't feel."

"I cannot take your Burden, if you do not bare your soul!" rang his words now, like thunder. And the night resounded, and the stars trembled.

"Yes . . . I suppose, you must open an infected wound, to cleanse it. Or an infected soul. Well then." And for the first time in many years, Nellval—who bad been so many things, her previous "lives" involving the pain of so many, and now but a tangled skein rolled tight in her deepest depths—allowed herself to remember. Doing so, she looked into *his* eyes, the fathomless eyes of the starry king, and—drowned.

She was swimming in the Sea of Pain of all Humankind. For one instant only, she knew the unspeakable *agony* that one mind cannot conceive. And the next instant, like a bubble of air, she burst forth out of that Sea, for her life. . . .

Gasping, she found herself looking at the hazy surface of his placid otherworldly eyes, no longer two pits giving way before her. "Who are you, really?" she asked, "*What* are you?"

"Who am I? I am you," he said. And then the eyes cried.

There was an odd stillness to the silver night, as it listened to the silent weeping of the starry king. Several large tears containing in them reflected starlight rolled from his eyes, inevitable, like the passing of seasons. Yet, not a single twitch came to the face. Its absolute lack of tension spoke of strange acceptance of all things.

His tears stopped. Again, silence.

And then Nellval felt a great *thing* lifted off her, a great weight gone from her soul. (And she noticed that the locks of his hair were now even whiter than her own—or, were they of the same infinitely pale shade, had they always been thus?)

She was free. A nothingness now filled her, a great empty bubble of air and nothing, of hazy moon-lit musings, and thoughts calm as silk.

The starry king said: "I have taken your Burden." And then began to shimmer, gossamer-fine, and fade away.

"Wait!" cried Nellval. Blood pounded at her temples. "Wait, Lord of Stars! You have taken away not only my Burden of suffering and pain, but also my *memory* of the self. . . ." Her voice grew small in the stasis of the night. "I have—nothing."

"Such is the price," came his dwindling voice.

But Nellval reached out with her pale strong human hand, and grabbed the shadowy fading being, took hold of him, and they *struggled*, in a weird instant of timelessness. In her embrace she held a universe of silver and stars and night, and it was a touch so ardent, yet so oddly sweet, so gentle, that as she fought him (so oddly familiar), she found herself instead caressing him. And she suddenly, inexplicably began to *know* who and what he was, had been, and to *remember*.

. . . Birds sang outside the ancient tower. The king, young and emaciated, lifted the gaze of his red sunken eyes from the lily-white corpse of a young woman, covered by rose-petals and her own fragrant hair, like rust. Death.

He could do nothing. Absolutely nothing. Here before him was a fact. Death.

He had no more tears left . . . The Sun had been shining the same way now, for the third month (During the second, he forgot the meaning of *sun* and *day*, and perceived only shadows).

How could she no longer be? How, O gods! She hadn't even been beautiful. Or exceptionally lucky, so gods had no reasons to envy her and punish. . . . Or him. He had been humble. Yet—a humble king.

Why? O gods!

When his moment of crisis had passed, he was left with a sense of nothing, an emptiness of soul. And when he looked again at the once-dear body of a once-living woman, he suddenly realized that it too, the body, the *thing*, it did not matter.

Nothing any longer mattered. He saw that flies came to sit on the corpse. And the definite beginning stench—or, had it been thus for some time now?

And the king, or the one who had once been king, lay down on the cold clean stone of the floor, and then, began to watch the day outside the window, calmly, relearning every nuance of the coral-gilded dawn and sunset, every shifting of things, and accepting them within his empty, dying heart. . . .

"That was but another life. . . . One life that I had lived, of so many." The starry king spoke to Nellval, in the instant of their struggle-embrace.

In answer, suddenly she began to weep, shuddering sobs rending her body, still holding him tight as a dream. And his gentle shadow-hands tightened about her, as he continued: "Yes, it is the futility of things, and consequent apathy, that had first killed me, and then made me see things in a different way, and to *care*."

"But you have cared for so many!" she sobbed, the young-old white-haired woman with a once-black soul. "I have seen it inside of you, and they had all been just like me, not better off at all, all hurting—"

"We are but one thing ultimately. One thing of pain."

"And you, are you then but a starry vaporous ghost, the magical yearning of my dreams? My conscience? You, who have 'taken' my burden and hate away, and then gave back *new* memories of things?"

"No, not a dream," he said. "I have been once a man. And now, I no longer know. For the moment, you might say, I am—you."

Nellval continued to weep. "You have taken so many Burdens on yourself!" she repeated, "so many Burdens!"

And his placid eyes were on her, and they had ceased the struggle.

"So many Burdens, starry king . . ." she whispered. "And what of your own?"

Was it surprise that flickered in the haunting immortal eyes? He then *looked* at her. "*My* Burden? What of it? I no longer have a Burden to call my own. Don't you understand, it is the things that *you* cannot bear, that I take from you? And the things that the others could not bear, they constitute my Burden now . . ."

"But—how can you contain so much within you?"

"How can I not? Who else is there, what god or gods," laughed (yes, laughed!) the starry king in gentle sorrow, "that can, or is willing to bear *my* Burden?" And his voice echoed out into the sky and stars of night.

Nellval thought only for a moment. "I have nothing now, really, nothing—to live for. And I have learned of myself. Go, for once in your own peace, you who were once a man—I will bear your Burden now."

And before a whisper of protest came from him, she reached with her hands (her fingers incidentally touching the silk of his locks, oh, the strange sweetness of it!) and took the dull crown of stars from his brow (it burned her like agony), placing it on her own white head.

As she did thus, there was a fire inside her mind, and the shadow-man standing before her without a crown, gifted her with a look of such empathy and awe and at last recognition, that her heart—having so many fatal cracks of pain in it—broke at last.

Who knows if she died or not then, but she was *changed*. *He* too, was gone now, truly, a smoky dream. Nellval *stood* alone in the night, among dark old graves and silver star-flowers, and the sleeping dead. The moon had dipped to the nadir, close to the horizon, and the heavens were filled with only a trillion stars.

Nellval once again carried her old burden within her. And with it, somewhere deep, she knew somehow there were others. And yet—

Nothing was quite the same. And the Burdens of the World, odd as it seemed, were not at all difficult to contain. Indeed, they seemed light as a feather, as night vapor. . . . Like a load of stars from the sky, ringing, light and silvery. For, there was now that ever-present "feel" of the Crown about her head, a sensation of agony so close yet so far away, and never quite touching her, that allowed her to Bear.

Only at one instance could it touch her, Nellval knew—not when she remembered her own, already receding burdens of death and unfulfilled love and betrayal, no. It, the agony, would burn only when she momentarily recalled (with such longing . . .) the hazy dream-memory that the starry king had given her, of his own past, and of the one life—the last—in which he had loved a woman with hair like rust. For when—so long ago, it seemed—Nellval's own white hair had color, it was thus, *rust*. And Nellval had recognized, in that silent woman's corpse, many lives ago, herself. . . .

But now, that was all irrelevant. She stood, and the world was once again before her. She had freed him.

The Starry Queen.

THE STONE FACE, THE GIANT, AND THE PARADOX

Brushing a constant sprinkling of ants off her bare knees, Janéh crouched on the grassy bank of the wild pool, mesmerized by her own reflection on the still water.

On the surface of the waters, her face floated pixie-like out of the upside-down sky. It watched her back from a unique angle only her perfect twin self could achieve. From the cloudy murk of the wild watery morass it seemed to emerge, wicked shadow and light resolving into two beautiful, odd, almond-shaped eyes of the Fair Folk, with a distant look imprinted on them.

A face, perfectly immobile.

Janéh hated it.

It was a rigid mask—the blank countenance of a strange young woman without shame or fear or humanity, and the heritage of her fey father who had appeared to her beautiful half-wit mother, like the Green Man of the Forest, on a lazy sun-drenched afternoon in May. On that same day, with the buzzing of bees, and a warm fragrant breeze blowing over two sinuous sweetly wrestling bodies, Janéh was conceived, while the sun played through the trees. Her simple mother, Mireah, was later known to mumble, in her more lucid moments, that he had been "glorious like spring itself", and "bright," and he "promised to return."

Mireah died, waiting for him to return, while Janéh grew to early womanhood. Janéh had a face that never cried, never smiled, regardless of what emotions she felt inside. She wore a mask of locked features that frightened little children of the village where she lived. They would see her, and start their running game, terrified and yet enjoying the sense of terror deep in their naive wicked minds. "The Stone Face!" they cried, and ran about squealing, in little ruffian gangs.

Janéh ignored them always as she passed, straight-backed and fey, and looking neither left nor right but only ahead of her. The little beastlings never knew that, out of pity, she avoided turning the peculiar gaze of her swamp-hued almond eyes directly on them. They also did not know or even suspect that she could run faster than any of them, and could catch them, if she wanted, easier than a breeze.

The adults of the village knew a bit more about Janéh than their offspring. The blacksmith's son had watched her once, hidden in a thicket, as she raced through the forest glade, like the wind itself, and her feet—he claimed—had left no imprint on the moss-covered earth. "She must have been chasing the stag, and she ran beside it!" he later swore to his fellow drinkers in the tavern. Not many believed the blacksmith's son, for he was known to tell a tale brighter than the rainbow. Besides, it was well known that the blacksmith's son, Gihen, preferred tales and songs and his reed-pipes, to pursuing his father's trade. This did not go over too well with the villagers, who were not too frivolous themselves, but hard-working and simple like the earth, and could understand nothing of the attraction that the glimmer of dew upon forest moss or the beating of a moth's wings in the heavy green thicket held for some fools such as himself.

But the villagers were more ready to believe when Ailan, the son of the richest merchant in these parts, came back from his deer hunt empty-handed, his beautiful dark eyes sharp as flints in anger. "It was Mad Mireah's daughter," he told them, "She helped the stag escape me by spooking it, and then ran after it! The witch, the fey changeling—she runs like a wild beast of the forest! It was her, I tell you, I wouldn't mistake her ugly Stone Face anywhere."

Ailan never mentioned to anyone however, that he had been aware of her for seasons now, watching with occult hunger the stone-frozen unearthly mask, and her Fair Folk eyes. He had been watching ever since he had once looked fully into her eyes many a winter ago, when they were still children, and saw a *mystery*. At that time also, he still knew no names for desires that were just beginning to move inside him.

And it was for that reason that he often went hunting in these parts, knowing that she roamed the forest like a wild creature. Often he caught glimpses of her through the trees, and once even saw her pale body as she swam in the little thicket-hidden pool. The sight of her body imprinted on his retina like fire, and sent demons of want leaping in the murkiest deep places within him. And because even then Ailan did not know— or would not let himself know—his own deepest self, in that instant he hated Janéh, hated with a passion the sight of her lithe whiteness that seemed untouched by the sun despite exposure to the elements.

Janéh lived alone on the fringes of the village, in the house where Mireah died. The young girl remained there because she had nowhere else to go, and because, despite her isolation, she considered it her home. When Janéh passed through the village, she hardly ever spoke to the folk on the streets. When she did speak, it was in a self-effacing, soft voice. Also, she had learned well, instinctively, to avert her eyes, so as to avert unnecessary attention and cruel mockery from the likes of Ailan.

Lamira and Nellis, daughters of the baker, who used to play with her sometimes when they were children, would speak kindly with Janéh when she came in to the bake shop to make a purchase. Often, she would receive the bread from the shop in exchange for berries or wild herbs that she was famous for gathering. The baker's daughters used the fresh herbs and succulent berries of the forest as ingredients in their baked goods. However, they usually talked to her only when the baker was not looking.

In the village tavern, Radiene the tavernkeeper, smiled at Janéh only when the tavern was half-empty, and no one could see his expression. Janéh dutifully came to sweep the floors and scrub the counters there daily, and in exchange, Radiene would give her a generous sum of four silver coins every month. He was also one of the few who dared to strike up a conversation with the girl everyone thought Faerie-born.

Janéh had, at first glance, a simple manner about her, almost like her mother. She spoke so little, some customers thought she was a mute. And yet, Radiene knew, there was wisdom lurking in her slanted fey eyes—for, once he actually glanced inside, he found humor, sharp wit, and of all things, compassion.

"Why don't you ever smile, Janéh?" he once jokingly said, when no one was looking. "I know folks have not been fair to you around here, but you are a good, hard-working girl, reasonable and with all your wits about you—unlike your poor departed mother, bless her soul . . . You should stand up for yourself more when people laugh, you know. If you don't, folks get the wrong ideas. It's a sad world, it is, but you must be friendly. Or they'll grow to mistrust you even more. And then, it'll be no turning back. . . ."

Janéh stopped scrubbing the counter-top, and raised her Stone Face and slanted almond-eyes to stare directly at him. The moment froze and distorted. And it seemed to Radiene in that odd instant of shimmering time that the Forest itself, crawling with *things* had touched him then, encroached into his own soul, with a chill of the pine-needle floor and mossy trunks of great trees, with a hiss of wind through branches of monolithic oaks, and with the silent alienation of falling leaves as they swooned gently toward the earth.

The moment had passed. And Janéh answered his question without artifice. "Master Radiene," she said, "thank you for the advice. I want to tell you a truth which may sound odd to you. I never smile because I—*cannot*. Not even when my eyes are laughing so wildly I would burst. In the same way, I cannot weep, or express surprise. *I cannot move my facial features beyond blinking or barely parting my lips.* In truth, everyone is right, to call me 'Stone Face.' Because I am that."

And again she proceeded to polish the counter with earnest zeal, averting her gaze and allowing her dark swamp-brown hair to obscure the Stone Face.

But Radiene felt a novel fear. And although still kindly disposed, he never again dared to speak thus to Janéh.

The small quiet pool was at the edge of the forest closest to her, and Janéh liked to come often near its still waters. When no more work was left to be done, she would come and sit and look into the murky greenish depths, trying to fathom the true bottom of it, past the mirror surface that reflected back at her the hated Stone Face.

As she sat thus, she would also glance now and then at the diligent rows of scurrying ants all around her on the grassy bank. When they crawled on her, she took deep breaths and simply blew them away, or gently brushed them off her, for it never occurred to her to harm the tiny creatures of the forest. She was a Giant, and they, the little ones, helpless before her.

Therefore, it was *she* who had to tread lightest, to control her physical presence, so as not to overwhelm.

Sometimes, hares came hopping past her in the grass—so still she was—and drank warily from the pond. At other times, a stag showed its antlered head, and lapped the clean water at the farthest edges of the bank.

Once Janéh saw a man walk past, with a light step and voice uplifted in song. She knew Gihen immediately, having seen him before in the forest, and her eyes danced in acknowledgement, while her face-mask remained still and rigid. The blacksmith's son grinned at her, and winked, all along singing like a lark, and proceeded on his way.

And another time, she saw a different man, haughty and loud, the sound of his boots crashing through the stillness. He wore hunter's green, and carried a crossbow, with heavy feral arrows meant for a stag slung behind him. She recognized Ailan of the village, and pretended not to see him, while he halted in his tracks and stared at her, breath in-drawn. He thought she did not realize he stood there, and revealed such a look in his eyes, which she had never seen him show when others were present. She had always thought he simply hated her, mocked her for her silent ways, but what she saw then was naked lust.

Soon afterward, she noticed the hunter often in these parts, and always he would halt by the pool to see if she was there, before proceeding on his way. Often he carried a bleeding carcass of the slain prey with him, seeing which Janéh's throat constricted into an anguished knot. Only—while it rent her insides, her frozen Stone Face remained like the surface of the still water.

Most recently, there was talk in the village that Ailan was in pursuit of a great living stag. Janéh believed she herself had seen the elusive creature once or twice, and thought more noble than any other sight of the forest.

On the day of his planned hunt, Janéh became the stag's shadow, following the animal through the forest so that the stag itself did not sense her. Never did Janéh think it unusual that she could move more silently than silence itself, or that she could match the beast's pace at will. There was only the occasional realization—when, throughout the day, the stag grew tired and stopped to feed upon the forest green—that the world also swung to a momentary halt, and then appeared to fall out from underneath her feet, while the sky spun gently and settled like a slowing carousel around the orb of the sun.

When the hunter arrived, the stag had paused to drink, and Janéh crouched right beside the creature, paces away. Ailan nocked his arrow. But with a scream that was torn out of her by pain itself, Janéh jumped forward to frighten the stag who took off like the wind. The woman in turn went running after the beast—alongside it—while branches and tree trunks flew past, and the forest blurred all around.

The hunter, Ailan, was left far behind, burning, furious, and his hissing arrow flew amiss.

For the rest of the day, Janéh never left the wild creature's side. She only returned to the village at dusk.

Odd looks greeted her from passerby. In the tavern, everyone stared, and the talk grew quiet, until she again left, having come only for her pay. It did not take long for Janéh to sense some wrongness, an emotion of brewing chill, even though she did not see Ailan anywhere, only perceived a *flavor* of him in the talk of the villagers. A psychic scent of displeasure started to waft on the wind, together with a trace of ghostly anger, of one man's raging voice that rang in her head. All this Janéh knew, being—she thought—fey and inhuman. She never heard Ailan's physical voice, never had to hear the actual words repeated by anyone on the streets. She simply knew that he told certain *things* about her to everyone in the village.

She was to receive the odd looks for the next several days, as she went about her tasks, and still there was nothing overtly amiss. At least, nothing that seemed to apply to her directly.

Until a half moon's turn later, it came crashing down on them all, the doom.

The elders of the village spoke in hushed tones. The children stopped playing on the streets, and hid their sweet wicked faces to stare from behind shuttered windows at the wind-blown streets.

It was the time they said, after the Cycle of a hundred autumns, that the Great One was stirring, and you could feel it in the wind. It was in the way the stag ran. And in the way the Faerie-born revealed their normally hidden fey powers to the rest of the mortals.

The Giant was coming.

"It is bad luck that Mad Mireah's daughter lives among us." said Farista, the most beautiful maiden in the village, as she took the bread from Lamira, the baker's daughter.

Since the baker himself stood there, sorting the fresh wheat loaves, Lamira said nothing, as always she said nothing to defy her father. But, as always, the non-act of silence induced a slithering feeling of guilt to start up in her, to chew at her gut. For, inaction also is betrayal. And Janéh—sad Janéh of the grotesque ugly-beautiful mask face—had been Lamira's friend.

But then came a fresh strong voice, like Lamira's unexpressed conscience itself. Gihen, the blacksmith-never-to-be came into the bake shop, slamming the door and making the tiny entry bells dance like angry bees.

"What's this talk of bad luck, I hear everywhere I go, good friends?" he exclaimed. "Not you too, Farista my Fair? Spreading rumors of that poor girl. Tsk, tsk—here, Nellis, Lamira, get me a sourdough or two, if you please—"

Farista snorted daintily. "Rumors, is that what you think?" she said in a chilly tone. "They say she drove away

Ailan's great stag, for she runs like the devil's own mare. They say she turned her Face to look at him, and now Ailan is cursed. He lies in bed all day, and there is a pallor sickness upon him. They say his bright eyes have lost their black fire . . ."

"They say the Fool sits on the Dung-hill, and the Cow dances on the Pot of Gold! Pah! Believe only what you know," sang Gihen, his wild baritone breaking out while Farista, Lamira, Nellis, and the baker all jumped back from the living onslaught of it.

"Out, out, ruffian, clown, you!" The potbellied baker shooed him out. "Go sing outside with your crazy Cows, you greatest Fool! I pity your father."

"And I pity your lovely daughters," retorted Gihen as he grabbed his baked goods and ran for the door, laughing.

Outside, his laughter stilled, for there was sorrow on the wind.

In the tavern, that incorporeal sorrow was drowned with ale, while somebody said rudely: "What foul witch-luck! I've heard the Great One comes at such times as these . . . It's a sign of such, for Mad Mireah's daughter lives among us."

"It is true," someone else noted. "Supposedly, He comes forth from the distant mountains where He sleeps for centuries until an unusually strong presence of Faerie kind awakens Him, pulls Him from the Sleep. It's happening now, they say. The breath of the Fair Folk is too definite on the wind. Soon He will come to stomp on us, on the village, on all our lives, for to him, we are but ants. . . . And all because Mad Mireah's daughter lives and witches among us!"

Radiene straightened his apron over his bulky frame and poured from the tap, silent.

And then someone else said: "Well, so she does. And what are we going to do about it?"

"Yes. What is everyone going to do about this living curse among us, this Janéh, whose mother lay with the devil himself?!"

All heads turned as Bremand, father of Ailan, and the man who owned half the village, entered the tavern. Bremand stood tall in his rich fur-trimmed clothing, his graying hair topped by a hat of ermine. Bremand threw a regal glance around the room, until the look of his heavy eyes met those of Radiene.

"Tavernkeeper," he said, "is that unfortunate still in your employ?"

"If you mean Janéh, yes, she is," answered Radiene quietly.

"Then I demand you let her go immediately, wash your hands of her, and forbid her to come into this establishment!"

Radiene frowned, and shifted his bulk, straightening himself involuntarily. "Isn't that for me to decide, Master Bremand?" he said in a low voice.

"Such a decision would not be necessary. Sirs!"

All heads turned again, for Janéh, Mireah's daughter herself, stood on the threshold of the tavern, just behind Bremand.

She looked different somehow. Everyone blinked, trying to fathom that difference, but then it occurred to them that she no longer wore women's long skirts, or dirty smock and apron. She no longer had her hair tied in a plain sorry knot at the back of her head. Instead, loose and fine, it came down her back, like long filaments of spiderwebs spun in the forest. And she was clad like a man, in coarse pants and doublet. No weapons she bore, and yet she stood, ready to do battle, a soldier.

Janéh stared with her horrific blank Face at them all. And then she began to speak, in a tone of voice that none had ever heard from her—loud, forceful, brazen.

"Master Radiene! I thank you from the depths of my devil heart for allowing me to work here, all this time. But now, friend, find another tavern scullion."

She turned to Bremand who, standing so near her, almost shrank away. "So, Master Bremand. How is your handsome son?"

"How dare you, hell-spawn! Even now you extend your witch thoughts to my Ailan. He is already bedridden in his chamber, from the unspeakable evil you had called upon him, the death-will, the beastly apathy—"

"The beastly lust," said Janéh. "That, and hurt pride."

"What?" The merchant stared.

"Your son lusts after me and pursues me, for more moons now than I can count. But he is proud, very much like you. Even admitting the lust to himself is unthinkable. And to others? What would all of you think? That Stone Face, ugly wicked Stone Face, has such an effect on fair Ailan who can have his pick of the best? Even I think him sick and perverted in desiring this—this—" Janéh struck herself on the chest, the only sign of fury being her trembling fist. "This pathetic creature with no heart, frozen in a stillness worse than death."

"Then maybe death it is that you should have, witch!" Bremand cried in rage, "Death, clean and holy to purge us of your presence, to drive off the fey curses of your Faerie kind, to free my son!"

"Yes! Kill the witch!"

". . . Let us stone her! . . ."

". . . Kill! . . ."

Radiene heard the swelling of voices all around, felt the almost physical hate, but was immobilized somehow, both in voice and movement. And incidentally, he began to perceive a rhythmic sound. Was it only blood rushing in his temples?

Janéh stood meanwhile, silent, and she looked at them with her Stone Face. Finally she opened her tight beautiful immobile lips, only once, to say with surprising calm: "I have done nothing. . . ."

But they did not hear her, for they were arguing whether to burn her in the center of the village, or to hang her before the church.

It was then that the first truly audible great rumble came from a distance, a persistent rhythmic sound that in its initial birthing they did not sense. But as it grew in intensity, it culminated at last in thunder. It made the glasses ring and dance on the tables, while the ground shook under each hammer-like blow.

Then, Gihen came into the tavern, dramatic, wild-faced—or, more so than was his usual manner—and he stood before them all, saying nothing, simply pointing outside with his hand.

And above the sudden general silence, arose Janéh's clear voice, calm, sardonic, and binding. "At last, then. Those are His Footsteps. You were all correct, and it is all my fault. He is here. The Giant has indeed awoken, and is hurrying all the way here to greet me. Or is it, to eat me? Or, to eat all of us and stomp us into pulp? Why, could it really be that I, poor Stone Face, whether Faerie-born or not, am so pivotal to the scheme of things, that a Giant has nothing better to do with his time?"

And in the continuing silence, the woman with the Stone Face, without twitching a muscle, or cracking her face-mask, laughed.

"Well then, idiots who would kill me for your own fear," she said finally, "I suppose I must go and meet Him."

And with that, she turned, slipping past Bremand, past Gihen, past the tavern doorway like a woodland mist, and was gone.

While outside, growing louder by an increment of miles, the Giant Footsteps thundered, and the whole village and the earth on which it stood, quaked.

Outside, the wind was strong. There was a light haze over the village and the horizon, where the sun was beginning its slow evening landing, while the sky shimmered like a mother-of-pearl mirage.

Janéh stood outside and blinked, for in the delicate haze nothing was as it seemed. In her unfaithful vision, faraway mountains momentarily rose and sank like yeast dough, while the clouds shifted and tore themselves into filaments of cotton.

For that reason she almost doubted the sight of the swiftly approaching shadow—yet another shifting mountain—which loomed from the far West, and which brought with its approach, rhythmic thunder.

She blinked, the wind drying out her eyes, and her thoughts raced ahead of her, out and above. And somewhere in the far distance they met with a great *presence*. Her thoughts—the winged things—sprung to *it* like offspring, and blended, giving her multi-dimensional sight. She could sense the *old one's* pattern of awareness. Through *it*, she towered over the land, her eyelids brushing the cloud mass, her brows like snow-capped peaks, and her lips the fissure-caves of a mountain.

So immobile, so rigid the Giant *face*, that Janéh felt a sudden unexpected affinity. For, she also felt thus, she too knew the frozen immobility of features that was beyond humanity.

Villagers gathered around her like frightened beastly children, yet Janéh did not know them, was only halfway there with them, and halfway thundering high above the earth.

The Giant shadow loomed, and in passing, momentarily eclipsed the sunset. Like encroaching night, the *being* swung *its* arms as *it* took each step, and eddying winds curled and wound into sudden vortex-funnels with each great swing, while the land trembled. . . .

    . . . *Dreaming* . . .

Janéh heard the Giant thoughts swoon like clouds, from high above. And she thought she saw panoramic memory-glimpses of ancient deserts bathed with a white younger sun, of seas that used to exist where mountains now reposed, of mountains being born, and of endless ancient sand. . . .

And now and then, there were instants of sight encompassing great Cities of old, of legend, of great human

Fleets upon long-dead oceans, as they fought each other like tiny ants, among the glittering aquamarine waves. And when the waters washed over it all and receded, again there was only sand. . . .

And there was another intimate *awareness*. . . . Only—just before Janéh could fathom its secret, she was slammed back into the full physical presence of her own being, as wild human cries arose all around her.

The people of this village watched from their temporary safety of distance as the Giant's feet crushed the barley fields of the neighboring settlements, only leagues away. The Giant moved slowly, like a dream-walker, and yet drew near with the swiftness of a heartbeat. And as the monolithic human form neared, *it* appeared less and less human, and more and more like a walking mountain—like a craggy brown mountain rockside hewn in the vague humanoid outline. The Giant never bothered to look down upon the destruction that *it* wrought, never flinched as *it* stepped upon toy houses and dispersing human insects. *Its* eyes—or the blotches of concave darkness that appeared to be in place of *its* eyes—*its* eyes were shut closed.

"Look!" the villagers cried, pointing. "They are trying to burn the monster!"

And at that point distant fiery projectiles were seen flying like tiny bees to harmlessly sting the Giant form, as the residents of one neighbor village attempted to fight back.

"We must get away!" cried others. "In minutes, that thing will be upon our own village. Load the wagons!"

Janéh stood like a rock, mesmerized, while all about her panic erupted.

"My goods, my precious warehouse!" cried Bremand. "Fifty gold pieces to anyone who would load my goods! A hundred for a wagon!"

But for once, no one listened to the richest man in the village. Instead, as he stood dazed with greed, someone ran into him on their way down the street. Bremand's fine ermine hat got knocked down from his head, and was instantly stomped in the dirt.

"We don't need your gold, Master Bremand," a man said then, "and you don't need it either. Let it be! Go instead, and save your son who lies ill."

Janéh felt a firm grip on her arm, and focused at last. Radiene was pulling her, with a worried face. "Best be on your way too, girl!" he said, "Like everyone. . . . Get away while you still can. Look, gods have apparently intervened, striking us all down, but giving you this chance. . . . Hurry now, and bless you!" He tarried for an instant more, gave her hand another squeeze, and was on his way.

"Bless you also, Radiene," she whispered at his wide back.

She blinked again, stared at the sunset. She felt light, almost reluctant to be fully present *here* in her body, for her winged thoughts still made her buoyant, still cried out to lift her like a feather to soar with the Giant *one*.

"So, what kind of a Fairy are you anyway, girl?" The mocking baritone voice came from behind, breathing over her shoulder, and she turned sharply, startled, almost knocking noses with Gihen, the blacksmith's son.

He stood, outrageous, calm as a mule, hands on hips, and regarded her with very steady clear eyes. She wondered for a moment why he was not running like everyone else. But then she remembered that this one was as crazy as she—or more so.

"I said, what kind of a Fairy—"

"I heard you the first time, don't shout. And don't call me 'girl,' either. You know very well I am Stone Face." She answered him in a similar manner, falling into the easy sarcasm automatically, as though she'd been saying such things all her life, not just since this afternoon. But then, Janéh realized suddenly, she'd *thought* sarcastic thoughts all her life, simply never voiced them before today. Her speech too had been frozen into a blank pattern—just like her face.

"I don't like 'Stone Face,'" said Gihen, while the earth around them pounded. "I don't like names that distort the truth, or don't fit things. Since I don't believe that you are Stone Face, even 'girl' sounds better. But forgive me, Janéh. What I was trying to say is, being so called Faerie-born, how come you do nothing now?"

"Do nothing?" said Janéh. "First of all, you Singing Fool of a blacksmith, I'm not even sure *what* I am—stark mad, or Faerie-born! No matter what you and everyone else may believe. Second, what would you like me to do, challenge the Giant to a duel? I might actually hurt the poor thing as He treads on my Stone Face and finds instead an unbreakable hard spot. . . ."

But Gihen watched her seriously, and he said, "Your eyes are like wild swamp water. Fathomless. Unreal."

"Oh, and is that supposed to be poetic and make me swoon?"

"No. It is supposed to make you think. Because it's true. And it simply means that you are—despite what you say—one of the Fair Folk. And you can't even admit it to yourself."

"Fine, supposing I am. . . . Shall we spend another hour standing here arguing about it?"

"I wouldn't advise it, Fairy Janéh." he answered. "Unless you would like to be stepped on. In approximately five more minutes."

"What then would you suggest, blacksmith-poet?"

"I suggest you make up your own mind. And by the way, since now I'm not leaving you until you do, you'd better make it up fast. And make sure it's a safe and satisfying solution for both of us."

Another time, and Janéh would've been furious with this one. But not now. Because he stood so steady and still, with folded hands. And what he said actually made sense and rang true. And because none of them had anything more to lose, except time.

Janéh brought her hands up to touch her face, to feel the cool skin of it—while all around, screaming people and horses and wagons rushed about, children cried in real fear, and the sunset burned. Her Stone Face felt the same as always. Immobile fine muscle around her eyes. And no curve came to her lips when she tried to force them into the grimace of a smile.

. . . *Dreaming* . . .

The Giant was so near. In six more steps *it* would tower over the church spire on the outskirts of their village.

Janéh rubbed her cheek. And then she felt a tiny sharp sting. By reflex she smote herself in that place, but luckily missed the tiny ant that got simply transferred from one section of her body to another, and continued to run down her hand. As always, she did not kill the little one, simply blew on her arm, and the ant was airborne.

And then it came to her, the answer that was there all along.

The Giant was Dreaming.

All she had to do, was bite it into awareness, in a way that she knew she could. In her own unique way, of the Faerie.

Janéh closed her eyes, and her thoughts sprung heavenward like small warm winds. With her thoughts, she raced higher and higher, until she was near the *great one*. And she found herself again floating among the ancient dream memory images.

Listen! her thought cried. *Awake and listen, ancient one!*

But the feebleness of her spirit-call surprised Janéh herself. The Giant's dream images, floating cumulus-cloud visions of ancient land and sea, were so much stronger, so prevalent, that in the dream-vapor her single thought sank and drowned.

What makes one feel an ant's bite? A poison? Its tiny focused intensity? Reasoned intent?

Janéh gathered herself, shaped her winged thoughts into a single precise arrow, and then, in spirit, flew. Her bright

Faerie-human essence rose, crossing the distance of miles, circling the great plateau trunks of mountain that were its legs, past the torso that was one solid abysmal cliff wall, and around the Giant's wizened head of white-capped granite. She neared the cavernous Rock Face with caved-in spots of darkness where eyes should be. She rose past the forehead of limestone, veined with silver ore around the brows.

And then the woman-arrow sank, dived and pierced the cheek of the Giant Stone Face, and she called it with all her will, called it in the ancient way.

A heartbeat of eternal silence.

And then the moving mountain stopped. On the very outskirts of their village, the Giant stood motionless, silhouetted against the sunset. And the aura of Dreams around it became a great funnel tornado. The Dreams whirled with an ever-intensifying centripetal force, and finally sank into the recesses of the great *being*.

In their place, a flower of *presence* bloomed forth. Dark eye-caves shook and eyelid-portals swung open to reveal Faerie *light*. A monolithic arm lifted, and a cupola-palm rested against the stone cheek to touch the place where the thought-arrow found its true bite. The Giant was Awake at last.

And as she found her essence cupped in the heart of this ancient indescribable thought-flower, Janéh knew at last the things that had always simmered just out of reach of her own awareness—things that were her fey heritage, and things that were simply deeper aspects of her humanity. Like a thin but unbreakable rime of frost, they had surrounded her since birth, waiting to break free upon her self-realization, and always hovering at the outer surface, containing her emotions and making her face into a living mask. Like miniature replicas of the Giant dreams, they accompanied her always—fluttering subliminal butterflies of Faerie power and human emotion, imprisoned by her self-denial, and in turn imprisoning her true self.

But now they were free. . . .

Janéh's thought essence flared like a lantern in the dark, expanded into a cloud of *sensation*. While at the same time, Janéh's mortal body, miles away, began trembling with a fever.

Gihen watched with a mixture of pity and awe as the fey woman before him shook, then suddenly doubled over and covered her Stone Face with her shivering hands. When he attempted to assist her, she struggled, brushing him off with inhuman strength. And she continued holding her face as she collapsed onto the ground. In the end, Janéh lay in the fetal position, palms covering the Stone Face, harsh feral sobs rending her, gasping for air. And he could only stand there and do nothing.

In contrast to her body's agony, Janéh's mind-presence flowered in an ecstasy of freedom. The Giant *being* surrounded her with a warmth of *presence*, and she knew it was both *male* and *female*, sky and earth, day and night. She also knew, at last and without a doubt, that the Giant's being was indeed connected somehow to her own self.

I have returned, my daughter. As I had promised once I would. To complete what I had started in you. You, who were conceived by the force of one of my Dreams taking human form, the one that visited your mother in a spring long gone. . . .

You see, without me, you would not be. And without you, I would have nothing to draw me to life, nothing to perpetuate this new Cycle which hinges on paradox. For, I come when my own blood calls. Only mine own, Faerie, can call me into the world. Only mine own, Faerie, can stop me. I come to be Wakened and then to be Thwarted and put down, back to the Slumber of time. I am the Timekeeper of the world, awakening at each End and Beginning, to mark the Passage of things, as must be done, now and always.

"You are the earth, and the forest, and you are my father." Janéh's soul spoke in understanding.

And then, unfurling its spirit-wings, her essence once again soared, and flew. She left the haven of the Giant's *presence*, to return to her flesh and complete her own self, at last.

Janéh took in a shuddering gasp of air, and raised her tear-streaked face to look up at the world of angry sunset and a man's still shadow falling over her.

Where the Giant had stood, there were but dark clouds quickly dissolving, as though an invisible gale-wind had come to drive them away, only to replace everything by empty skies and an odd silence.

"It has been accomplished," Gihen said in quiet awe, looking down at her. "Like the songs and stories had told. Like the legend."

"You hardly know what you're talking about, blacksmith-poet." responded Janéh tiredly, wiping dirt-smudged tears and blowing her nose in her sleeve.

But Gihen ignored her words. Instead, he stared at the smudged face before him upon which a host of very definite grimaces succeeded one another as she cleared her throat, and then was replaced by an even more definite smile.

A *smile!*

The Stone Face was grinning at him, stone no longer, and as human as anything he had ever seen.

"I am different . . ." she whispered then, running her fingers in reverence over the curved apple of her cheek, and stood up from the ground, "Look! I am—"

He looked indeed, and saw her true at last—saw what he had always known she was. The only things left of the old were her slanted weird almond eyes. . . .

At that moment there was much shouting all around them, as more and more people picked up a cry.

"It is her! Janéh has saved us!"

". . . The Giant is gone . . . Faerie-born magic has saved us!"

Gihen laughed, shaking his head. "Pathetic, isn't it? Yes, now they admit it, the blasted fools. And as always knowing so little, they have made an instant heroine. Pah! Where only an hour ago they were ready to kill."

"But you—blacksmith-poet. You do *know*. Had always known, haven't you? Your fool's songs had been fragments of wisdom—"

Janéh could say nothing more, although she wanted to say so many things to him, because at that moment, she saw Bremand the merchant approaching them all, and at his side, the stiff haughty figure of his son.

Ailan did not look ill. In fact, having come out of hiding, he appeared rather healthy and well rested, even elegant. And his always-proud beautiful eyes now shone with an even greater eternal ice.

One thing was different, however.

It is said that eventually there comes a balance in all things. Eventually, justice has odd ways of manifesting itself in this world, human mortal and Faerie. When truth is denied, it still struggles to be, and in the process, transforms the very thing that stifles it.

Ailan had struggled so hard to deny, even to himself, what he had felt toward Janéh—an emotion that in its uncorrupted form might even have evolved into love—that the inevitable change had taken hold of him.

Thus, he now stood looking at them all, fair and tall as always. But his raven locks framed a blank absolute Stone Face.

A THING OF LOVE

It was said that Faelittal the Executioner had neither a soul nor a living human heart. A soul had never been given to her, it was rumored, by the will of gods. And a heart—that fragile organ thought to be the seat of emotion—her heart, or any semblance of it, Faelittal had long since cracked in twain, splintered, and then ground the fragments to dust, ever since her sword had first cleaved, with exquisite precision, a human neck.

She would do this, cleave human flesh, without a single twitch of her pale sublime face, without a blink. They who witnessed executions, had the chance to observe this, for unlike any other executioner, the queen's sister looked into her victims' eyes and wore no mask.

Lyksandias, the queen, called for executions frequently. To her they were "things of love," the means by which people were taught the letter of the law, unhealthy displeasure was subjugated, and the seasonal canker-sores of different thinking were uprooted. The queen's rule was absolute, and those not quite aware of this fact, were forced to taste the sweet mercy of her judgment. Lyksandias was unyielding in her "love."

All manner of men and women were executed. Ordinary villains, freemen, and those involved in trade, were normally hung. The warrior class were shot by marksmen, or strangled with a silk cord. That same cord was offered to the more affluent women and upper class ladies—the latter also had the choice of treacle-flavored poison.

The priesthood was allowed by the queen to burn heretics at the stake. There were of course numerous other means, enough to fill a tome.

And then, there was the High Execution, either by great sword or ax, to be performed as the highest form of chastisement of traitors to the queen. Faelittal was the loftiest practitioner of this art.

Originally, the somber sister of the queen merely bore arms as a warrior in the service of the God of Defense, one of an elite honor guard, first instituted in deep antiquity. Once it had merely been ceremonial in nature, but at present, things were turbulent, and threats real enough to warrant the presence of a genuinely skilled guard elite.

But Faelittal rose above her already exalted rank. She was an ascending meteor, and a warrior's static role could not sustain her potential. Icily composed, placid in demeanor, and brilliant in perception, Faelittal became the original High Executioner.

"My little loyal tigress-cub," the queen would say, with a fond yet secretly awed look, to her not so little younger sister. She in turn, would look down at Lyksandias, column-like, from her man's height and stature, and reply: "I am yours to command, my bright sister, O queen." And there would be a certain look in her eyes that was not there at other times.

Lyksandias had many lovers. Indeed, this was one of the original reasons that the High Executioner's position came into being. It was some years ago that Faelittal had to slit the throat of a maddened young aristocrat who personally threatened the life of Lyksandias. He had achieved the fleeting rank of consort, but beneath it all was planning treachery and the queen's overthrow. And Lyksandias decided to turn this into an example.

The dead but still warm body was carried to a public scaffold where Faelittal, with emotionally eloquent, uncovered eyes, threw down her warrior's emblem, and instead, donned the ebony cloak of night and death. There was one difference to this cloak however—a fine silver starburst graced its back, a symbol never previously seen.

The High Executioner's symbol it became. And on that day, with a long shining blade, Faelittal executed the body of the traitor.

With time, other such occasions arose, and the queen's sister gained fame for her weird elegance and impassivity while dealing out death. Some went before her pleading and crying, up to the very final stroke that cut their life. Others stood in dignity, and there were yet others that had to be carried up senseless, not able to fathom the horror and hopelessness of their positions. To all of these Faelittal showed only a blank oddly receptive face. She was neither cruel nor sympathetic—simply aware. It was at such times that a superstitious fear of her first occurred to the onlookers, for they could understand most other kinds of affect—pity, guilt, fear, even sadistic glee—but not *this*. And so, they concluded certain things, one of which was that she had no heart, was not really human.

A female demon in human form.

The queen heard of these rumors and laughed. It only helped maintain the particular nature of her reputation. Faelittal however, did not laugh. Not being the jocund kind, she merely shifted the expression in her already ambiguous eyes.

That had been a long while ago. Now, yet another man stood to be executed by the queen's judgment, a young nobleman of wide popularity both with the court and the masses. He was of a good family, but too liberal, frank, and outspoken. And that became his downfall.

He was Remialt, of the house of Kellen. He had never been the queen's lover. And yet, when he insulted the queen's authority, Faelittal guessed by the particular nature of her sister's reaction, that Lyksandias had wanted him.

The court, meanwhile, was aflame with rumors and turbulence. Such a turn of events was indeed unprecedented; no one expected Remialt to say or do what he did.

For, the Kellen had stood up in the presence of all court, and called the queen a "golden whore." And then, still facing her with unflinching eyes, he brought into question her competence and the regal status that had been hers by birth, through a centuries-old chain of succession.

The queen, normally in suave control of herself, allowed a tremor to pass her lips. And then, ignoring the present court, and saying nothing to him in her beautiful despotic dignity, she summoned Faelittal. Which meant that here was to be no mercy.

The queen's sister entered, wearing the usual impassive face, looked at her victim to be, then paused.

Remialt's dark-eyed gaze was so keen, so righteous, that he caught her attention. Therefore she asked him, in her rarely-heard soft voice, something that only a privileged few condemned were entitled to hear: "Is this true, O man, what you say? Do you really believe and stand by your words?"

"Yes," he answered firmly, meeting her eyes with fierce conviction. "I will always stand by my words."

"Then," Faelittal said blankly, "by my hand you must die."

And the guards took him unprotesting.

The eldest son of the house of Kellen was then given the customary week to prepare himself for the High Execution.

The following day half of the court donned mourning, and there was outrage. The family Kellen went about like the living dead, their tragedy wedded to dishonor. Rumors, angry rumors, sent mercurial sparks everywhere, and those who understood such things, predicted that at last the queen had done something that would bring consequences beyond her imagining.

"The truth . . ." everyone whispered, "he had simply spoken the truth!"

"But truth is not to be." The old and blunt lord Kellen grieved, for in his advanced age he was at last broken. "My son will die. Oh, why couldn't he be like all others, and be satisfied with—with *self-delusion?*"

There was no answer to this. Only, the Kellen younger son decided to do something that might let him retain a measure of sanity, retain a belief in some form of ultimate truth. Chiarn Kellen secretly went to plead for his brother's life, before Faelittal.

He was a dark, thin, and tall youth, Chiarn. He would have appeared wraithlike, if not for the proud stiffness of his posture and keen searching eyes. Toward evening, as he was finally allowed into the High Executioner's presence after his long wait, he never lost that pride, only gained an edge to his inner anger.

Faelittal stood before a small window in a dark room, looking out somewhere. She turned to him, a silhouette, clad like a man, and he still could not see her very well. *She must be afraid*, he guessed, *to face what I have to say.*

"Who are you?" said a woman's quiet voice, as she looked at him, he was not sure how intently, in the twilight.

"Chiarn Kellen. The second son. You are to execute my older brother on the third day from tonight."

"Ah yes." She paused. Inside him, blood pounded; anger and outrage seethed, as he wanted to cry out, strike her. For, like a post she stood, face unreadable, taller than him, and somehow *eternal*.

And he felt then, without even beginning to speak, that no matter what he would say, no matter how he pleaded, he had come all for nothing.

"I am here," he began, hopeless and awkward because of this new awareness, "to speak for my brother's life. To find out,

O High Lady, if there is anything I can do, if there's any way to convince you—"

"To spare him?" She cut him off. "You must know that I only do my sister's will. Why speak to me and not her?" Her eyes, like a night animal's were liquid and glittering, while her face was shadow.

Why indeed? He paused, as if this thought had never occurred to him. And then, in a voice that to himself sounded cold, rational, he reasoned out loud: "Maybe because she will not be moved. And you—you have less to do with this, less personal involvement. What is my brother's life to you, but a trifle? To be thrown away or spared, think, how really insignificant! You have no real interest in his death. And therefore, I presume, you might be swayed. Somehow. Please . . . spare him. Have mercy on our family! In the name of all and any gods, name your price!"

He waited, and in the dusk he thought he saw her faint smile.

"I have never been swayed before . . ." said Faelittal. "Luckless boy. You've come here to ask me this, knowing very well what my answer would be, beforehand. But your pride insisted. It insisted that I would treat *your* words differently somehow, honor *your* request. Out of a parade of luckless lives, I would be impressed by the unique plight that comprises yours. Don't you know, boy, who I *am?* Don't you know that I have no sympathy, no senses, and no heart?"

In his overflowing anger he was never to be sure if it was irony that he heard in her voice.

"Then I call all curses upon your head! Dark, ancient, fierce curses to consume you, to swallow you whole!" he blurted, the knot in his throat that had been building up all along, about to release a flood of tears. "You are a beast indeed, a she-demon! I am not afraid of your anger, I tell you this straight; I would kill you now myself, and you would see I am no boy, but a man!"

"I see . . ." she said—soft, tired words. "I have insulted you. So then, O man who is not a boy. Kill me, if you think you can . . ."

In response, a thin pale dagger gleamed with faint residue of evening light in the folds of his clothing. But before he could even move, she was at him, like a black leopard, across the length of the room. Her lukewarm fingers clamped his wrist and held him there. And then, with a gasp from him, and a flick of her hand, his dagger clanged onto the floor.

Down, down, was lost in the darkness. What futility.

She continued to grip his wrist as he first snarled in frustration, and then hot silent tears burst forth, as his body shuddered, and slowly he sank to the floor. On his knees before her, he silently shook with sobbing. "My brother . . ." he cried, "Remialt . . . my brother! My b-b . . ."

And then he felt a light touch on his hair. She had released him and now—odd, passive—stroked his soft dark hair. "Child . . ." she said.

And in her voice there was no evil, yet no soul.

In surprise, Chiarn stared up at her, then grasped her feet with his two hands, and buried his face and his hair against the coolness of her stark leather boots. "Lady . . ." he mumbled, choking on his words, drinking his own snot and effluvia of agony. "Oh, lady, he—he loves life! There's a noble fair woman who is waiting to marry him, this very autumn. And—and there is so much that he would do yet, for all of the family, for—me. . . . Like before, I remember, we would go riding together at harvest time, and he'd give me crunchy apples smelling of autumn sun, and . . . and oh, how he chased me through the house when we were boys . . . And once, I remember—he mostly smiles, but—I remember I had seen him cry. Only once! Our mother lay in fever. And at dawn, she died. And he would touch my hair, lightly, just as you have done, and—"

Sobs cut him off, as the room went reeling before his eyes and now the pressure of weeping was more than he had ever known.

"Poor youth . . ." said Faelittal. "You do not sway me. You cannot."

Chiarn's anger burst forth anew, incredulous. He stared with volcanic eyes up at her distant face-shadow. "Don't you—love anything? Care for anything?" he whispered, no longer sobbing, in shock.

The Executioner spoke words that were soft, impassive, and immensely meaningless to him. "I love. That which is truth."

"What of the queen? She is your sister, do you love her? Love, love, love, do you love? What would you do if she were condemned to die?"

For an instant he thought he *saw* something move in her, a flicker of the shadow.

"You do not—ask the proper question. . . ." she replied, with the telltale gentleness that made the fine hairs along his arms stand up from his skin. "What I would do as a sister is one thing. As an executioner—another. . . ."

"Then you would execute your own sister! Gods!"

"Yes. Only *I*. You—" she paused, inexplicably gathering herself for something—"You do not *understand*."

"Yes, I don't understand. . . ." Chiarn was beyond shock, beyond anything. Suddenly composed, he was feeling a slow fear move within him. There was something so peculiar about her, about the whole situation, he now knew—something far more complex than he originally guessed. A gathering of paradox. And yet so far he could not explain it to himself.

"You are not human, O High Lady . . ." he ventured.

"Wrong," she said matter-of-factly. "I am human. If you'd moved fast enough, your dagger would've killed me. Only—praise gods it did not. For I must be the one to kill your brother. Know, that only I can do it the *right* way."

"The right way?! There is a right way to *kill?*" His voice was back to the emotional morass, sarcastic bitterness.

But the next words she said, froze him.

"Yes. There is a right way. As the High Executioner I have been given this knowledge. Now, ask me no more of this, boy!" She was brisk now, harsh. "It is already too much that you have heard. Because of your brother, and the nature of his offence—or better yet, the nature of his person—I have tolerated you. Only because of *him* . . . Now, go!"

"But—" Chiarn began, a knot again in his throat.

"Go!" Her voice boomed. And then, almost as an afterthought, her parting words followed him. "Do not think, Chiarn Kellen, that you have come in vain. For—you have clarified for me *what* exactly is to be your brother's death."

The incomprehensible words rang in his head as he walked on wooden feet. Later he only remembered that the whole time they had spoken, there had been no candlelight, and he had never really seen her face.

At dawn of the execution day, Faelittal came to stand at the high Palace Walls, a customary ritual before she performed her Act. Already, crowds of sickly-curious onlookers milled beneath, staring, whispering, and pointing at her, from the city streets far below.

Chiarn stood, one with the crowd, somewhere down there also. He had never been present at such an event, and now was perversely compelled to witness every minute detail of this day, every single one of her movements. . . .

As usual, the crowd was a many-faced beast. "Kill him, dark Lady!" they cried. And yet others cried, "Spare him, spare the fine son of Kellen!"

The midnight figure of the High Executioner, oblivious to all, stood without moving. Only when the sun broke past the horizon with its incandescent rose simmer, did she raise her hands skyward, and invoke the god that she served.

And then, she left the Palace Walls.

Somebody next to Chiarn nudged him, to whisper: "Who knows why she does this every time? Before she kills 'em? I don't—gives me a chill in my back, it does! Feels like—like you're one with *her*, one with the *condemned*. Like it's *your* execution being prepared, not his!"

"I don't—know," Chiarn answered faintly. He wanted to run somewhere, badly, but something gripped him here. He had to see, to *see* the death of his brother.

At noon, multitudes filled the center square of the city. It was almost impossible to keep them away from the scaffolding where the condemned was to die. As the sun reached its zenith, Faelittal appeared, swift and tall and dark. She wore the cloak of death, and at her side hung a long heavy sword. Since the victim had not yet arrived, she stood idle, and observed the crowd with receptive eyes. Those nearest who accidentally met her gaze, felt something acute and intimate pull at their insides. Consequently, all came to avoid her eyes.

Soon, Lyksandias arrived, ceremonially clad in ancient royal garb, so bejeweled and ornamented that she was like a precious gilded temple doll. She then sat down on a throne erected for her, to watch.

Last of all, Remialt Kellen, in plain white clothes of a penitent, was escorted in. His cropped hair and shaven face however, suggested something far from repentance—a defiant madness. But underneath it all, sensitive to him, Chiarn read the blank inevitability that is the end result of despair. Seeing it, he, already high-strung, was now sick to the stomach.

It was a primeval fear. . . . He, Chiarn, was sensing it for the first time fully, the fear of death—his self rebelling against the way of things, a sudden wild bird beating against its life-cage. . . .

"Oh, by gods . . ." people next to him were saying, "strange, how I never remembered, since the last Execution, how truly awful the whole thing is. . . . The long wait, the—why, if I'd remembered, I wouldn't have come to see this one!"

"Yes, there's no spectacle in this thing, I now understand," a woman said in despair. "I feel ill. It's as if I can sense exactly what the Kellen is feeling, I am in his place."

Meanwhile, Faelittal continued to allow her gaze to travel about the audience, looking at each and all. It was only the condemned himself that she appeared to ignore.

"Sister," said the queen somewhat in haste. "Proceed." And her royal voice again almost shook. Lyksandias, too, only now remembered how odd, how terrible these moments in the Executions had always felt. Why did she never think not to attend? Why come and masochistically pain herself?

Faelittal's normally soft voice now boomed. "Remialt, heir lord to Kellen! Are you prepared to die?"

The prisoner did not even blink. "As well as any man!" he retorted in a strong voice of defiance. Only Chiarn saw the deeper tiredness in his gaze. Somewhere a few feet away, a man's shaky old voice sent up a keening wail. Chiarn recognized the voice of his father. His heart twanged. In the selfish microcosm of his own personal preoccupation with mortality, he had almost forgotten all about *that*. His father—their father.

On the scaffold, Remialt flinched, hearing it also.

"Speak your last words," Faelittal said.

"My only words are for the house of Kellen." The condemned man bowed in the general direction of his father, his eyes hungrily searching the crowd. He waited, and then said simply: "I hope that *he* who hears me now, blesses me. . . . I have only spoken the truth."

And then, impassioned, he exclaimed: "And I still say, Lyksandias your queen is a golden whore! *You*, all of you have the means, the power to end this—"

He was cut off by a heavy slap on the face by one of the guards. But Faelittal raised a threatening gloved hand at the abuser, and Remialt was released.

She beckoned Remialt to draw near. And then, for the first time, the High Executioner truly looked into the eyes of the condemned man.

A timeless moment. A nothing. All his despair, wildness, righteousness, soul—immortalized in a still glance. And then, all she said was: "Come, O man. Meet your true death."

Holding his breath, Chiarn watched his brother, watched with a sick hunger every movement of his face. And it was then that maybe he alone, of all those present—knowing Remialt the way he did—saw an instant of *difference* in the expression of the condemned man. An expression of peace replaced the stifled anxiety and despair on the face of Remialt. It lingered for a fraction of an instant. And then, it too was gone. Instead, what was left was an odd, familiar, blank *receptiveness*—where had Chiarn seen this before?

All around, the multitude, like a single beast, sucked in its breath. And now Chiarn knew that he was not the only one who had sensed all this, stood in bizarre full empathy with the condemned. *In fact*, he now thought, "awakening," and also surfacing for breath, *I am not unique at all, not different from them. . . . They too can feel! Because—because I can feel them in turn! It is like a great self-reflecting mirror with an endless gallery of reflections stretching unto infinity, all echoing each other back at themselves. I feel Remialt's emotion. The crowd feels it. I feel the consequent emotion of every person in the crowd. And every person feels the emotion of every other person, including myself. . . . And what we all feel, is Remialt's approaching death. . . .*

It is ours, it belongs to us.

Faelittal the Executioner meanwhile, silent as the sun's shadow, removed the great sword from its sheath, and raised it high overhead.

The condemned man, with blank *receptive* eyes, as though he predicted her every next move, in perfect sync with her, stepped forward in silence, then sank on his knees before the neck-rest, and the basket. He slightly inclined his head forward.

The frozen dilated eyes of the glittering doll Lyksandias, and the rest of the crowds were upon his figure.

When the sword fell, it made no sound. Neither did the head, as it fell into the basket ready for it. So clever the blow, that for several instants the headless torso remained upright, as though unaffected by it all.

Another pulse-beat, and the crowd wailed, as the psychological spell—that had lasted since dawn—was broken at last. They were all free of it, free, and so the people—to show themselves that their will was theirs again—made audible cries, exclamations, gasps, or whatever it is that affirmed their beings under such circumstances.

Chiarn could at last avert his gaze (something that subconsciously was his only goal, since dawn). To quickly take his mind off the approaching numbness of despair, he now began making his way toward his old father, where the rest of the Kellen gathered. For the Kellen, a time of grieving and consolation was at hand.

On her throne, Lyksandias, stricken by something she herself could not explain, recalled again that this was exactly how she felt after each High Execution—as though her being had been ripped inside. And yet, this feeling would always "close up," and recede deep inward, and she'd forget. . . . Truly, it was already beginning to do so now.

Faelittal stood alone. Odd, how everyone's attention had all of a sudden shifted now, away from her, from the corpse, from the scaffold. Such was the ending to all High Executions— no cheers went up; no harsh crowds screamed for more blood. Never. In the end, they desired above all to leave the place. Already the square was emptying.

Faelittal stood column-like. Her keen faraway gaze took in the exquisite form of her sister, royally escorted, and briskly leaving the square. She never looked back, had already forgotten the dead man.

And when Faelittal was sure that there was no one left to observe her—that is, no one who would observe her and *understand*—she too took a deep breath, like a sleeper surfacing, and felt all her senses, all *feeling* and *sensation,* rush back into her, on soft delicate sterile wings of truth. And then, because now the sun shone brighter, the air filled her lungs with crispness, and the fresh scarlet blood still dripped from her sword's blade in a small pool at her feet, she blinked, and there was wetness in her eyes.

One of the guards under her command covered the body, knowing automatically the routine. Faelittal did not need to see the one she killed. And yet, the wetness continued in her eyes, and would not stop.

It was not the *man* she was crying for—it was the wretched *body*. The poor flesh and the nerves, that had to feel the harshness of the parting, the rent neck muscles and the spine. . . .

Faelittal knew that the *man* himself had felt nothing—his silver cord of life she had gently *severed* beforehand, when she looked into his eyes. She had learned enough about him to do it properly, from the necessary conversation with his younger brother. *Too bad*, she thought, *that the youth Kellen would never know how he had in fact facilitated his brother's gentle way of dying.*

Faelittal always allowed a condemned one's relative to meet with her, so that she would know the nature of the fine fabric of their souls. For, souls were exquisite things, unique, yet one could be fathomed through a close other. . . .

And always, she would release each man's soul, gently, with the utmost care, and then execute merely a body—like that very first time.

Only, *these* executions were different. *Fear* and *responsibility* for each death had to remain here, to rest heavily on someone, for the sake of balance.

And for that purpose, there was the great crowd, the "audience." They were executed vicariously. And the queen also. . . .

But why, one might think, did she bother with it all, Faelittal? Why tolerate the whim of the queen, the tyranny? So much easier it could be just to end the dark reign, to render Lyksandias powerless, to *execute*—

Faelittal watched the rose-stained sword in her hands, and thought, as always she did afterward.

There were so many others in the world, like Lyksandias, too many. Remove one, and another would spring up—overt or subtle—to take up the reins of power.

But as long as Faelittal stood as the High Executioner, that dark ultimate power and responsibility was in her skilled hands. She would do occult justice with it.

But even more so, Faelittal stood crying for Lyksandias. Because once again, for what innumerable time, the queen, having her soul opened for her to the truth through such costly means, allowed it again to close up. She had turned away, gilded and radiant, having forgotten.

And Faelittal the Executioner wept, because she knew so intimately the fine nature of her sister's—and hence, her own—soul.

THE BALANCE

The world's greatest wizard, Liir, having reached the pinnacle of his learning, decided one day to view the ultimate mystery.

Having cast a trinity of mighty spells that whisked him out of his earthly body and his present state of existence, he—or at that point, to be precise, the entity—found him/her/itself in a space and time continuum unlike any that human words can describe. Amidst the pulsing vibrant energy of a cosmic nebula that was the universe, Liir saw the Male Principle and the Female Principle, both represented to him in their respective human shapes, locked in a great eternal embrace/struggle.

Liir perceived this struggle with an awe that only the wise of the highest degree can experience. What a marvel, what a sublime paradox, the entity mused, that the universal balance hinges upon this eternal strife! Neither of the Two shall ever give way before the other, or else all crumbles in an abysmal apocalypse! What an inconceivable thought! And yet, Liir thought, how perfect is the universe—for these two great Principles are absolutely equal in strength, and nothing shall ever come to outweigh the balance of One in favor of the Other.

In that cosmic instant, the Man, noticing all of a sudden that They were being observed, paused in his divine Struggle, and turned His radiant god-visage to the entity.

Liir thought he distinctly heard these words:

"What's this? Who are you, mortal?"

It was at that point that the Woman, having found the way clear before Her mighty fist, knocked the Man out with one perfectly aimed divine blow.

DEMONKILLER

The woman burned. The flames were nowhere to be seen yet they moved, streaming in delicate filaments, in her mind. The manic flames, invisible, incandescent, stood all around her eternally.

From the outside no one knew how she burned. No one could tell that she looked out at the world through a veil of bluish-gold flame and that from her perspective all faces appeared to her bathed in an auric firelight.

For example, this thin dishonest man who now stood before her in the stark room—he too did not know.

And thinking how he did not know that a carnelian-ocher dancing flame came to lick his chin like a hellish goatee, and how it made him appear, the woman considered it while her bemusement came out in the form of a subtle lowering of eyelids.

"Did I not pay you enough?" said the thin man in alarm. "Did I not reimburse you well for your efforts, Lord Priest?"

"Don't be afraid," said the woman who was thus addressed, and whose long-unused given name was the word for "flames," Agnias. "Do not tremble so," she added softly as she suppressed her antipathy and watched the licking fear eat him alive. "Our debts are settled, you have what you wanted, and I have my coins. Go now. I am tired and will rest."

"Yes, oh yes!" he exclaimed, backing out the door. "Thank you, Lord Priest!"

He was gone long before the rust-hued flames of his aura had faded from the room.

She watched the dying embers of those repugnant flames, the last feeble terrified sparks that managed to cling to the bare white-washed walls and doorway. She sat down then, on the sparse narrow cot in the room, cool, and free of him at last.

At last she was alone.

Cool white walls.

Demonkiller.

No matter where she went, no matter how well she covered her face and tall form, effaced her being from prying eyes, someone would notice. For the violet eye-jewel sunken between her brows in the location of the third eye gave her away. It was the mark of one who held power over the demons of this world and all the ethereal ones beyond. Mark of the warrior priest of Anrah.

And thus they would find her, seek her out and beg her until she relented. They offered her gold and precious stones in reward, land and riches and other ephemera. But she relented only because pity was her weakness, because she could not bear to see their personal flames dance madly about their faces— flames that raged along with their emotions and fears and made her mad also.

At first, so long ago, it seemed now, she had tried to ignore the petitioners. But the peculiarity of her demon-sensitive nature made their disturbed flames follow her, seeping into her mind from a distance of walls and floors and houses and city streets. And so she had to put them at peace, to calm those flames. Which required for her to agree to their terms and perform the task.

The task was always the same.

"My brother is possessed! He pretends innocence during day, but commits murder in the night," they would say. Or else, "You must help my wife! She has not been herself for these last three years. There is a demon incubus that comes to her every night, and she has been barren, refusing the marriage bed."

Others would say, "Our liege lord has been good to us all these years and suddenly he is not himself but a madman, taking away the last of our paltry land, punishing minor crimes with terror."

There were also feeble priests of other less warlike Gods claiming their temples to be haunted, old women who complained of sudden ailments in the family, guardsmen who insisted upon unpassable roads where horrors lurked.

And always Agnias had to exorcise the demon cause.

It was said, a woman could have no power over demons. They called her Lord Priest, for the warrior priests of Anrah were all male, and she had to sacrifice her sex in order to be one of them. Thus, Agnias was a woman in body but had to maintain a charade of man's attire and swear celibacy.

She had not wanted this burden, never wanted to be one of them. How then did it come to pass? She had been sold into servitude to the Temple of Anrah when she was six—a scrawny, starving orphan with no name and no memory of where she came from. The slave trader had lured her with a false smile and the aroma of baked bread that he carried with him for just such a purpose. Driven by mindless hunger she went with him despite his sickly auric flames which she saw quite well.

It was her first conscious choice.

Because of her intense eyes, thin pre-pubescent body, and unusual height, she was assumed to be a boy-child. Later at the auction the Temple retainer had picked her out of the lineup for that same height and straight-backed, angular sharpness.

She was not stupid even then. In silence she made her plea to the Gods. Having lived on the streets she knew what fate generally awaited girl-children and preferred this risky unknown. And some deity must have heard her, because no one bothered to remove that part of her clothing which would give her away.

The austere priests gave her the first robe. It was the color of burnt umber and humility. They shaved her clotted auburn hair, like low-burning flames, and called her Agnias in memory of that hair. That night she lay on her pallet, small girl-child hands pressing against the bare scalp, the naked cold. She clenched her eyes shut, clenched her jaws, and after some time heard inside her a keening. She was not sure who it was that made the sound, except that now her last sense of *woman* was gone with that hair.

She would only earn the right to wear her hair when she received her seventh robe. Meanwhile the priests assigned her and other boys her age the lowest tasks of the Temple.

Five summers passed while Agnias drudged in silence, more remote than any of the children in her group. At the end of the fifth year the violet jewel of Anrah was embedded between her eyebrows, and she was the only child who did not scream at the piercing of the skin and skull-bone.

It was only when she lay in the stupor-illness that followed, together with the others of her initiation group, that her femininity was discovered. Since the holy jewel was already within her flesh, it was too late to dismiss her from the Temple.

Thus, true hell began.

Still weak, slipping in and out of consciousness, she was brought before the high priest of Anrah who looked at her with terrifying eyes. The raging flames stood above his shriveled head like a pillar, greater than any she had ever seen.

"Blasphemer!" he hissed, and slapped her on the cheek. The pillar above him grew wider, threatening to engulf her, to obscure her own protective flames. For the first time Agnias made a choking sound and shrank from him, looking at the spot above his head.

Noting her strange reaction, the high priest astutely comprehended what she saw. He too had a glimmer of her ability, and at times could envision a burning corona around the faces of others. "Why do you draw away and look above me?" he said. "What do you see?"

The child stared with horror in her eyes. "Great fire, my Lord! I see monster flames that come to quench my own!"

"Do you see these flames on others?"

"Others have different flames. Never as great as your own."

"And yourself?" continued the high priest. "Do you see fire about you also?"

"Yes . . . It is like a curtain. It licks before my eyes. Do you not have it also?"

It was at that point that the high priest inhaled deeply. While the fires above his head settled to a natural low simmer, he resigned himself to this girl-child in their midst. She was different and for that reason she would remain.

Besides, he liked what he saw in her eyes. A strength. An awareness.

His voice remained stern while he admonished her. "From now on," he said, "you are to be as the other boys. It matters not what you were born—you will grow to be a man in the House of Anrah. For it is the only way. Since you already bear the violet mark of Anrah on your forehead, you have been fated to learn His Mysterious Way and we may not send you from here.

"When your woman's time comes and your body changes, you must control the natural urges that will come to you. It will be difficult and you will be tempted. You will also tempt others in this Holy House. For that reason you will be given separate sleeping quarters. In the future you will avoid others whenever possible. And if at any time one of us comes to seek you out in secret, or threatens you, you must come directly to me, whether it be an initiate or a high-ranking priest. Come to me at any sign of unusual interest from any one of us—steady eye contact, odd changes in expression, stolen touches—"

"I understand," she interrupted softly, this child of eleven years, with averted eyes.

She had interrupted the high priest of Anrah.

And yet because she was so different he allowed it.

"My Lord," Agnias said. "Am I then allowed to stay?"

"Have you any other home?" the priest answered. Uncustomary words of mercy on his part.

And then recalling himself, his voice returned to ceremonial ice and he pronounced, "Female child. I address you thus for the last time. Are you truly prepared to bear the burden of the Way of Anrah? If so, swear it, using your name, and Anrah Himself will witness. You will be made an exception to all rules, and allowed to put on the second robe of the initiate."

What other choice does she have? the high priest thought, observing the young form before him.

Agnias thought also, as she proceeded to speak the words of a unique oath to Anrah, which no woman had ever yet made. *Even under duress, there is always a choice. It is the one I make.*

When she was done she was dismissed back to her former silence and the tasks of the newly made initiate.

After she had left the room, the high priest dismissed all of his retainers and was alone. It was then that his sunken face dissolved into ease, and he allowed himself to shake with the strength of his suppressed emotion.

For he had seen the immense glory of the flames, like a beacon, all about the child.

She, unlike all others, was radiant like a rising fire-sun.

During the ten summers that followed, Agnias learned the secret arts of the God. Together with her peers she learned the rituals of summoning and of control, of demon nature and human nature. She learned to wield the staff, the sword, and the bow, to throw and to strike, and to use her body as a fluid weapon of defense. Anrah was the God of Wisdom and Darkness and the Solitary Way. And eventually, it came to Agnias that her own nature somehow coincided with this. The life of the warrior priest was her own.

With time she exchanged her second robe, pure white, for five more. The last one she put on, deep violet, was that of the full priest. They anointed her and other priest initiates like her and yet unlike.

For no woman bore the title of Lord Priest. And no other priest had chosen never again to let grow the hair.

Her first exorcism Agnias performed involuntarily. In the year of her sixth robe, ebony-black, one of the initiate-priests in the Temple appeared to come down with a rare malady of the spirit. He had meddled in demon-calling far beyond that of an initiate, and one of his callings had taken hold of him at dawn, at the very moment of invocation.

For days, to no avail, priests of full rank struggled to release the unwise initiate. Hour upon hour the young man lay motionless in his cell, frozen in a dull blissful stupor. His eyes had rolled to the back of his head and his face bore a complex expression of agonized ecstasy. Meanwhile his pulse became softer and milder while his skin grew clammy to the touch.

Finally the high priest was to be summoned. Agnias was one of the three initiates, all black-robes, to attend the stricken unfortunate until the high priest's arrival.

They entered the possessed man's cell at high noon, at the time of day when demons were at their weakest. The moment Agnias laid her gaze upon the possessed, she knew what was wrong.

A form of black flames, vaporous, vaguely female, had straddled his chest. In a sick parody of sensual bliss the demoness moved back and forth, undulating, gripping his shoulders with her black long-nailed hands, and her head was leaned forward over the face of the ailing man. With her lips placed on his forehead she was slowly draining his life-flames, Agnias saw. Lower and lower they flickered, dull red, mortally weak, until he had almost no aura left. Another hour of this, thought Agnias, and the man would be beyond help. His body was already dying and all that kept him breathing was the will of the succubus, her terrible fire-bond.

Anger exploded within Agnias. While the other two black-robes stood back in somewhat nervous silence, completely unaware of the auric sight before them, she stepped forward to approach the bed. With her strong large hand she took hold of the black fire-form and was not surprised to find it solid. The feel of its midnight flames was agony-cold and yet it became weightless in her grip.

Agnias ripped the demoness off her victim's body as though she were a rag doll and hurled her across the room. The man on the bed shuddered, gurgling, while his dying self-flames flickered sadly. And on the other side of the room the black succubus wailed. With a screech that no one but Agnias heard, the demoness sprang back at her. And for the first time Agnias beheld an unbound demon's face.

Raging horrifying darkness. Burning ocher eyes. Long, skeletal feline teeth.

It all lunged at her and should have terrified. And yet somehow it failed to affect her. For the outrage within Agnias burned golden, stronger than any notion of fear.

As the demonic she-form came at her, Agnias swung her fist and landed an explosive blow against the demoness' face, which again sent the thing reeling and screeching across to the other side of the room.

All of a sudden this began to amuse Agnias immeasurably. Because this time the black flame-wrought succubus did not move but cowered several feet away from her against the wall, snarling in a low guttural voice.

But then, sadistic, Agnias neared the hell-creature. She herself felt mad, demonic, with the unfurling of her unexpected power. She leaned over the demoness and stretched her hand over the horned black forehead of burning ice.

The she-demon thing immediately shrank away. Agnias could see that her simple touch was causing it acute pain.

Agnias did not see however what the high priest beheld at that instant when he at last entered the room. The sight that greeted him was that of a great burning tornado of golden-bluish flames that danced about her own human form. This golden fire filled the room and the radiant flames ate away, merciless, at the demoness. No need had Agnias even to move a finger—the demoness would soon be undone before her like candle wax.

Agnias was a human torch.

This the high priest saw. And he stopped, and he let her finish off the demon on her own.

She had saved the victim's life. And from that day, she, more so than any other, was named *demonkiller*.

Agnias left the Temple upon her full initiation to walk the land, as was common with the warrior priesthood. In her wanderings rumors of her abilities preceded her. Although the priests of Anrah all wielded powers to put down demons, none could do this with the ease of Agnias. They had to chant words of power, to concentrate their wills. All Agnias had to do was enter a room, to make a demon squirm.

Almost two summers had gone by, during which her head remained clean-shaven and she was kept busier than anyone else stemming from the House of Anrah. With each demon confrontation Agnias felt her power unfold and less effort necessary to accomplish her task. She was always weary immediately after and yet oddly energized. The weariness came from the demon struggle, while the energy sprung from some barely-tapped place deep inside and was fed by the rejuvenated fires that crowned her satisfied customers after each task well done.

And always at the end her greatest reward was peace.

Only, peace—no matter that it was so well earned—was not to be hers today.

Less than half an hour passed since the thin frightened man left her presence when Agnias heard soft footsteps ascending the staircase of the inn. And then, an equally soft knock on her door.

And already she could feel *his* flames.

"Enter," she said. "The door is unlocked."

Silence.

And then the door creaked, opening.

Still seated on the cot, Agnias moved her head to watch. Through the crack in the door she saw only darkness in the hallway. She knew she was being observed.

Then it opened wide and a tall cloaked form entered the room.

Agnias saw electric blue and lavender flames consuming the cloak and hood. And when he lowered the hood, she saw the fires spring unrestrained heavenward above his blond hair.

"You are the Lord Priest of Anrah? The demonkiller?" he said in a voice used to petulant command. He observed the woman before him—her smooth clean-shaven scalp, the surprising lines of her face, the violet Mark of Anrah, her clear tired eyes.

She was not what he had expected. Fragile, refined, gentle, even. Ambiguous.

He re-evaluated his first impression quickly enough, when her clear eyes turned on him, and he saw a quickening of intensity.

"Who are you?" she said simply. "What do you want?"

"Who I am does not matter. What matters, is that I will pay you like you've never been paid before."

Agnias sighed. He noticed how indifference returned to her eyes. "Payment doesn't excite me. You are a Lord, I assume. What is the nature of your situation?"

Again, silence. She wondered at his hesitancy. His flames were agitated, true. And yet it was not the same kind of urgency, panic, that she had been accustomed to with the rest of her supplicants. This one was excited, but different somehow.

He spoke at last. "Lord Priest," he said. "I am a— *collector*. Of rare things. Rare and marvelous and unique. I collect—demons."

Agnias laughed softly.

"What a strange thing," she said. "Why would anyone want something so foul? It's like saying you collect scorpions or mortal illnesses."

"Scorpions are in fact collected to extract their poison, for medicinal purposes, Lord Priest."

"Poison can be used as medicine, true," she said. "But the primary use of poison in this world is murder."

"I understand," he retorted softly, copying her manner. "And yet, my reasons are aesthetical. To me demons represent the beauty of unbridled power."

"Unbridled indeed. How do you expect to contain a demon? Put it in a jar as though it were an eastern jinn? Try it and watch the jar crumble into dust just before the demon breaks forth to consume you—a true story, and fools have been known to attempt this. My brothers of Anrah keep records of such idiocy."

"I have at my disposal a powerful magus. He will pronounce the necessary words of binding to make the demon obey me. He has done so a number of times before, with success."

"Is that so?" Agnias said, her clear eyes focusing on him. "Then why do you need me?" And then she added, "Your magus is a charlatan. For, like thoughts, demons cannot be bound, only seduced and shackled temporarily. Eventually they turn on you and destroy you. We who follow the Way of Anrah know it only too well. Therefore, I'll have no part of it."

The man was silent, patient. Only she saw his growing furious passion by the nature of his flames. He was hiding it well however. Not a trace of unrest on his young insolent face.

"Lady—I mean, Lord Priest," he said. "Please. You are my last hope. All I ask is that you set the victim free of this particular demon that I desire, and the rest is up to me—"

"My Lord, you and your fool magus will have hell unleashed upon you. Tell me of this poor victim of your demon."

The blond man saw his chance. "The demon is within a young innocent woman," he said. "She does not know this. She is the one I would have as my wife. And this demon I desire to bind and keep with me for the rest of my days, to grace my collection."

He observed bewildered sorrow in her eyes.

"What unusual priorities. Even if you succeed, do you think your poor wife would appreciate having her demon tormentor always nearby? In a gilded bird cage perhaps, right next to your wedding bed? You are cruel in addition to being a fool."

Strangely enough, he smiled. "Well said," he retorted, "I've been called that and other things."

"What should I call you then, besides epithets?"

She said this last thing roughly, for there was immediate charm in his smile, and perversely it touched her. It changed his face. And it warmed his electric-violet flames so that they burned clean.

"I am Maquon."

Agnias rose. She approached him, stilling her mind with long-practiced ease, negating his pleasing warmth. She looked plainly in his eyes, and said, "Take me to this demon."

An hour later, they exited the carriage in front of the tall front gates of an expensive villa, on the finer side of town. The blond man, Lord Maquon, led her past liveried servants, into the house.

Agnias, who stood as tall and upright as the man, followed him soundlessly, disregarding narrow glances of the house servants, all of whom were better dressed than she was. As many of her brethren of Anrah, she wore humble gray clothing of coarse wool and cotton over her deep violet robe—so as not to incur attention.

They stopped before an ornate door leading to a boudoir chamber.

"My betrothed, the Lady Niadde is within," said Maquon softly. He watched her, and Agnias noted something strange about his gaze, a gossamer veil of impassivity sliding into place. It made her pause and look at him also, closely, intently, before entering the chamber.

She opened the door and saw an opulent room. In a deep chair before an arch-window of stained glass sat a pale striking woman. Her eyes were closed. Her form was so still that for a moment she appeared to be an old thing made of wood. Flaxen hair fell loosely about her mother-of-pearl face and shoulders.

And there was nothing extraordinary in the bright violet-electric blue fire-corona above her head, except that it was robust, just as the fires above Lord Maquon. Indeed, it was possibly identical—his exact flames.

Behind Agnias the door shut firmly, and Lord Maquon stood regarding her in silence.

"You lied to me," Agnias said calmly. "Why?"

There was movement in the chair as the blond woman rose with stiffness and stood looking at her. "I am Lady Niadde," she said in a brash voice of power. "My brother lied so that you would come here of your own will. Free Will is the first step, when it comes to Binding."

"I see no demons to bind here, only two idiot youths," Agnias said. "I can certainly use ropes to attach the two of you together. Or is it that you are suggesting that I myself am to be bound?"

"There are no demons here, it is true," Maquon said, nearing Agnias while his sister took a step toward her likewise. "I used that as an excuse to get you here, knowing your compulsion for acts of nobility. I've been studying you for a long time now. . . .

"One thing that I told you is true—I *am* a collector. Only, I collect Things that Cannot Be Had. I've obtained truth from a liar, darkness from light, fire from water, laughter from pain, and a child from death. What I want now is no demon, but *yourself*, a woman who is like a man. I want to draw forth desire from you who had sworn to feel none."

As he spoke thus, Maquon stopped before her, his face with its intense clear eyes inches away.

For the first time, Agnias revealed a bitter smile. "There are other women who are like men. There are other celibates. Why do you choose to pursue me with your nonsense?"

"I will have what I want," said Maquon.

At which she sighed. "You see before you a sexless priest of Anrah. I am a man in your eyes and mine, and will be for as long as I live. You do not want me."

"No!" exclaimed the Lady Niadde. And then she added, "You are a woman, and no Oath can change that, no dark misogynist God!"

The woman's words were oddly sweet, like a long-needed balm, as though they came welling from her own subconscious. They touched Agnias even though she made a point to ignore them.

But now Lord Maquon reached out to Agnias, touching her shoulder like a tentative butterfly. "Lady . . ." he whispered. "Please . . . give me a chance."

And because he was so earnest—and because pity had always been her weakness—she looked at the man, her own eyes serious and steady.

"I see," she said softly. "And you think it a worthy act to provoke me to break my Oath? My Lord, you shouldn't have bothered. Don't you realize how easy it would be to feel desire for you? Am I not alive? And as such, it is natural to hunger. You are beautiful, as men go, Maquon. I know, for I have spent a decade of my life in a House of men. In that Holy House there were all kinds, some as fair as you. If not for my Oath, I would have allowed my heart to break many times. Only—I had not. Just as I will not allow it now and not *ever*. Although once I had no choice, I now *choose* this way for myself and honor a promise given long ago."

"Then I would break you!" Lord Maquon cried. "For I must have what you refuse to give, *despite* your will."

And at this senselessness, all traces of her compassion fled. Inner fires arose angrily, once again dancing with intensity before her eyes. "What you must have is not before you," she said in a cold voice. "Enough, I will not tarry here."

And Agnias turned to exit.

"No!" he exclaimed. And then, "Now, Niadde, speak the words to bind her to me, now!"

Before Agnias could take another step, the figure that was Lady Niadde began to utter quick guttural noises punctuated by odd screams. Or at least it seemed the sounds issued from her, for she was now akin to an animated doll, and the language that left her lips was arcane and ancient, like cobwebs in a dusty vault.

Agnias recognized words of power wielded by magi of considerable learning, words that had been taught to her when she wore the fourth, red robe of Anrah. Words of desiccation, words of dust.

Normally they would have no effect upon her, she knew. And yet because of her own state of doubt, her vulnerable introspection caused by the strangeness of the moment, immediately she sensed a lassitude come to blanket her senses. And she recognized another power was at work here—enough power in fact to be the result of twin focused wills, or of something more. . . .

Brother and sister with a natural talent for powerwielding—the surprise of it must have caught her off guard, and in that second she lost the opportunity to resist.

The room started to turn, and twilight obscured her vision. A conflagration was upon her, violet and electric blue. Sensual power surged through her mind. Before she even had a chance to gather her own forces, her limbs melted like warm honey and she felt herself dissolving. Her last awareness was of the strong arms of Lord Maquon closing tight around her, warm. . . .

And then, all around, his *flames*.

In a haze of radiant delirium, she fought, and she dreamed. His flames were everywhere, scalding, and he was alongside her, his skin warm, warmth spreading like mead. . . .

Lips extracted her pulse-beat from the hollow of her throat, her life-flames. Somnolence came, willing her to become translucent, half-flesh half-spirit, and to give in to the intimate need, to give herself up and to burn. . . .

Demon!

Maquon was not a true man. She knew it at last, saw through the impossibly intricate fabric of the illusion that he had cast around her, a never before seen manifestation of demonic power at its highest.

This was not a mere demon, but one of the highest Lords of Darkness, one who had the power to appear fair and radiant and to disguise the nature of his hell flames.

A demon who knew her enough to ply her true weakness.

The knowledge struck Agnias like a splash of cold water, and reason returned. She struggled in her mind, focusing her true vision, seeing herself as she really was—standing in a bare room with no one else there with her, only the demon essence. She was engulfed in corrosive ruddy vapor and at its edges was black fire, the fabric of hell.

It was eating away at her, eating her life-flames. And she was but a fly caught in a monstrous web.

The demon was greater than any she had ever seen, like a shadow form of ship-sails. It spread itself languidly about her, its immense semi-corporeal flesh unfurling in an invisible wind, filling the room. Tatters of dark smoke wafted like writhing shadows. Agnias saw now that the form that had appeared to her as the Lady Niadde was merely a wooden mannequin dressed in woman's clothes, seated in a chair.

The demon, this thing of impossible power, had lured her here in order to destroy.

No! cried Agnias with her mind, striking out against the enveloping hell flames of darkness. Her clean essence of gold flames burst forth like a flash of sunlight but immediately the flare started to dissipate and was sucked into the corrosive foulness all about her.

Anrah's Chosen, mortal woman, you are mine now, crackled and roared and howled the flames as the demon lord Maquon spoke at last within her mind. *Give in.*

Agnias felt that she could not move. Her body's muscle control was no longer her own, and her limbs felt heavy like wet clay and then weightless and numb like cotton. She was being consumed and her essence drained.

Tell me at least what you truly want of me, you who call yourself Maquon? she cried, her thoughts pulling together in weakness, barely shaped by her will alone.

Anrah, said the demon simply, as it continued draining her.

Agnias was now so weak that her body crumpled to the floor. She lay in the stark chamber bathed in waves of red and darkness, and she thought with the last great focusing of her fading being.

If I give you Anrah, if I show you the way to my Lord, will you follow, demon? Do you dare face the God?

Show me, he replied. *I will follow.*

First you need to release my essence, Agnias whispered, her thoughts faint like smoke now, barely there.

But the demon flames laughed in answer.

And Agnias knew in that moment that she had lost. It was a sharp realization, and a wave of final despair came to her.

In her final thoughts Agnias saw herself feeble and small, a girl-child in the House of Anrah, denied even her last vestiges of self, lying on a pallet. She saw herself from the inside and outside looking on, her cold clean-shaven head. She was holding herself, holding the place they had shaved her, the bare scalp, touching the place that was missing. . . .

He abandoned you in that moment, spoke the demon flames, as they consumed her. *Anrah took away what is rightfully yours. He pillaged your female self. Neither man nor woman are you now. You have denied yourself, cut off your feeling, your needs, your true life, all these years of service to Him, all for nothing. And now, die in emptiness, mortal.*

The elements of truth that were present in what the darkness said weighed hard upon her. Agnias lay, no longer feeling her body at all, only her last fading essence, its crown of flames, that pillar that normally stood above her in glory. It was fading fast, its filaments fine like smoke, like fine hairs breaking off and dissipating into the eternal dark.

She lay and slowly died and watched them go.

And something came to Agnias just before the end. A faint butterfly-soft spark of clarity touched her, engaged the last embers of her reason. And she felt her true self, that which was her connection to Anrah, the network of cords and lines of life-force, twisted and braided together.

She felt the lines, like a million strands of hair. They were all around her, and they faded only as she let go, as she allowed them to float away and sever her connection to the life force.

Only a few left now.

No!

She cried out and she allowed herself to feel along the line of the last strands even as they tore, away and upward. . . . And like lightning she knew that this was her true connection to the God Anrah and to life itself. The choice to maintain the bond was hers.

As always, the *choice* was there before her.

She reached out and held on to the single filament, while the darkness closed in, and she forced her essence to reach out and to sprout forth more of herself, to sprout new filaments of light.

They burst from her essence, from her bare scalp, long and glorious strands of life force, standing up like a cloud of flickering light, like floating seaweed made of fire.

And with each new bursting of light, each new achieved bond of redundancy, strength returned to her, and Agnias was a vessel filling anew.

She could feel her body again, felt the currents of blood moving through her veins. The filaments meanwhile grew and grew, filling the room with a web of fibrous light.

Her auric mane of light-hair stood up and the demon form around her shrank away, beginning to shriek, for she was now the one consuming him.

The demon Maquon was reduced to a shadow form imprisoned in a tangle-web made of her auric hair.

Agnias blinked and opened her eyes in the physical world. She saw his vaguely male human shape of soot-black scales and bits of flesh seething with maggots that grew in him, a head crowned with horns; saw his long fangs and eyes like pits of hell. As she stood up from where she had lain on the floor she observed the monstrosity before her, immobilized on the physical plane by invisible bonds.

The demon crouched, contorted, next to the wooden mannequin seated in a chair.

Agnias regarded them both for a moment before she reached out with her hand to place it on the demon's forehead. It was the last touch she made before forcing a demon's ultimate destruction.

The air moved thick and fluid, like water, before her and just for a breath Maquon took on his pleasing man shape, his clear beautiful human eyes imploring her, willing her to give in. . . .

Agnias sighed and then continued to touch the thing before her, as it shrieked and burned and then was no more.

She breathed hard, for she was now truly alone in the room. Only herself and the wooden mannequin. The doll lay motionless, its head covered by a wig of fine soft female hair, like flax.

Agnias touched it softly, lingering for a moment before she turned to leave the room. And then she touched her own scalp, as though to reassure herself.

It was smooth, clean-shaven, bare skin softly defining the shape of the skull underneath.

And as Agnias looked out at the world through her usual curtain of personal flames, she knew them for what they were at last, Anrah's gift and acknowledgement of her fullness of self.

A glorious auric secret mane of hair.

THE SLAYING OF WINTER

Iliss moved through a dead world.

Snowflakes finer than dandelion seed floated down gently, sparsely, brushing against her face with feather lightness, while the tundra around whirled by. A solitary bird soared overhead—a Northern bird—and trained a strange look of its sharp eagle-eye on the being below.

Iliss huddled in the voluminous fur garment which she had bought back at the old roadside shelter-station. This peculiar cumbersome thing she wore as a beast wears its own skin came with a hood that left only her eyes and a slit of her face exposed, and it was unbelievably warm.

The trader had called the garment *shuba*. The station was on the boundary of things, and beyond it began the Northlands. There too, she had traded in her Southern mount, a sturdy gelding, for a sled and team of dogs—strange, unfamiliar means of conveyance. Iliss felt remotely sorry for the small furry beasts, so much like tame wolves, that were to be tied in pairs in front of the sled, and who obeyed a raised or lowered long stick called *girg* by the Northsmen. But then, all sensation was remote, so in truth she felt nothing.

Iliss shivered despite her relative warmth, hating the cumbersome feel of mittens on her calloused fingers and the wreath of fur around her face restricting her field of vision. Her posture was immobile. Her left hand clenched the leather reins in a kind of death grip forced by lack of familiarity, by lack of trust. The right hand was rigid, holding aloft the long *girg* stick high above the dogs' heads—they would run forever thus, until she lowered the *girg* on the ground.

How much farther to go? How much farther. . . .

Iliss was better used to the freedom of the Southern steppe. Give her the tall grass, the quick short agile horses, the unrestraining soft leather trousers and vest of a plains warrior, her trusty knife at her belt, and a light bow and quiver on her back—she needed nothing else. Let the hot dry wind wash her face like honey. . . .

Here, there was only the cold. Iliss never knew there could be so much cold in one place at one time. Everything, the sparse craggy trees black against the white land, the steel sky, the gray sun low on the horizon, all was raw cold, a tomb of diamond ice. Around her the land dipped and fell and rose again, as hills of snow—dull, mysterious with shadows, then suddenly sparkling in the sun—rose to meet her.

If there is anything to this burial ground, Iliss thought, *it is not for my people. But now it is a fitting place for me.*

The cold stung her face, clawed at her eyes, hungering at the edges of her bitten eyelids. She had cultivated no weapon against it.

Where was she going?

She had been told to follow the faint trail in the snow, using various visual landmarks and the sun as her guide. Back at the shelter, the trader's eyes had acquired a focus when he saw the fine heavy coins she offered. She knew their only value had been as a metal, to be melted down later and wrought into a blade maybe, or a wash basin. Metal was rare here in the North.

And again she wondered at herself, why bother? What purpose did it serve, her coming here into the deathly lands, her hopeless quest? Indeed, in a subtle way, her mind was not her own.

For Iliss remembered no tale, in all of ancient lore, of anyone who had successfully killed a God.

Such was her intent.

In her own home plains, among her agile, dark, sloe-eyed people, Iliss had been a warrior, and she had known shame. Iliss stood taller than any woman, possessed eyes the color of an overcast sky, and an arrogant walk. Harsh-tongued, she was quick to lash out at others. Quick in humor, she had boasted before the Gods.

Yet when her home village was raided by a strange enemy from the North, her old parents and her only brother butchered, and her sister Naiass raped, Iliss did not have the courage to commit the suicide customary of her people, the Killing of Shame.

And the people spat at her, mocked her—they who had better survived the Northern raid. They turned their backs in shunning whenever she passed by. And they ceremonially rubbed out all traces of her footprints with the left toes of their leather-clad feet.

Iliss forgot her youth, her boasting ways and resorted to being a shadow, her eyes transformed into stone. At last, when Autumn drew to a close, and it was Winter, she left them.

She had ridden alone through the plains, farther and farther North, haunted by Naiass, her younger sister, crouching like a beast in her thoughts, her clothes stained and torn, hair clotted, filled with the smell of human sorrow and neglect.

Having lost her mind, Naiass had lost all facial expression. She had become timid like an animal, reacting with only a hazy disturbance in her vacant stare when someone approached. Iliss had been unable to come near Naiass. And the villagers, out of pity, did not bother to drive the mad one out farther than the outskirts of the settlement. After all, the mad were watched over by the eagle-eyes of the Gods.

Iliss herself was touched. She had lost her mind in the older, quiet way, unlike her sister. Her sense of revenge she had confused—swallowed it with her soul's pale lungs, not her heart's black guts—and now she breathed it endlessly, instead of passing it through herself like offal.

Instead of hating the Northsmen, she hated their Gods.

It had been the will of the Gods, people said, that her family be killed, and she should have died also. Northern Gods were just as powerful as those here in the South. They dealt equally among Themselves, gave each side allowances for deaths and births.

Iliss had said nothing and she did not hear them; these days a wind rushed through her ears and her veins in a clamor. One name rang interminably in her mind. The barbarians had invoked it as they slaughtered her family. *Trei*, they called Him, the Winter God.

"*Trei*," she had mouthed, numb-minded, as she and her brother fought the raiders, while her old father bled in the burning house. *Trei* became the abstraction of hate, cold and ugly. If He had a human form, she could imagine her hands tightening around His neck, squeezing, crushing, making a moist welling blackness. . . .

And because there was nothing else left, no end to her living shame, Iliss decided to go North. She would go to its farthest reaches, where it was said the Gods could be found among the sparkling mountains of ice, and where the sky held strange colored lights, like the splintered rainbow. And there, among the wondrous splendor, she would find *Trei* and slay Him.

Then, she would die.

Clenching the reins and the *girg* with stiff fingers, Iliss was carried farther and farther along the barely perceptible trail. There were adequate supplies of grain and dried meat in the back of the sled, and extra warm blankets. The grain was for her own consumption—for since that dark day she had stopped eating flesh—while the meat was for the dogs.

One last point of honor Iliss refused to part with at the shelter-station. A long knife of finely honed iron she had kept close to her body, tied around her left upper thigh. This knife she had used when fighting for her life.

Her knife, first taken from her and plunged into beloved flesh, brother's guts spewing . . . Her knife, regained too late while Naiass was broken—little smiling Naiass—her soft eyes agonized, then glassy . . . Screams, crackle of fire, her mother's hands charred . . . Smoke, and Northerners with long pale hair, rose-skinned, shrieking, clawing at her, *Trei, Trei, Trei,* then bleeding, limbs severed under her slashing knife. . . .

Her knife.

Iliss was jolted out of the familiar circle of madness as a howling of wolves came in the distance. It was dangerous to be caught thus, alone in the wild. But the thought of danger was sluggish in her brain, like all other thoughts long since had been. Her dogs, yapping nervously, carried the sled around another hillock, while the howling increased.

Not even evening yet, she thought. *They come out to hunt early.* How perverse everything was here, in the cold land. Even the wolves were unlike those in the steppe.

They warned me, the next settlement is less than a day's ride ahead. A Northern settlement. Would they allow a stranger to stay overnight? If they only knew my intent.

The dogs' ears all prickled, stood on end. They became hard to control. With a grip that made her lose all feeling in her hand, she held the reins and thought of how many wolves she was capable of fending off on her own.

At the next turn, amid a sudden unexpected cluster of sparse evergreen bushes, a scene met her eyes. It made her throw the *girg* down immediately, halting the dogs in their tracks.

Truly, if they were but to move a couple more feet ahead, they would touch noses with a wolf pack.

There were six or seven of them, great beasts, overgrown with thick gray Winter fur which is so prized by the Northsmen. Immobile, their jaws scowling, pink mouths shocking against the surrounding snow, they froze in a half-circle around some *thing* huddled against a hill slope.

Iliss held her breath, even though she knew the wolves had already sensed her and the dogs' presence.

The *thing* was human. Naked to the waist, with light fair skin turning blue from the cold, and hair the color of corn, he had only a fur pelt to cover his lower body, and fur boots on his feet. His hand gripped a long knife as he froze in a half-fallen, half-crouching position, his own teeth bared at the wolf pack in a lupine scowl.

There was blood on the ground. And only then did Iliss notice the corpse of a pale wolf lying in the deep snow, just before him—between him and the rest of the wolves.

Her body reacted ahead of her thoughts. Her hands went for the long blade hidden at her left thigh, and although encumbered by the *shuba*, she was agile. One precise strike of the knife at a furry throat, and a beast expired. She felt nothing. Before it had time to hit the ground, she was already rolling away, plunging the blade into the other nearest wolf.

Snarling, they turned on her, while two went for the boy. She realized her mistake too late, knew how badly she had broken the delicate balance with which the boy was holding them at bay. Again the thought came, *How different these wolves from the ones at home, how insolent . . . Monsters of ice and cold . . . And how useless I am even here, again. . . .*

And then—as she thought this, fighting now for her life as much as for the boy's, and watched him fall under the weight of one of the gray maddened things—from the corner of her eye a different shadow moved.

A larger man shape, fur-clad, appeared as if out of nowhere, having been concealed behind snow-covered shrubbery. He balanced an axe in one big glove-enclosed hand, and with the other tossed a wolf in the air. That one had been ready to sink its teeth into the boy's bare throat. The man screamed something in a harsh unintelligible tongue, as he threw off the wolves like they were mere snowdrifts, while the boy began to whimper something in return, not quite daring to cry.

Iliss had taken care of another wolf. But then, it must have been the heavy clumsy clothing again, for she was not quite quick enough as the last of the beasts leaped at her exposed face. There was a strange, somehow familiar look in its intelligent eyes—she could not tell if it was the gaze of a hunter or a victim.

A sorrowful bitter look.

The man saw this and whirled around, leaving the boy. He dropped the axe and reached out with his gloved hands for the wolf's neck. What happened next Iliss had no senses left to know, not even time to blink. There was only a frozen instant of movement, a glimmer of his pale skin, a face surrounded by a fur hood, and then the wolf was no more.

But then, dropping the beast, the man suddenly came for her. There was an odd Northern smell on him, of unworked animal fur, oil, and raw leather ... There was a flash of pale eyes, much like her own, a harsh furious face. Suddenly he swung with one fist, with a look of pure hatred, and Iliss felt a powerful blow to her head, then excruciating pain. Her last sluggish thought before the world went dark, was of surprise.

Northsmen ... all insane beasts ... And I too ... Trei.

I liss awoke to warmth, like honey, and a dull headache. For an instant she had forgotten. Her mother would be putting more straw on the fire now, just before she prepared the morning porridge. . . . Her head throbbed. And then came truth.

Mother's hands charred. . . .

Like a vile illness, reality started in her stomach and radiated through her body. She was alert as a wild animal, but did not move. No need to let whoever might be there know that she was conscious. She lay, breathing lightly, her eyelashes fluttering slowly higher, in a trick manner of seeing without actually opening the eyes, she had learned long ago.

The smells around her were foreign—like the strange man, of skins and oil and animals. Mixed in was a pungent deliciously smoky flavor of spiced food. From someplace away, a fire crackled warmly.

She sensed with her skin that she was completely naked, lying on top of something warm and furred, her body comfortable enough in the hot air that she could be uncovered.

Nakedness meant vulnerability, so Iliss opened her eyes, no longer concerned if she gave her last advantage away. Her people disapproved of physical nudity; it was immodest, and one could hide no weapon nearby. And now her only weapon was gone.

Iliss found herself lying on the floor of a small room, quite odd, for the floor and walls were all covered with animal pelts. Soft marvelous fur was everywhere, of all shapes and colors, fox, and rabbit down, beaver, and even bear and wolf pelts, rusty, spotted, gold and cream, pure white, smoky silver, rich earthy colors. It was overwhelming, for never had she imagined such riches in one place—a hunter's most avid dream. The Northsmen were masters of the hunt, she knew, even more so than her own people.

There were no windows in this room, only a small chimney-opening in the wall next to a pit in the corner, surrounded by stones. There was one low door, and it was closed. In the pit burned a bright fire, sending warm red-gold shadows to leap among the furs and along the wooden rafters of the low ceiling overhead.

And if she were but to look closer, with the vision of her soul, it might have seemed to her that the spirits of the animals came for the last time to animate their own skins, and danced sadly in the firelight. Only, the eyes of her soul were shut, for even now she was breathing the endless cycle of bitter darkness with the soul's pale lungs. . . .

Iliss took a large wolf pelt to cover her lower body and her breasts. She then tried to rise, wincing from the sudden pain, and fell back. She seethed at the madman who hit her, imagining how she would put her knife through his eye sockets, scooping, twisting. . . . What had she done but help the boy? Who were they anyway? Where was she?

At that moment the door creaked open and, stooping, an old woman entered. She had wrinkled skin along her face and bare arms, flax hair, bright pale eyes. Walking barefoot, she wore a sleeveless cotton dress trimmed with animal fur. And she carried a wooden bowl of some hot pungent foodstuff—the same aroma Iliss had smelled earlier.

The woman's expression was not quite blank enough. A brightness, a curiosity was in her quick eyes.

She neared Iliss who sat up despite the pain, her expression cold. The woman looked at her, crouched and offered the bowl. She waited in silence.

Iliss took the bowl. The woman continued staring. Then with one finger she touched her own chest and said, "Ulav."

Iliss understood. However, out of spite, she let her eyes remain empty.

"Ulav, Ulav," repeated the woman, pointing at herself. Then she pointed at Iliss and waited.

Iliss stared. "Curse you," she said clearly in a level voice. "Filthy barbarian hag. Since you don't know my own language, I can say anything." And then she shrugged, tiredly. With a finger pointing at herself, she said, "Iliss."

The woman nodded, with just a hint of a smile, and immediately repeated. She did not leave.

Iliss took a sip of the stew, then frowned. It was too bland despite the pleasant spicy aroma, and too foreign. But she was hungry.

While she ate, the woman examined her closely, in curiosity, then reached out to touch her hair. Iliss' hair was dark as untempered metal, copper-brown, long and fine—but tangled and filthy at the moment. She grimaced, then mocked in her once-customary tone. "Never seen the like, have you? All of you, pale-haired *gazhigs*." She spoke self-indulgently, knowing the woman could not understand.

Ulav again touched her hair, then brought it to her nose.

"Yes, stench of rot." Iliss said. "Didn't wash it for many moons now. And I'm not going to."

Then, because of a spasm of pain in her head, she grimaced. "Won't wash it ever, old bitch," she continued, "since I am rotting already, all of me, walking carrion. It won't be long . . . Maybe you will help me along, eh?" She grinned. "Send me off to the sweet House of the Dead."

The woman in the meantime had noticed that Iliss used a pelt to cover herself. Ulav took the pelt in both hands and pulled it down, until it slid down below her breasts.

Great full vessels, ripened by the Goddess of the Land, they are, and your hips are strong and wide, her mother had once told Iliss in pride. *You will bear and feed daughters and sons.* And like Autumn fruits her breasts had swelled, when she was but ten summers, and many a man in her village had cast a longing glance at them, and at her willow-strong body. It had been ten more summers since, yet Iliss had known no man.

With one wrinkled hand, Ulav reached out, placed it on one of the breasts, and felt it for signs of motherhood. Iliss slapped her hand away.

"No, old woman," she exclaimed with anger, "I have no milk, no brats to feed. I only wish I were a man now, with a man's body. No sorry children would then spring from my flesh only to die like carrion."

A new dark thought came to her. What if they were keeping her alive to breed with their men? Iliss knew nothing of Northern ways.

The older woman Ulav seemed upset by her sharp reaction. She muttered something in her vague tongue, and frowning took away the half-empty bowl of stew. Then, without another word she rose from her sitting-crouch, and left the room, shutting the door behind her.

Time went by, and Iliss' temple throbbed more quietly. Alert, she listened to the remote sounds of the place. The door of her prison remained firmly closed.

Then, noises outside. Several male voices arguing, and one female voice which sounded like Ulav. Iliss thought she heard her own name being mentioned. Then the door was roughly opened, and what appeared to be a crowd of men and women paused at the entrance. Three or four actually bent their heads from the low ceiling, and entered the room, while the rest stood milling at the doorway, looking on. Among them lurked urchins of all ages, like a flock of blond geese.

The men were all tall, great boned giants over six feet, wearing wolf-pelt and woolen-made vests and fur leggings, with tall boots. The women, large and stately, some slender and others full-bodied, were dressed in long wool and cotton dresses lined with fur and embroidered with colorful designs. All had long hair like Autumn hay, of different shades, ranging from sand amber to the palest flax. Women wore scarves and kerchiefs over their hair. Older men wore beards, and the younger were clean-shaven. Necklaces of strung animal teeth gleamed, their ivory paleness blending in with the pale rose-tinted skins, muscled arms covered with fair down. Hardened faces with pale eyes—sky, cornflower blue, gray steel—stared at her. Their looks spoke of curiosity, disapproval, even faint desire. But mostly, *alienness.*

Iliss felt her body becoming like the trunk of a dry tree. She wrapped herself closer in the wolf pelt, her shield. She stared back with stone eyes and looked *through* these beings so that she would not have to look *at* them.

She observed that, of the four men inside the room, one was extremely old, shriveled like a root and tiny next to these giants. His white hair was parted in two long braids, and his beard likewise. There was a torque of metal at his wrinkled throat, and another clasped his head. Quiet confidence suggested he was chief among them.

To his left stood a younger man, with a ruddy wool band tying back his hair, a fine face, and deep water-hued eyes. He examined her boldly.

On the other side of the old man were two younger men, with kin resemblance between them. The shorter one with the lighter hair and kind eyes, watched her in sympathy. The man next to him, with a sallow face and sharp pale eyes like her own, Iliss recognized. He had been the madman who dealt her that heavy-fisted blow.

And then the man who hit her, spoke. First he spoke in their alien tongue, and his tone was respectful, for he was addressing the old man. The other nodded, said something. Then the first man turned directly to her.

"You are named—Iliss," he said imperfectly, in her own language of the plains.

"Yes," she said, not bothering to be surprised. "And *you?* Who are all of you? Why am I here? What—"

He interrupted her rising voice. "I am Waevan," he said. "And these are the Gowirak People. You are in our village." He paused. "I know your name, but I know nothing else. *Who* are you? Why have you crossed into our lands? Your kind does not show here often."

"Why did you hit me?" she said. "I was trying to help the boy. He was surrounded by wolves—"

His eyes, so phlegmatic, came to sudden angry life. "Enough, curse you!" he said in a voice of a growling bear, and for an instant she was reminded of that wintry scene where he, the wild stranger, fought the wolves. "Idiot bitch! You stupidly disrupted my son's *ugainn* ceremony! You almost got him killed! He was showing himself a man, by facing the great wolf pack alone, by earning their trust and assisting their fallen brother. There was no need, and yet you attacked. You killed many innocent wolves, and made me kill more of them for nothing. If only you had minded your own business. . . ."

If it were not for his foul pronunciation of her native tongue, Iliss might have been impressed.

But just as suddenly, the anger left his eyes, and he was again bland, washed out. His hand made a helpless, scornful gesture. "But—what did I expect? You, a foreign barbarian. You know nothing of our ways."

He paused, his gaze averted. "Truly, I see now, I acted too rashly, in anger. I shouldn't have hit you. You knew no better." His voice dwindled, in empty silence.

Then the old man—who was intently following the exchange and, as Iliss realized, probably understanding some of it—spoke.

"You—Iliss—he tell," said the old shaking voice, and a withered hand pointed back at the younger man.

Waevan spoke again, "Veddr is the Eldest of us, and his Voice is heard Loudest. He is here to help decide what is to be done with you."

Only now did Iliss feel a small twinge of worry. "What of my dogs and sled?" she said, pretending not to hear.

"The dogs and the sled and *you*, all belong to me now," replied Waevan. "The first two I keep. But you—I have no use for chattel like you. That is why I have called all here. So that one can fairly choose you."

"Your words," Iliss said, her eyes focusing on him with intensity, "are like fresh cow dung. 'Choose me?' Of what do you speak? We belong to none but the Gods. In truth, what you say is beginning to stink so loudly that even the Gods can smell it, all the way to their Silver Halls! And just like dung, Northsman, your words diminish in effect the more you air them out of that big stupid cow-lipped mouth of yours—"

The old man Veddr suddenly burst out in wheezing chuckles.

Waevan was undaunted. "Veddr is somehow finding joy in your speech," he said in a bland tone, ignoring her meaning. "Maybe he will consider you for his own household. Likely, there's work for you near the cook pot and he and the wife could use a Southern foot warmer—"

Continuing to chuckle, old Veddr shook his head. And the equally old and tiny, kerchief-covered woman whom Iliss only now noticed behind him, leaned forward and raised a shaking hand to hold her nose.

"Ah, then maybe not. Because not unlike your speech you seem to stink." Waevan added, "Veddr's wife prefers a clean household."

Iliss heard nothing in that moment. The insides of her head were spinning with vast empty skies. *You know nothing. Know nothing of Southern ways, and nothing of me. Try to cage me, Trei. . . .*

Her eyes bright with energy, she glanced around the room. "So, stink or not, who wants me? Who thinks to hold me?"

There was silence. Then Waevan said, "If you think you can run away, you are wrong. When a man of the Gowirak binds a wife, or a chattel, it is with the help of the Gods, with inseparable bonds.

"More dung falling from your mouth," she said. "All bonds sing out to be broken." But at the mention of Gods, a shadow came into her eyes. "When a Plainswoman is forcibly bound down, she either dies or claws the enemy's heart out of his breast."

"What nonsense. That is not true," he said quietly. "I know the ways of the Plainspeople."

"Not well enough." She shrugged. "Besides, I speak only for myself." And she sat back, emotionless, among the furs.

Suddenly the young man with the water-pale proud eyes spoke. He pointed at Iliss, addressing all, then Veddr alone.

"It seems that Gavvar will take you." Waevan translated, showing no reaction.

"I wish him luck," she replied, seething in anger, and gesticulated a raw Southern obscenity with her right hand.

"You are the one who is in luck," Waevan said, ignoring or maybe not understanding the gesture. "Gavvar is one of our best warriors. He will provide well for you, and all the women will envy you. I don't quite know what he sees in you—"

"I don't either," she said. "Maybe *this*?" And she made the finger gesture again.

"Your skin is too dark. And your hair, too—"

"Too brazen?" she finished for him. "Yes, of course, go on. Speak. You're a pale-skinned *gazhig* whose whoring mother shared a nest with a featherless crow. And when convenient, you pretend not to understand or hear what I say. . . . Well, listen to this, or ignore me if you like: I plan to kill him—this so beloved warrior of yours—at the first opportunity. Just before I kill your God *Trei*."

Silence. It came to Iliss suddenly that, for the first time since she had spoken, this was too much.

Most of these people did not understand the language of the Plains, nor the gestures. It was the word "*Trei*" itself, her intensity, and her way of spitting it out, that made them sense something dark in her intent. However, there were several that understood.

And then, slowly, recovering from the sickness of her meaning, they began to speak, to raise their voices. The room was in turmoil.

Veddr's voice sounded, and then again came uneasy silence.

And Waevan turned to her, dark-faced, and said, "No one will take you now, wicked chattel. You have spoken like a mad one, words of blasphemy."

She shrugged. "Your God is doomed. Doom-doom-doom," she said, and grinned. "*Trei, Trei, Trei.*"

They looked at her in horror, while her mind embarked on a dizzying flight in the great empty skies, and she loved every instant of it.

"Why don't you kill me?" she said. "You kill all others. You come to our plains and you . . . kill."

"The insane are in the Hands of the Gods . . ." Waevan whispered. "No one shall touch you, madwoman."

"Rather, the Gods are in the hands of the insane, see!" And she laughed and waved her hands about, making the obscene gesture for the third time.

The Gowirak began leaving the room. Before he left, Gavvar threw her one peculiar glance. She saw lust in it. Veddr, shaking his old head, muttered something to Waevan before stepping out in the wake of his wife.

When all had gone, Waevan turned to Iliss with his expressionless blank face, saying, "I should indeed kill you now. You have shamed me before the village."

"And what of your Gods? I am in their Hands." She smiled.

"I care for none . . ." came his suddenly harsh whisper, and he leaned close, staring into her eyes, never blinking. And still there was no emotion in him. The licking flames danced in his pale irises.

There was a long pause. And then, what he said next made Iliss' skin suddenly prickle, as a remote true fear came to her.

"Listen, mad one . . ." Waevan spoke, violet shadows on flaxen hair, glass eyes. "You intend to kill *Trei*. Yes, I can see it in you. Mad you are, and it is impossible. Yet, of all things . . . of all things, the Slaying of a God may be done, if at all, then by one who is insane. You shall kill *Him* who is Winter. . . . And I—I, too bear a grudge against the Cold One. I, of all men, shall help you."

Iliss awoke to cold. It cut her like a bared nerve, the sense of weakling dawn, freezing cold in her nostrils, and a haunting monochrome whiteness that seeped in slowly from the outside. She lay in the pile of furs, unrestrained, and still nude, lay against another cold body, which she recognized as the man Waevan.

White skin, large rough features, carved like fjords of ice. And yet, he was like a young boy, a child asleep before her. And he had not touched her. She remembered vaguely how he had come in the night, silent, and bedded next to her in the furs as though she herself was but a dead animal skin.

And then, it must have been her steady observation of his still form that woke him up. He inhaled the deep awakening drought, and then turned to meet her direct gaze.

Iliss continued staring at him, insolent like a wolf.

"What do you see, woman?" he asked, simple from sleep.

"You," she said. "Wolf-killer who beats strangers. Did my presence here make your dreams darker than they already are? I hope you squirmed and dreamt of the wicked pitch-black night."

To her surprise, and for the first time, Waevan laughed. The sound was soft, more gentle than she could have imagined from someone his size. And then he spoke, and again there was remote strangeness in his voice. "How do you know my dreams? How do you know if they are like your bottomless Southern night, or if they are like the Northern Rainbow?"

"Oh, I know. They're like fresh cow dung . . ." grumbled Iliss, and then quickly got up, fur draped loosely about her, and started to do a shivering stomping-dance in place. She herself was blue from the cold.

"If you were one of our own women, you'd have fed the fire through the night," Waevan said, more like a sad statement of fact, throwing a look at the dead fire-pit.

"But I'm not," Iliss said with derision. She turned on him, a pallid wrathful spirit in the gray dawn, and was cold, sharp with intensity. "Well, my master Waevan, a new day is here, while a certain God still walks the face of the land."

He looked up at her, again appearing to misunderstand, a vagueness in his gaze. "Breakfast is eaten downstairs," he said. "Come and meet my kin."

"What, you expect me to walk naked?" she said. "Give me my clothes back. Or else, I will indeed show them all. *Trei!*"

In the room below, Iliss ate a meal with Waevan and four others. Ulav was there, turning out to be his old mother. There was also the younger man whom she recognized from the night before as the one who had watched her with sympathy. He was Waylak, younger brother of Waevan. And here was the boy of no more than ten summers, Vati, together with his smaller brother, Daiva, both Waevan's sons. Vati was the one whom she had attempted to save from the wolves, and now he sat glaring at her.

Eating in silence they all watched her, cautious—except for Waylak, who smiled once and greeted her with awkward words in her own language of the Plains. This was a surprise—which of course she did not show, but stared back at him briefly, like a glacier. Ulav nodded grudgingly, still appearing to resent her, and placed before her a steaming bowl.

"Today we will be going hunting," Waevan announced after long moments, repeating it in his own tongue. He ate without looking at anyone, and his voice was strong, and yet remote.

Ulav paused eating. She said something in the Gowirak language. Even Waylak and the boys appeared startled.

"It is not a season to hunt anything," explained Waevan, throwing a gaze of sightless eyes in Iliss' direction. "They do not understand why I want to hunt now. I will tell them I must hunt for something. And since this is my house, I need not explain my actions."

Iliss nodded, her eyes lowered to the food before her. "When do we begin?" was all she said, in a soft voice.

"I go too," said Waylak suddenly. His accent in the Plains-tongue was even worse than his brother's.

Waevan replied in Gowirak, and she could tell by his tone that he was displeased.

To her even greater surprise, Waylak turned directly to Iliss. "Woman, you are his wife now, tell my brother I too want to go!"

"You are quite wrong," she said, one brow rising. "I am not his wife. I am not his chattel. I am not even his friend. However, we go to *hunt*, together. Or else, I go alone. While you—whether you come along is not my business."

Waylak was shocked into silence. But then, Waevan said impassively, "Well. Come along then, brother, come along with us."

And that was that.

In the South, there is much legendary lore woven about the art
of the Northern Hunt. They speak of the raw skill, the barbaric
strength of the Northsmen, the terrible enemy that they make.
They craft tales of ice-lit Northern lands, and the stalking
warriors who can read animal tracks of gossamer lightness in the
snow, even after a new snowfall comes to obscure them. No
beast escapes, for they can track even his shadow. Their
relentless hunt even extends into the southerly Northern Forests
of evergreen, bordering the tundra. . . .

Iliss remembered those Southern tales when they set out.
She wore a man's Northern clothing, and carried her knife. It
was interesting that Waevan allowed her this much, in his blunt
indifference. Between them lay a wordless temporary
understanding that they would both cooperate until they
achieved their mutual, secret, deadly goal.

Waylak and Waevan sat before her in a large sled, the
likes of which she had not seen, long and intricate, placed atop
wooden needle-rails, and driven by a pack of dogs twice the
number of her own small pack. She, together with the supplies,
sat behind them. Her place in the rear of the sled was a sheltered
nook that, she supposed, was reserved for the likes of "women-
chattel" like her, and that would serve as warm tight bedding
overnight. And she did not care.

Iliss was in her customary dark temper. She hummed a
little children's song the words of which she had turned around
and made adult—obscene, some would say, or maybe only very
sad. It was all about broken innocence and death and war. It
rushed like the wind in her mind.

The air was crisp and dry and sharp as sunlight over ice.
As they flew over curving ice-dunes of the tundra toward the
unknown, their faces almost swallowed by garments of fur, the
beauty of this North, of this striking glorious place almost

touched Iliss. For a second only, it scratched at the armor of her heart's outer door. And then once more, she knew only the icy haze of sunlight and the humming wind.

Somewhere ahead, was the enemy. *Trei*, the abomination, walked the land.

"We may ride far," Waylak cried to her from up ahead, wind singing at his back and cutting at his every word. "My elder brother does not say where we go, only that we hunt. And I obey his wisdom."

In answer, she sulked, and said nothing to the kind brother. And thus they rode through endless expanses of white light, and the sun rode low at their back.

The land stretched barren with snow. Occasionally there were clumps of evergreen, and even more rare, trees of pine and fir, amid exposed rock. Once there was a shadow over them, quick and violent, and she again saw the Northern bird, *sirnak*, brother to the eagle of her native Plains, circling the sky. Otherwise, there were no signs of life.

"How much longer?" she ventured at last.

Waevan almost did not answer. "Soon," he said after a pause, looking in the face of the wind.

"Where do we really go, brother?" Waylak again tried. "If I knew, I might be of some help."

"We go North. As far as it takes us. Where there is Mother-of-Pearl in the sky. . . ."

"To the land of Gods!" Iliss said.

And at her words, Waylak showed pain, and he bent his head sadly. "I was afraid of that, brother, that is why I came along. And now my fears are justified. This woman's madness has tainted you also, and her words of blasphemy awakened your heart to the old anger. . . ."

And then Waylak turned back to Iliss, saying, "My brother's wife was taken from him by the will of *Trei* Who is Winter. Treiga bore the name of the God, but He did nothing to protect her when the Ice Winds came. As she slipped into death, there were no prayers that would bring her back. And Waevan my brother went mad from sorrow, all that Winter, until the snows receded in the Spring. He had cursed the God and sworn revenge, until there was no more pain left but hollow silence which he then bore for three Winters. And now he was almost free of the dark. Until you brought it back."

"No! She comes as a sign of the Gods, brother!" Waevan cried then. "Don't you see, she comes because it must be done! She will be the one to assist me—"

"Assist you?" Iliss began. And then she said nothing more, but thought, *If I must, I will fight you before the God for the privilege of destruction.*

"Then you are both insane," Waylak said, his eyes tragic. "But I am responsible for you, my brother, my closest of kin, and I will be at your side. Only—you will never find a God unless it is fate indeed, unless a God is willing."

"Will *Trei* run and hide from me?" whispered Iliss. "Not so. I will follow until there is no more North in North, until I run into the face of the sun, or of night."

"Soon, woman . . ." Waevan said. "We will have what we both must have, and we will touch the Northern Rainbow."

But Waylak's next words made them both alert like razors. Turning back to the trail that they left behind, Waylak pointed out a fleeting speck of blackness, trailing like a far-off star behind them. "We are being followed," he said. "And the pursuer has been behind us since the beginning of the trip."

They stopped to eat and sleep, when the crescent of the sun came to barely skim the horizon. The Northern sun never truly rose or set, knew Iliss, but in her wildness of heart, she had not kept proper track of the seasons, and was not sure if it was true Summer or Winter. It mattered little to her single-minded purpose.

"Who follows us?" Waevan said, as he fed the dog pack. "I don't understand."

"I know who," Waylak said. "It must be Gavvar. He is a bright warrior, brother. But what you never noticed all these seasons of blind sorrow, is that he had always wanted to be like you, always wanted to have what had simply been yours. And now he lusts for this woman."

"Well then," said Waevan softly. "He will come upon us soon, to make a challenge here in the wilderness, and I must be ready for him."

"You?" Iliss snorted. "I would think it is my own concern to handle this one. . . ."

"And if he kills you, who would be left to destroy *Trei?*" Waevan mocked her.

"If he kills me," she replied, "I will leave that duty to you."

Thus, they waited. And then they slept fitfully through the night, huddled together in the shelter of the sled, keeping sporadic watch.

Iliss did not care if the very stars fell out of the sky overnight, cared even less if someone came upon them or not in the darkness, and slept through her own watch. If he had any honor, Gavvar would not touch them in the night.

And she was right. When it was dawn, a man-shape greeted them with a loud voice of challenge, and there was barking of the dogs.

Before Waevan was even on his feet, Iliss stepped forth, free of the fur *shuba*, to facilitate her movements, icy wind swinging her dirty copper-brown long hair into a thorn-tangle about her tanned face. In her hand was a long knife.

It was indeed Gavvar, clad in rich furs, striding toward them. She saw a glimmer of water-pale eyes that glanced her way intensely. And then the man haughtily ignored her, looked past her toward Waevan, and made his challenge.

Voices were mingled on the wind with the barking of the two dog packs as they strained to fight, like their masters strained.

"I have made my will known before the Eldest, before all Gowirak," Gavvar said in her own broken language, so that she too would know his intent. "And again I claim this woman, mad or not."

"Then speak to my face, *gazhig*, address me, not this one!" Iliss exclaimed, stepping to block his way.

From behind, Waevan's voice was low, apathetic. "I have no claims on this woman, Gavvar. But we are on a hunt now, on the most important hunt of our life, and to tell you the truth, you waste our time with this nonsense. Go back to the village, young buck, and when we return, make your claim then."

"No, Waevan. She comes with me, now. Fight me, if you are man enough! I have waited long for this moment. . . ."

Waylak arose on the other side. "Gavvar," he said quietly. "What foolery is this? If you challenge my brother, you must challenge me also—"

"Be silent," Waevan said to his brother. And he came forward, carrying his own great axe, stopping next to Iliss to whisper harshly, "Out of my way, woman. . . ."

Iliss gave him a long silent look. And then, like a bolt of lightning, her right hand swung, and her fist connected with his temple. So swift was she in landing the strong accurate punch, so unexpected her action, that Waevan did not even make a whimper as his giant form crumpled onto the snow.

"Don't!" she cried at Waylak whose first reflex was to come at her. "Or you'll join your brother on the ground. Rather, be kind enough to get him out of the way."

And then she turned her attention to Gavvar. "Now," she repeated, and this time was not ignored, "you will address *me*."

Gavvar's eyes filled with fury. He lunged at her in a manner that was uncertain, still full of surprise, so it was easy to avoid him. Iliss was well versed in hand combat, and as she slid away, she also managed to twist his great tall frame, and made him fall on the ground.

Gavvar sprung back with lightness, suddenly fierce, and no longer careless. "I will make you pay for this shame, woman," he hissed. "I wanted to have you in honor, but now I will have you here, right on the snow. . . . And when I'm done with you, I will carve you open—"

But Iliss sprung at him with an inhuman cry of hate, and rabid eyes. Without the furs she was blue from the cold, but quicker by far, and was made even stronger by the urgency of her heart.

One second they danced the warrior stance, circling in the snow, the next they were a mass of movement, and the next, Iliss plunged her long knife into the man's only exposed part, the vulnerable throat.

She killed him with a sobbing growl of fury, and twisted the knife in place. She watched with her own incandescent gaze the agony in his water-pale eyes, the moment of disbelief, the shock, and finally something else, remote and alien, a welling of moisture. His eyes cried, not stoic at the last moment—cried silently, as a young life was extinguished.

She wiped the knife in the snow, stood up, her expression like the night. Waylak had been frozen all this time, not interfering, horrified, watching her from his dazed brother's side. And only when she finally turned her eyes to meet his, he ventured to speak.

"There was no need to kill him . . . like that," he said. "You could have knocked him out, like Waevan. And we would've been safely on our way." He paused. "Woman. There will now be an old heartbroken mother, back in our village. Gavvar was too young. You didn't have to kill him."

Iliss looked at Waylak grimly. And then she smiled.

"But I wanted to kill him," she said. "He stood in my way. And—I just wanted to see if his dying face was like my own brother's. You Northsmen killed my family. I am finally paying back."

"Then I am sorry for you . . ." said Waylak. And he did not meet her eyes again.

They traveled, driven, without pause, for two full days. When Waevan came around, rubbing his aching head, he only nodded at her, saying, "A blow for a blow, that makes us even." Only, there was a different expression in his eyes, a kind of remote appraisal that was a mixture of anger and acknowledgement. Before continuing, the two brothers laid out the dead man on his own sled, covered him, and bade the trained dogs return to the Gowirak settlement. As they worked, they threw occasional strange glances at Iliss, which she chose to ignore.

At dawn of the third day, they saw the Northern Rainbow.

The sky was a dark glorious cupola of colored lights, and the sun floated on the horizon, lending glitter to the hollow great expanse. The land had become bare of all but the whiteness, and there were no more tracks of beasts of any kind.

Waylak looked around in awe, and spoke softer than usual. "Tread softly, my poor brother, for here it is. The Land of the Gods. . . ."

"I know," responded Waevan. "The Lights in the sky are Windows to their Silver Halls. . . ."

And Iliss noticed at last that there was something different about this man Waevan. Imperceptibly, over the last several days, he had changed. It was a gradual change like moving ice. He seemed to come awake from an old dream, and, unlike her, harbored a regret.

"Must you go on?" Waylak said. "I fear, my brother. I truly fear now. This place is sacred somehow. And we bring with us a taint. . . ."

In answer, Waevan only frowned and glanced at Iliss.

"You . . . need not go on," she said, for the first time in earnest.

"Neither must you," Waevan said. And he looked in her eyes.

But Iliss ignored his meaning, smirked, and turned her eyes away. "Having come this far, you may wait for me here—if you like. I may not come back. You may return to your Gowirak hole. Or you may dissolve into the sky, for all I care. While I go on alone to meet *Trei*."

Waylak cast his gaze down, while Waevan said tiredly, "Then go, woman. I set you free. I will not go with you, for my own hate has at last burned out."

In the heart of the North, Iliss stood alone. The twilight-day sky domed above her, while the sun touched the rim, and the Northern Rainbow glowed.

She stood, raising her head to the sky, and opened her mind.

I am here, Trei. *I have come at last.*

Silence.

And then she saw *His* shadow cast upon the ice. A great fur-shape, a Northern beast as great as half the sky, shimmered in the air before her, and a Voice sounded in her temples.

To the death . . .

The White Bear growled like thunder, and came upon her, while the North winds screamed.

But Iliss fought back, larger than life, in a fury of hate, like a Southern maelstrom of burning darkness. She grasped the Fur of the Bear, touching glaciers of ice, and slashed with her dull gray steel. And the blood of the Bear came forth like water. . . . And the eyes of the Bear, water-pale, cried wordlessly as *He* dissolved before her.

Iliss withdrew her knife and blinked. But there was only the surrounding whiteness and the Bear was gone, while the canker of hate in her heart still burned, the same as before.

Like a bear herself, she howled her frustration to the sky, and the emptiness answered in echoes.

And then a Howl came in answer, a chorus of all winds, from behind, and she whirled around to see *Him* again, this time a great silver Wolf.

The Wolf bounded down the sky, gathering solidity as it neared her. It stopped an instant before her. Intelligent burning eyes, so familiar—hunter and victim. And then it pounced.

Iliss dropped her knife, and used her bare hands to grasp the vulnerable part of *Him*, the throat. And then, with all the strength of her, she tightened her fingers, and squeezed. . . .

She thought she saw traces of a burning Southern village, the crackle of flames. And in her mind's eye she saw all her dead. And her sister, Naiass, with shattered bottomless eyes. . . .

There was a sound like the breaking of bones, and the neck of the Wolf snapped. And as *He* too became vaporous, *He* gifted her with a look of intensity and sorrow.

Again, silence. And all around, the white. A burning hole of emptiness in her soul.

Damn you, Trei! *Why?!* she cried to the skies. *Why must I have no peace even now? I have slain you twice!*

And then the Voice came softly to whisper at her ear:
You must slay me for the third time. . . .

The Northern bird, a great sun-white *sirnak*, dropped out of the sky and landed on the ice-whiteness before her. The Bird folded its wings, and sat regarding her out of its one beautiful piercing eye.

Come . . . said the Voice. *Slay me now, for the last time. And you will be free.*

And yet the Bird did not move, but watched her. Suddenly vacant, glassy eyes. It waited.

Iliss could not move. Indeed, as she stood there, she realized that she could not bring herself to move; something inside prevented her.

The God was there, before her. The Bird sat helplessly on the snow.

In the sky danced the Northern Rainbow.

And Iliss released a long tense breath, with it releasing *something* that had been with her for a long, long time. Out of her soul's pale lungs into her heart's dark gut it moved, churning. . . .

Fading from black to gray smoke, to nothing.

She bent down then, and gathered a handful of crystalline whiteness in her hands, shaping it into a ball. And when the ball was well formed, she took careful aim and threw it at the Bird.

Her throw was gentle, a light toss. And yet, when the snow came to scatter on the white plumage of the Bird, there came an aftershock of light, so bright that it echoed across the sky and resounded in the Northern Lights.

Like a whisper, the Bird was gone. And in *His* place stood a translucent figure of a Man.

The God, *Trei.*

And Iliss looked at *Him* fully, and she heard *His* Voice.

You have slain me three times over, Daughter of South. And the final killing took away the final hate. Now I grant you that which has driven you to me.

"That which has driven me . . ." she echoed.

Your sister's mind. Your own mind. I release you all from the Winter Ice.

And the God came forward, bathing her in the Rainbow aura, and enveloped her in arms of light. And *Trei* kissed her on the face, and on the forehead, and on the eyes.

Know this, said the God. *It is not I who sends death to your kin. It never is. North and South, you all destroy yourselves. And with each killing stroke of the axe, or sword, or arrow, you slay me also. Over and over, a million times. And for each beast that runs or crawls, for each bird that soars, I too feel the moment of their slaughter. Each skin cries out to me, until I can no longer hear the Wind or the Sun for their clamoring cries. . . . For I am a part of you all, a part of your passing, and will always be. I am the World's Winter.*

"I see now . . ." Iliss said. "I remember seeing You looking at me from out of the eyes of the dying. . . . That wolf, those animal furs, the Northsmen, my brother too. . . . It was You I saw, Your name I heard, but I did not understand it then. I saw You and believed You to be the cause. While all along You were but dying with them. . . . Forgive me, *Trei.*"

Forgive yourself, said the God. And in the blink of an eye, *He* vanished. Iliss knew this time *He* would not return, ever.

And Iliss stood free, beneath the Northern Rainbow.

"You may stay here at Gowirak, if you like, woman," Waevan said, watching her expression. Searching for something. Former madness?

Iliss was tired. She looked at him with her direct clear gaze. "I have killed *Trei* thrice over, and this is all you have to say to me?"

Waevan's mouth strained to hold back the ember of a smile.

But her next words drowned his budding warmth, replacing it with inner regret.

"I cannot—friend," Iliss said. "I must return and see something for myself. Return South, to my own Plains. There, I must look into my sad sister's face. To see for myself if the God spoke true, and if indeed Naiass no longer has Winter in her eyes. . . ."

For the first time in a long time, the world that Iliss was seeing blurred. In her eyes was a thaw, rising water.

"And then, maybe—" she continued. "Ah, by Gods, who knows? I might want to venture to the farthest South of Souths, where the other Gods dwell. And there I may witness the Birth of Summer."

SUN, IN ITS COPPER SEASON

The ageless young woman reposes upon a settee of gossamer silk, propped up by pillows and fanned by servants.

She is ancient, really, despite smooth skin and clear eyes. She has been here always and there is no record of her arriving, or even beginning. She has not sprung forth and she has not been engendered. For her, such a condition has no meaning.

When the woman sleeps, so does the world; so do we, you and I. When she wakes, the sun floats up from the rim of the horizon. It happens exactly as her eyelids rise, fringed by soft colorless lashes. One is cause, the other, effect. Eyelids, sun.

The woman is mostly silent. She spends her waking moments staring into an incalculable distance of internal space with vacant eyes, and replies in a soft voice when spoken to. But she never begins a conversation with those who serve her, never makes demands; never initiates, only responds.

They scuttle around her like insects, coming and going, bringing her fresh linen and silk, ripe fruits upon gilded plates which she absentmindedly takes and suckles as a child would feed upon a mother's teat. Juices of the fruit run down her pale skin, but she pays no notice, and so the servants who attend her must periodically wipe her chin with steaming cloth.

Her throat is dry and she wets it from a goblet of antique metal upon which are rendered in relief warriors and lovers and godlike beasts, running along the circumference, woven into each other as leaves of a vine. Thus, tiny metallic lovers beget beasts which in turn beget warriors, who sweeten into lovers, cycling unto eternity. Inside the goblet there is only well water, cool and pure, for the servants have learned over the years that she will drink no wine, no spirits or brew, no squeezed or fermented life-blood of tree or beast. She is austere in her needs. And yet, intricate records of her needs are kept in neat volumes bound in thick bejeweled leather, and the servants refer to them when in doubt.

The woman, when awake, sits upright upon the settee, then reposes on one side or the other, and sometimes stands up to walk in a smooth gliding manner across the great hall. She is silence upon marble as she makes her way down the myriad stairs and into the gardens outside, while the sun beats upon her pallid flaxen head of hair, unadorned and simple like her skin.

Hours might pass as she stands with her face in the wind, folds of fabric pressing to define her slender maidenly shape, her eyes unresponsive to the sun's glare and never slitted as with a normal woman or man. Eyes are changeable; they are often without centers, like pieces of flawed glass containing nebulae of murk and cloudy matter interspersed with translucence.

The servants eventually touch her arms and gently lead her back. It is usually when the sun begins the second portion of its westerly journey and shadows slant and lengthen upon the ground into stick giants.

Her repast is once again wholesome and simple, fruit and fresh loaves of barely-sweetened wheat, and handfuls of nuts. She eats no flesh of any animate creature, beast, fowl or fish, no meat of the living. More than once over the crawl of decades the servants might test her desires and offer her roasted flesh steeped in piquant spices, but she seems to know its cadaverous nature without tasting, and moves her head in impassive refusal.

The woman is led twice each day to a bathing chamber, where she is disrobed like a child and made to enter a warm wading pool that rises only to her waist. Seated upon smooth carved stone in the center, she grows still but not somnolent, a carved marble bust rising out of the liquid. The bottoms of her small but prominent breasts quiver over the surface of the water which speeds outward in concentric circles underneath each breast at every breath-caused movement, while her pale almost cream-gold-white hair is let down. The hair sinks, unfurls like seaweed in the water, creating more dissonant ripples, and the servants attend to it and to her skin which never shows evidence of sweat or seems to need cleansing, but which is cleansed twice daily nevertheless, until the woman is as pristine as the marble upon which she sits.

When the morning bath is done, the woman returns to the great hall or the gardens. And if it is the evening bath, she is led forth with much ceremony and a procession of scented candles to the chamber of sleep which contains her grand bed.

The bed fills the room's void and is a centerpiece. The chamber's cathedral ceiling is pointed into a pyramid needle at its apex. There are windows near the top of each wall, displaying the darkening sky and the emerging stars. They are visible to her only as she lies, watching the space overhead, focusing upon the receding high point of the ceiling, and allowing herself the stillness of oblivion which encompasses the world.

But first, long before the eyelids close and the sun is released to depart, there is ceremony.

Candles are carried in by the procession of maids, servants, personal attendants, and those apprenticed to the serving staff unto a third generation of servitude, and deposited in the room, everywhere, upon each flat surface, until the chamber is bathed in soft glowing light and it seems they are all afloat within the sphere of the sun itself, so bright is the place. After the light warms the air with scent of dried forest—for each candle is a cornucopia of different flowers and pine sap and obscure lesser herbs, all sending up their faint secret essences into an aerial union, mingling only in their extinction—after the air is charged thus, the servants commence the task of unraveling the layers of bed coverings.

They remove brocade and silk and flax and cobweb-fine translucent coverlets, throwing them up to soak in the scent and the warm glow. When the softest inner sheets are revealed, the woman is led into the chamber. She steps upon a footrest; her robe is taken from her. Nude and blush-on-lily-white, still fevered from the bath, she sits, then sinks slowly into the bed, with her hair falling around her in wet filaments, strong and resilient like freshly watered summer grass.

The servants begin to cocoon her, fluttering sheets and gossamer and butterfly-wing softness everywhere, drenched in the maddening essence of forest. As each layer falls, other servants stand waiting, pliant; each of them waits their turn to extinguish a candle with a single breath, one flame per moment. One at a time the candles die, so that the gold glow is barely diminished and the light fades in an infinite gradation of loss, as down yields to water—gentle yet selfsame and unaffected in essence.

As the light departs, the room gains indigo. It presses down from on high, deepening mist with rich hues carrying shadows. And at last, when only a handful of candles glow, soft incense-drenched smoke rises from the sea of extinguished wicks to mingle with the heavy somnolence in the air. The final brocade coverlet is pulled up and swept to curl against her chest, and the woman lies still, gazing into the overhead expanse.

Servants stand back, exit in catlike silence, and the last candles are extinguished.

Now that candlelight leaves the chamber, the tall windows near the ceiling come into prominence. They ring, it seems, in the sudden fullness of light; they glow with sunset, their smooth unstained glass shards reflecting gold and rose, or maybe violent crimson through the metal mesh grill mosaic that binds the pieces.

She is alone.

The woman lies motionless, sometimes exactly as she had been placed, her hands resting softly against her chest, or swept up to lie against the softness of her pillow, brushing against her cheek.

She takes breaths, deep, even, ever-lightening. Her eyes are wide-open pieces of glass in the twilight of the room.

One more breath of thick forest, of burnt grasses and flowers and candle smoke, already dissipating.

Another breath, of indigo and blue.

The ceiling above her is a point into which all lines flow. Lines of wall converge, and disappear into the microscopic heart of nothing, receding inward, rushing, falling.

She too is falling, focused; becomes a line, then a point. She recedes inward, into herself, and the world recedes from her.

With eternity approaching to engulf, her eyelids come down at last.

And in the same breath, outside, the sun is gone.

It is night; her night.

The woman sleeps.

A t first glance, the routine is unchanged. She surfaces out of the sleep darkness and with her first deep intake of breath, pale slate dawn touches the eastern horizon. She continues to breathe, stirs gently, stretches, and as her lids flutter, the dawn turns metallic mauve, then gilded rose. Shadows in the room around her recede to the corners and blue drowns in pallor. When she opens her eyes, the windows once again brim with the hues of the approaching sun.

The routine is unchanged on the surface of the living mask, and yet, in all things there is only change, as the world knows. A breath that is taken is the same yet different in each taking. Each day, each night is unique; indeed the cycle consists of unique moments and the only anomaly is the possibility of any moment being the *same* as the last.

One such unique silver-pale morning of the many silver or radiant gold or subdued or exuberant mornings, with clouds poured over the sky and fading out the sun overhead, the woman sits in the garden. She is silent and her face is a dream, and yet, as the servants attend her—today of all days the king is here to observe her and the ceremony must be even more pristine for his sake—today the most observant of them see an enhancement in the fine quality of her stillness.

To say the woman is often as a statue is to give a statue the benefit of a human animus. The woman is infinitely more still and stonelike than stone itself, for in her stillness she incorporates all her surroundings—stone, garden, the breeze blowing with humid warmth, sunless overcast sky, the world. She is greater than all of these and contains not only a single human animus but the billowing life force of the world. And in this, she is lesser than any one inanimate object, for she is fundamentally not *one*. The woman is a mortal woman's shell containing something else.

And this morning the shell contains either less or more, depending on how one looks at it; it is stiller than stone and quieter than the sum of a statue's marble pores. It is vast in its barren void, as though her internal form has somehow unfurled into the next stage of finer intricacy, opening great previously non-existent spaces that are now vacant and require to be filled.

The king approaches and stands before her, curious and youthful in his vigor, confident in his sovereignty. Youthful, and yet already he is embarked upon the declining nether slope of a man's years. He observes, as always, as he has observed for many years of his rule, how the woman sits and breathes and looks out and through him with eyes of tainted glass upon the gardens—or palace hall, or bed chamber—all and any of the places gifted to her by the kings of antiquity, for she was here long before any of them, and they could do no less than honor her, as he does now in his turn.

The question is asked, as always, "Is she satisfied?"

Her answer comes after a short pause of breath, and as always it is the same, faint "Yes." The notion of satisfaction is outside her bouquet of experience, but she must always acknowledge their effort and intent.

All is well; all is as should be. And yet the king senses something new in this woman-statue's pores, possibly this minutely different quality of her silence; always she secretes it, her peculiar aural sweat. He senses the lack of it this time, the indescribable absence; senses it with his own body, and not quite with his conscious mind, and for that reason pays no attention to himself—not yet.

When the audience is done—as always it is unclear whether he attends her or she attends him—the king departs and she, in her grand palatial estate of ancient honor, is forgotten in the morass of his other regular concerns of state.

But the woman continues being new. She is fed by servants, according to the book of her needs, and she takes very little this day, it seems—this morning and then later this day. Even less enthusiasm is shown for her simple meal than usual, and she barely chews and swallows delicately pungent chunks of warm freshly sautéed vegetables, and occupies herself by dragging a crusty corner slice of bread against the sauce. She watches it leave streaks upon the plate, which all culminates in a floury collapse into a snow-storm of crumbs. Then she does not move or raise a finger to wipe the tiny droplets of the afternoon rain as it begins to come down in the gardens.

The woman is led inside, and as she enters, stepping across the threshold, she turns momentarily, and her gaze is like a flitter of a lost bird. Her eyes fill with something vaguely

unbalanced, an inconclusive emotion. It is all gone in a blink—
as though she momentarily reaches out and searches for
something not there and then relapses to the receptive apathy of
herself—and she continues into the grand hall and the rest of her
afternoon.

Some of the servants notice this hesitation, this questing,
this faltering. One maid in attendance frowns briefly to herself,
wondering. Another looks behind them furtively, also seeking
with her gaze anything suspicious, anything out of the ordinary
out there past the occasional fat raindrops.

The third, most astute of the three, notices a man walking
away in the distance along one of the gravel paths. She pauses—
for he is only a receding speck, a drop of sky water himself—
and she thinks. From this distance he is no one she recognizes by
sight; neither a gardener nor a caretaker, nor a servant in
attendance. Possibly he could be a guard, one of those newly
assigned by the king. He could be a messenger or a vendor or a
complete stranger who took the daring opportunity to take a
walk on the woman's personal estate grounds and savor the air
of her reclusive gardens.

All the maid knows is that he walks with a straight back
and at a steady unhurried pace, and his hair glimmers at times
like burned wheat while at others it is burnished rust. At least
this is what she whispers to another servant that afternoon with a
lurid smile and a secret palm held against her mouth.

None of this is a concern, of course, or a point of
significance, for while the woman has an infinite array of maids
who gossip and speculate about her unfathomable nature and its
habits and peculiarities, she is uniformly held in the highest
regard by the serving staff, a regard close to awe.

Thus, the words of this one maid, who, as the afternoon
wears on, very likely suggests in some innocence, in simple
humor, that the woman they all serve has at last seen an
irresistible handsome man and no doubt can no longer eat or

think or *sleep* and will now pine away with emotion for him—
the words of this maid are nonsense, and taken as such.

And yet, it is a curious coincidence that the nonsense of
one serves to parallel the reality of another.

Because when the time comes for the fall of evening, and
the bath is drawn and the ceremony and ritual is concluded (with
the maid being one of the usual participants, doing her common
part to blow out a golden candle), the woman lies at last in her
grand bed in her chamber with its needle-sharp up-swept ceiling,
and she observes the seething twilight and the expectant death
throes of the sun through shards of window glass set in metal
filigree, and she looks and looks and cannot stop.

Her eyelids. They are incapable of lowering and staying
closed for more than a blink—no matter the thick drowsy smoke
and incense suffusing the air—and flutter up immediately as
something assails her, so that her eyes glimmer with moisture in
the blue and indigo, dilated and fierce and altogether wild, for
she is burning with a fever of thought. No peace comes within
moments, minutes, hours. No soft receding warmth to make her
heavy and waterlogged and receptive, capable of giving in,
letting go in the usual way. No narrowing of self into a
diminishing point of the mind-funnel; instead, the droning urge
of unresolved distress, something, something.

Receptivity is forgotten.

And while the sun snags upon the edges of the west, a
poor caught fly in the celestial cobweb, the world also waits, in
puzzlement.

Night will not come. They who live in the world
malinger and observe their timepieces—pounding pendulums of
grandfather clocks, running sand in the hourglasses turned over
and over in vain. Structures ring with ticking clockwork bursting
with coiled springs and gear-mounted mechanical movements
along clock faces displaying what should be deep hoary times of
darkness; under other circumstances they would be correct.

But not this day without end. Not this dark-less fevered night that is not.

All through this the woman continues staring, and her eyes strain, opened wide and terrible in a newness of need, of unresolved intent which is alien to her, and which is a form of agony.

She tosses among the soft linen and silk and mounds of malleable pillows; she is sunken in this supple, resilient, tender heart, a flower of newfound hell without release.

As long moments line up in a procession of futility, of shadow candles to be blown out and springing back into existence, of repeating movement and retreat in a perverse parody of rapid eye movement of dreams, the woman feels her forehead burn. It has been thus for some time, hot scalding skin, but she senses it now for the linen around her has grown so oppressive with her body's heat that she must throw it off.

Coverlets are pulled down, discarded; delicate fabric billows up and away, beyond the bed's shadow-obscured horizon, and slides over the precipice into the unknown that lies beyond the edge of the bed-world. Fabric sinks beyond the edges in a parody of the sun which does not. The woman turns, flings her arms overhead, pounds the pillows, scratches silk with fine delicate fingers that now resemble claws. She then rips what is left away from her, draws the fine laces around her throat and pulls, undoes knots that she had never once tied on her own, pulls, rips, shreds. . . .

Her diaphanous gossamer gown is in tatters, a mass of broken moth wings, and it slips around her flesh, bunching with the bedding, high over her pale thighs; is non-existent.

The woman moans, parts her lips with thirst for oblivion, becomes a snake of movement. She is turned over, and the line of hips and waist is a parabolic curve, a wave of motion, as she undulates.

Servants come into the bedchamber, solemn and terrified. They crowd around her, one by one, some offering fallen coverlets to her, others murmuring in soothing voices filled with stifled distress.

"No!" she cries, sitting up suddenly. Her hair falls about her, tangled, a loose skein. She is flushed, and overhead the windows pulse with unrelenting eternal sunset.

She gathers herself in a fœtal position, legs bunched up, hands clutching her feet, face tucked against her knees, while hair serves as a curtain.

"No," she says again, this time in a faint breath-whisper.

She is without sleep, and sleepless, she is a madwoman.

With her we are mad also, while in futility the sun beats the wings of its corona against the horizon.

The king is notified. But there is no need, for the king already knows, has known all through the unrelenting twilight of this false non-day-non-night, the endless unresolved sunset. The king stands on the balcony of his own distant bedchamber, resplendent and wistful, and considers the way the sun floats on the rim over the palace gardens that face west—the sun, a plump waterlogged persimmon in a bowl of sky cream.

The mechanisms that keep track of the hours tell him it is now just before dawn, or it should be. A passing flicker of thought comes, how is it that sunrise and sunset are so interchangeable; but then, no—dawn is crisp and cool in its austere quality of light, while sunset always ends in rich, warm, earthy sun-death. Cool-to-warm is the difference in the tonal quality between the two—rose to mauve, violet to indigo, yellow to amber. Sunrise and sunset are never the same and now, the king thinks, now is a mockery, for the sunset malingers in the wrong notch of the day's chronology.

The world has gone wrong.

Florid rumors flow and speed along from servant to maid to page to those outside the woman's estate. Only lovers are sleepless, only the grieving, the impatient, the needy, the wicked, the guilt-ridden, the ever-burning, the inspired, the cursed, the tormented. Only the weak, the ill, the insane, the dying. So many onlys.

Which of the above is she?

Is there yet another reason undiscussed, not yet conjectured?

The maid, who has seen the strange man walking away down the garden path, insists that he is the one tormenting the woman's imagination. The notion is curious and is considered, then spread via the lightning lines of gossip, moving out in concentric circles of wagging tongues into the depth of the world.

Meanwhile, as minutes and hours spill into day two of lingering faux sunset, while the woman cries out in her centerpiece bed, her sleepless flesh burning, lily turned to blood rose, all existence is disrupted and begins to feel the strange consequences.

Flowers, poised upon the brink of folding for the night, stand limp and wither with effort of holding still. Field crops are not fed the sun's light directly and there is no relief from the ambient warmth except in the long giant shadows that slant toward the east, behind all things. Beasts move about in restless somnolent worry and nervous birds flitter from the branches, unable to find a place of appropriate deep shadows to hide in, in order to have peace of night. They have not slept either, diurnal and nocturnal, their inner clocks suspended in an unnatural pause. Indeed, all living cycles are disrupted. If this continues, there will be further dissipation of life's most basic structures, followed by death.

The king meets with his close advisors, then with a council of the wise and educated and versed in the occult. He is told things which he digests, then he in turn speaks. The maid's rumor has reached here also, and a general order is issued to find the strange man and bring him before the court.

Meals are served as they wait. Elsewhere, the world attempts to sleep with the sun beating against the sky's edge. Curtains are drawn to create the illusion of night, and some are deceived into temporary peace and slumber. But the natural world has no curtains to be drawn—unless they be thunderclouds—and neither the king nor his wise advisors know of a way to control them to overcast the sky.

In the false second afternoon's third hour, a man is escorted by guard into the presence of the king. The man is not in his first youth but he is virile and he matches the description provided by the maid, for his hair is burnished rust running into wheat husk. Indeed, how is it that the maid can be certain of the details? For she had seen him from the back, walking at a considerable distance, with only his hair glinting. . . .

Yet the man is somehow determined to be the one and same.

The king begins to question him.

"What is your connection to her? How does she, a recluse, come to know you?"

The man looks up once, then replies in a gentle unaffected voice, his slate-gray eyes again lowered in simple humility before the king.

"I don't know. Nor can I imagine. . . ."

He is tall, and up-close the maid who kneels at the king's feet can only stare and grow warm with blush, for he is handsome beyond her imagining.

"Who are you?"

"A man."

"You are insolent! Who are you?"

"I am . . . no one of consequence. A traveler."

The king bristles at the humility and sees only contradiction. But he speaks as he knows he must.

"Traveler of no consequence, you now become someone of singular importance. You will be made presentable, and then you will be . . . presented. To her."

The stranger raises his face once more, this time in possible protest, or maybe only confusion. Lips part, but nothing comes forth, since nothing plausible can; only a light exhalation of breath.

In moments the audience is over—for each moment is now twice as precious as it had been only a mere day and a half ago—and the man with bright ruddy hair is taken to be cleansed, fed, manicured, and examined for physical defect. The results are deemed acceptable, fair even. And thus, he who is of no consequence, is taken to the ancient great estate in the same gardens in which he had strolled casually days ago, as witnessed by a maid. The maid in question never suspects the effect her moment of vision has on the fullness of fate.

The woman is sprawled amid soft crumpled bedding in the morass that is her bower. She has refused all food and drink and her skin is deeply flushed, while her chest rises and falls in a pattern of arcane illness.

The book of her needs—indeed, her refusals—lies propped upon an easel while several servants hover nearby, turning the saffron pages, looking inside as though it were a balm, a temple, a source of all answers. But there is no answer to sleeplessness; indeed, such has never been recorded. And yet they continue to shuffle through the text, slogging like tired students over the same material they have seen too many times already in preparation for the master's final test.

The stranger, now transformed into a groomed man of court, enters without a sound. He is accompanied by the king's guards but they fall back at the entrance, allowing him the illusion of intimacy.

And thus, he enters, his supple goatskin footwear silent upon the floor, his tunic sleeves of linen and vest of crushed velvet moving about him in tailored folds of perfect obedience. His hair, a brazen cap of copper glow.

Is it that copper hue which she first notices, as she turns her head side to side in mindless discomfort on overly soft pillows?

The woman pauses. She then grows still as a wild creature, frozen. Her eyes are fixed upon him, while servants stand away, then hurriedly retreat from the chamber.

"You . . ." she whispers. "Why, oh why did you come?"

He bows in reply, and in his expression there is a halting pause, a subtle veneer that suggests a lack of understanding and a lack of recognition.

"O woman . . . I am not sure. I don't—I cannot know you—"

"Oh, but you do, you do! Nay, you will. . . ."

She mutters, interrupting him, half rises from her reclining position, heedless of her nudity, and then sits up completely, curls into herself, pulling her knees up.

She raises her hand in a most natural childlike gesture and beckons, "Come."

He approaches.

"Touch me . . ."

"What?" he says.

"Here, lie by me and touch me. You must touch me and make me forget. . . . So that I can—remember."

But he stands before her, his head leaned to the side in semblance of uncertainty.

"Here," she insists. "Pleat my hair, braid it, untangle the strands. For I can feel each single strand, and they don't know it,

I can feel each one being tugged or set loose. The point of sensation beneath each hair rings in my mind and separates my thoughts."

And so he reaches forward and puts the long fingers of his artistic hand upon a lock of her hair, fallen like late summer hay. His touch is asexual, that of a creator testing new material. And yet it seems a warm autumn glow comes pouring from underneath his fingertips and her hair is now a few shades more ruddy instead of its usual sun-gold flax.

He touches her for long moments, then sits down at the tall bed and takes her nude fœtally-folded body and . . . unfolds it. Receptive, she falls open like a puppet, an unrolled handkerchief, and reposes against his chest with her back.

His hands lie austerely upon her arms and waist, holding her, then move gently, hands of a monk, over the rest of her, pausing along each convex and concave surface to encompass her outline and render it to memory.

Minutes flow and they grow still together, and then it seems there is no beginning nor end to their flesh. His expensive court clothing given by the king is taken off one piece at a time, and she in turn touches him along his exposed planes, places her long fingers like flower petals along his chest and back, draws locks of his hair into her palms and separates each filament to test whether he too can feel each one.

They lie against each other, sometimes moving, sometimes stilled like the seasons and the moments of the day— both in eternal motion and yet completely still when considered separately. The light of the infernal sunset outside the tall windows seems to take on a succession of warm hues, then cool, pulsing like a flame of a gas lamp.

Eventually he cradles her, lulling the woman into somnolent lassitude. She exhales once—her once-fevered body cooling into natural repose—releases a pent-up breath of long-needed peace, then sinks back into him. As his lips descend upon her slackening mouth in a gentle co-mingling softness, her eyelids flutter closed.

The next moment, night slams upon them all.

The world sleeps in darkness, for the sun has broken its tether at last.

The dawn comes with her shudder of in-drawn breath and opening eyes, and the unnatural morning rushes forth without any preliminaries, bursting, pulling the sun out of its netherworld into the here and now. The woman sits up, gasping, face still murky with shadows of oblivion, gray circles under her eyes. It has been a night of fierce unspeakable dreams, such as she has never had before, and she is worried out of the last one into stark wakefulness.

The man lies still asleep, limbs tangled with hers; nude and strong, faithful and reliable, he reposes at her side. His hair spills richly on the pillow, and she puts her fingers with fascination upon the nearest strands.

Her touch wakes him—yes, he too can feel each single filament—and his own eyes open. The first thing she sees is the blue of sky—changeable and not really a true color. He watches her, simple, perfectly open to her, and his lips are drawn into an immediate smile; a natural reflex. He then relaxes his mouth so that the smile departs for a moment of resumed control, but remains lurking in his sky-eyes, permanently. He watches her, warming her with the hidden light of the smile, for long drawn-out moments.

And then, he exhales, in regret. And as though the world senses something of it, the morning sun is overcast briefly by a rolling morass of slate-gray cloud.

"It is time," he says. "Time for me to go."

Her lips part in immediate agony, but only a breath comes forth instead of a torrent of words. "Why?" she whispers, controlling all the ocean of words, all things fighting to come out of her. "Why must you go?"

"You know why," he says.

She jumps up, sidles off the bed and stands before him, her sylvan sleek body ethereal in the semi-cloud illumination.

She looks down.

"It is only difficult to perform one's function when there are others like oneself . . . to *compare*. When there are no others, when you are alone, it is easy. It is *right*."

He nods. "It is so, as you say."

"We are alike, are we not, O man?"

He wants to smile again, then hides it firmly, ruthlessly this time. He will not slip up again.

"You make the days, while I string them together into weeks, months, seasons, years . . ." he says. "We are not meant to meet, for it disrupts our . . . function."

He pauses, drawing breath deep into himself, considering whether to say more or not. Then, continues.

"It is required that we forget. Things such as ourselves running in parallel alongside each other, never meeting, define the world's fabric."

She watches him, stilled. "There are," she says, "threads that sometimes bend, sagging like waves, in the pattern of a cobweb. Burdened by heavy dew. . . ."

"It is all my fault," he says. "I have passed through your gardens many a time before—times immeasurable. For I walk past you four times a cycle, each time bringing new colors of the season. . . . And I have never seen you, nor you noticed me, walking softer than silence."

"What happened?" she says. "This time, this one different time. Was it you or I who stumbled first?"

"This time I could not pass you by."

"No," she says, "It was I, who cast my gaze in your wake, and by seeing you when I should not have I have stumbled."

"Does it matter now?" he says. "There have been so many times when I wanted you to hear my footsteps. In the snow, or along the wind-stirred gravel kissed by your own sun. Upon fallen leaves, or sprouting shoots of new grass."

This time it is she who smiles.

"And you think I did not know it?"

He nods again.

They are both silent while their heartbeats retain an even strangely similar rhythm. He gets up then, and takes the linen, plainest of the garments that had been granted him, leaving the expensive velvet and goatskin behind; he would never use the sorry skin of a beast in any case, and indeed his feet will always be unshod as he walks, for he must feel the earth. . . .

She watches him, recording each of his movements inside her, while outside, her steady sun travels the eastern sky toward the distant west.

Before he exits, he looks at her once.

"You will sleep tonight," he says.

It is neither a question nor precisely a statement.

But she replies, "I will do as I always must."

"It will no longer be easy, as before," he says, and his eyes never meet hers.

"It will *be*."

She says this, knowing that it will never again be easy for him to walk his measured footfalls either. And that the next time he would walk by her garden, he might choose twilight or night as his moment of passing, so as not to tempt either one of them to stumble again.

She knows it is for the best. And yet, the weight of knowledge has settled upon her, and she is now loaded with it, impregnated with the awareness.

She is aware—her vast mind reeling—of the even more vast, impossible fullness of time.

As for him, the man walks out of the chamber, past the guards whose eyes are open with duty and vigilance and yet who miss his passing completely—as from now on they always must. And he is not seen by anyone ever again.

The woman takes a sobering breath and proceeds with her own manner of being, while the days and nights will now proceed into their proper gradual lengthening. The days and nights will march on, steady, as the falling and rising of her eyelids, each day a breath.

But somehow, autumn will linger unseasonably this year. Only once, only a season.

Autumn without peace.

LADY OF THE CASTLE

Ruricca NoOnesDaughter knelt on cold stone in the courtyard of Rainn Castle. Exceptional wind stung her eyes as she held the body of Lord Sedal Rainn in her arms.

The arrow had dropped from the sky, it seemed, guided by that mad wind, entering his unarmored breast, kissing his silk shirt with a point of steel, and leaving a rose of blood. No one had seen it coming.

Ruricca *heard* it—in her mind, it *scraped* against the air.

Thus, she had been the first to run to him when he cried out, the first to uphold him after he fell from his mount and lay in startled weakness on the cobblestones. She had moved faster than anyone, faster than the Lord's son. As a result, Lord Sedal's last words were directed to her before he died:

"You, who are at my side, in responsibility and mercy . . . you are the one who by law must hold the Castle."

Shocking words.

Kimre Rainn had come breathless, a minute too late, past the crowd of silent people gathered around the incident, and threw himself upon his father's body, sobbing in silence. His long ebony hair soaked up crimson where it touched his father's blood. And when he lifted his face to her, there was stark fury mixed with anguish. Apparently he knew very well what had been said to her, knew the tradition of his father and the father before him, and had always counted on being at his father's side on his deathbed.

And now, his birthright was swept away from him by this nothing, this nameless waif who looked not a summer older than fifteen. He had seen her only last evening in the great Hall, performing with the other jesters and gypsy fools that had come to dance and sing and tumble, thus earning bread before his father. She had done some pathetic sleight-of-hand, dressed in a vulgar costume of rainbow colors and tiny bells. And then later, she had drawn a small harp and sang, and her voice was admittedly better than expected—good enough in fact that the Lord his father had called her to him and she sang to him a ballad of his own choosing.

After the song had ended, Kimre remembered noting her pale fluid features underneath a fool's cap, and the timbre of a clear voice announcing to the Lord Rainn that she was Ruricca NoOnesDaughter.

What an odd name, he thought. *Theatrical, no doubt. What silly affectation.*

"And how shall I reward you for your graceful singing?" Lord Sedal had asked with a nostalgic smile still lingering on his features.

"I need nothing, my Lord," she said, bowing, half-dancing before him. "I've already eaten, so it appears I've already been paid."

But the old gypsy woman from the lower table had glanced intently at her, and Ruricca nodded, saying, "On the other hand, the fates change, and I need something after all, to repay the good widow Chiccose who has let me ride with her people. What would you give me in your wisdom, my Lord?"

And Lord Rainn had then ordered a purse of coins to be brought to her, which was immediately passed on to the gypsy.

Ruricca took one coin from the purse before handing it away, and with a bright laugh she threw it up in the air, so that the Lord and all gathered in the hall saw a shining upswept comet of light. The coin came spinning down with the reflected fire of the torches, and landed in her open palm. Glancing down upon it, the smile had left her fluid features, and she looked at the Lord with a knowing intensity. "Do not go outside tomorrow, my Lord," she had said strangely then. "My thanks for your gift."

Kimre remembered all of it as he now stared, in anger and with some other complex emotion, at this odd girl-woman who was holding his dead father and whose face was pale like the Castle walls.

She was now, by a wicked quirk of fate, the Lady of Rainn Castle.

"I am sorry, my Lord . . ." said Arwes, the captain of the guard. "The attack happened so fast that we had no time to—"

"Who did this to my father?" Kimre interrupted, his voice rising like a storm. "Was it a Blackeyre arrow?"

"It appears so, we saw soldiers wearing Lord Devath's colors in the field below. . . ."

"And you did *nothing?*" The young man's voice cracked in accusation, heedless of the effect of such a display.

"But my Lord—"

"Don't call me 'Lord,'" Kimre exclaimed hoarsely, raising a proud horrible face. "You must not call me that ever again. I had failed in my duty. You have a new Lady now, and you must swear to her."

And the people stood silent, with heads lowered, because all knew he was right. The law of this land dictated that the one who had risked his life and was at the present Lord's side at his moment of death, was to be the next Lord. However, to make certain that the death was not in fact prematurely contrived by the candidate, each new "Lord" would go through a trial period, while the death was investigated in a thorough, scrupulous manner.

Thus, because of the unusual rules of succession, loyalty to each Lord of the Castle had been guaranteed by the heir who was always to remain at his side, to watch and guard. For, the Castle was different from all others, it was said, a place which cradled within it an occult secret. This secret was protected by each generation's Lord of the Castle, while many outsiders had sought to breach its surreal mystery.

Ruricca looked at the stricken young man with the black hair who leaned against the corpse, only inches away from her.

"I am so sorry . . ." she said in a faint voice, "I was merely standing here . . . I tried to help . . . Sir—I mean, I did not mean to—get in the way."

His expression blank, he looked at her in withering coldness. "It is done," he said. And then he lifted his father's body, bearing the precious burden with reverence, and carried him into the Castle.

Ruricca was left standing in a circle of Castle folk. She had risen from her kneeling position only to be walled in by stony faces, alien eyes. They looked at the thin pale young waif in a gaudy coat with silent accusation. And beyond the silence there was fear—a fear of the future.

Ruricca's period of trial and judgment was about to begin.

There was no actual memory of the first time someone called her "NoOnesDaughter." It must have been the cranky widow who would chase the playing children of the village from her herb garden in some faraway place, long ago. The woman used to find them running through her plants, stamping on the delicate herbs, and she'd call out someone's name and threaten to tell their mother. When Ruricca's name was called, she sometimes wondered why she was simply yelled at. No one ever said anything about her parents.

Ruricca's earliest memories were of an old woman who smelled like violets, leaning over her. The name the old one called her, "Ruricca," meant "question," a puzzle. She had found out later that the same old woman, whom she had always known as "grandmother" and who had cared for her until she died when Ruricca was approximately nine, was not a relative at all.

Was I left in a basket on the doorstep? She wondered upon occasion.

Later, Ruricca would find herself wandering everywhere and nowhere. She had discovered early on that she was very clever. She'd been able to learn many crafts and trades from the people she occasionally had the luck to stay with. She would sleep in barns after having done chores for a farmer. She'd enjoy a meal after assisting a baker at his scalding oven. She could weave, sew, carve wood, mix pigments for a city artisan, play all kinds of stringed instruments after having willingly drudged for a music-maker. Most of these things she learned by deceit, late at nights. Most of these things, and more.

Chiccose, the traveling gypsy, had come upon Ruricca in a small town only several weeks' ride away. Ruricca had just learned how to juggle by watching Chiccose's own son, Chern, and his little daughter Chiarra, perform at the town fair. Later she had gone to the other corner of the fair and had gathered her own little crowd by juggling some stolen fruit with the élan of a professional. And even later that evening, when two gypsies held knives at Ruricca's throat, she managed to wriggle out of their grasp, pulled trick figs out of their ears, and made stern Chiccose laugh—an unprecedented feat.

"I like you, little girl," Chiccose said then, winking her raven eye at the smiling waif.

"I am not such a little girl as you think," said Ruricca.

"I know . . ." said the wise gypsy. "None of us are—and you are like us."

"I am NoOnesDaughter."

"You were once someone's daughter, and today, if you choose, you can be mine."

Ruricca smiled brilliantly, almost like a gypsy, except for her blue eyes, saying only, "I will travel with you for the time being."

And that was how things turned out. Ruricca quickly learned all the slickness and dexterity, all the wisdom and the lies that Chiccose could dole out. Watching the old gypsy at work from behind a curtain of hanging amber beads, she learned how to spread the Tarot deck and how to peek into the eyes of each victim-customer for clues. When Chern practiced throwing knives outside, she observed his perfect aim, and the grace of his movements. And when little pixie Chiarra ran about the campsite with her silver bracelets and veils, twirling artfully, she smiled at her and then stole all her veils for one night, to practice a faerie dance in the moonlight.

It was thus that Chiccose caught her, and from that moment on Ruricca became a part of the traveling gypsy show.

Ruricca NoOnesDaughter entered Rainn Castle, flanked by ludicrous guards. However did they think she could escape? That is, of course she *could*, but how did they know?

Inside the great Hall—where only yesterday she jested and sang before the Lord—there was spare torchlight and hollow silence. A tall older man stepped away from the crowd of servants, and she recognized Neral the head steward. He had been kind to her and the gypsies before they even performed for Lord Sedal, feeding them ample fare from the Lord's own table.

Now, he looked at her with troubled eyes, while saying in a gracious tone, "My Lady . . . we bid you welcome."

But there was no welcome in any of the other faces surrounding her.

"I—" said Ruricca, stumbling a bit in an attempt to sound as a proper noblewoman, or at least her notion of what that form of speech entailed, "I'm rather unsure as to what to do at this precise fate-purported juncture. Exactly—that is, I am not exactly what you would call a noble and pure-bred lady at all, or not quite, in all sooth—or truth. I am verily but a simple jester and juggler and occasional masque player for your entertainment and idle delight, as you well know from last eve's performances. Indeed, here I only tried to help. . . . This is all a sad mistake. Oh, what am I saying, I mean, it is a dreadful bungle, a veritable howler, nay, blunder, a tragedy-inspiring gaffe and *faux pas*— you are familiar with the Frankish language, are you not, I mean—"

Silence.

And then Neral pushed forward a young woman in a clean apron with rebellious eyes. She stepped forward with a short bow and then said, "I'm Jessea. I'm to be your personal maid, m'Lady."

"I don't require a maid," said Ruricca softly.

From the back, came snickers.

At which she added, "But a maid obviously requires a lady. I mean, forsooth."

"Do not make it more difficult for them than it already is," said a cold voice from the back, as Kimre Rainn descended the stone staircase into the Hall.

Ruricca had the urge to bow, out of habit. Instead, she gracefully nodded her head in acknowledgement, saying, "You are quite right. It seems I have no other choice but to be a lady for the moment. I have wronged you—Kimre. I want you to understand that you are, despite everything, still master of this Castle."

"Impossible," he said in bitterness. "You are the Lady, and I am now but a knave. And it is only by your grace that I may stay here."

From the outside they heard a minor commotion, and then a little dark girl hung with trinkets, came running into the Hall. She was followed by a tall handsome man and older woman, while the rest of the gypsies remained peeking in from the outside.

The gypsy Chiccose had a colorful paisley shawl drawn about her shoulders, and her coin necklace sparkled about her neck. Smiling with a flash of metallic teeth, she addressed Ruricca.

"It appears that fortune has smiled upon you, little one! Will you now share it with your wandering family?"

"It is a dubious fortune," said Ruricca. "But I will certainly give you what I can. After which, I fear, we must part company."

"What?" said Chiccose, staring at her with suddenly dangerous eyes. "You would throw out your adopted mother?"

But Ruricca stared back at her with a soft smile, undaunted. "Of course, my dear Chiccose. But I also give you a nice rich box of gold coin for a parting gift, which is more than you could conjure in a year. Am I not a good adopted daughter?"

At which the danger immediately dissipated and the old gypsy laughed raucously. "Ah, but that makes all the difference in the world, my dear! Besides, we were leaving anyway. You know we must. . . ."

"You always do."

"I'll miss you . . ." said little Chiarra. "Will you forget me now that you have a whole Castle of children?" She had noticed little faces peeking from behind the stern servants of Rainn Castle.

"I never forget." Ruricca's expression was gentle. "Especially a sprite like you. But now you must go."

Ruricca turned to the steward. "Sir—that is, Neral, as my first Lady's request, I ask that you give these people precisely all that they need. But not a snippet more."

She glanced back to the gypsies. "Go, my friends. I do not say goodbye."

As steward Neral followed Chiccose and her kin out through the back, Ruricca once again turned to face the servants of the Castle, Kimre standing among them.

"Now," she said, "let me begin by telling you a story of a Lady who was *not*. . . ."

Lord Devath of Blackeyre Keep was informed that his arrow had found its true mark. And as fate would have it, Rainn Castle was now not only defenseless and verily his for the taking, but its new Lord was a crazy traveling jester, a curmudgeon, a fool! Apparently, Kimre, the deceased Lord's son, had not even been there to receive the succession.

Lord Devath laughed for at least ten minutes over that one. He then ordered his men to gather a small riding party, for he would go visit his future seat of power. The secret of Rainn Castle was practically in the palm of his hand.

Devath was large and corpulent, with small deep-set eyes encircled by folds of deceit. He was reputed to be well-versed in the dark arts, and his vassals had a superstitious fear of his dark consuming looks. After all, was it not the *geas* placed by him upon one of the soldier's arrows that had ensured the murder of Lord Sedal Rainn? So it was spoken among the halls of the Keep, in the kitchens and pantries, in the fields and stables.

The Lord of Blackeyre arrived at the high walls of Rainn Castle, and his minions set up a luxurious tent. Pennants of black and sunflower gold were raised, and they tore about in the high wind—the same wind that had directed so well the arrow.

Lord Devath idled in his tent, sending two messengers to the gates, to announce himself. From the comforts of the pillowed seat he could hear his messengers' fanfare, and their properly insolent voices.

And after a minute of silence, he heard a response.

"The Lady of Rainn Castle," exclaimed a young bright voice from the walls above, "has better things to do than entertain murderers. Begone while you still can, or you will regret it!"

At that point, Lord Devath started again laughing, and this time could not stop.

K imre watched the thin waif dressed in bright rags as she toured the Castle. He had offered to take her around and show her all things of consequence—anything in order to escape the main Hall, where the silent body of his slain father was laid out in state, waiting for a burial two days hence.

It was odd how she'd refused a change of clothing when she was first taken to the master's chamber. Ruricca had looked at the grand room in awe, her pale blue eyes moving fast to take in all baroque detail. Later, as they passed the hot kitchens, she paused to smile tentatively at Mabel the cook, and asked if it were all right to try a piece of cookie from a pile that was cooling on the plates.

Mabel was a portly woman who was always in a slightly irritated mood—probably from constantly being in all that heat.

"You're welcome to as much as you want, m'Lady," she snapped, never looking around, as she was removing a tray of breads from the furnace. "It's all yours now."

"Then may I offer some to you, Mabel—that's your name, isn't it?" said Ruricca, as she popped a large chunk of baked dough into her mouth.

The cook stopped in her tracks. "What?"

Ruricca was momentarily speechless, while one side of her face resembled a chipmunk, as she was trying to chew and swallow and answer at the same time. "Hewe, hawe some," she finally managed. And then, swallowing, said, "Maybe you should turn that oven off and take a small break to enjoy these wonderful things. Oh—and may I offer some to those little people that are hiding around the corner? Come out, I know you're there."

As she said this, a small band of children with serious round eyes appeared from behind the door to the kitchen. Kimre hadn't even realized they were there, while this jester-girl obviously had better ears.

"So," said Ruricca, as the children crowded the already crowded kitchen past the flabbergasted cook, "I propose a trade. A cookie for a name."

"Bella!"

"Anida . . ." said two little girls.

"Feran!"

"Jigge!" yelled out two boys.

And as the four children and the cook sat down to chew the goodies, Ruricca turned to Kimre and offered him a fresh crumbling piece.

Kimre felt a sort of rebellion rise within him, an anger—at himself, maybe—because for a moment he had actually felt like grinning at her. But then he remembered who she was and what had come to pass. And he said softly, bringing a whiff of chill to the hot kitchen, "My Lady, I am afraid there's one thing you must know, one thing I must show you before the day is through. It cannot wait. Especially now that Lord Devath of Blackeyre Keep is camped outside our walls—laughing. So, I must ask you to come with me. . . ."

Ruricca gulped down the last bit of cookie, and wiped off her thin sunken cheeks. "Of course," she said, "I almost forgot—the secret of Rainn Castle."

They climbed the tallest tower of the Castle, which in turn became a spare turret, with barely space for a staircase. Every five feet, there were tiny portal-windows on the walls, making the turret as hole-ridden as Swiss cheese. Unbridled wind sang a symphony in the Swiss cheese—ahem—turret, and Ruricca felt giddy from a peculiar dissonant combination of height and claustrophobia, as she climbed the steep stairs after Kimre.

At the apex, the stairway ended at a small locked door.

"It's in there," said Kimre, crowding his tall form against the ancient stone walls, standing aside to let her pass. "I've never been allowed inside, only my father could enter. There's no key, supposedly. The door opens, they say, only to the true Lord of the Castle."

"You mean you've never even *tried* to open it?" said Ruricca, her brows sweeping up in fluid surprise. "Not even when you were nine summers old, all alone, and it was nearly midnight?"

"I was never alone," said Kimre. "And I don't remember being nine, nor staying up past midnight."

"Remarkable," said Ruricca.

She then approached the door, gave it a slight push, and with a creak the door moved inward, showing a wide slit of light streaming from the inside.

"Come on," said Ruricca. "It is shamelessly unlocked. In addition, I see no trolls so far, nor any other questionable or highly deplorable and outright ghastly things."

"But—" Kimre began.

"Oh, for goodness' sake, don't make me carry you across the threshold like a blushing bride."

Was there a quiver at the corners of her lips? Kimre was never to be sure, because she had entered the forbidden room, and he had no choice but to follow.

Inside, the light source turned out to be the burning sunset. The tiny room had a sharp conical ceiling and four huge windows—more window than wall, to be exact—and each one matched one of the compass directions. Through the west window came a direct wall of light, golden-mauve, like the setting sun. The east window showed a sky of royal blue, with scattered points that were early evening stars. The north and south windows showed portions of the sky in states of chromatic flux, flowing from gold to indigo.

In the center of the room stood a short table upon which rested four objects. One was a sword, long and heavy, obviously wrought for battle, and encased in a bejeweled sheath. Another was a thick tome, covered with weathered leather and bound with inlays of gold. The third—a globe of fine luminous crystal, resting upon a silver stand. The fourth and final object was an inkwell bottle, made of mother-of-pearl and fine eastern glass.

Ruricca and Kimre bent near the objects, noting an inscription etched upon the table: "The Lord of Rainn Castle must sign the Book."

"There's no pen," said Ruricca.

"Look," said Kimre. "There's a quill pen encased within the crystal sphere! I suppose you must break it open and get the pen." He paused to think. "Oh!" he said suddenly, "I have it! You must use the sword to break the crystal, so that you can get the pen, to dip in the ink, and sign the book!"

"Right," said Ruricca. "And ruin a perfectly good crystal scrying ball. If Chiccose heard this, she'd have a gypsy-seizure—one of those highly theatrical nasty things that can go on for longer than the death of the Prince of Denmark and the star-crossed lovers of Verona combined."

"But it makes perfect sense!" Kimre frowned.

"Only if you've been reading books of faerie romance. Well, have you?"

Kimre felt an overpowering urge to take her by the collar of her bedraggled patchwork coat and slap her—once, twice maybe. Maybe even three times or more. Instead, he said, "So, what then must you do?"

As they stood there, the sun appeared to sink progressively before their eyes. It must have been the odd structure of the room, but darkness came to the visible sky almost in minutes, while outside it was probably still light.

However, while all the four windows outside filled with stars, the globe that lay on the table retained in it the glow of the sunset. Like a phosphorescent lamp, it illuminated the room.

Ruricca, her face bathed in greenish-indigo glow, circled the table slowly, then, opened the book with a snap. In the center of the first page, there was a careful faded drawing of a circle, barely visible on the antique parchment. The circle was subdivided into various radii and quadrants—twelve, to be precise—and a number of smaller circles were drawn within. There were also very odd looking symbols inscribed all over the circle, symbols that luckily Ruricca recognized quite well.

"It is the Zodiac," she said. "And this appears to be someone—or something's—astrological birth chart. This room is obviously a place of observation, allowing one to view all of the sky. And the message, to 'sign the Book' very likely means to observe and record the astrological Signs. Only, to what end, I am not sure yet. I wish I knew more of this, like the gypsies."

"Actually, I do," said Kimre in a soft voice. "I've studied the arcane art, in secret from my father."

"Good," said Ruricca, looking at him intently with her blue eyes. "In secret, you say? Then there's hope for you yet."

Ignoring this yet another provocation, Kimre leaned closer to observe the drawing. "It is indeed a birth chart," he said. And then he frowned. "The chart of someone born beneath the Sign of Aquarius the Water Bearer—which is myself. . . ."

"Interesting," said Ruricca. "This suggests that you might be the destined Lord of the Castle after all. Tell me, what other things have you been learning in secret from your father?"

"What do you mean?"

Ruricca's fluid features danced with sudden animation. "Well, I think I've seen all I need here."

"But—" said Kimre.

But she was already out of the room and bounding down the stairs three at a time, like the acrobat that she was.

Kimre bounded after her.

The wind arose into a gale around the highest turret of Rainn Castle.

R uricca was outside in the Castle courtyard. It was just after dawn, and she had called young Shawn, the Lord's hawk-keeper, to walk outside with her, and bring a couple of his best flying birds.

"'Tis not a very good place to fly 'em here," Shawn was saying, sullen from having to be awake even earlier than usual. "The wind, it is very strong here, m'Lady."

"Indeed." Ruricca smiled. "But you are such an excellent hawker, and I see your birds are the strongest and most beautiful in the entirety of this fair land. You should have no trouble at all."

"Really? You really think so, m'Lady?" said Shawn, his features starting to loosen.

"I know so," responded Ruricca. "I have seen a lot of fine hawks, but only yours retain the same undaunted bearing and spirited pride in captivity that is found within creatures of the wild."

Shawn was grinning wide. "Thank you, m'Lady! Why, I was never told such a nice thing as that by anybody! The former Lord—God rest him—used to say I was lazy—"

"Shawn," said Ruricca with a sparkle in her fluid blue eyes. "I want you to fly the hawks, now, and I will watch their graceful flight."

"Immediately, m'Lady!" Shawn said, beaming, and released the birds from their jesses.

Two creatures with wide gray wings, bounded like angels of silver into the morning sky. They circled the towers, fighting the strange wind, and Ruricca watched intently the erratic pattern of their flight.

Later, after Shawn had lured them down, and after thanking him sincerely, Ruricca returned inside the Castle.

In the Hall, she saw the tall gaunt form of the deceased Lord's son, standing in silence before the open casket. When he turned to her, she saw true anguish in his loosened features, for the first instant. And then, noticing her, he pulled all traces of emotion inward as though retracting a living rope, and was again made of stone.

"Kimre," she said gently. "What do you think really killed your father?"

The young man became very still—if a rock can become even more fixed in its stasis.

"You don't need to hide from me," she said. "I know."

A terrible pause.

"Then enough, by gods!" he exclaimed. "It was my own folly and my own inability to control what I didn't properly know that were the cause of my father's death!"

"You stirred up the winds. . . ."

"I only tried to guide the arrows back upon their own heads. The soldiers of Blackeyre were at the foot of the Castle, and when they started to shoot, I thought I might take advantage of the situation and try out something I've been practicing—in secret. . . ."

"Yes, I remember now . . ." Ruricca said with a faraway stare, "I remember feeling the winds surge just before the arrow took flight. Soon, I felt their tempestuous struggle against someone—*you*. And then, I felt that someone falter—never falter like that, Kimre—"

"I swear, by all I hold sacred, I never meant for it to be thus! I lost control! I—"

"And when you did, the winds reacted in natural antithesis, guided by the subliminal will of your very enemy, Lord Devath."

"Yes, but how do you know this?"

"I have a sense for these things. . . . Rather nasty and intrusive, no doubt, but—" Ruricca approached him, looking straight into his eyes. And then she added, "But don't be afraid, I've no plans to tell anyone else."

"Still, how did you know—"

"Oh, a number of clues. Those bizarre winds over the castle. The fact that you were strangely the only person not there when Lord Sedal died. Your extraordinary anger at me. And then, one glaring clue—when you set up those four silly objects up in the turret room, there wasn't a speck of dust on any of them. Meaning, either they were magically self-cleaning—which no true sorcerous objects ever are, most being ancient and quite filthy, not that I would know, of course—or some diligent maid came into the room to clean it every week. And that, according to your own words was impossible, since the room was forbidden. Which left the only possibility, which was yourself."

Ruricca paused, a mischievous twitch on her lips. "Oh, and by the way, Jessea my nice chatty maid told me last night that the 'mysterious' turret room was simply your study."

Kimre's mouth dropped. And then, pale as the corpse lying before them, he hung his head. "What will you do, now that you know?" he said. "I know I deserve to be condemned for murder, I should confess before all. . . ."

"The details, of course, are your business. And it was manslaughter, not murder—which makes a difference. But, I will not tell. Instead, I will help you get rid of Lord Devath's threat upon Rainn Castle."

"Since I can remember, I've always had this sensitivity to the air, the currents, the flow of the winds . . ." Kimre was telling her. They were back inside the tiny turret room with the great windows, at the top of the world, and it was high noon.

The four windows displayed an even, brilliant sky of cornflower blue, with not a cloud in sight. In the far distance they saw a haze that was the horizon, with green fields and forest land—all belonging to the Lord of this Castle.

Kimre stood before the table while Ruricca glanced through the same book that she had first seen yesterday.

"Heaven be my witness, I wasn't trying to delude you as much as you think . . ." he said. "It's true that I like to come up here, but these objects had been in this room ever since I could remember. My father showed me the astrological chart of my birth, and I've been intrigued ever since. And this book really does have to be signed by the Lord of the Castle. You guessed correctly—'signed' refers to astrology. Each Lord's birth chart is carefully added to the book that is some sort of chronology of Rainn Castle. I suppose mine doesn't really belong there now, but my father had been so sure I'd succeed him—"

He paused, finding it difficult to speak. And then he said, "But as far as I know, neither this book nor any of these other things, is the occult secret. All the book does is talk about various Lords' births and acts of kindness and mercy that they had done throughout their lives—nothing heroic. And nothing very occult about it. Indeed, my father never told me. . . ."

Ruricca was silent, intent on leafing through the worn pages of the book.

"How—do you know so much?" he said again. "Who are you, really?"

"I am Ruricca NoOnesDaughter," Ruricca said absentmindedly. And then she looked up from what she was reading, and there was an earnest expression in her eyes.

"Why do you keep saying that?" he countered in soft insistence.

"Maybe because I like the sound of it." She smiled. "And the fact that it means hardly anything. . . ."

"You—feel the winds also. Tell me, how does one really maintain control over such a force?"

At which Ruricca laughed. "Oh, but you don't. That is impossible. You must *trick* the winds. Suggest *ways of movement*. Convince the air that it needs to do what you intend it to do."

"Oh . . ." he said.

"Now," said Ruricca, "regarding your problems with Blackeyre, I have an idea. We will need to go outside, where the winds are still blowing strong in confusion. And first, we must calm them down. Help me carry these items downstairs— although they're about as magic as my foot, they may come in handy."

Saying that, she picked up the book and the crystal orb, while Kimre followed her with the sword and inkwell bottle.

On their way outside, Ruricca called the children of the Castle to follow her, and they did, visions of cookies-to-come filling their imagination.

"Listen to me carefully," Ruricca said in a bright cheerful voice to the children. "We are going to play a game. Now, it is very important that you do exactly what I say."

She turned to the oldest of the girls. "Bella. You will take this Book, and hold on to it tight. And you will pretend to be the North Wind. Don't worry, I'll explain in a second."

She turned to the youngest of the boys. "Feran. Take this sword and be very careful. You are the South Wind."

The youngest girl, Anida, was then instructed to take the crystal orb, and be the East Wind. Finally, Jigge, the oldest boy of the four, was given the inkwell, and dubbed the West Wind.

"Here's what you'll do," Ruricca began, "I will call out the name of a wind, and that person has to start doing what I say, as quickly as possible. There will be a lot of running and jumping—"

After she was done instructing the four children, Ruricca approached Kimre, and took his hand. Kimre was startled by her very light touch, a breeze almost.

"Before we begin," said Ruricca, "I want you to practice calming the air currents. Now, remember that air is sly and changeable and very perverse. The winds will often do the opposite of what you suggest. At first, they may surprise you, confuse you. But—if you watch them carefully, a pattern will emerge at last, a pattern of logic and movement. And then, with the greatest subtlety, you can insinuate yourself within that pattern, and make it sing for *you*. . . . Now, watch me."

The wind was jerking spasmodically all around them even as Ruricca spoke, and the children stood ready with serious faces and sparkling eyes.

And Ruricca allowed herself to feel the rough gusts, like ghostly hands upon her hollow cheeks, tearing at her eyelashes, blowing from all directions.

Especially the South. She singled Him out, and then could feel Him, as He slapped her cheek repeatedly with the breath of dry scalding heat. She could feel and hear and *sense* Him.

"South Wind!" cried Ruricca. "Take the sword and attack me as though I were Lord Devath himself!"

And as little Feran came running at her, squealing, pretending to pummel her with the sheathed sword, there was a sudden lull in the air. A pause. Kimre could feel the great *presence* as it stopped suddenly to consider. And then, perverse, it began to fall back. Kimre could actually *feel* its decision, separate from the other three elementals, and its consequent action—the opposite of what Ruricca had instructed the little boy to do. And in a sudden flowering of comprehension, by way of example, Kimre knew what this was all about.

The game had begun.

Lord Devath had sent for a division of his soldiers to arrive at the base of Rainn Castle where he'd been sitting in his tent like a potted plant since the previous day. Apparently, laughing had gotten him nowhere, for even without a proper Lord, Rainn Castle had formidable walls and strong gates to breach. Reinforcements were thus necessary.

Not too late after dawn, his soldiers had reported seeing hawks flying above the Castle walls. The birds were flying as though they were drunk, one soldier had said, as though they were struggling against some inexplicable force.

"Your magic over the Castle must still be strong, my Lord!" said the captain of the soldiers to Lord Devath, bowing with a knowing smirk. "The same forces that you conjured to defeat their puny Lord yesterday."

"Yes, well. Of course," Lord Devath said. He had no idea really, what had caused Sedal Rainn's death, but as any sound and practical despot he appreciated the opportunity it created.

"My Lord!" said another soldier, running. "There is something strange happening around and outside the Castle! The winds are rising to gale levels, and it is impossible to remain standing next to the Castle walls. Your sorcery seems out of control! You must stop it now, or it will be too late!"

"Winds, eh?" Lord Devath mumbled. And so he stretched his bulky frame, rose up from his planted position, and slowly came outside the tent.

Around the Castle, the air had become blurred like a funnel. Lord Devath had to squint from the dust that was blowing in their direction. He then uttered a number of pungent curses.

High above the Castle walls, on the other side, four children were running, laughing and chasing each other in a large circle around the perimeter of the courtyard—in the direction opposite the blowing winds. In the middle of the courtyard, stood a gaunt young man with ebony hair and eyes closed in a grimace of intense concentration. Next to him stood a thin waif dressed in a bedraggled rainbow coat. She watched the man with a tiny smile of amusement.

"Winds . . ." said Ruricca softly to the children. "Stop running."

And although Feran and Bella and Jigge and Anida came to an obedient halt, the winds beyond the walls continued to spin and blow madly, while Kimre remained focused with his eyes closed.

"Good," said Ruricca. "You've gotten the hang of it so that physical props and bits of scenery are no longer necessary."

"Can we play some more, m'Lady?" giggled little Anida.

"Of course, East Wind. Only, a little later."

Kimre opened his eyes.

"You can stop now," she said to him. "I believe Lord Devath is appropriately alarmed right now. You can defeat him very easily by natural means if you send your soldiers and Captain Arwes down there."

There was something disturbing in the expression of Kimre's pale eyes. He looked at her, steady and unblinking, and his eyes were like occluded glass.

"Do you know," he said in a soft voice, while the winds continued roaring a few feet away, "that I could kill them all now, with a mere thought? That I could extend the winds so that they wipe clean the whole land, as far as the eye could see?"

"I know," she said. "But you must not."

But as she grew silent, Ruricca felt his rebellion, felt it in the strange new gusts of air that started to pummel and tear at them, disturbing the pocket of calm that had been within the Castle walls. The air currents tore at her stringy listless hair, sent currents of chill down her back, whistled through the sleeves of her old coat. The children stopped smiling and began to huddle from the unusual cold.

From the outside below the walls, came yells of fear and pain, as Lord Devath's men were subjected to some new unspeakable onslaught.

Kimre's hair was a wild black storm, and it had risen, flowing above his head. His eyes were expressionless as he faced Ruricca, and there was a shade of a smile on his lips.

She saw *within*, saw what he was seeing, the tumult, the black thunder. . . .

In the sky above, black clouds began to race, appearing out of nowhere, converging.

"I'm afraid, m'Lady . . ." Anida whimpered, while Jigge held her against him, speechless.

The sky meanwhile grew black.

Destruction! Death! Ruricca could sense it building around them, flowing outward, while the clouds hung in darkness over the Castle and beyond. She could feel *hate* and *guilt* and *fear*. She could feel his regret.

"Stop," she said to him. "Please don't take your own pain out on everyone else. . . ."

She could feel his presence, almost read the edges of his thoughts.

No! the thoughts cried, *Destruction!*

A few steps away, huddling together in the dark, the children began to cry.

Ruricca took a big breath. She then closed her eyes and said: "*That's quite enough!*"

And immediately, there was a universe of lightning—millions of brilliant razors split the sky—and then, impossible thunder, deafening above their heads, deafening the children's cries.

And then, came rain.

Torrents of water spilled from the sky, and the midnight cloud mass seemed to empty itself in seconds, lightening the edges of the sky with each instant. At the same time, the winds began to dull, slow, shocked into surprise, and weakened by the outpouring of a strange emotion in the very air itself.

The winds had settled. The torrential rain slowed to a gentle softness—as *she* had asked it. . . .

And in that soft rain, Kimre stood weeping silently, while the waters from the sky glided down his cheeks, mixed with his tears.

"I see, *Lord* Kimre," said Ruricca, as the drops of water trickled down her lashes, "that at last you understand the secret of Rainn Castle."

Later, all the Castle folk had gathered in the great Hall. Kimre had stood before them all, and had spoken in a clear sad voice all the truth of what had happened, all the details of Lord Sedal's death. When he was done, a number of people were crying, and Kimre stood with his gaze trained to the floor.

"I am responsible for my father's premature death, and I'm at the mercy of the Lady of the Castle," concluded Kimre.

Steward Neral approached Kimre. "It's a terrible mistake to make," he said sternly, "but if your father were still alive, I believe he would forgive you, knowing your fair intent."

Arwes, the captain of the guard turned to Ruricca, saying, "What should be done, Lady? He's been a good son to Lord Sedal, all up to this. And if I'm allowed to speak, I know Kimre, ever since he was a boy he'd always meant well. After all, he did save us from Lord Devath's siege just now, with those frightening storm-winds! Blackeyre was lucky to get out alive, and I swear he'll remember it for the rest of his days, and never again try to take Rainn Castle!"

"Please, m'Lady," said Mabel, the cook. "You've been exceeding fair to us, and we ask you to be the same with him."

"Yes, Lady, please . . ." a number of other voices joined in.

Ruricca had been standing in silence, listening to their words. She looked now at all their faces—earnest, full of entreaty. She looked at Kimre who, having confessed all, had a kind of peace around him, despite the resignation. And she looked at the open casket a few feet away, where the body of Lord Sedal was waiting for burial.

"I suppose," she said then, "I must do what is only fair under the circumstances—Kimre, do you believe it's the duty of the Lord or Lady of Rainn Castle to do what is best for the good of this place, for all those who live here?"

"Yes," he said, looking openly into her eyes.

"Then I must insist that you, Kimre, are now the Lord here. I renounce any claim upon this noble stronghold, and surrender all the duties to you, who had shown the most responsibility and *mercy*, and protected the good people who live here and who so strongly believe in you."

"But—" began Kimre, shocked, while around him happy voices swelled.

"I think it's time you buried your father, Lord Kimre, so that he can now truly rest in peace. And then, get back to the real business of running this place. Meanwhile it's time for me to be on my way also."

Even later, after Lord Sedal had been properly put to rest, Ruricca and Kimre were alone in his turret study. He, sitting with his head between his hands, she, chewing on a cookie from a batch just fresh out of Mabel's oven.

"I didn't tell them *everything*," Kimre was saying. His countenance, no longer petrified with denial, was receptive and sorrowful. "I didn't mention that if it weren't for you, I wouldn't have been able to *stop*. I would have killed and killed—"

"But you didn't. You may not know it, but you'd stopped just as I broke open the thundercloud. It was all quite simultaneous. And I did read your thoughts clearly, after the rain came. You understood that *mercy* is the secret of the Lord of Rainn Castle. Mercy, like the rain bringing release to the angry storm."

"Maybe you're right . . ." he said, his eyes brimming with liquid. "I remember in that moment of absolute furious power, hearing the crying of the children. . . . Their frightened faces, their hopelessness. . . ."

"You're not going maudlin on me now, are you?" said Ruricca, wiping chocolate and crumbs from her face. "Because if you do, I'd rather jump out of one of these nice windows, and splatter over the stones below."

"No you won't," he said, coming alive. "I'd call the winds and lift you to safety before you even had a chance to reach the ground."

"Think you can do that, all by yourself?"

"Try me." He was now grinning. And in that moment Ruricca felt a definite warm breeze tug gently at her hair, despite the fact that they were inside and all the windows were shut.

"Ruricca NoOnesDaughter," he said, and the sound of his voice came soft as a whisper. "Would you stay here if I made the winds dance and sing for you?"

"Not a chance," she said with a little smile.

"But my father had named you Lady after all. . . ."

"And so, for a while, I was." She sighed. "But I think I've done all I can here. You're well on your way to learning control—not over wind and rain, but over your own *self*. And law or no law, you make the best Lord. Goodness—you make the one and only Lord, for certainly I'm no such thing!"

"And where will you go?" he said. "Back to the gypsies?"

Ruricca NoOnesDaughter shrugged, then touched him softly on the cheek. "Where do you go when the whole world is before you?"

And with that, she left the Lord of Rainn Castle.

WOUND ON THE MOON

As the late afternoon sky stood lavender upon gold in the great city, the thief was imprisoned for the highest crime there was. The stranger had raised her eyes and gazed at the Al-Eralir, lord of Aerhad-el-Raas, as he rode by in a procession, surrounded by obeisant slaves, haughty, beautiful, and cold as death.

The great multitude all around had sunk to the earth in worship, the faces of men and women hidden, the eyes shut tightly, so as not to risk a sacrilegious glimpse of the Al-Eralir, demon lord. But she, an outsider, had stared in curiosity first at the graceful magnificent stallions which walked, bejeweled, and barely under control of the crimson warrior guards of the Al-Eralir.

And then her gaze had slid higher, from the mirror-bright trappings of the great black beast in the center of the procession to a mounted figure of stonelike bearing. She was stricken by the sight of empty amber eyes in a perfect face. After he had passed by, the blood-clad warriors of his guard brutally captured and manacled her, not giving her an instant to react.

Under more normal circumstances the thief *could* react, swiftly and ferally. She could, when provoked to physical violence, move lithe as water to strike and leave no trace. Only this time she had looked and tarried much too long, as if something in the air of this huge city dulled her wits. When they took her, she did not even desire to resist.

From the start, she had never admitted that she was a thief.

It must have been the agility in her eyes and the brightness, that made them all assume, and she went along, passive and uncomplaining. They were intense gray-blue, those eyes of hers, and peculiar in their own way. Peculiar, maybe, because neither the jailer nor the guards had previously seen such eyes in a commoner, and even less, a thief.

The jailer also noticed her oddly fine looks, as he searched her for valuables. She had then, to facilitate his efforts, surrendered two rings, a neck chain of precious metal, and the ready information on the nature of her occupation. All this to end the further probing of his lecherous fingers. The jewelry took its permanent place in the jailer's collection, but he only guffawed when she told him she was a warrior. And the thief was moved on for further inspection by the jailer's next superior.

One of the crimson guards believed he saw a glimmer of a dagger in her boot. But that came as a second thought, after the definite stirring of desire at the sight of a slim leg and calf encased in masculine trousers. Her body was limber and well formed.

The dagger was confiscated. And then they had wheedled a name out of her, Lyren, by force of threats. That had been one thing she was loath to part with. However, threats were threats, and for one who was dead in Law already, cooperation meant an easy or not-so-easy way to end.

Knowing what was good for her, Lyren did not resist when they stripped her and gave her a penitent's rags to wear. Thus she was to appear before the demon lord himself whose lips were to utter her punishment.

"When you are summoned, bitch, dirt beneath His feet, you shall fall flat on your face. Then you shall crawl to His Seat, never lifting eyes from the floor," she was told, and a guard dealt her, as a reminder, a lash of the whip. It fell across her cheek, cutting a thin crimson welt that burned like hot coals. She never flinched.

Afterward they threw her into a cell, dark with rotting night. And when true night came to lie over the city, she slept, knowing what was to come.

They said that Aerhad-el-Raas, pearl of cities, stood the first in the way of the rising sun, before all of the lands of men, in the East of all the easts. It was the hallowed Seat of the expansive unconquerable Empire which from the city took its name.

In all of the Empire of Aerhad there was no other such city, no other such exquisite luxury, and no other such decadence. Contrasts prevailed throughout—beggars and lepers lined the squalid bazaars with their fly-covered bodies, and man-filled rags huddled in filthy alleyways and under the bridges crossing Urthad, the River of Smells; in the rich quarter the streets were paved with gold, sparkling crystal fountains ran with wine, and from the palaces and gardens of the nobles came exquisite music and softly muted laughter of courtesans.

Over all this ruled Sahtiel, the beautiful demon lord, whose mother was said to be none other than the moon herself. The previous Al-Eralir, his mortal father, built Aerhad-el-Raas, city of cities, and his son added the Empire.

Sahtiel surrounded himself with beauty in the truest sense. Godlike in appearance himself, with golden hair running like honey to his shoulders, skin of pale ripe olives, features reminiscent of a statue from a holy shrine of Cxeris, and amber eyes of the mountain cats, Sahtiel attained twenty-three summers, conquered the East in another three, so that rivers of blood irrigated the lands, and then decided he had no more desire to see ugliness in any form.

In the luxurious rooms of the Palace of the Al-Eralirs musk and incense were burned day and night, and the sweet scent carried out into the gardens to eclipse the fragrance of the roses with its sensual delicacy. Beautiful youths served the Al-Eralir, for he was known to take only male lovers. His crimson guard was composed of the finest warriors who served their stern master with fanatical loyalty, for his charm had conquered their souls. It was told among the people however, that the present Al-Eralir, having demon blood in him, held strange orgiastic and occult feasts, where terrible perversions were practiced.

Sahtiel had decreed that no commoner was ever to lift eyes outright at him, and no woman approach him without crawling upon the ground, so as not to defile him with their baseness. He also gave orders never to have the sick or the ugly within his sight. All this was on pain of death, for the Al-Eralir had no mercy. And the punishments he dealt out were such that instant death could only have been a blessing. . . .

It was before the demon lord that Lyren, thief, and stranger, was to be brought forth.

In the morning Lyren awoke in her cell, and the understanding of the way things really stood smote her. The day before had been like a daze, in which she only remembered two cold amber eyes, lovelier than any human ones she had seen, and terrible. But now her practicality had set in.

Utter fool! What in Aldiz's name made me dawdle like that? He resembles someone—

She did not finish the thought, the implications of which were too unclear to pursue. Instead she forced herself to ponder on the purpose of her presence here in this accursed city of the corrupt.

Somewhere in Aerhad-el-Raas was Haderi, alive, she knew, for the carnelian stone in her earlobe remained warm and pulsing with his heart. Her blood-sworn promise to him still stood, and so did the half-conscious love which had managed to insinuate into her relationship with him since the last summer of their travel companionship. Haderi, unlike her, was not a renegade *sehjir* warrior, but a thief, one of the most sophisticated and highest-placed in the Guild. He had taught her all the tricks and the grace, which now helped her to pass easily for one of the Guildmembers.

Lyren remembered the strange skirmish in a small town tavern, which involved her and Haderi with a group of men from the city. Haderi killed one with a throw of a knife, and she bowled over two others. They had left the place swiftly, but not before she had seen a bit of oddly rich clothing show from under the folds of the cloak of one of the fallen men. Like a cold wave came the suspicion that these were disguised noblemen. Indeed, the land ran with rumors that nobles from Aerhad-el-Raas often came and went in the semblance of commoners, for perverse entertainment. And if it were so in this case, then the two of them were in great danger.

Her suspicion came true, for the next morning Haderi left her on some private business and did not come back. Never quite sure of his intents, Lyren waited a week. And then she knew that a venture to the city was now inevitable.

She had once promised herself not to approach Aerhad-el-Raas closer than an arrow's flight. It was as if some inner sense stood as a warning against the lure of that decadent trap. Only now the moment of truth was at hand. The business contract that had first bound them was now only second-place.

Lyren had to rescue the man she had been hired to protect, for his own sake.

Curiosity killed the moth, ran a common saying among the people. Only Lyren would never quite see the truth of it, not even when she was entering the city where there were so many perilous things to be curious about. What harm would it do, she had thought as she stood with the multitude before the procession, to glance one time at the Al-Eralir? How in the world could she be noticed among the crowd, and even then, why couldn't she swiftly escape? Lyren was not aware however, that the crimson warriors knew which sorts to watch more carefully than others. She, as a stranger, had not prostrated herself quite as correctly as necessary, or soon enough. She had hesitated. And that drew their attention.

Lyren thought about death, as footsteps echoed down the prison corridor, and her cell door fell open. Two guards entered, roughly lifted her from the cold stone slabs of the floor, and removed her outside.

Before being brought into the demon lord's presence, Lyren was made more presentable by two slaves who brushed out her short, higher than shoulder-length dark hair, and gave her water to wash the grime off her face and hands. The rags remained, for the sake of humiliation, but the Al-Eralir was to see no dust or disarray.

The great arched doors opened before her, and she was pushed from behind to fall forward on her stomach into a great dimly-lit chamber.

For several instants she was too surprised to do anything, only lay feeling the cool mosaic of the exquisite floor tiles against her cheek. A harsh whisper sounded from somewhere nearby: "Crawl!" it hissed. She opened her eyes and saw, at the level of the floor, the feet of the guards who lined the two walls.

By Aldiz, what a fool I must be making of myself, she thought, as she began to slither along the floor. She had a long way to go.

"O, Exalted One," a voice from someplace spoke out, "this *nothing* huddled before you on the ground, penitent and groveling, has committed the ultimate crime of seeing your Visage. Pronounce, if you will, the manner of its death."

Lyren liked this not at all. *Neither am I "huddled,"* she thought, *nor "penitent"—for I do believe I'd do this again, given the chance, only with greater caution. And even less am I "groveling." Aldiz knows, I don't grovel. This bastard assumes too much.* And abruptly, unexpectant to herself, she gave an audible snort of contempt.

Rarely had it been that such a simple thing as that could have so great a meaning or such a peculiar effect upon a room full of people. Almost, echoes were heard from that one sound, so silent became the great chamber.

And then something prompted Lyren to repeat the great crime, the terrible crime that had gotten her here. She looked up.

The young man with long golden hair, half-reclined on the great, filigreed throne, observed her blandly from underneath the lazy slits of his bored eyes shadowed by a fringe of long sable lashes. *Eyes too beautiful even for a maiden*, Lyren thought.

At his feet sat a dark-haired youth with coal-black eyes of a doe, dark-skinned, and delicate-boned. He was watching with a sleepy look the proceedings, his head languidly leaned to the knee of the Al-Eralir. Sahtiel's elegant hand was absently toying with the strands of the boy's silky hair.

Lyren's raised eyes met the look of the empty golden ones. And then suddenly, there came a spark of interest in those yellow melted amber eyes.

Sahtiel carelessly glanced at the ragged beggar at his feet. *It was human, of indefinite sex.* The Chancellor had promised it was to be the last one for the day, not to be put off because of the magnitude of its crime.

Chancellor Razd proceeded to describe in his usual groveling voice the crime. It was another one of those who had "looked."

Sahtiel listened in silence, listlessly, absentmindedly stroking Jieri's hair. Jieri. This night they had not slept much, for the Al-Eralir had experienced a resurge of passion toward the youth, which was beginning to wane since last week. Now Sahtiel wanted to lean down and breathe in the scent of Jieri's sweet silken locks, but held himself back for the sake of maintaining the formal atmosphere of the audience chamber.

Razd finished his speech. The human on the ground suddenly squirmed, making a very definite snort of derision. And then it raised its head of dark unclean hair. In a young face two uncharacteristically piercing gray-blue eyes met his. Sahtiel involuntarily felt a reminiscence of *something* wash over him. His interest was quickened.

"Gods of Aerhad!" exclaimed Razd. "The wench dares to look at you once again, O Glorious One! Order her maimed limb by limb, her breasts cut off, her womb filled with molten lead. . . ."

The woman on the floor slightly turned her head in Razd's direction, and her remarkably clear eyes filled with cold anger.

"I'll maim you, hairless devil, monkey, son of—" she hissed, no longer caring of the consequences.

Razd's mouth fell open.

And then Sahtiel laughed.

Every crimson guard watched in silence as the Al-Eralir laughed, his voice cold as crystal, inhuman, echoing in the great chamber.

The woman watched too. Only there was no awe on her face. She seemed quite annoyed.

"When you're finished, great Al-Eralir," she said in a strangely calm voice, "do proceed to condemn me for your idiotic crime. Aldiz help me if I listen to any more of this without reverting to violence. I wonder, can demon-kin withstand strangling?"

"What is your name?" said Sahtiel, and she saw his amber eyes were now alive and burning.

"My name is mine. To give or to keep. Why is that boy looking at me like that?"

Jieri was staring in near shock at this pile of common rags, which suddenly began to speak back to his lord.

Her insolence was so new that Sahtiel involuntarily straightened in his seat. "Rise," he said quietly, "Come here."

"Now *such* orders I like. The floor was getting cold."

She stood before him, wrapped in nondescript concealing rags, but he saw that she was tall and slender. And again, those eyes of hers were indeed remarkable. Sahtiel had not previously seen such brazen clear-eyed insolence in a woman.

Her head leaned slightly to the side. "Well, what now?"

"Yes, what now?" he said. "I will not have you killed yet. Who are you?"

"I am Lyren."

"You give me your name, when before you refused."

"I am deliberately provoking you." She bared her teeth in an angry grin.

Sahtiel glanced around the chamber. "Leave us, all of you." His gaze included Jieri.

"Illustrious One—" began Razd.

The amber eyes burned.

When the chamber was empty, the Al-Eralir turned to Lyren. "I do not know your motives, but you intrigue me."

"I intrigue many people—is it permitted to sit down?"

"Sit, here, by me. Tell me things."

"By Aldiz, you're not as blood-thirsty and cruel as I thought. I expected to be torn and maimed—immediately."

Lyren sat down in a light crouch before the throne, her clear eyes trained on his. Despite her unsightly appearance, there was grace in her movements.

"I hope, O Al-Eralir, that you don't mind my stink. People brought forth from prison customarily give off an odor. Have you considered cleaning the place, ever?"

"Your words are too clever," he mused. "You must be a thief."

"Hm, we were speaking about odors—"

A smile passed his fine lips, sensuous and pale. "Nevertheless, I shall call you thief." He watched her closely, in silence, studying, it seemed, everything about her.

"Interesting?" Lyren asked. She was feeling discomfited by this.

"So, thief," he said. "So, you hint with utmost subtlety that you desire a bath. And a change of clothes. Should I allow you that, I wonder? Or maybe it might be more interesting to have you beheaded?"

"Not at all. From what I've heard, you've overused the method already. Besides, that wouldn't *look* nice at all. And I know you don't like things that don't look nice."

"*You* don't look nice." The golden shadowed eyes watched her, unblinking.

"Ah, but again, *that* can be remedied—"

"I wonder." The mockery was very subtle from underneath the indefinite expression of the refined face, but once again she knew, by the slight curving of his lips, that the verbal game they were playing pleased him.

"If you, O great Al-Eralir, don't try me, you'll never find out."

"Well then, you have stirred my curiosity," Sahtiel said, and summoned slaves to the chamber.

Lyren was indeed curious to look at, later that day, after she had bathed and donned an elegant masculine outfit. Her once listless hair now fell in dark soft curves around a pale fine-featured face with its evocatively clear intense eyes. The dark expensive material of her well-fitting caftan and trousers emphasized her willowy stature, almost too tall for a woman. As she walked to Sahtiel's quarters, those who saw her pass often mistook her for a young handsome nobleman going on the demon lord's business.

Sahtiel had invited her to dine with him that night, a particular honor. Lyren hoped that his interest toward her would not wane before it could be beneficial for her and her search for Haderi.

As Lyren approached the lord's quarters, unchallenged (she was given permission to walk around freely), she thought wary thoughts. People had said strange things about the present Al-Eralir. He was not human, they said. He had no compassion. And many doubted if he had a soul. His refinement was so acute that it had turned into perversion. He took beautiful youths from the finest families of the Empire for his lovers, putting to death those who displeased him.

And they said that he did other worse things.

Lyren paused before the guarded doors of the private quarters, frowning at the two crimson guards (who probably would've loved to frown back—the Al-Eralir's short-lived favorites were envied and disliked, often for good reasons). The doors were opened for her, and she entered into a luxuriously furnished room, once more, dimly lit, as it was characteristic of Sahtiel.

Rich exotic carpets hung on the walls and covered the floor, while mosaic tiles decorated the ornate ceiling. Lyren however, immediately turned her attention to the great arsenal of weapons hanging on one of the carpeted walls. She turned around, and seeing no one in the room, quickly advanced to examine the objects closer.

Among the barbed pikes, spears, battleaxes, swords, *Ahri* knives, daggers, throw darts and discs, she saw one sword that took her fancy. Lyren had made it a habit, since in the employ of Haderi and the Thieves Guild, never to carry weapons more conspicuous than a dagger. Now, lacking even her one small throw-knife confiscated by the jailer, she remembered with involuntary envy her own longsword which she had had to turn in to the Guild for "safe-keeping" before beginning her work with them. This sword before her, slim and of a simplistic workmanship, brought memories of times both good and bad. And Lyren, on a newly learned Guild habit, did not hesitate to take it down from the wall.

She slid the blade out of the long scabbard, weighed it in her hands, then tried the feel of the handle with both hands separately (she was ambidextrous). Then came the practice swings which she felt compelled to try. Lyren was deeply engrossed in a very pleasant practice bout with a ghostly opponent, when a voice sounded from behind.

"The elegance of your movement fits the weapon. The sword is yours."

Lyren had thought, since the beginning, that his voice was oddly memorable, and now, once more, the clear quality of the sound jerked her out of her concentration.

Like crystal breaking . . . beautiful, she thought, as she turned around, somewhat embarrassed by her display.

Sahtiel, his golden hair a stream of pale liquid honey in the semi-twilight, had come in through a small hidden door, and was watching her for several moments now. He wore a long white robe with a wide ornate belt over ankle-length trousers, and his perfectly proportioned body was arrow-straight. Despite the fine-boned semblance of diminutive delicacy, Lyren realized that he was taller than she.

She was unable to hold the words back: "Is it true what they say, that you are the son of Ilenvis, the moon?"

His dark arches of brows moved slightly upward. "And what *do* they say, thief—or should I say, warrior?"

Lyren lowered the sword and approached him. "They say, O Al-Eralir, that you take blood—human blood—and you drink it from a silver vessel when the moon is full. And then, your mother descends from the sky, leaving the sphere unattended. She comes to you, out of love, to tell you the truths of this world and others. And you kneel to her—" She paused. "And then there are other things, darker ones that you do, which I don't comprehend. . . ."

Sahtiel looked at her, silent, his expression indefinite. At this proximity she was better able to examine the details of the face, and sensed a welling of apprehension. The peculiar charismatic quality about him was beginning to have its effect on her.

"Must I tell you everything, my thief?" he spoke then, and drew his face down to hers, so that their eyes were inches apart. And then his hand touched her left earlobe. His fingers brushed against the carnelian stone, warm and living.

"What is that?"

She blinked, coming out of a reverie. "Nothing. An earring."

"No. It is more, I can feel it. It is some kind of a living transfer link. With whom?"

She was surprised, then wary. "Whatever do you mean?"

The amber eyes glowed. "Do not attempt to withhold anything from me. You *know* what I mean. With whom?!"

"What does it matter? With a friend."

"Why?"

"By Aldiz, what is it to you?" she exclaimed, now angry. And then she felt a wave of fear at the sight of an even greater anger, cold, and strange, in the golden eyes.

Lyren lowered her gaze. "I am looking for a man," she said, "A man of the Thieves Guild. I am his hired bodyguard. This—" she pointed to her ear, "is to establish permanent contact. I know he is here in the city."

"Is that all?" The eyes were still cold.

"Yes! What else could there be?"

"You said, 'a friend.'"

"I lied. My employer."

"No, you lie now."

"Demons be damned, why do you insist this? What do you care?"

"His name is Haderi-e-Relavis. I know him . . . well."

"You—how did you—"

Sahtiel watched her intensely.

"How did you see what I was thinking?" Lyren said.

"Didn't you know? I had glanced into your soul. My Mother gave me the gift together with Her blood."

"I suppose she had also given you the right to freely assume power over everyone?" said Lyren, angered by the indifferent arrogance.

"I do not assume. I *have* the power."

"Hah!" Lyren snorted and turned away from him. There was a pause.

She paced the room. "Well then, find him. Find Haderi for me, if you truly can."

She did not see as Sahtiel smiled. "I have already found him," he said.

Lyren froze.

And then she felt a chill sweep down her spine as a hand came to lie against her left shoulder, from behind.

"You shall have Haderi tomorrow," he spoke softly, close to her ear, "In exchange for—for this. . . ."

Surprise came too late, as she felt the languid yet hard pressure of warm lips against her throat. As his other hand slid around her waist in a tightening embrace, she managed to breathe:

"And how do I know the—truth of what you say? . . ."

"You have my word," answered Sahtiel, Al-Eralir, as for the first time in his life he felt passion toward a woman turn him to fire.

The nightingale stopped singing some while ago, replaced by the morning birds, when Sahtiel opened his eyes. In the tentative rose glow of dawn coming through the great arched balcony windows, Lyren lay asleep, the slender body naked under the light silk covers of the great bed. He drew closer to watch the face in repose, washed by the last blue shadows of the fleeing night. She was not just fine-featured, but truly beautiful, he saw now. The aristocratic lines of the face reminded him of something, only what, he could not recall. Under the dark brows, her long lashes lay against the pallid skin of her cheek, and the dark soft waves of her hair flowed in disorder against the pillow. Her pale full lips were parted slightly. So pale. . . .

She was so very fine and dark and pale . . . His mind blurred for an instant, and he thought he saw, in the strong angle of her chin, in the heavy line of her brows, a youth. It was as if a man were lying beside him, not a maiden.

This was how he had first seen her, with her defiance, her manner of nonchalant ease, and her quick witty answers. The way she dressed also aided the illusion, in particular the night before when she was practicing with the sword. Sahtiel was infatuated with her, with the illusion, until the two were intertwined into one complex object of desire. And when he discovered the body of the woman, the novelty only kindled the desire further, so that all night he burned, his passion greater than that ever experienced before.

Sahtiel watched her and thought of what he had done. From the first he had known, despite all her words, that she loved Haderi, and the memory came to him of the raven-haired thief who had once stolen his heart and his soul with a glance. Haderi had had the same, almost the same effect on him as Lyren. Haderi was quick, clever, brilliant, and his dark handsome elegance was noticeable everywhere from a distance.

And Haderi, although the mesmerizing golden beauty of the demon lord had touched him, did not submit to his advances. He was not usually a lover of men. And women, as Lyren knew, also held little interest for him whose life was quicksilver and ambition.

Sahtiel hated him then, after the handsome dark thief had rejected him. That had happened years ago, when the Al-Eralir breathed with the passion of conquest of the East. Somehow Haderi had escaped his wrath, maybe because Sahtiel had not tried very hard to apprehend him.

But now, once more, Haderi was within reach. It was a strange discovery for Sahtiel to make that the thief was even now imprisoned in the dungeons of the city for a reckless act of murder of some nobleman.

Sahtiel thought only briefly before doing what he did, thought very briefly how he had once loved Haderi, and then, how Lyren loved Haderi, and how he now wanted Lyren. And then, still loving Haderi, and newly loving Lyren, he summoned a guard in the middle of the night, when she slept in his arms, and told him to throttle with a silken cord a dark handsome man in the thirty seventh prison cell on the right, the one with a tiny window facing the east, and the rising sun. . . .

Lyren woke up from the cold. It was a cold that slithered its way from her left ear to the rest of her body, insinuated unnaturally into her blood, so that it seemed to slow in her veins. The carnelian stone burned with cold.

Her eyes flew open and she sat up in the great bed. Next to her Sahtiel lay back on the pillows, his eyelashes shadowing the amber eyes, watching her lazily and indifferently.

She stared at him, at the indifference, and suddenly a great surging tidal wave of emotion came welling in her, a wave of anger.

"He is dead," she said, softly, and her clear eyes shone bright.

He spoke nothing but at that moment something slowly forced the corners of his lips upward. A tiny cynical smile.

Lyren remembered that tiny smile. It was a catalyst. She turned on him then, turned on the Al-Eralir of Aerhad-el-Raas.

"He is dead!" she cried, "You betrayed me!"

"I did not betray you."

"What?! You dare say this now, when you gave me your word—"

"My word is still yours. You shall have Haderi as I promised."

She stared at him, suddenly cold in anger and understanding.

"Yes," he said, "You see now. You did not specify *how* you wanted him. I give him *dead.*"

"But why?"

He reached out with a hand to brush his fingers against her cheek. She did not draw back, but flinched. There was a tiny trace of a scar there, a whip scar. It had healed incredibly fast, overnight.

He ran his fingers along the scar. "Because you are beautiful," he said. "And Haderi was—beautiful too. There shouldn't be such beauty together, as yours and his. Dark with dark. No. . . ."

"You are mad . . ." Lyren said softly.

"No," he continued. "Dark should be with gold. I am gold. . . ."

"By Aldiz and all the gods, may you be damned, but you're mad!"

And Sahtiel laughed. It was a crystal clear cold laugh. "No. I am not mad. I am omnipotent. Which, in itself, is a sort of madness to those others who cannot know what I know or have. . . ."

"And what is it that you know and have?" said Lyren as she stared closer into his eyes.

They were golden and cold with emptiness. And he did not answer.

Suddenly Lyren sprang from the bed, throwing back the covers, and stood naked before him. "So, you think that you know and have things greater than the rest of us ordinary mortals?"

And then, she ran to the open balcony, past where the gauze lavender curtains fluttered in the morning breeze.

Before he could react with surprise, she was on the balcony, looking down, high above the city, her lovely willowy body tinted lilac and gold by the rising sun.

The breeze was strong where she stood, and dark specks of birds circled the towers and turrets of the palaces nearby, blue-gray against the lightening sky. Aerhad-el-Raas, drowning in the pale milk-fine mists of morning, spread all around her, immense, boundless, teeming with confusion of lowly life. Lyren, her hair flying in the wind, looked around her, then raised both hands to the sky, and cried, sending great echoes resounding against the walls of stone and the emptiness of the great abyss:

"Hear me, O Aerhad-el-Raas, city of the mad and the meek! I, Lyren, challenge Sahtiel Al-Eralir to a duel! Let the Al-Eralir fight a woman, if he has any courage in him! Let him fight me with sword, a duel of honor! You, O corrupt rotting city, hear

me well! Hear me well and bear witness to my words! Witness
now this Formal Challenge!"

The echoes rang and dwindled into living silence. She
lowered her hands and breathed in the pure air. The deed was
done.

At the doors of the balcony Sahtiel stood, naked as she,
his countenance full of surprise, anger, and odd sorrow.

"What have you done?" he whispered. "What have you
done, O fool? Now I'll have to kill you . . ."

She barely turned her head at his voice, and her eyes
were calm and intense and clear, as she answered: "No, demon
lord. Now is the time that I wound the moon. She has forgotten,
I think, what mortal pain life contains. Through her son She shall
remember."

At midday all the city came to watch the duel of Sahtiel Al-
Eralir of Aerhad-el-Raas, and the woman *sehjir* warrior. By
law, a Formal Challenge could never be ignored or refused, by
beggar or lord, or the one to abstain from the duel would have
been forever termed coward and less than a man. A Formal Duel
was usually to the death, but this was never specified by law.
The winner determined the final terms.

At the Field of Combat, just outside the city, space was
cleared, and a wide square platform erected, for all to see. All
around, thousands milled, seethed, expectant.

The two opponents were given only armor and
longswords, according to the rules of combat. Sahtiel, slender,
elegant, clad in silver, stood before Lyren, easily swinging a
longsword. The helmet with its white plumes hid his face under
its visor. Lyren faced him, equally armed with a sword. She
wore black.

"Foolish thief," spoke Sahtiel, "I did not want you to die."

And as the Duel was called to begin, Lyren answered, cold and impassive, swinging her sword up for a strike: "Fight me now, demon lord. Fight while you can."

They came together, two birds of prey, to tear each other's hearts. Lyren was swift, but Sahtiel was fire. Their swords flashed white in the sun, as they met and separated, leaving searing lines of light in the empty space. The crowds were silent, watching.

Never had Lyren met such a skillful and strong opponent. And she remembered in snatches how people had spoken of the Al-Eralir's prowess. In the time of Conquest, he had ridden in front of his armies, merciless destroyer, brilliant swordsman. He sliced human flesh like a reaper in a field of wheat, yet he was never wounded.

"The moon must indeed love Her son!" Lyren cried, breathing hard, in a tiny free moment.

Laughter was his only answer, as he increased his attack, pressing forward, and forcing Lyren several steps back.

"However," she gasped, "she does not love you enough. It is said—it is said that the sun also loves His children . . ."

"Save your strength, my thief," came the clear cold voice, as he dealt her a blow that nearly shattered her sword.

"The sun," cried Lyren. "The sun loves His children! The sun, Arev, loves His daughters. And He loves His one daughter so much that He has given her a gift . . ."

Sahtiel advanced on her, step by step, lightly, tirelessly.

"It is a great rare gift," she continued, "a gift of feeling mortal pain, of being tired and then resting, of ignorance and then experience, of indifference then love. It is a gift of living, of being mortal. Here, look at this scar on my cheek—I bleed and can be wounded! For I, Lyren-e-Arev, daughter of the sun, have this gift from my Father . . . And the moon—the moon, Ilenvis, had forgotten. She had forgotten to love Her son enough to give him true life."

Sahtiel seemed to falter for an instant, and his sword left a crooked arc in its wake, before striking hers.

"You, O Al-Eralir, have never been alive truly. You have never loved. Haderi you destroyed, as you now attempt to destroy me, because we are both alive, more alive than you'd ever be, and you, having nothing, had unknowingly wanted that life for yourself. I fight you now not for revenge—there can be no revenge for an act of one who is not alive, not humanly alive. I fight to give you mortal pain, so that you would feel, so that the moon would know what She has done.... This city—its darkness is the work of Her hands, Her misdeed. I free you and it.... Let the wrong be righted!"

Suddenly, swift as light, Lyren swung with the sword, the same longsword that he had given her in his half-love, half-life. He was somehow, for a single instant, petrified, his reaction too slow. Her sword cleaved his in half, and continued its fall to slash through the light silver armor of his right shoulder, and then his flesh.

Blood, red human blood sprang forth in a fountain. It ran and stained the silver, like a great rose flower opening its petals. The wound was not fatal, yet deep.

Slowly, without a sound, he sank to his knees. The handle of the broken sword fell out of his limp hand.

Lyren stood above him, not triumphant, not sorry. "It is a hard way. To learn life," she said softly, almost kindly.

The silence was universal, profound, all around. Laying down her sword, she reached out with her hands to remove the silver helmet from his head. The golden hair spilled out in a stream of radiance to lie about his shoulders. His face was of marble pallor, and the gaze of his exquisite eyes lowered to the ground. The cruelty was absent from the countenance, together with strength.

"If what you say is true . . ." he whispered, then was silent.

"Look, O people of Aerhad-el-Raas!" Lyren cried. "Look upon His face! Look freely, for you are now free!"

Like great rumbling thunder the voices swelled, all around.

Lyren turned back to Sahtiel. "I shall not kill you," she said. "I almost loved you once, lord. You, like Haderi. But I can't now. Now that I know what you could have been . . . I pity you . . ."

Suddenly she took hold of his hair, gathered it behind him, and taking her sword in the other hand, cried out once more:

"Behold, O Aerhad-el-Raas, free city! Let this make him a man!"

The swordblade came down, shearing off the great golden mass. She held it up for all to see.

And Sahtiel, Al-Eralir, wept, for together with the cropped hair was gone his pride.

The sky stood lavender upon gold over Aerhad-el-Raas, as a rider left the city on a great black steed. Immediately behind, a train carried in state the body of a handsome dark man with the marks of strangulation on his throat. The rider, Lyren, warrior, stranger, and someone else, never looked back to see the young demon lord watching her from the highest tower in the city. His wounded shoulder was bandaged, his hair short-cropped, and his face pale with sorrow and mortal pain.

That night, people said, there was seen a blood-red wound-blemish on the face of the pale full moon.

REVULSION AND THE BEAST

You chose beauty over truth, my beloved. And beauty chose you.

Beauty is wise.

She had seen all the way down to your innards past the mangled coarse fur and the crumpled boar-skin, past the eyes of hell and the maw of midnight. . . .

She had seen down, deeper yet, to the level of smallest things, where boundaries break down and the edge of a knife blade is a wide plateau, where dust motes are suns and the nigh-invisible thing that makes up who we are is connected to all else—that is how far down she looked. There, at last, among the infinite worlds nestled within the span of a teardrop's membrane, was your single point of light.

And she latched onto it.

Beauty is relentless; she pulled you forth.

Later, in your accursed castle, the two of you played the game of stripping outer layers and the shedding of skins—nothing more, really, than a lovers' tension-dance. You tried to open her, grant you that much, but all you had was her radiant surface. And since there is nothing more impenetrable than such homogeneity, you were convinced that she was thus throughout.

She, on the other hand, peeled you layer by layer in her mind, ever clasping your point of light, until she saw the beast facade crumple, and underneath a simple wounded thing—a human thing.

Beauty is wise and relentless.

I watched you as you returned triumphant to our father's house, how you proclaimed her as your wife and lover, and the mother of your children unto the ages. From my recessed window in the attic, I drank in the sight of your previously grotesque form now transformed into a similar keen beauty as hers. You were sleek and perfect like my sister, but more angular, as befits a man. I longed to put my fingers to the electric surface of your blond hair. Just to feel a shock. . . .

At last, you were a true man in their eyes. My father, the old bourgeoisie of the town, the righteous circumspect clergy, all accepted you, since now they could be certain of the fine, stiff velvet of your doublet overlying a man's body. Though, despite what you may think, and no matter their initial indignation, they had accepted you even earlier—not admitting to themselves even, that, in the world, property is sufficient proof of humanity.

With them it was instinctual as soon as father had returned bearing twenty oak chests filled with old doubloons and faded ancient lace encrusted with pearls and faceted topaz. They had accepted you with the sensual need that this town has for gold and old nobility, even though you were the Beast. And protest as loudly as they might, they would have had you ravish my sister in your old horrifying form, without a blink, if you'd but also revealed that you bore the title of Prince, or if a drop of regal blood diluted the ebony ichor in your beastly veins.

Only, we had seen you as a man long before all of this even began. We, daughters of this house.

When you cast your lure of seeking and glanced into the scrying mirror, looking for your fair redeemer, we also could see in our ordinary mirrors the reflected shadow of your burning hell-gaze. Bonds had been established even then.

We felt you in our guts—nay, in our wombs—my sisters and I. And she, the Beauty, she felt you in her pupils. For a fortnight your burning hell glanced out at us from all reflecting surfaces in our house, and riddled our nightmares. Tormented, we walked at all times with lit candles. And because of your intrusion, we in turn glanced into each other's souls. Thus, when you chose her with a single impulse of need, we all knew the moment.

There was one other moment of significance, when in passing you had seen me, and you had recoiled, as in all fairness you must. For I am thus, not to be borne, even at the level of my soul. I am called Revulsion.

You had seen me and recoiled, you who were the Beast. I was exactly like you, but deeper than the skin. For the part of you that was the quagmire on the outside was what filled me throughout. I was dark all the way *in*.

And in my homogeneity, I frightened you.

My sister, who is both Beauty and Wisdom, is the only one who had never feared me, the only one who could see the nature of my darkness. Beauty would come to me and sit in my monk-like cell, as I reposed against the grand faded pillows of soft antique linen, my form shrunken with muscular atrophy. We would remain thus in silence, while the sun traversed the haze of sky outside the small window, past the curling vines of ivy.

We sat listening to the calls of birds outside, and the rush of the wind as it moved past the towering walls of our ancient house. I saw the meandering lines of rivers in the distance, and the faraway lumps of shadow that were the mountains. I saw the roads and the rooftops of the closest houses, and the single needle spire of the cathedral, piercing the sky.

They say that the needles of the church-spires are sharp, so that they could pierce heaven and prick the soul of God, so that He would remember us, hear our cries, and look down.

I spent long hours calling Him with my mind. Calling, so that He would take me away.

But the only one who ever heard or remembered me was my sister, Beauty and Wisdom.

I call her Wisdom even now. That is my own singular name for her, for while beauty fades, wisdom remains everlasting.

Wisdom sat by my side, and took me by my clammy misshapen hand. And sometimes she would tell me rambling tales of distant wonder, in a breathy childish voice that had imprinted upon me so well.

Her voice dispelled, for a moment, my dark. And when she, my only visitor, would depart, leaving me to my self, I remembered again what I was, remembered and allowed the thick stagnant waters of self-revulsion to rush back, to cover me. And in the twilight, in the long hours of night, before I ravaged sleep—for sleep, too, would refuse to come to me voluntarily, so that I had to hunt down and plunder *it* for a taste of gentle oblivion—I burned with the emptiness, the ugly filthy hatred of the self.

And sometimes, in flashes, I remembered you, my beloved.

You are never mine; I know it well. But allow me this false sweetness for a moment, if only in my mind. Thus, my beloved.

Ever since the first time you insinuated into our souls, looking for her, there was a link established. I know not whether my other sisters felt it as strongly as I did, for they, not unlike Beauty, had real existences, while I spent every moment here, decaying. It is no wonder that their momentary awareness of you would be eclipsed with the richness of their own private moments, the moments of their daily lives. The reflecting surfaces, the mirrors of our house revealing glimpses of hell shadows, were all quickly forgotten.

I, on the other hand, lived vicariously through all of them, and most of all through you and Beauty. At odd hours of the night I would be disturbed by pricklings of intensity, by touches of your mind and hers, as you loved each other in the tumult of darkness. In the cool mornings, when lilac haze stands upon the world outside and the sun is still swaddled in yesterday, I felt touches of crisp air upon your cheeks as you walked the gardens of our father's house. And at high noon, when warm heady scents arise from the distant harvest land, I could feel the coolness of your hand in hers as you shared a repast of mead and freshly baked bead. Each sweet, rich, fierce burst of flavor, each bite, was mine also; still is.

I suppose this link will always be there, until my own life ebbs away. And while I feel the moments of your life, can you feel my *being* also? I hope with all my dark heart that you do not.

This mirror must reflect one way only.

Do not feel or hear me, my beloved. My intrusion upon your light would stain you, would sully you and my sister Wisdom.

Only once had my intrusion served well. That one time, I know it had, for I had cried out to both of you, and it came from my deepest hidden wilderness, the profound true voice of my being.

It was when you lay dying, still locked in your Beast form, on the grounds of your fearsome castle in the deepening twilight. My sister had broken her promise to return to you, had forgotten you in the familiar joys of living in our father's house. Your pain was so acute that it had reached out to me, and rebounded through me like a sympathetic string. I rang with pain, tolled with it, played it. I was pain; hence, I was you.

In my tiny cell, I had cried out, and my voice was but a whisper, yet it reverberated through my mind like the bells of all the cathedrals put together.

And Beauty heard me. Not you, but *me*.

She heard my pitiful cry, the cry of sister Revulsion, and she remembered. And through me she saw you.

Only for a moment, I was your divine link.

But that moment was enough. What ensued next is known to everyone, and the result is blessed history.

I am glad to have served you well, that once. Maybe it is the reason I was put on this earth, the reason to justify this creature that is myself, this Revulsion?

But, no matter. You chose well, my beloved, by choosing beauty over truth.

For truth is, Beauty loves you from her heights, while I love you from the bowels of hell which is all the same throughout, all *me*, and my need for you is dark like my homogenous being. There would be no relief, and I would pull you back down with me into the beastly abyss.

Beauty is wise, but Revulsion is a madwoman.

I WANT TO PAINT THE SKY

The child observed her older brother as his brush danced over the vibrant canvas. The painting was concealed from all view but his own, bursting with meticulous detail, and almost complete.

"I want to paint the sky!" she said at last and reached with her small hand for the thickest brush in the youth's holder.

"No!" Meost said sharply, moving the container quickly out of harm's way, for he had seen her handiwork on the white walls of his workroom, and wanted none of it on this canvas.

The little girl pouted, and then forgot about it, as she was likely to do all along. Out of the corner of his eye, the older brother watched fondly, in secret, as she paused, forefinger in mouth, considering what to do next.

"Go away, go play with mother," he said sternly, lips quivering with secret humor. "I must finish this painting for the beautiful golden-haired lord, the one you've admired through the glass bead curtain. Yes, we saw you staring, little twit."

"I am not," she said. "Not little."

"Ah, then you're my big twit. Now, go, Evirie! Quickly, boo!"

She squealed and ran from him.

And Meost once again picked up his brush. Odd, that she had spoken thus, for of all things he had yet to paint the sky. . . .

Summers passed, and time had painted tiny streaks of gray and white distinction upon Meost's dark auburn locks. He was now the Master Painter in the land, and Lord Astean himself considered him one of the Treasures of his realm. Many an image of beauty and vigor had Meost given to the Lord, creating his likenesses, and anything else the Lord desired.

Evirie, now eighteen, was an apprentice to her brother's craft. For the first five years, she was only allowed to watch him mix pigments, pour oils, and streak canvas with white ground. On the sixth year, a brush of her own was given to her—not too large, and neither too small. She was not to use it yet, not until she was ready. Meanwhile, she could stand over her brother's shoulder and stare in fascination as he wrought marvels of rich color upon whiteness.

Lord Astean himself, beautiful as a blond god, often sat for portraits in Meost's rather small studio. Over the years, dozens of the Lord's likenesses hung in the Halls of his Palace like mirrors of his life.

First, was the portrait of Lord Astean as a youth. It was the same one for which he had sat that first time, long ago, while a little girl stood behind a glass bead curtain and watched her brother paint the beautiful golden haired being with great violet eyes. Then, she was too young, and beauty had merely meant wonder and brightness, like the rising sun, or a rainbow hung upon the vault of heaven.

Next, came portraits of Astean as a hunter, a warrior, a warlord. In the first, he rode a young white stallion, in the second, a great black warhorse, and in the third, a gilded chariot.

In each portrait, his hair was golden, spilled like a river of dawn, and his eyes violet and clear.

Evirie longed to take out her own brush and try a likeness of the Lord from memory. But she knew she was not ready yet.

Later, Meost painted his liege Lord as a statesman, a ruler, a sovereign. He was shown standing upon the summit of a colonnade, or was poised behind a writing table filled with symbols of wisdom, or else, was seated upon the Throne of ivory and amethyst—the ivory being like his skin, and amethyst paling before the depth of his eyes.

And in the last three years, Lord Astean asked to be portrayed as a bridegroom. He was immortalized thus in a bower of roses, beneath a full moon in the garden, before a single candle in a boudoir. These last three portraits were to be sent to a Queen of a distant Eastern land, who was being considered as a potential bride.

The Queen herself was beautiful as a dark beast of the forest, with skin like olives, and hair like the absence of light. She had her own Master Painter at Court, and he had created many likenesses that were sent to Lord Astean.

Astean fell madly into awe with her, and was stricken by the finesse of the paintings. He had called Meost to him and requested a portrait of himself, this one done to such perfection as yet unseen anywhere in this mortal plane of being. This portrait was to be returned to the dark Queen, and was to impress her beyond her ability to be impressed.

The portrait was done (while Evirie cowered behind a thick curtain of velvet and watched the golden beauty of the subject being portrayed), then was delivered to the Eastern land, and the Queen was duly impressed.

"Such a Treasure indeed he is, your Master Painter," she had written to Astean. "And yet, my own Painter, Livekke, can match him in skill and artifice and subtlety of execution. Moreover, Livekke can exceed him in the sense of Prophetic Wonder that only the Truest Art can possess."

"Is that so?" Lord Astean had exclaimed, his amethyst eyes narrowing in darkness. And yet, there was nothing he could say now to his Bride, for the Queen, whose given name was Civelas, was on her way here to his very own land. And supposedly, her Master Painter was accompanying her as one of the Wedding Retinue.

In the meantime, Evirie had ceased merely watching her brother work, and was now mixing her own pigments, making her own boards and stretching canvas. With them, she would walk in the fields and in the forests, and in the flatlands where the sun drenched green grass, swans flew overhead, and jack rabbits pounded through the sparse growth. There, she would set up her materials and paint the land, the earth and sky and creatures that inhabited both the realms.

She then showed her completed images to Meost, and for the first time he stilled in wonder, drawing breath. Her images were neither alive nor realistic like a mirror. Rather, they were fabulous, brazen, impossible, unreal—and thus divine.

More real than anything he'd ever seen or painted in all his years. For, Meost knew in his wisdom that true fantasy is the only reality.

"You have wonder within you indeed, Evirie!" he whispered that first time. And suddenly, for the first time in her life Evirie was sad, frightened. For, she saw in her brother's honest loving eyes that she had surpassed his own craft.

Lord Astean met his Queen in a chamber built like a faceted jewel. She arrived, walking on a bed of silks that were strewn before her by running slaves, and the soles of her feet were more delicate than the cheeks of some maidens of the Lord's Court.

Civelas looked into the amethyst eyes of her Lord and bridegroom, and was stricken by the first blush of wonder. For, just as Livekke's wondrous masterpieces could never prepare Astean for her beauty, neither could Meost's one Portrait of Portraits express the true living radiance of the golden Lord.

But because Civelas was more proud than even Astean could imagine, she forbade herself any further inner pleasure at his sight, and instead announced in a cool tone that before the Wedding, there was to be one other thing that would finalize their union. Without it, Civelas insisted, she would refuse to marry this blond god.

"Name your price!" said the blond god himself, as he trembled from the beauty of her, and was taken with a fever of imagined intimacy. . . .

"You have a Master Painter, do you not?" Civelas said. "I propose a Competition, to see which one is greater, your Painter or mine. They shall both paint—what should they paint?" And she carelessly turned behind her to ask a courtier who promptly answered like a mannequin: "Why, a scene, of course, Your Majesty."

"Indeed, a scene. Let me see, a dawn maybe? Or, no, better yet, a sunset. Let it be a sunset over your Palace."

"Certainly," Astean said, thinking that since Meost knew the Palace so well, who else but he would win such a Competition.

But the Queen was not done.

"They must both paint, in one specified day, a scene of a sunset over your Palace that would happen *two weeks from that day*."

"What?" Astean said.

"I didn't think My Lord was hard of hearing," said the Queen with a light, beautiful, ironic sneer. "But in case you misunderstand, I mean for our two marvelous Artists to be placed in isolated cubicles, locked away from all views of the outside world, and not allowed to communicate to anyone who might give them an idea of what the trends in the weather are for the next two weeks. Thus, they are to sit and paint from *instinct* only, from the raw innermost urgings of their gut, what they think the Palace would look like in that one moment of sunset, on that one day."

"What madness!" Astean exclaimed. "That is sorcery, not Art!"

"Not at all," she replied. "Not sorcery. Merely a test of measure of one's Artistic Prophetic Vision of Wonder. The only definition of True Art."

Lord Astean stared at her, overwhelmed for a moment by her obvious superiority, not to mention her innate ability to add capitalized emphasis to certain spoken words. But then, since that was not to be tolerated, he smiled, and his amethyst eyes were lovelier than candlelight.

"Then so it shall be. I accept your challenge on behalf of my Master Painter. And I assure you he will win."

But the Queen only smiled back, with her lips, but not her eyes. "Indeed," she said mockingly. "He ought to win, if I am to marry you."

Evirie came upon her brother Meost sitting with his head lowered, forehead pressed against his hands, a look of empty sorrow on his normally transfigured face. "What is it, Meost?" she asked, touching his shoulder like a dove.

"Nothing, little twit. . . ." he whispered. And then added: "Nothing, for I am a dead man."

He told her about the upcoming Competition, told her of the secret conversation he'd had with Lord Astean, of how he begged on his knees to be spared this, but instead, the Lord promised he will die and his family be forever dishonored, if he were to fail.

Hearing this, Evirie wrung her hands, and then hugged him to her chest, and smoothed his auburn and silver locks.

They sat silent and hopeless thus, together. In two days the Competition was due to begin.

The next morning Evirie went to see Lord Astean. She had never been in the same room with him when he was openly aware of her presence, nor had he ever acknowledged her existence any more than one would note the arrival of a light breeze in the room. For the first time, the gaze of amethyst eyes directly met her own, and Evirie was struck with the first vertigo of self-acknowledged intimacy. In that primeval contact a spark of wonder was born, and her heart was in that moment irrevocably changed.

"Rise, Meost's little sister," the Lord said, gracious and yet heedless despite the meeting of looks—as though a fine veil was drawn over him, preventing the true focus of his gaze.

But she remained kneeling, both from terror of what she was about to ask, and because her knees had grown weak at the sight of him, grown weak from such a proximity to beauty.

"My Lord, I beg you! Spare my brother!" she began.

But before she could finish, the golden god frowned, and exclaimed, "What nonsense! What is it that you ask? Begone from my sight! You are never to be allowed into my presence again, and I promise to tolerate you in the same house, but only if Meost wins. Now, get out, idiot girl!"

And Evirie crawled out on her hands and knees, leaving behind a shattered illusion, and one spark less of her soul's wonder.

O n the designated day of the Competition, the two Master Painters were escorted under guard to two tiny isolated cubicles filled with artists' materials and some water and provisions, and enough candles to last them overnight. They were to begin their work at sunset, and finish all by the first light of dawn. Next, the two completed paintings of the Palace were to be taken outside, surrounded by official witnesses, and publicly exhibited for two weeks. Finally, in two weeks' time, all were to gather to watch the actual sunset that was to be depicted on the paintings. Whichever painting depicted a truer picture of the sunset was to be declared the winner.

Meost was given snippets of advice by well-wishers—for he was a good man, and was well-liked at court and everywhere.

"The safest thing is to draw a sunset that would be most likely this time of the year," they all whispered in his ear.

Evirie agreed. And filled with everyone's practical ideas, Meost took a big breath, and like a resigned condemned man, entered his cubicle.

The next morning, at dawn, he emerged, under guard, carrying a beautiful exquisite scene of the Palace bathed in orange and lavender and topaz yellow, with small snippets of cotton clouds scattered in the sky.

On the other hand, Livekke held in his hands a dark stormy scene, just after a rain, with a dark thundercloud still hanging over the Palace, and the grasses of the cultivated lawns exquisitely drenched. Not a bit of warmth was there in that sternly beautiful sunset, only grays and faint bluish lilacs.

Everyone laughed, of course, filled with relief. This time of year, it never rained, and this foreigner Livekke obviously didn't know what he was doing.

Meost breathed a little easier after that, and Evirie also. All they had to do was to survive those two weeks and pray for normal excellent weather.

Lord Astean walked like a peacock, sharing their preliminary joy, while the Queen only smiled quietly and changed the subject of conversation whenever her Bridegroom would become too unbearable.

By the end of the first week, the fair weather changed, and faint clouds started developing on the horizon.

Seeing that, Evirie knew with a start that a dark premonition she did not want to admit to herself was coming true. Armed with an inner sickness, a wrenching, she prayed before a candle to any and all gods in the pantheon.

Meost acquired a permanent troubled shadow over his eyes. And when by the middle of the second week the clouds gathered thicker, his shadow had thickened also, and bore in it traces of death.

The night before the eventful designated day at the end of the two weeks, it rained. The rain came in a downpour all through the night and into morning, and did not let up all afternoon. The sky was gray like a dove's wing, or a bitter man's smile. Clouds grew like thick funereal veils over the Palace.

In Evirie's room, a single candle burned as she knelt, praying violently, to gods that refused to hear her or simply refused to reply.

And because of that, she snuffed out the candle eventually. With eyes like ghosts, she dug and rummaged through a small box of her most intimate belongings, until she found her brush.

She had not touched it yet, had not used it ever, this first brush that was a gift from Meost. Neither big nor small it was, but just right.

When the sun began to lean toward evening, through the thick soup of the cloud mass, Evirie snuck outside, carrying with her a parcel. Inside, were some paints, oils, and thinners, while next to her heart, wrapped in a silk handkerchief, lay her brush.

Her thoughts were somewhat mad, broken up, random. "I am going to re-paint his painting . . ." she whispered to herself, over and over, as she ran through the wet streets of the city, "I don't care if everyone already knows what it looks like, I am going to re-paint it. . . ."

At the Palace, the two paintings were exhibited side by side in a brilliantly-lit glass hall, under heavy guard. Both the Master Painters were already present, also under guard. Livekke had a pleased look on his little clever face, while Meost looked like a dying man.

Seeing that, Evirie's innards contorted, and she stood staring through the fine glass into the well lit hall and watched her brother's slowly dying eyes. She watched the bright orange shades of his painting, trying to memorize each hateful line it seemed, each garish mockery of the present reality. She stood thus, and forced herself to look and remember, and rain once again started to fall—or, was it something else running down her cheeks?

In an hour, it would be sunset.

Lord Astean was in a thunderous mood. "Why not dispense with the formalities," he mused outloud. "Meost has lost the competition, and might as well be executed now, before the sun sets."

But the Queen stopped him with an elegantly raised wrist, and a little smile. "Not yet, my Lord," she said. "Not yet, according to the Rules. However," she added, "may I recommend my own Executioner? Just like my Master Painter, I assure you, he would do the superior job."

At this, Astean flared. "Never fear, Madam, I think we can manage ourselves in this one instance!" And the Lord's Executioner was called to attend and stand ready.

Half an hour left, and all watched the sand run out of hourglasses, or the pendulums swinging on the great hall clocks.

Finally, it was time to go outside, and tediously witness that what was universally known to all since this morning.

No one saw a shadow of a young girl streak across the lawn, carrying a small box of supplies, and a brush that was neither too large nor too small, but just right for her slender-fingered beautiful hand.

Unknown to all, she spread out her box of paints, and poured out the oils. Oddly enough, there was no canvas yet, or at least not one to be seen.

For about five minutes she was busy mixing. As crowds began to fill the lawns before the Palace, she had a jar full of bright fiery crimson ready, and then a persimmon orange, a cadmium tangerine, and a sage yellow. Then, in another large container she had white, and in three little ones, some violet, lavender, and finally, wondrous gold, with real gold leaf ground and sprinkled into the oil. . . .

At exactly one minute before the first clock was expected to strike, she took out her brush from its cradle of clean silk, and she dipped it into crimson.

As the Lord and the Queen came out onto the Palace Lawn, accompanied by the two Painters, their masterworks, and an abundance of guards, Evirie raised her eyes fiercely, and then exclaimed in a remarkably loud ringing voice that carried all through the gardens, and made heads turn.

"Wait!" she cried, fierce-eyed. "It is not over yet, for if I must, I will paint the sky!"

She reached up with her brush, and suddenly, like a great comet, the brush exploded, and began to grow in size before their very eyes.

It grew and grew, and was taller than the Palace walls, then taller than the highest trees, then as tall as the height of swans' flight. And yet, the brush end that Evirie held was still neither large, nor small, but just right.

The other end, meanwhile extended into the heavens, and fanned out.

And suddenly, high in the sky, came a great smear of crimson red. The crimson passed all across the dome of the sky, and in its wake, the gray darkness of the storm clouds was obscured, erased, literally painted over.

Evirie dipped her brush, and it plummeted from the heaven like a falling star, growing smaller until it could easily fit into her jar of orange. And then, up it swept again, and grew, and left streaks of burning orange light next to the smear of crimson. Orange blazed, overshadowing the clouds, and was like a window of warmth through which the setting sun could suddenly reflect.

The next time the sky-brush dipped, it touched yellow, and then carried it up into the air, and splattered droplets of saffron like dew, like early evening stars.

Next, Evirie dipped into white and gold, and she spread it liberally over the horizon, right around the sun itself, which she touched up with more orange and gold and white. The remainder of the thunderclouds was fluffed over with soft cottony whiteness, tinged at the edges with rosy violet and soft sweet lavender and lilac.

Now, the sky above the Palace blazed with glory, and all that was left was but the Palace walls themselves, still stained with dull grey and indigo. Evirie took the remainder of her paints, and dipped the brush in all at once, making a pattern of rainbow across the sun. She extended it and tinted the shadows of the Palace walls, and now they danced and glowed, and sang with many-splintered light!

She had remembered Meost's painting quite well, as she had watched it through her tears, and now, here it was, drawn on the very fabric of the world!

There was a clamor among the people, and the faces of the Queen and the Lord bore shock akin to insanity. Neither one of the two appeared particularly beautiful at that point, and Evirie made a mental note of it. She must remember it the next time, for it might come in handy when it's time to paint a new Lord and Lady of this land.

"I declare this Competition void!" the dark Queen cried. "And our Marriage plans likewise! I return home to my own Far Superior Realm!" And saying it, she stormed back into the Palace, followed by most of her attendants.

"Well, go then!" Lord Astean cried in her wake. "Go, and may you be damned with all your Artistic Prophetic Wonder!"

Meanwhile, the two Master Painters were released by the guards. Meost came toward his sister, and took her hand that held the brush—which had grown all small and normal-sized at this point—and placed her hand against his heart.

"What's the matter, big twit?" Evirie said, looking at him with exuberant eyes. "Haven't you heard me say it enough times, that I want to paint the sky? It's rather Artistically Prophetic, and possibly, mildly Wonderful."

"You saved my life . . ." he whispered with awe and profundity welling in his eyes. "Who and what *are* you really, little twit?"

"I don't know. . . . And I am not little. Really. I am—"

And at that, Meost smiled, and thought he knew who his sister was, at last.

But maybe, he didn't. Not quite.

For as they walked together in the rain drenched grass, and Meost paused to stretch in freedom his arms that had been bound unkindly at the last minute, ugly red welts were revealed at his wrists, caused by rope burn. And his face, though now animated with joy and relief, still harbored old shadows of concentration, wrinkles of primeval exhaustion. In addition, his head was newly blanketed with so many noticeable gray hairs that now there was almost no auburn left.

Evirie stood somewhat apart from him, watching him from the back, letting him breathe free, and observed the wind of a golden evening sweep with kindness against his hair.

She then quietly took out the brush that she had hidden in her pocket, and she raised it once again before her. And she strained, and thought, and felt something, with all her intensity of being.

There was no paint left on the brush tip. Nor did it grow to gigantic proportions. Rather, it shrunk inward, seeming to disappear into the dust motes of the air, or the recesses of her mind. And as she barely moved it through the wind, tracing her brother's outline, the streaks of silver in his hair seemed to disappear also, fade into the onrushing twilight, until only a few were left—just enough to shine like tiny threads of light.

When Meost turned again to her, she had already put away her brush discreetly, and he had seen nothing. Only she noticed that his face seemed now at least ten years younger. And there were no traces of wounds on his strong beloved wrists.

She smiled at him, full of his peace tonight.

Tomorrow, she knew suddenly, she would go and paint someone a new heart.

LORE OF RAINBOW

One day, when the world was new like a phoenix's egg, a woman looked up at the glaring sun fifteen times too many, trying to determine the exact color of the transparent gem she was carving, and then happened to look back at the contrasting blackness of the poor shop in which she worked. As she did thus, tiny splintered rainbows seemed to dance in her field of vision, and there were blind spots of color that refused to go away.

"In the name of God—whatever his or her great name may be—" she swore, "there are just too many colors in this world!"

Her son who intently played with the flawed gemstones discarded at her feet, looked up at the sun, blinked, and said, "Don't be silly, mother. One can't have too much of a beautiful thing like that."

"Much of life *you* know. . . ." She grunted, thinking of her lazy beautiful husband in the back room, who slept on their humble bed like a king, until high noon, every day, while she, eyes tearing from strain and dust, carved gems worthy of a king's lily skin, into exquisite pieces of jewelry.

All this was exchanged for a pittance, so they could have gruel and meat.

"What would you do, mother, if there were no *red?* Or what if there were no red, or pink, or coral, or scarlet, or violet, or *lavender?* Especially lavender? How would you tell your rubies apart, or distinguish rubies from amethysts? Or—"

"First of all, Diall, they are not *my* rubies," said the woman whose own name was Ilvidre, meaning "lavender," in the tongue of the land. "Had they been mine, then we wouldn't be here now, living in this hovel—not that it really matters at this point . . . And secondly, when you come to be my age, believe me, you would not care the least bit if a stone you are working on is red or puce, and your only concern would be to tell the difference. Now, enough of this nonsense, sharp-tongued child. Leave me in peace, and rather go tickle your father's toes with a feather. It might awaken new thoughts in his dormant head."

"Your age? You are not even twenty-seven summers, mother!" cried insolent Diall, giggling, as simultaneously his mother tweaked the left one of his ears, prepared for his next words to come, as they always did. And as always, they ended in a verbal draw.

But for the rest of the day, Ilvidre, carver of gems worthy of a queen's ivory throat, sat at her work, thinking of colors and the reasons behind their proliferation. Her husband, whom she had chosen only because she had once thought she saw lapis lazuli in his eye-sockets—the hue of which quickened her blood, and had marked him in her mind as hers—woke up later than usual, blinded by the sun through his closed lids, and complained that there were no shades on the window, and no porridge in the pot. Ilvidre ignored him, saying only once that his hands were in their place, weren't they? Did he know their use, or did he have to be shown yet again how to fill a pot with water and grain?

The husband, whose blood was of the noble Families, almost as fine as the king's (or very likely finer, but such talk was not encouraged), was silenced only for a moment, remembering his place and the reasons why he had been given by the king to the best jewel carver in the land.

"Ilvidre, take anything your heart desires," the king had spoken seven summers ago. "In exchange for your craft I offer you anything in my power."

And his secret thought, of course, was that she would ask to have himself.

But Ilvidre who stood tall and young and filled with the beauty of the life-force—the same force that danced with angry sun-fire in the facets of colored glass—did not want the king with his cold agate eyes like the night, and the frost sprinkled on his sable hair. She, who wrought perfect beauty of reflecting surface upon stone, chose nothing of material riches (they ceased to have value, after always passing through her hands like ephemeral wandering guests, so that she grew detached from their kind), and instead took a youth fair as light, from the king's court, to grace her everyday existence, to inspire her work, as her mate.

He was called Andelas, and light ran in his blood like the pale streak in his twilight hair. But there had been, it seemed, too much strange languor in his veins, together with the light, which made his blood heavier than it should have been. Or maybe it was the other way around, and the thinness of the fine delicate blood caused his veins to constrict, to stifle, and thus reduce the potency of his life juices?

Every day, Ilvidre noticed, the workings of the rich, slow earthly indifference manifested more strongly in his heart, and his thoughts turned sluggish with what she thought was lack of effort. And then came gradual sorrow.

Constantly submerged now in his gentle depression, he watched his wife at her work, and the colors of the gemstones blended in his mind, because of his encroaching apathy (the causes of which were mystery), and he no longer saw their brightness as she did, their uniqueness, or their differences.

"What has happened to you, my love?" Ilvidre wept secretly, during moonless nights. "The weight of our mortal realm, this earth, has quenched your soul's life, and you have lost your bright will in the drowsiness of its slow pull. . . ."

Nothing answered her but the wind, the secret friend that caressed her neck at times most unexpected.

Twice, winters displaced summers, and Diall was born. Diall was like his mother, bursting, fiery, quick with the life-force, and soon insolent wisdoms fell from his lips like dew drops. And Diall was like his father once had been—bright and dark all at once. The earth, Ilvidre knew, which made all things heavy, had a fingerhold on him also. All he had to do was let go, and she would start pulling. . . .

"But no—you, my son, you I'll never allow to give in to the Burden!" Ilvidre thought in passionate anger, as she lived her days in her sea of shimmering facets and colored light. And joy kept her working, whenever she saw her son strong and virile like herself, as on that one day when he brought to her attention colors.

It was true, colors were in the world, everywhere. They gave things properties which allowed some to be seen, while others to be hidden, and made some things more valued than others.

"How curious," Ilvidre muttered mostly to herself, words tumbling, while her husband—after having eaten what little they had, and poured out with words the daily batch of sadness in his soul—sat looking at the road. "Have you ever considered, my Andelas, that if there were no differences between blue and white, men would likely not be able to tell apart mountain crystal from sapphires? Or diamonds from colored glass?"

"Diamonds in themselves have the property to cut glass," Andelas said in dark lethargy. "Therein lies one difference, at least. Another difference is that we have much glass. But there is not a single diamond in this house that we can call our own." His irony bordered on inexplicable sadness. He never actually meant to say what he did; what irked him was not poverty but a curtailment of freedom.

"And is that what really bothers you?" she said in sarcasm to counter his irony, thus fighting fire with flame.

He was silent.

"Do you still blame me for my choice, my love?" she whispered suddenly. "Is it really that our life is so reduced that matters, or that we were once happy in a different way?"

"Ilvidre . . ." he said softly, you do not . . . understand."

"You refuse to do your share!"

"And you are proud!"

"And we are both fools." She sighed. "You know that I would never take from *him* anything if I can help it."

"I know. Yet the king would give you anything if you asked—not that you should ask. Not that we need anything, really. Nothing. We need nothing. . . ."

"But you are in need of something! You are pining away like the last snow in spring . . . Tell me, husband, *tell* me, I beg you, why?"

Andelas, whose eyes had once appeared lapis lazuli, regarded her with bland weakness and sorrow, and said: "I loved you, Ilvidre. I still love you. But I have no more strength to live. With you, or with anyone, anywhere. I am going . . ."

"Father! Where?" Alarm was in Diall's voice for the first time. "Who will tickle the soles of your feet with a feather? To whom will you now tell stories of ancient, holy, foolish wars, heroes, and kings?"

But Andelas averted his former gemstone eyes, while the wind tugged at his single pale lock of hair among darker ones. And then, taking nothing from the poor shop, not even an old cloak to cover himself from the wind, he went out the door. For a moment his shape blocked the sun.

"Do not fear, boy," Ilvidre spoke, resuming her carving, "Your father is only half-mad. He'll return. His rumbling belly will lead him back, in less than a day, you'll see." But she knew, even as she was saying these words, that she was lying. And Diall knew it also.

Andelas never came back.

Autumn displaced summer, and then came winter. Winter was the time when few colors of any kind could be found, in all the great expanse of the world. Even her jewels now seemed faded. The eyes of Ilvidre weakened, her vision slowly misted over, until her perfectly-honed sensitivity for colored light was blunted.

One day, Diall, who helped her sort the finished gems, found that she had left three pale turquoise stones among similarly hued sapphires.

"Look, mother," he pointed out. "Couldn't you see the depths of the sea in these, unlike all the rest?"

"Stop mocking me, little jester," she quipped, angry and yet smiling, just as a fear had crept in, began feeding on her.

"I must find him," she said with resolve, waking up the next morning.

"Do you mean, father?"

"And who else would I mean? Not some lofty god of shiny gemstones and facets, you think, sweet beastling?"

It was needless sarcasm, and she felt sorry the moment she said it. But then, she had to continue. "There is something, Diall, something about your father and the nature of his blood—your blood too—that is more than you think. His Line goes so far back, so far . . . Lost in the twilight of ancient things. Its roots drink from a divine well. Even the king, that gray-haired tall man, the one you have seen only once in the Parade, and thought so handsome—"

"Handsome only like a solitary bird of night, mother. . . ."

"Handsome, nevertheless—he, the king, his line does not even come near yours."

She paused. "Diall. You know, through tales told by myself and your father, of the lesser gods—they, who are not quite like Him Her Who Is One."

"Yes—the Tilirr . . . I remember the stories you told."

"A beautiful ancient word. . . . In our tongue we call them 'Lords.' And although one speaks of them but in stories, they exist, as the grass, and the wind, and the land exists."

"And father? What—"

"There is something unearthly in the blood of your father. What exactly, I don't know. Whatever connections there are—"

"But you used to say he is worthless, lazier than a sloth—"

The eyes of Ilvidre flared. "Do not," she whispered then, "do not ever speak like that about your father again."

Tears welled in Diall's eyes, for her voice hurt more than her hands had ever done. "Where is justice?" he sobbed in anger. "Why can you say these things then, and not I? Why?"

But she had no answer to give him, and for once, in his bitterness, there was no verbal duel and he had the last word.

Feeling the deathly sorrow and fear gnawing at his heart, and the world slowly fading before their eyes, Ilvidre left her son to tend the shop and sort the king's gems, while she went into the wide land. She spoke with its people, young and old, and asked, endlessly asked.

Questions relating to all things and their properties.

It was true, she was told, by ploughmen in the fields and vagabonds along the roads, painted prostitutes on the stone-paved town streets and corpulent shop-keepers in their bursting stalls, silk-clad haughty nobles from atop their tall mounts, thin dark priests with ascetic eyes, and dreaming philosophers in warm taverns—it was true, they all said, something had happened, that the world was changing.

Things were losing the fine quality about their edges, blurring. . . . Strange apathy, like all the great weight of the earth, came to hang over the souls of things, washing out the colors. Dawns and sunsets were less vivid; dew glistened on flowers of paler hues; the sun blinded in a more ordinary way than it had done before. There was less whiteness in the white of snow, and less violet in the summer dusk; red was pale, washed out, in the shadowed heart of the rose, and blood, red human blood (besides being seen to run more often) ran with darkness from the vein.

Ilvidre went to see the king. She carried a great diamond, of the palest most delicate violet, as she remembered it when she had carved its myriad facets. But when she dropped it on his open palm, the king saw a great smoky crystal, which was, in a matter of heartbeats, effaced into nothing by the ghostly light it reflected.

"It is one of your diamonds, my Lord," spoke Ilvidre.

"Why then does it resemble coal?" asked the night-eyed man, remembering the jewel-carver as she was seven summers ago (when his blood convulsed in his veins at the sight of her youth, her softness and her hardness, her life). And now, in the uncertain light, she appeared a wizened old woman, then suddenly a child. She held, ensconced in ethereal layers, the full range of her years, and was *different* each time he blinked.

"It resembles coal because in its basic makeup it *is* simple coal," she replied. "Diamond comes from carbon. You know that, my Lord. By their nature, these two are the same. It is but that underlying reality is becoming visible. All states of being are superimposing . . ."

"What would you have of me?" he asked, softly.

"Give him back to me," she said. "Give my husband back."

The king was genuinely surprised. "I have given him once, and I never take back a gift. What then has become of Andelas, your husband?"

"If anyone, I would think you are the one to know. I have searched the land. He has gone, like a frightened hawk. And with him—look around you—with him has gone the fineness of things, the color."

A moment of facet-sharp reality.

The king sighed. "Do you think, in truth, I can hold one who is of the Tilirr? I would not have 'given' him in the first place, if his will had been against it. But he had wanted you . . . He had chosen you, not the other way around as you were given to think."

"No!" she whispered. And then: "How perverse, how relative things are . . ."

"Yes. So they are indeed. Who knows, really, whether it was more your will or his?"

And in the fullness of the moment, will it matter?

"Yes," she agreed, her voice trailing off. "Who knows. . . ." And then added: "I will continue searching."

And meanwhile, the world continued to change. *It is beyond human hands, now*, she thought, watching a gray dusk falling, or seeing a silvery sea, with but the palest aquamarine shadow lurking in the farthest depths.

Colors faded. In autumn, leaves fell no longer golden, but dark as clay, and the ripe fruits seemed frostbitten, or out of season. Mushrooms were hard to find, complained the poor folk, because there was nothing now to distinguish them from the pebbles and the rocks. Grass came up in the spring, resembling anemic sprouts, and then, slowly, faded even further.

One more winter, and there was no more lavender.

Ilvidre wept, because she slowly felt her name, and hence, her self, losing meaning. Soon after, fiery orange was gone, dispersing softly, gently, like warm milky vapor over a boiling pot. And yellow followed close behind. In their stead, things were gray, vapid smoke. Only red, blue, and green remained, pallid and weak, but being so tenacious in their nature, still a part of this world.

And there was growing unrest in the land. Wherever Ilvidre traveled in her aimless search, men seemed to become more desperate and bitter, arguments arose from weak and fallacious causes and pointless clamor, and longer became the memory for evil. The soldier's trade took on a vital relevance, while that of the assassin, flowered.

Ilvidre's wits clouded, akin to her vision. Like a shadow, the madwoman entered taverns, wandered narrow alleys, or walked lonely roads alongside fields, which lead from one more town to another, indefinitely. No longer had she any need to ask. It was enough for them but to see her eyes, vacant, receptive, that souls were unburdened to her.

Her thoughts did not dwell long on anything, yet her hidden memory grew rich with the accumulated lives of others. Outwardly, only the rare flicker of light upon razor-fine facets in gems, registered in her mind—the occasional bracelet on a lily-fine noble hand, or an earring dangling in a soft female earlobe.

In the meantime, at last, the world went black and white. Like a curtain it came down, one morning, definite in its abruptness, whereas before, in contrast, the previous gradual fading of things had been so vague, so dreamlike.

She woke up that morning to a dawn of silver, and it must have been the sudden sense of inescapability, the terror that gripped her heart—and everyone else's—which made her stare wide-eyed, in hunger, at the world, at her hands, spread her fingers wide, in disbelief, because what she was seeing could not be real. Ilvidre's sanity, if not her vision, came back in all its clarity, as she looked around her, finding a gray place. . . .

"Andelas!" she then screamed, and came running, wildly, into the open fields of morning. Above her, the sky contained all gradations of black and steel, quickly lightening.

When the sun rose, it shone like a polished blade.

"Andelas!" she cried again, puzzled, confounded. And then: "Someone, in the name of mercy! Anyone!"

There was no answer. The wind kissed her, gently.

"Why . . .?" she said, softly, to the wide expanse. "Why is all this? Surely not because of one man's withering soul? And surely, not because of my words? All I have done is live my life, and see my color. How then do you dare take away my sight? Infinite wondrous hues of the rainbow, where have you gone?"

Morning birds sped overhead, with the wind.

"Tilirr!" she cried. "Lords of Rainbow! Why have you forsaken this world?"

She paused then, allowing herself to submerge into a remote mind-place of avid remembering. She stood and searched deep within her great collective memory, for traces of old names. . . . Like a boiling stew, there came memories of living orange . . . Somewhere, someone had mentioned the name. And then came other memories, like flashes, of green, and red. Blue shimmered somewhere, and yellow glowed like hoarded gold. And again, somewhere in the deepest velvet hollow of her pupil, the softest place, she had found, buried, violet. Thus, she had all their names.

"I will it," said Ilvidre. "I will it that you answer me, all Seven of you: *Melixevven!* She who is orange joy! *Fiadolmle!* Lady of green! *Werail!* Lord of red passion! *Koerdis!* He who is blue truth! *Dersenne!* Sacred lord of yellow!"

She paused, with an inexplicable knot in her throat, and in a quieter voice, invoked: "And you, gentle one . . . Violet lady of love . . . You who has a claim on lavender, and hence, on my own soul . . . *Laelith!*"

But she knew that she had named only Six, and did not know the Seventh One. And from lack of knowledge, while sensing that there had to be Seven (such divine symmetry occurred to her in that moment), and yet also sensing that some things had to remain mystery, Ilvidre called on the name of Andelas, and doing thus, named him white.

There was a shimmer on the face of the sun. Blood, rushing in her veins, hurt with its intensity. And the wind, her ever-present lover, began to die.

Silence.

Nothing different in the chromatic gray and black make-up of the landscape. Yet . . .

Ilvidre heard voices. Like a memory, muted, they sounded in her soul.

. . . Insolent one. . . ! What claim do you have on us?

And then all about her, things began to convulse.

First like a rippling in the hot air, mirage-like, then violently, with the clouds accelerating in the steel sky, and the sun beginning a dance of gray fire. She could no longer feel earth underneath her feet.

The voices in her mind increased, and then echoed out into the open land around her, ending as dim thunder hundreds of miles away. Next came the wind. Ilvidre, an island in the universal chaos of swirling black-grayness, slowly began to distinguish the seven odd shadows right in the center of her visual field. They, too, were islands of constancy, becoming brighter, gently, softly, until she knew them for human shapes—no more, no less. Yet suddenly she was aware of something else.

Red-Orange-Yellow-Green-Blue-Violet . . .

White.

The colors, although of the lightest saturation, were a wondrous sight against the black. They stood on that fine narrow margin between existence and unreality, half-tangible shadows, and Ilvidre knew them for what they were, although she could never quite make them out.

"Andelas," she whispered, "I claim him."

Red shimmered. She could just perceive him, *Werail*, a massive male figure in the armor of millennia past.

What are you? His voice rang, like air. *What claim have you on One of us?*

"Very simple," said Ilvidre. "I, mortal, demand what is mine. Or at least, I want to hear him tell me why he came to be what he is, why he chose me or allowed me to believe I had the free will to choose him."

Don't you know? breathed *Melixevven*, the soft orange voice. *In part, he was ours always, and you have but helped him know himself in the process of choosing.*

You have helped him become Tilirr.

"Rather, I have frightened him away, the weak one that he is, thinking that he could be something more. I thought he would eventually do what he must—what all of us do," said Ilvidre, her voice bright with disdain, bitterness, and a host of other emotions.

You did not frighten him, whispered violet (and Ilvidre felt her heart wounded to its depth by the voice of *Laelith*, so that she wanted to weep), *You let him know what he is by insisting that he embrace what he was not. And thus he indeed became something more. He remembered a different world than this limited one . . . You let him come to us, as he withered away, burdened by the unforgiving weight of the earth.*

"But by leaving," Ilvidre cried, sobs rising in her throat, choking her, "he took away my world also, my own! He took away the color! I cannot let it be, for it is my life!"

Not he—the earth was leaching itself of all the joyful brightness. He only took a small part of the fabric that is you. He took it for himself for the reason of loving you. And yet it does not concern us any longer . . . You, your world . . . sounded blue *Koerdis*, like a gust of winter.

"But, why? I cannot understand! Beyond love, what bond lies between him who was Andelas and my own only brightness in life? What misdeed of ours? For it must be a much broader thing, and the fault could not be mine alone, since I am too paltry to deserve such a universal punishment . . ."

There is no punishment, spoke *Fiadolmle*, greener than spring.

No punishment . . . whispered *Dersenne* in golden radiance, *but the passing of things . . . The time for change has come. Andelas was the forerunner . . .*

Tears came down her hollow cheeks. Ilvidre looked at them, at the Six who had spoken, and then looked at the One who had been Changed.

"I have named you," she said. "Speak to me, my own *Tilirreh!*"

He will be mute now, said *Dersenne*, again. *Until the next age. Now, out of the light's opposite space, the darkness, another comes to displace him.*

"No," said Ilvidre, "I want back that which he took away. I demand."

What reason do you give that might offset the pain of this existence? And by what means do you demand? said *Fiadolmle*.

"The reason of constancy. The world is now less than it has been. And I have no means, except for my self, my own constancy."

But your world is inconstant. It can no longer hold us, don't you know? sounded *Dersenne* with golden sorrow. *The souls of men have all sunk under the pull of disillusionment, the weight of the earth. If Andelas, having but a trace of Tilirr blood before fully becoming, could bear it no more, how do you think we could, who are Tilirr?*

His leaving had no direct relation to ours, echoed *Melixevven*. *Before he even felt the urge, we were already fading. Except that the passage of Tilirr is slow like the shadow.*

"And now you are but shadows before me. Yet—you owe me . . ."

Yes, spoke *Koerdis*, a cold wind. *In truth, a balance must remain.*

"Thus," whispered Ilvidre, her heart constricting under the immensity of what she conceived, "I lay a claim upon one thing that will restore balance, and that is color. I claim all of you. Somehow. A part of you must stay."

And how do you propose to do that? mocked *Werail*, in rolls of thunder.

"I will fight you, if necessary. In any way I can. I will grab hold and not let go. . . ."

No one mortal can hold Tilirr. No one.

"Has any mortal ever tried? Who knows," whispered Ilvidre, "If I can but hold on to One of you. . . ."

Hold me, then! cried *red* thunder.

The world was suddenly turning upside-down, while Ilvidre felt a burning hand, brighter than any incandescent red coal, clasped in hers. Nothing existed but that hand. It burned, like a scream of loving hate in her mind.

And screaming, Ilvidre snatched her hand away.

She was better prepared however, for the second one.

Yellow sun. A golden hand, so bright that it was intangible, rested in hers. And because it was intangible, Ilvidre grabbed, with a fierceness of the desperate, only empty air . . .

Hold me, mortal . . . came a sultry whisper, and suddenly a bountiful *green* whirlwind burst upon her willing palm.

Vines laden with leaves sprouted, erupted like a forest, and there were so many things, so many living winding things all at once, that Ilvidre did not know what to hold, or how. And as she considered it, in that fraction of a second, all was gone.

Then came *orange* laughter. It bounced off the earth and sky, and rang in her ears, in her mind, exhilarating, breathless, while a semi-transparent slender hand, like bubbling honey, touched her own. Ilvidre's nerve endings rang. She could not bear the tickling, tingling sensation, and her hand, spasming involuntarily, let go of the amber one.

In the next moment she was enveloped in arctic winds and water, *blue* and icy. A touch of death clasped her palm, cold like untempered truth, and all her feeling in the hand was suddenly gone, the harshness of it being too much to bear. The water flowed through her frozen palm, while she watched it pour by, in futility, unable to grasp with her paralyzed fingers.

And then all the world blazed *lavender.* In the palm of Ilvidre's hand rested a presence. Neither cold nor hot, nor lukewarm, it was like a paradox, wonderfully gentle and firm, wonderfully right . . . Feeling came back to her fingers which closed in reflex over that which she held.

Yet with the touch, something dawned on Ilvidre, something brighter than anything she could have imagined, brighter than light itself. Ilvidre beheld the soul of *Laelith*, and could not bear what she then knew. It was intolerable, and sensing that her heart was about to break, the mortal woman slowly let go, knowing that a part of her would go also.

Last of the Seven, Andelas stood before her. Nearing her, silent, he extended his hand (so familiar—she remembered every crease in his palm, every moment when it caressed her, skin against satin skin).

In those instants that they touched, Ilvidre saw once again his face, sallow and radiant in beauty, the dark hair with one pale lock, like silk, and the lapis lazuli eyes. . . . All was the same, except for the eyes, which now held in them a flood, everything in the universe, yet did not know her. His hand in hers was warm, human, indifferent. It was so easy to hold him, quick, just let her fingers close over his, tighten, quick—

But Ilvidre suddenly realized with absolute certainty that she did not want to hold him at all. She had come to know from the touch of Laelith, among other things, the nature of love, and knew now that this was not what she would do to her chosen one. No, not this grasping selfish thing; love was a season—not to be held down nor contained within a limited human vise, but to be swept into, consumed and *lived*, for as long as it endured.

Strange emptiness.

Ilvidre opened her fingers and let her hand sink. And then she backed away.

"You have spoken the truth . . ." she whispered, as the Seven regarded her. "Holding you back is futile. And now I know why. So then, O Tilirr, begone . . . And take with you . . . my life."

The wind, previously subdued in the background, began to rise to the level of awareness.

But no movement came from the Seven presences. All around, the world stood black.

"What now?" she whispered.

A promise. To you . . . whispered *yellow*.

Ilvidre looked into the fathomless eyes of *Dersenne*, and saw it, contained there—a glimmer of hope for the millennium to come.

And then, with the next blink of an eye, her memory closed, and that which she knew was buried deep in the primeval kernel of her being, mingled with the nature of her blood. Ilvidre herself was now changed.

Tilirr, like tendrils of bright vapor, faded out of existence.

She stood in the open field, her mind grasping at some elusive memory, sweet and out of reach, while tears came down in a constant violent stream.

The king sat in his high seat in the great hall, and listened to his people crying outside the window, calling his name. They called for death, someone's, anyone's, to be wrought. His hair was like gray winter, overnight, with but a thin raven streak.

Before him stood a young boy with bright, desperate, and forceful eyes.

"There is no color," he said. "Yes. But the deed is not of human making. You know it cannot be! Think, my Lord, of what you are accusing my Family. . . ."

"I do not accuse . . ." said the king with tired eyes. "The people need a culprit. They do not understand and are afraid. I must give them what they clamor for, a sacrifice."

"And do you, my Lord, do you understand?" exclaimed the boy. "How do you propose to alleviate their fear afterwards? And can you aspire to know in full the workings of this world?"

"You speak far beyond your age in wisdom. Yet when you come to know the human heart, you will know that it is ever so changeable. . . . And you will know that it is but the immediate present that ever matters. Memory fades and time sweeps it clean. Do not think of the future, boy-child. Tomorrow will dawn, gray, and they will still see the same darkness all around. And then, yet another tomorrow. And finally, they will forget. . . ."

"And in the meantime I must die. To postpone a fear. . . ."

"Yes . . ."

The boy hung his head. *I will never come to know the human heart,* he considered, with strange irony. His defiant anger was gone then, replaced by real childish emotion. "So then, let it be," he whispered, "I will be their symbol . . . Like a holy, foolish, ancient hero."

And the king rose from his seat, stepped down, and bowed his head before the boy. "Forgive me . . ." A trembling voice issued from the king's chest. "You are indeed her son. . . ."

"He is my son, yes!"

Ilvidre stood in the great hall. She had come from afar, knowing in her heart that there was little time.

"Diall. Come to me."

"But I must die, mother!"

"Nonsense, little demon, I will not expect or allow you to die before your own mother." She turned to the king, "No, I will not."

"Why have you come back, O woman?" said the king, death-sorrow in his eyes.

"I have come for this boy of mine, what else did you expect? And I've come to tell—of the Rainbow."

"What? What is there to be said?" There was pleading in the man's voice.

She looked him over, hawk-hard, looked through him.

"Let me speak to the people . . ." she said. "Let me speak to them of the Rainbow. Already it is a forgotten thing. And that must never be."

In the silver dawn of morning, when the first gray sunrays came in slivers to part the absolute black night, the woman Ilvidre took her son by the hand and went into the center of the city. There a crowd had gathered, to listen, or to sacrifice at whim. They cried out the name of the king, but because he did not come, listened instead to a woman's strange words.

And she told them. . . .

"Look upon the rising sun, O people, and tell me what you see!"

In response, the crowd convulsed.

"Darkness! Gray light!" someone cried.

"Nothing!" came from others.

"What are you, witch?!"

"What has happened to the world? We are blind!"

"Death! Death to us all!"

"Where is the king? Let him show his face!"

She looked at the maddened sea all around, Diall leaning close to her. And then, to his shock, she pushed her son away, forcing him into the hands of strangers, into a blanket of anonymity, while leaving herself exposed.

Diall protested, but she silenced him, for this time she was to have the last word.

To the crowd she spoke.

"You see, all of you, only what you choose. The rest you discard into oblivion. But, ah—memory is such a fickle ghost.

At the same time most divine and accursed, it breeds guilt and conscience, allows cause and effect—and thus the notion of justice and truth. Memory is the sum of our choices, our shape, our color, our wonder, breath to breath; it gives us the pattern of continuity of self, known as life. I, too, am mortal, with a mortal memory span, yet I have touched the *Tilirr* of Rainbow. And now I tell you that their passing is not because of any one mortal's fault. It is because of *all* of you and your fickle, accursed, divine lack of attention, your willingness to ignore, to take for granted, to let what is important slip away. . . ."

"No!" they cried. "Not us! Find us a guilty one, find us, and we will sacrifice him to all and any gods! Mercy, O gods!"

She looked with glassy pale eyes back at them, at the rage, and exclaimed: "If you do not believe my words, then come, touch me! As I have been touched by the *Tilirr* . . . Touch me, all of you vultures, if you must, tear me apart! Hold, if you can, the memory. . . ."

And as they rushed to surround her—hands clawing, scratching, ripping into her as if they could indeed swallow and consume her flesh and with it the thing that was gone—all who touched her body were suddenly prompted to look up at the sky, their minds in whirlwind.

In the center of their vision, the sun shimmered, pulsed, and then went through the whole spectrum of colored light, for the duration of a single moment—like a jewel with endless cut facets that reflected inside it a sequence of a lifetime.

And then they knew.

There arose a great weeping in the land, for at last the people could no longer hold the lie like a curtain before their eyes.

The world had no *color*.

Indeed, beyond that one instant of sight they could not even remember what it had been, only that there was *something* they had forgotten, and it had been glorious and bright.

And for most this knowledge was enough.

From his lofty palace window, the king watched, gray tears welling in gray eyes. A gray wind blew.

When the crowds were gone, leaving her to herself, to what was left of her, Ilvidre had somehow remained upright. She was like an ancient trusty pillar, cracked beyond repair but still standing, her clothes and flesh torn to shreds, and her face a dying mask. And yet her eyes were brighter than the sun with the hidden knowledge and hope, buried in her blood. Even now the blood was leaving her, running to stain with some black meaningless shadow-hue the too-heavy earth. . . .

Blood was memory. What was its color?

And yet she was not alone. Diall, the boy who had spoken wisdom, had come crawling to her, then stood for a moment, mesmerized, clasping his mother's waning body, and watched the sun.

In his eyes stood a shimmering rainbow.

SWANS

I continue to knit even now, as they stir up the flames below me.

They hadn't bothered to tie my hands, out of pity maybe. Or maybe, this freedom is his final love gift to me.

My fingers move rapidly, a storm. They work the needles, pulling rough strands of colorless wool into loops and stitches, starting the last sleeve of the seventh shirt. Meanwhile, my mind wanders, lulled into a moment of peace, of times blurring.

I blink. And I wake from a recurring daydream of a deep velvet black sky, with sprinkles of sugar which are pinpoints of light, pale saffron and green.

The wonder of it stands to engulf me. In spirit I sail the boat of gossamer that is my body—their bodies, all. I inhabit them. This is the flesh of a swan, covered in pearl-white down, but turned to huelessness by the night. Above, below me, beating wings, none of them my own. On one level I feel nothing, hear a vacuum of silence, while on another level I hear the crackling of the rising flames.

I stand, tied at the waist with loose bonds which connect me to the stake and yet allow me to move my hands and work violently. My fingers express what I myself cannot speak; they tear at the wool, and weep and rage as they pull upon the string and form the loops. The fingers wail in silent agony of twisting contorting fury at the helplessness.

I am mute.

If I speak a word, if I laugh, or make a sound, it will all be for nothing. All of these damned seven years, for nothing. . . .

That had been the hardest, keeping the silence. My vocal cords have atrophied, and I swallow, feeling the flaccidity at the back of my throat. I swallow the air of twilight, the smoke rising from the crackling fire below, and the hollow silence.

Keeping silence became difficult only on the fifth year. That was when he found me. Before that I had lived alone, surrounded by the seething forest. My little hut had nothing in it but piles of wool, and everywhere, swan feathers. The wool was spun together with my hair, a perfect uninterrupted strand. Endlessly I had to start over, every time my hair woven into the string broke. For, that continuity was a part of the bargain.

Or was it? I no longer remember if my own hair had been part of that promise I made, a requirement for the bonds of enchantment to fall. But I was obsessively compulsive. . . .

On that fifth year, it had been hard not to make a sound when he took me with him out of the forest—while I trembled in terror and held on to the bundle of completed and unfinished shirts which he allowed me to take with us—and brought me out into the alien city where he was lord. There, among strangers, he placed me in a building of marble and glass and filigree, and had me dressed in heavy brocade, velvet and silk.

I became his mute queen.

And then, one night, silence became hardest when he came to me and held me to his body with a sweetness that melted my limbs, and gently stroked me, enveloping me with warm lassitude. At some point, while the night breeze poured garden fragrance upon us from the balcony, his gentle touch became one of strength.

The world narrowed in around us. Strength was pressing down, stifling me with pleasure, molding me into pliant shapelessness; force was in the fabric of the world, pouring into my flesh. And then he moved within me, delving into places I never knew I had. As he moved, the rhythm eventually did something to me, which nearly caused me to cry out. Only, I did not; I bit his shoulder instead, like a little snarling bitch. He would laugh later, calling me his wild little one, his beloved she-beast from the forest.

He still has that wound on his shoulder, from my teeth. It is a wound-mark of my love and silence. He will have it tomorrow when I am no longer there. A mark to remember me by.

My fingers flying, I knit the last shirt, and wait for my brothers, listen for the distant sound of beating wings. They will come, I dare to know, in this twilight, and the rising crackle of flames of the pyre below me. . . .

They will come.

Their coming will rescue not only them, but it will rescue me from myself, from my mad promise of silence. For today, as the flames burn, night falls upon a day which is nearly the last day of the seventh year of my muteness. In truth, I don't know what day it is, whether it is a week short of my vow or not. Really, it doesn't matter, for even if such were the case, I would be dead tonight, and all would be over anyway. This is my last chance.

The moment is now.

Silence had been hard, nearly impossible, when I had given birth to the child. It is a child that had been taken away from me in secret injustice, which is the cause of my standing here on the burning pyre. Then, I had cried in wordless agony in my mind, birthing it, birthing the fruit of our sweet rhythmic movement in the dark—he and I moving, sweet power flowing all around, and he riding me deep. . . .

They say that pain and pleasure are two opposites of one singular thing, and you must have one to justify having the other. The pain of birthing had caused me to clench my hands against the white linens until my knuckles felt no blood flowing, and I had no sense left in my arms. They had given me a bit of wood to bite on—as they give all women in that moment of personal hell—and I was glad for it, just as I had been glad for his shoulder in that melting warm pleasure-dark.

I birthed and I gnawed the wood to the quick.

And I didn't cry out.

Later, they let me see the child, touch her, put her to my pale white flesh. A contrast of flushed newborn pink and rose against adult pallor.

She suckled me, took my breast between tiny lips, and I trembled with a feeling of tenderness and fear, a dichotomy of intensity that caused tears to well in my eyes, while my vision doubled from the effort to contain myself, and to keep the silence. . . .

And then, while I lay in the post-delivery stupor, someone came and took her away from me, took my daughter, that tender little being, away from me. She only had time to drain the right one of my breasts, while the other remained heavy with milk and aching against my heart.

I didn't even have the chance to learn her sweet newborn smell.

And when they took her, I did not cry out. I only allowed my mind to scream in white agony, for I was too ill and weak from giving birth and from holding on to the silence all throughout. I was too ill to rise and go after them, to stop them and to bring the child back.

I took the piece of wood, what was left of it, and I weakly struck it against the walls, against a metal basin at my side, against the posts of the bed—weakly, yet with all my strength.

I was still striking the wall the next hour when they found me. The sound I was making had been so faint that no one could have heard me from outside my room.

For, even then, I did not cry out.

It was then that he came to my side. He questioned me, shook me by the shoulders, then moved away and cried in rage at those who stood around him, accusing them justly of neglect of me and the child. Eventually he quieted, and came forward on his knees and placed his dark raven head against my naked breast. For once, I felt his trembling silence to match my own.

The room emptied, leaving us, and long he remained on his knees, his face buried in my soft breast, until finally, in the tumult of the gathering dark, our intermingled madness and grief, I let him take my breast, lying full and aching, and suckled him like a babe. . . .

And I never spoke a word.

And now, I blink once more, this time because the smoke had gotten strong around me, and the fire burns closer with each breath. I huddle the finished six shirts stuffed tight inside my heavy upper clothing, away from the raining sparks, while like a madwoman, I knit, and the sleeve is nearing completion.

I cough, even then in silence, choking on the burning air of approaching death.

And then, in the deepening twilight, I can almost hear it, the beating of wings.

My eyelids close, and I find once more the solace of a dream where I am flying in a soft body of down, stretching my slender neck forward against the onrushing wind. The air is clean and cold, and I can breathe freely as I open my beak and scream out, while my brothers join me, and everywhere is the pounding of wings. . . .

After the child was gone, he would not come to me for months, leaving me to nocturnal solitude. I could not write, never having learned the art, and thus could not explain, nor even express my sympathy, my equal sorrow to him, who was my king, my lord and lover.

And eventually, when the days of autumn narrowed into dim light and the trees had lost their fiery leaves into a brown ichor that littered the cooling earth, the sixth year of my silence was nearly at a close. It was on one of such deep long evenings that he finally broke his coldness, and he came to me by the warm blazing hearth. There, I lowered myself down on my knees before him, and I buried my head against his feet, and washed them with my mute tears. The shape my body took before him was calling out for his forgiveness.

And he read the unspoken language of my form correctly. He took me, enveloping me in the warm strength of his arms, and because his need for me was so strong, he allowed himself to forget all past, to let the veil of pain between us slip away.

Once again we were lovers throughout the dark autumn and then winter nights, lying in a sweet cocoon of intimacy while the winds raged outside, and patterned frost obscured the window glass.

When spring came, I too had quickened once again, and the child grew within me like a beloved fruit of tenderness. It was once again nearly impossible to keep the silence, because I wanted to laugh, to cry out with joy, when I felt it kicking the insides of my womb.

I sat in a rocking chair, warmed by gentle sun through a faint curtain of gauze, knitting the sixth and then starting the seventh shirt, while my child danced within me, and the day of its birth drew near.

I remember that day even now, as smoke stifles me, and my fingers barely continue moving in their automatic deathly rhythm, no longer filled with sensation but rather agony, as they fold the needles and pull the loops of string.

When the child was born, he had made sure that we were well watched, and this time spent all days in our company. My infant this time was a boy child, lusty and pink with health, and I grinned with pleasure feeling him at my breast, feeling the smoothness of his tiny cheek against my flesh.

For days, we were living an idyll. And then, one night, someone came—and this time I knew her, the old woman that was his own stern mother—and took the child away, while I found myself heavy with drugs that must've been poured into my cup half an hour earlier. I fainted, as I ran after them, so that I was found on the floor when someone had come to check up on us.

This time, he came to me with insane eyes. He struck me several times, and I wept, but did not cringe, for in my self-hate I had wanted him to strike me, wanted to feel the pain for what I knew I had deserved, for not having prevented this terror the second time. For, this time I had no excuse. And I had not cried out.

His judgment this time could not be prevented. I was locked into a tiny room, bare of luxury, with a single poor cot. There he visited me for a week. He raved, he begged me to speak on his knees. He would throw me on the floor and strike me with his feet, and then would come down on his knees and beg me to strike him in return. He begged forgiveness, which I gave him with all my heart, as I remained mute and tenderly stroked his hair.

And then he would rave again, and at one point, he forced me back on the cot, and in a bizarre fury was overcome with lust—a death lust—and he rode me. When he was spent, he fell upon me weeping, cradling my body against his in a pitiful embrace which I knew would be our last.

For, the next day, I was to be burned as a dark witch, a changeling, a mute sorceress who would never speak the words to clear herself. Such was the law, and not even the lord or his beloved could rise above it.

And even then, I did not say a word, did not cry out. Only one thing was left for me. I continued knitting, because that one inexplicable obsession he would never deny me, not even now.

I knit now, with my eyes closed, while smoke rises above my head. The thread no longer has a single hair from my head running through it, but that can no longer be helped, for there is no time, and I must continue the best I can.

The sleeve is almost finished.

The beating of wings. . . .

Am I hallucinating this, or is it indeed so? Could it be that suddenly, the air is clean of smoke around me?

I open my eyes, and see shadows of deep pallor, illuminated into golden whiteness by the nearby flames. They fall down from the sky upon me, while all around, cries of the multitude are heard.

And from a great distance, far in the crowd, I see his sorrowing eyes. He watches me. Even now.

He loves me, I know he loves and wants me, and I cannot even defend myself in his eyes, cannot tell him I am not guilty, cannot even tell him what truth I know.

This I think, while I hallucinate the beating of wings around me. My dream brothers have come to save me, and to save themselves.

The last stitches come rough. Indeed, I am not quite done, but something truly does fan at my head and I smell less smoke than I should. . . .

What could it be?

Something is beating at me violently, as I blink, thrown into a dream—or is it the here and now?

I have no brothers. Never did.

They were but the singular yearnings of my lonely mind, a soft dream of white feathers and family.

And yet, why is there a commotion in the crowd?

And why does he suddenly come running forward, with an insane cry of hope issuing from his beloved lips?

The shapes of light come hurtling at me from above, their beating wings keeping away the flames. And with a mad instinct, I scramble and remove the shirts that lie hidden at my breast, unwrapping the first, flapping out the coarseness, and letting it land over the flying shape of whiteness nearest me.

I blink, and the twilight air shimmers, and I see a miracle taking place. The form grows, elongates, and takes on the shape of a man.

Without thinking, I move and unwrap the second shirt, and toss it even as it is unfolding upon another flying being, and it also transforms. . . .

I continue thus, four more times, until six male shapes stand around me, putting out the flames among the clamoring yells of the crowd, and all I have is but one shirt left, the one with an unfinished sleeve. It, I toss finally at a single smaller younger bird shape that flitters, wings beating violently in my face.

The swan also dissolves before me, another man, this one a youth, this one with an incomplete leftover wing where his right arm should be. It is just about where my hair had ran out and I had continued knitting without it. . . .

The seven brothers that I never had stand around me, while looking above I see the rest of a great white flock, like a pale gossamer cloud obscuring the blackness of the sky.

My lord, my beloved, rushes to me, but the seven stand tight, protecting me with the whiteness of their arms like wings, and in that moment I know that I can speak at last, I can break the silence.

And thus, I open my lips, and take in a deep breath, and then I cry out.

And the scream that issues out of me is not quite human, but wild, hoarse, terrifying, filled with seven years of pent-up truth and agony, seven long years of frustrated terrible pleasure, pain, sorrow, wonder, love, and madness.

It is not human, that cry, for my vocal cords had lost their ability for speech a long time ago.

It is the scream of a swan.

THE STORY OF LOVE

It is such an easy thing; all stories are the same. They are histories of the act of taming with love. Men tame women, women tame men; fathers and mothers mold daughters and sons; siblings twist each other; children temper parents; strangers weld bonds with those who are nameless in the wilderness. There is bending, breaking, twisting, and contortion.

But the end result is always the same. One yields a part of the self to the other. And in the process the tamer is also remade. Some become two complacent beasts, two intertwined halves. But it is more often that they acquire custom-shaped notches and edges that can be made to fit not just one but several others; often there are more than one such, so that individuals can come together in groupings, united from different angles and directions, their surfaces roiling with receptivity. . . .

In the end, they are all weakened and strengthened as tempered steel—which is both soft and hard, unbreakable and flexible, a thing wrought of disparate materials that have undergone unifying *change*. Steel is love, its product on the physical plane.

He who has allowed the change that is steel is the God of Love.

This is one such story.

"If he says that about you once more, if he strikes you again, then you should run away, child," said the old nurse. She spoke thus every time, then immediately apologized for her impertinence, as though her words could be swallowed back.

Crea shook her slender wrist, so that her fingers swept back and forth past her swollen lips. She did not dare move her neck or face, because the blood streamed from her nose with each breath; movement would make it worse. She gestured to the old woman for silence, since the nurse was hard of hearing and had to be reminded to keep her voice down. "No, please," Crea whispered. "It is all right. I need to keep my thoughts to myself, and to curb my tongue. . . ."

The nurse sighed loudly. "Your father is a cruel man, may the gods forgive me for saying it. What he says and does is not right."

Crea shuddered, and said nothing. Her thoughts painted the monster, images coming in fragments, how he taunted, how—vampiric—he fed on her outbursts of emotion, and how his hand and his leather belt rose over her while the blows came like strikes of lighting, never predictable, always finding the place most vulnerable to pain. . . . He was very careful not to damage her face or body directly, since she was a beautiful girl—extraordinarily so, some people in the household said— and she would bring a great bridal payment. Only this last time he lost his mind in a more distant place than usual and forgot to find reason, forgot to be careful, forgot to use a cloth between his tools of punishment and her skin.

Crea's nose was bleeding and there were streaks against her cheeks where his hands had made contact as he slapped her at least three times before sanity returned and he restrained himself. Her neck had been scratched with the edge of the brass buckle. He had just barely missed her eye.

"He drinks and becomes an animal . . ." muttered the nurse, her voice again ending on a loud note.

"Animals are wronged when you say this, Na-Ma. And he is the same without drink." Crea spoke with her gaze averted, but her voice was clear and cold as a razor's edge. Always such a polite child, patient, receptive, pliable child. Such clarity, hard as diamond, was a first.

The nurse missed the fine nuances, the difference in her charge. Instead she pulled the girl—nay, a young woman, soon—behind her, to clean her up and put unguents on her wounds.

"Old drunken beast," she repeated, accustomed to blaming wine to excuse and mollify most flavors of wrongdoing.

"Even when he goes without a drop," Crea whispered.

Nahad Eri-Devi was a wealthy merchant, having made his fortune by selling leather goods and other fine merchandize. His caravans traversed all the routes of the great deserts of the Compass Rose, from city to city, from oasis to the very edge of land where the port cities rimmed the earth like jewels on a string of coastline. With years his belongings compounded; he built himself several fine homes in at least three cities, and in each he had a wife who held her own court over a small harem of concubines, and knew little of the others.

Nahad was the father of three large healthy sons and a brood of daughters, and he visited them frequently at first. But then with time he settled in one of the cities and stopped driving his caravans himself, handing this task over to his sons.

Here, in the port city of Wahadia, perched between the verdant coast of paradise and the edge of the desert called Hell, where date and olive trees grew in abundance and the climate was mild, he sat in his gardens and ate and drank to his content, while his wife of this house grew sickly and finally the gods chose to take her away to the next layer of the world.

Nahad grieved for her.

At first he did not know it, but when he drank and the empty place inside remained empty, he understood that he grieved and that she was gone forever.

Grieving was inexplicable. She was merely a wife and he had two others. Mostly, he knew, it was akin to the loss of property, doubly bitter that he could never see or possess it again, not in this world.

Out of reach.

Nahad's only daughter of the departed wife in this house, was a lovely child, an ethereal peri, one of the bright angels, called Crea. Nahad wanted to love her, but all he could think of was that her mother was gone. And all he could do when he saw her was fly into a rage.

Nahad spoke dark evil words, prickling, biting. He had always used words to lash out at others before, but now it had become a particularly bitter and flavorful pastime, like savoring a wine that had gone past well-aged richness into the realm of vinegar, and it was painful to consume, yet he must, for it still had in it a ghost of sweet. His words wounded and were skillful in finding the exact weaknesses—for he was an astute, intelligent man with a sharp eye for human character. Thus, he knew exactly how to tear apart his daughter.

At first it was only words.

But as his drinking increased and his solitude deepened, he started to use the belt and the strap to strike her. The sons—her brothers were always away with the caravans, and they neither would nor could do anything to interfere. And the other daughters of the house, daughters of the concubines, did not feel charitable toward Crea, the offspring of the one wife, simply because they could not have her legal place and thus could not offer simple mercy past the curtain of rank and status.

Crea had no one to turn to, no one to stand between her and the maddened inexplicable rages of her father, which grew in frequency. There was only old Na-Ma, her nurse, and she could do nothing against the lord of the household. Na-Ma, whose name was Biseli, could take her away afterwards and minister to her hurts in her small servant's chamber. Na-Ma Biseli was her mother now, and as such, she was all Crea had.

Nahad Eri-Devi had high-ranking visitors. Shiar Muetal Gedar and his sons were here, upon the recommendation of the ruler of Wahadia, to discuss an extravagant caravan venture to the farthest East. And Nahad received them with a feast worthy of the highest.

Dishes of gold were brought out and polished, servants raced to the markets to return with the freshest succulent pheasant and lamb, fruits, and delicacies, and the kitchen roared to life. The daughters of the household were hurried to the baths and maids went to work scrubbing stone tile and precious sandalwood inlay.

Crea was told to attend her father and his guests in royal garb, and to make herself a vision.

When her father's servant left, Crea, whose facial swelling had subsided but whose neck still bore a slow-healing scar, stood and laughed, then shook with weeping. Na-Ma stood at her side, patting her back, then started to run about and open clothes chests and rummage through jewelry boxes that had once belonged to the deceased wife, Crea's mother.

"Wear the white and gold dress of your mother, child," said the nurse. Make yourself into a proud queen. Make them see you and want you. It is one way for you to escape."

Crea nodded. She then gathered fresh linen and vials of scented herbs and entered the bathing chamber. As the water ran from the height of heaven into the stone pool, she scrubbed her ankle-long dark hair and anointed it with myrrh, so that it shone like threads of black steel in the sun, and reflected secret red fire. She polished her skin and teeth and nails with pumice and sponge and camel hair, so that only clean flesh remained, and she dried herself in whiteness of sheets that had been soaked in rose water.

Na-Ma brushed Crea's hair unto crackle of dryness while a skilled kohl-artist drew lines on Crea's eyelids. Crea herself took out a fine powder-box and applied white dust upon her face and neck to cover up any traces of punishment. She then stood while two women lifted the white and gold dress above her head and guided her to the sleeve-holes and adjusted the layers of fabric laden with jewels and pearls. She stood while veils were wound and ropes of pearl braided through her heavy rivulets of hair. A pearl and jewel netted headdress was lowered over her forehead and her earlobes received rubies and chains of gold. A thick choker of intertwined carnelian, rubies and amethyst covered the scar on her neck that even the powder could not conceal.

In the end, she was a queen, an immortal, and as she entered the feast hall of her father, the silence that met her was of worship and awe.

Crea stood like a column of shimmering gold light before four seated men at a feast table. One of the four reposing on cushions was her father, and he looked grim and satisfied and smiled formally at her. The other three were the Shiar and his two eldest sons. The Shiar stared in unabashed appreciation, and laughed openly, saying to Nahad, "You have a goddess for a daughter, my friend!"

His sons stared also—Ayal the younger with a gaping mouth, nearly salivating at the sight of her, and the older son, Belam, in stricken silence.

Crea did not move her gaze from one to the other once she had glanced at them all in a single sweep of the room. But as she stood, receiving their examination, she knew that the gaze of the eldest son was the most intense, was the one that scalded and burned with cold fierce need.

"My daughter, Crea, come and serve my guests the perfumed elixir of roses," her father said to her.

Crea approached the side table and lifted a tall metallic decanter with a slim neck encrusted with jewels. It had been filled with the most expensive sweetest liqueur, a prize among drinks, for it was steeped with rose petals and honey and had retained the scent of sun drowning in a blooming garden. Crea moved as a gliding swan, her slippers silent, her veils and chains of gold gently slithering and metal tinkling. She stopped before the Shiar first, bowing to her waist, the decanter extended before her. When she straightened, she took an empty dessert goblet from him and filled it with a thread of crimson, slowly, watching the viscous liquid rise to the brim.

While she stood pouring, the robust but already graying Shiar examined her closely. He noted her waterfall of hair, the extravagant eyes which did not require kohl to burn like coals, an impossible fragility of her arms and fingers, the perfect mold of her face and delicate lips, the asp waist in contrast to the rounded hips and abundant breasts resisting the confines of a golden bodice. In all his sixty years he had not seen such striking female beauty.

His sons had not seen such glorious charms either, for they were silent and motionless with discomfort and amazement while she came to fill their goblets, lingering only for as much as could be deemed proper before each.

Crea's thoughts came hard as blades as she performed the task. *This son, or the other, maybe? The father? If they find me pleasing enough, if they choose to discuss my bridal worth. . . .*

She considered the possibilities as she moved, and her thoughts guided her veils and delicate raven filaments of her hair to sweep along and caress the frozen eldest son in passing, for she thought he was the most petrified by her, and hence the most affected. He held the goblet she had filled for him and watched her move away, and his lack of motion contained a bottomless well of promise.

She felt his gaze burning her, cutting her from the back, and there came a corresponding chill deep inside of her, electric currents running, of waters beginning to boil. . . .

And she had not even noticed what he looked like, or what had been the true color of his eyes.

None of it mattered, if he would take her away.

After the feast had ended, Nahad called his daughter to him. He stared at her unreadable perfect face, still decorated with kohl, and her dress of gold and white that he remembered another wearing.

A bolt of fury came to him at the thought, at the association. But he only said, "Shiar Muetal was taken with you and asked for you. And the bride payment is acceptable."

"He asked . . . for himself?"

"No, for his son."

Crea began to tremble.

"Which son?"

"The eldest," her father replied, vacillating between fury and a good mood. "I am considering now whether to accept his offer. I don't know if you would bring in more if we wait, or if this is the best anyone could give. Three hundred coffers of mixed precious stones, gold, sandalwood, and salt. Maybe I should tell them 'no?'"

He mused sarcastically, watching the girl's reaction, knowing the offer was generous beyond belief and that he had already said yes to the Shiar. He paused, waiting for her.

"My Lord Father," Crea said, "if I asked you one way or another, would it make a difference to your decision?"

"Of course, petulant child—of course . . . not."

He did not smile; she knew this was exactly what he would do and say—whatever she preferred, he would commonly do the opposite. And because this one particular thing was so important to her fate, she replied, "In that case, Father, I bow to your will, and leave the decision to you."

"Good. You are a wise daughter, and now, indeed, a blessed and fortunate one. And you wear this dress for the first and last time."

The Shiar's eldest son, Belam Gedar, married the impossibly beautiful daughter of Nahad Eri-Devi, and took her from her father's house into his own, in a distant city that lay somewhere deep inside the desert called Hell.

For a week they traveled by caravan route, accompanied by several small chests of her belongings. Crea's Na-Ma was allowed to continue with her longtime charge, and the old woman rode inside a smaller covered wagon behind her mistress and her new husband.

From the start, Belam treated Crea as though she were not of this earth, an ethereal creature of heaven. He did not touch her on their wedding night, lying next to her like a dead man, stiff and hurting with need, but terrified to sully the perfect maiden at his side. Crea lay motionless and lifeless also, waiting for something to take place, knowing what to expect, and yet the night deepened and she remained alone except for his faint breathing, quiet and tense. She knew he did not sleep.

Earlier on the day of the wedding, still in her father's house, Crea had at last taken a good look at Belam and found him to be not particularly handsome but pleasing, with dark hair and expressive kind eyes. Belam was a tall and large man, not given to fat but muscular and thickset, and his mannerisms were gentle. As many men of greater size he compensated by making himself smaller, stooping slightly as he walked, and subduing his voice and gestures. He was different as night from day, compared to the desiccated wiry slenderness of her saturnine father. His tone was soft and Crea found it like balm after the sarcastic barbs that she was used to receiving.

And now, as they lay next to each other yet miles apart, she almost wished that Belam would do with her what it is that husbands did with their wives.

The next day, the second feast day of the wedding, they remained strangers, woken by late morning sun and smiling servants and the festivities continued. During the day Belam was attentive and soft-spoken, never quite meeting her eyes, always anticipating all her needs—except for the one—and in all other ways acting the perfect besotted groom. But the night of the second day was a repeat of the first.

They woke on the third day and Crea felt a small seed of anxiety take root in her. All the care and kindness of her new husband for the rest of the third feast day did not alleviate the worry. At last when the evening torches were extinguished and the bedside candles snuffed out, the two of them lay next to each other, Crea with her heart pounding loudly, and Belam—he was like the distant abyss.

After long moments of breaths taken and deafening silence, Crea opened her mouth and said, "My husband, is there something wrong with me?"

The man barely breathing at her side suddenly stopped. It was as if he had died. And then, in the faintest star-glow seeping in from the window outside, she saw his body shudder and he half rose in the darkness, and leaned over her. "My wife . . ." he said, taking a deep breath, "you are so beyond me in perfection, that I do not dare impose on you."

In the darkness Crea felt herself going hot as the sun in zenith. She turned her face to his darkness and said, "I am no different than you, my husband. Please . . . do not fear to break me. I can withstand the same flames that forge steel. And I am yours willingly."

The darkness around her became warm, as though indeed embers of night started to burn with a black fire, and the air itself was simmering on the verge of boil. Belam shuddered, taking in a deep breath, then reached out to her, and she was enveloped in his touch and his need.

That night Crea learned the selfless sensation of becoming steel, as it is tempered—but first, consumed—in the flames.

After the third night, the morning of the fourth and last day in her father's house, the sun saw them wake, entwined and at peace, to the prospect of the journey that lay ahead. The journey itself was a monotonous stretch of sun-dazzle in the desert, punctuated by feverish nights in the marriage tent during which Crea and Belam discovered what is meant by the human mortal struggle to become one. The impossibility, the urge to reach out past one's skin was fueled by the sense of always something more to come. And they loved and burned together, finding no end beyond each end, only a collapse of edges, of lines of separation. . . .

Such was their distraction that the journey was over before either one of them expected.

Belam's native city filled out the horizon, first as a shimmering mirage, then a conglomeration of turrets and domes, all one incandescent mass of white and gold. Past the gates the caravan entered a splendid and teeming place of bazaars and walled gardens and in the center a lofty palace of the Shiar—a pinned butterfly with upswept wings upon a spread of verdigris velvet.

Crea observed it all with silent wonder. And indeed, after her first joining with Belam her husband, Crea often felt silence overcome her, a sort of blissful state that required no communication, no expression of outward needs, no speech. She was brimming with peace and contentment, and freedom had been achieved for her, freedom from self-pain. There was no longer a vampire feeding off her soul. The physical hurts had been secondary; it was the words that poisoned and sucked her dry.

But now—here and now was a balm of oasis in the desert. She smiled sometimes, to herself, as she felt the wind caress her face, and when Belam came to her, she simply looked at him, and her eyes were wide open and receptive. She almost always said nothing while her gaze continued to recite words that hung transparent in the air between them.

It did not take them long to fall into a fair routine. Days and weeks flowed into months, and Crea was feeling herself grow abundant with life, as a child formed in her womb. She met her husband's caresses with warm selfless abandon, letting him love her, and basking in his desire, simmering like warm creamery butter upon a skillet, burning, dissolving, gone. . . .

And yet, Belam was such a passionate man that sometimes he looked at her with a small worry, searched her face for something, seeing a lack of a thing that he could not express.

She had told him she loved him as much as he spoke, sang, drank, exuded love to her. And yet, something was not quite there. She was like a stopped-up subterranean well, where the waters are building at the other end, while only a small trickle is allowed to come forth between the piled rocks.

She was unfinished steel.

Months and seasons went by, and the child's time of arrival had come. Crea gave birth to a daughter, a tiny being as perfect in beauty as herself, with skin of rosy peach and hair as dark as a garden at midnight. Belam was ecstatic, and so was the old Shiar, even though this was not a boy-child. There will be enough time for that. Now, was a time of exultation in the joy of being.

In the meantime, Crea's father sent occasional news from home, and every missive from her native Wahadia brought by messenger was a bile-churning potion to her. She never opened the scrolls immediately, always set them aside on the table in her chamber and pondered the golden crinkled parchment.

Inside, her father wrote in a dry sarcastic tone of daily happenings, his caravans, a word here and there of her brothers, and his general business news. He never asked how she was, only told her of his side of things. And his side was like sand in the desert.

Not once did he tell her things of the heart, only concrete happenings of the world.

The letters came regularly, every season, and Crea's daughter grew to be a lusty infant. Her name was Cozaat, given in honor of her mother's mother, and Crea wrote of her existence in brief emotionless terms echoing his own, saying that she hoped her father was satisfied with the outcome.

She expected at least a sentence of pleased acknowledgement.

Instead, the next letter from Wahadia contained an angry rant in which her father blamed her for shaming him and their family by not providing the Shiar's son with an infant boy and heir, but a useless girl child like herself.

Crea read the letter, growing cold as the deepest part of a stone well, even though it was the height of noon and the air rippled with heat. She then crumpled the parchment and took it to the nearest hearth, where she cast it in the fire.

She did not send a reply to her father.

From that moment on, he was like a lump of ancient forgotten evil, and she thought of him not at all, only in the merest tiny moments of passing. With time, her father's formal letters became less frequent also, and then ceased altogether.

By then, Crea had conceived and dutifully given birth to two healthy sons, and her daughter, Cozaat, was now a girl child of seven.

"Look, my dear, a letter from Wahadia!" wheezed and panted old Na-Ma, now shriveled and ancient, hobbling into the room with three children in tow.

Crea, graceful as befitting a future queen, and yet somber, as was her habit these days, lifted her serious face from her sewing task at hand.

She was still beautiful, radiant with early autumn's glow—brushed satin of the palest cream of persimmon—and somehow even more ethereal, despite having borne three children. And as she looked at her wizened old Na-Ma, she suddenly felt her heart constrict with old agony, as she heard the name out of the past, "Wahadia." Stitches of silk halted, while a needle pierced her finger with sharpness.

It was a letter from him. It had to be.

The old beast was still reaching out his claws toward her.

"What does the letter say?" Na-Ma said impatiently, unable to hide a wrinkled smile of anticipation, for she missed their old home despite all things.

Crea paused for a fraction of a breath before she set aside her needlework and took the parchment. Inhaled the air of heat and her new home. Then she looked at what was rolled inside.

After moments of slow comprehension dawning, she looked up. "My father has lost everything . . ." she whispered.

"Na-Ma. Our family is ruined. He is . . . he is asking that I go back . . . that we must speak. That I come to him."

Na-Ma's face was stricken. "What happened? What will you do?"

"First, I must speak to my husband."

Belam read the scroll, then was silent while Crea watched his beloved large features, so expressive of emotion. This time they were deep and motionless, like the first time he had seen her.

Her father's whole fleet of caravans had perished, together with two of her brothers and all of their cargo. It was a combination of great sand storms that winter season in the stretch of merciless desert, and the fact that the ships that were supposed to bring back additional goods never arrived at the port city. Nahad Eri-Devi was now a pauper, with two less sons, and only debts were his consolation. In his letter he addressed both his daughter and the son of the Shiar, asking for assistance, for mercy, and—without words, but implying—forgiveness.

Crea stood motionless as Belam her husband began to pace the room, and then, she was silent for long moments after he came to her and took her in his great enveloping embrace.

"We will go to him, immediately, my love . . ." he whispered, his face hidden near her earlobe, covered by the waterfall of her still-raven hair.

After a pause: "Yes . . ." she replied. "We must go. I—must go."

Belam stood back to look at her face. "What is it?" he said. "There is something else, I know. I know how much pain your father has caused you, and I understand that this meeting may not be your true heart's desire."

She shook her head. "It doesn't matter, my husband. You and I know that I must go to him. It is my duty, even though I do not forgive him—I cannot."

Belam looked at her with such tenderness that she caught her breath. "He is a hard man, your father," he said. "I . . . know. He is like raw, unworked iron."

And Crea felt his mouth cover hers, and she stifled her sobs and let herself be consumed.

She spoke nothing.

For the first time in a long time, Crea readied herself for a journey back to the place of her earliest beginnings. She steeled herself to it, to the pain and bitterness mixed in one fruit.

Belam watched her, and as always he found one thing lacking in her, one thing for which he had no words.

Finally, on the evening before their journey was to commence, he stopped his wife with a gentle hand. There was something very important he had to ask; something that he wanted to ask her for a long time.

"Crea, my beloved," Belam said. "As we return to the city of your birth, to Wahadia, I have one thing to request of you. . . ."

"What is it, my husband?"

It was as though he was afraid to speak. "There is," said Belam, pale and drawn, "there is a temple in Wahadia. I am sure you remember it, a small jewel of a shrine, built of rose stone and white lilies. It is dedicated to the one who is known as the God of Love."

Crea's face was focused upon him.

"I ask you," Belam continued, "to stop there, and to pray to the God of Love. Beseech him, so that he will grant you, in his infinite mercy, the will to . . . love me."

Crea was stone. And then she exclaimed, "My husband! How can you think that I do not love you? How can you, after all these years and three beloved children of our joining, think such a thing? What is it but that I worship you and kneel before you, and accept your love with all my being?"

Belam's eyes were filled with pain. "And yet," he whispered gently, "you do not love me. Oh, you are grateful and you are pliant and gentle and all-accepting of me, but it is only because you are dutiful, and this is how you know to be, to . . . survive. You do not love me in truth, not as I love you."

"Belam! What you say—"

"It is an easy, small thing I ask of you, my wife," he interrupted, putting his fingers against her lips, lighter than a kiss of a feather. If you indeed believe you love me, and will do this thing for me, I will be satisfied. Whatever comes of it—ask the God. Ask him for Love, and if he does not grant it, I will be satisfied for the rest of my days to have your affection and your loyalty, as you have always given it to me."

"Oh, Belam! Oh, my husband!"

But he kissed her, this time furiously, his passion such as though this was their last day together on the mortal plane.

The following day, they started the journey to Wahadia.

After weeks in the desert called Hell, the sight of the verdant coastline and the port city was a welcome relief. Crea felt her heart pounding, and her shallow hurried breaths echoed in her temples. The arid desert air was suddenly carrying drafts of moisture and the perfume of ripe sweet fig, quince, and black currant. Only an hour, and she would enter the familiar streets, would see her father's house, and then, him. . . .

The old monster.

On the way to the home of her childhood, they passed the sacred place of temples, and true to her word, Crea bowed to her husband, then took a white lily from the vendor at the doors, in exchange for a generous gold piece, and entered the temple of the God of Love.

Inside, the air was lavender twilight, streaming upwards to a skylight. In the niche near one wall stood the life-size God Himself, made of precious metals and wood, and polished marble stone.

Motes of dust whirled in the light cast from the skylight above, and they were like dust falling from heaven, powdering the form of the God with immortality.

Crea knelt upon cold stone.

Sirume . . . Her thoughts cast upon the rain from on high, and she willed them to enter the chamber, to echo in the lavender twilight, to reach the One who was Love.

Sirume, if you hear me, I beseech you to . . . open my heart. My husband, my beloved Belam, believes I do not love him. Show him that I do! And if indeed my heart is not full as it should be, then fill it completely; fill me with your Love! Show me the Love that I must have, give me the Love that is You.

I beseech you with all my being.

Let me love.

In the temple there was only silence. She heard the solidity of quiet in the shadows, the flitter of moths and the birdcalls from the outside. The God's hidden face was in shadow—as it always must be, for none of us can ever look upon the true face of Love, only its reflection—and there was nothing out of the ordinary, not a breath of answer in her mind.

Crea took a deep breath of resignation, and stood up, then placed the single white lily at the small altar bowl at the God's feet.

She then backed out of the temple, careful never to turn her back on Him, and hence, on Love.

Outside, Belam waited for her, and they resumed the journey.

Her father's house was the same as she had left it, all those years ago. Crea stepped upon the cool stone of the courtyard, and looked at the old date tree growing toward heaven in the center, casting a long familiar shadow.

And yet, as she walked inside, she saw the difference immediately. There were no servants. No fine draperies covering the windows, no hangings on the walls.

Instead, silence and dust and desolation filled the rooms.

Her sisters and their mothers, the concubines, were all gone too, having left the house of the old father who could no longer maintain them. Indeed, there was no one, a tomb.

Crea took several wooden steps, while her heart thundered in terror, fury, confusion, resentment, and a measure of guilt. Belam followed her quietly. She then walked the long corridors, calling out to her father, and when there was only silence, she too became mute, and continued her search.

She found him at last, on the long terrace, looking out over the abandoned gardens growing wild in the back.

A stooped silhouette of a man, Nahad was seated on a stool, leaning as a wooden puppet against the railing, gazing forward into the white-gold distance.

At first, she did not recognize him, so small and dried out he was. So thin.

And then, as the breeze moved his hair and beard—long white filaments of it where there used to be black—she saw his familiar gesture, a lifting of fingers to balding scalp, as he swept his meager locks back.

She saw his form, hateful and astringent and filled with obstinacy even now.

She saw him, a ghost of himself, and yet, the same man who tortured and abandoned and condemned her.

She stepped forward, meanwhile feeling herself going from hot to cold, to scalding, to incandescent white, as the sun. She stood, burning, while *something* opened in the air around her and inside her, and she *knew* at last.

In that instant he turned, looked at her, still silhouetted, and then, as he recognized her—recognized the stately woman as his daughter—he spoke in a shaking voice, brittle with misuse. "Crea? Is that you? Did you bring the dress of white and gold?"

He stood, and in that moment Crea neared him and then took him by the shoulders, and she shook him in remembered fury, only this time he was weightless as an ancient twig, a dried out mantis.

He was dust in her hands. If she only willed it, she could strike him so easily now; it was her turn.

"Father?" she cried, feeling something inside completely rupture, as the wall of waters breached the rocks, and then it came forth, welling, flooding, rushing, the river of time and history and past, present, and future; the possible and the impossible, the what-had-been and the what-could-be.

"Father . . ." she whispered, choking on the flood, and seeing the sick, the old, the insane, the forgotten in front of her; seeing as she had not seen before, looking as she did through a veil of self. Indeed, pain wove the most opaque, thickest of veils around the self, one that swallowed all light, letting nothing pass through to the other side. . . .

But now, the veil was breached, cast aside, ripped by the force of the flood. Pain was an afterthought, an old tossed rag.

The God of Love had granted her this moment of sight; it is nothing more than what love always does. Love—not dim and blind but so far-seeing that it can glimpse around corners, around bends and twists and illusion; instead of overlooking faults love sees *through* them to the secret *inside*.

"I have the dress of gold and white, father!" Crea exclaimed, holding on to the old thing—creature, being, man—that was all alone and cold and clammy with self-hatred. "I brought it here for you, to give back to you, so that you could again have her and remember. . . ."

And the old one shook as she held him, so much smaller than she recalled him through her eyes of the past, and she noticed that now he held on to *her*, reaching out for her with his gnarled claws, holding on so as not to drown, for she alone was there with him, even when he himself was not. "Crea . . ." he whispered. "My true daughter. . . ."

Behind her, Belam reached out and put his hands upon both of them, enveloping the old man and his beloved in a single embrace of forever.

"He has answered your prayer, my love . . . not as you or I asked it, but as only the Gods know is our true intent."

It is unclear whether Belam or Crea said those words, or if they spoke them in unison.

But it is clear that many new arms of Love were opened that night—adding to the infinite arms streaming outward in unconditional embrace from the burning center of the Compass Rose.

Author's Note

The fantasy, fairy tale, and fable collection you hold in your hands spans twenty years of my short fiction writing—from the first published story "Wound on the Moon," written when I was a high school senior and published in 1985, a few months after my graduation, to "The Story of Love," completed in 2005 and nominated for the 2007 Nebula Award.

In the process of reissuing this definitive edition I decided to include three additional previously uncollected stories: "The Balance," "Demonkiller," and "Revulsion and the Beast." As a result, there are now *two* retellings of the *Beauty and the Beast* legend in this volume, one each of hope and despair, darkness and light.

ABOUT THE AUTHOR

Vera Nazarian immigrated to the USA from the former USSR as a kid, sold her first story at the age of 17, and since then has published numerous works in anthologies and magazines, and has seen her fiction translated into eight languages.

She made her novelist debut with the critically acclaimed arabesque "collage" novel *Dreams of the Compass Rose*, followed by epic fantasy about a world without color, *Lords of Rainbow*. Her novella *The Clock King and the Queen of the Hourglass* from PS Publishing with an introduction by **Charles de Lint** made the *Locus* Recommended Reading List for 2005. Her debut short fiction collection *Salt of the Air*, with an introduction by **Gene Wolfe**, contains the 2007 Nebula Award-nominated "The Story of Love." Recent work includes the 2008 Nebula Award-nominated, self-illustrated baroque fantasy novella *The Duke in His Castle*, released in June 2008.

Ancient myth, moral fables, eclectic philosophy, and her Armenian and Russian ethnic heritage play a strong part in all her work, combining the essences of things and places long gone into a rich evocation of wonder.

Vera lives in Los Angeles and is working on a number of book-length projects including *Lady of Monochrome*, a sequel to *Lords of Rainbow*, a new Compass Rose milieu novel *Gods of the Compass Rose*, the *Airealm* trilogy, and medieval-gothic *Cobweb Bride*.

In addition to being a writer and award-winning artist, she is also the publisher of Norilana Books.

Official website:
www.veranazarian.com

PUBLICATION CREDITS

"*Rossia Moya*," **The Age of Reason**, SFF Net, August 1999.

"Beauty and His Beast," **Sword and Sorceress #8**, DAW Books 1991.

"The Young Woman in a House of Old," **Strange Pleasures #2**, Prime Books, June 2003.

"Absolute Receptiveness, the Princess, and the Pea," *Bookface.com*, July 2000.

"Bonds of Light," **Sword and Sorceress #10**, DAW Books 1993.

"The Starry King," **Sword and Sorceress #6**, DAW Books 1990.

"The Stone Face, the Giant, and the Paradox," **Sword and Sorceress #12**, DAW Books 1995.

"A Thing of Love," **Sword and Sorceress #7**, DAW Books 1990.

"The Balance," *Marion Zimmer Bradley's Fantasy Magazine*, Issue 9, Special Short-Short Issue, Summer 1990.

"Demonkiller," **Sages and Swords**: *Heroic Fantasy Anthology*, Pitch-Black Books, April 2006.

"The Slaying of Winter," **Lords of Swords**, Pitch-Black Books, December 2004.

"Sun, In Its Copper Season," *Fantasy Magazine*, Premiere Issue, November 2005.

"Lady of the Castle," *Bookface.com*, July 2000.

"Wound on the Moon," **Sword and Sorceress #2**, DAW Books, 1985.

"Revulsion and the Beast," *Jabberwocky*, Prime Books, July 2005.

"I Want to Paint the Sky," *Bookface.com*, August 2000.

"Lore of Rainbow" original to this collection, Prime Books, September 2006.

"Swans," *On Spec*, "World Beat" Issue, Volume 13, Number 2, #45, Summer 2001.

"The Story of Love" original to this collection, Prime Books, September 2006.